OUT OF SPACE

Jim Ottewill is a freelance music journalist with more than a decade of experience writing for Mixmag, Vinyl Factory, FACT, Resident Advisor, Hyponik, MusicTech and more. Alongside journalism, Jim's dalliances in dance music include partying everywhere from cutlery factories in South Yorkshire to warehouses in Portland, Oregon. As a distinctly small-time DJ, he's played records to people in a variety of places stretching from Sheffield to Berlin, broadcast on Melodic Distraction and Soho Radio and promoted early gigs from the likes of the Arctic Monkeys and more.

"As gentrification, lack of funding, stifling politics and the pandemic continue to pummel nightlife, it feels all the more poignant to chart the past and present of raving, while questioning what's next. With lively and forensic research, clarity of thought and a passion for keeping clubbing's resilient spirit alive, Out of Space is less of a commemoration and more of a rallying cry." **The Face**

"Ottewill's book is tireless in its seeking out of new buzzes in grassroots clubland, LGBT collectives and local scenes, all of them ensuring euphoric highs for future generations of ravers." **The Wire**

"Jim Ottewill lands in Glasgow, South Yorkshire and beyond to write this comprehensive rave chronicle Out of Space. In an era where nightlife spaces are increasingly endangered, Ottewill posits his record of the past as a pugilistic rallying cry." **Resident Advisor**

"Most importantly, the book goes beyond the four walls of each club to the urban sprawl that surrounds it as we're taken on a local history tour. The author reminds us that clubs and parties, despite operating on the fringes of society, are an integral part of our culture, and many of us have gone through our own rights of passage, often travelling miles to experience our favourite clubs. Clubs and their supporting infrastructure not only have a heritage worth saving but also one worthy of capturing for posterity in a book – something which Ottewill has done justice to." **Now & Then**

# OUT OF SPACE

## How UK Cities Shaped Rave Culture

Revised and Expanded Edition

Jim Ottewill

First published by Velocity Press in 2022
This edition published in 2024

velocitypress.uk

Copyright © Jim Ottewill 2024

Printed and bound in Great Britain by Clays Ltd, Elcograf S.p.A.

Cover design
Hayden Russell

Cover image
Hendo Wang on Unsplash

Typesetting
Paul Baillie-Lane
pblpublishing.co.uk

Jim Ottewill has asserted his right under the Copyright, Designs and Patents Act 1988 to be identified as the author of this work

All rights reserved. No part of this publication may be reproduced, in any form or by any means, without permission from the publisher

ISBN: 9781913231637

# CONTENTS

**Introduction** | Do You Remember The First Time?     1
**Preface** | The Death of the Party?     7

**1** | Went out for the Weekend, It Lasted Forever...     13
**2** | An Ode to Past, Present and Future Temples of Bacchanalian Excess     45
**3** | Scouse Powerhousing and the Secret Agents of Change     77
**4** | Synths, Steel, Klang and Bassbins in the People's Republic of South Yorkshire     108
**5** | In the 0121 | Brum, City of Almost a Thousand Sounds     146
**6** | Close Encounters of the Remote Kind | Dancing at the Edge of the World     179
**7** | 'I Can See Clearly Now My Brain Has Gone' | Raw Rave Vibes Inside the Nether Regions of the UK     210
**8** | The Only Good System is a Sound System     244
**9** | Future, Past and Present Sounds of London     277
**10** | Inside the Utopian Metropolis | Searching for the Nightclubs of Tomorrow     320

**Conclusions** | Escapism | Hedonism | Community | Euphoria
    – Themes for Great Cities     361

**Endnotes**     387
**Acknowledgements**     415

For Kathy, Dre and Stan

# INTRODUCTION
## DO YOU REMEMBER THE FIRST TIME?

Jarvis Cocker coyly winked these words at us through a fringe back in 1994. An *'Acid House Memories and Memorabilia exhibition'* poster[1], created by Jeremy Deller for a fictional event at the Tate Liverpool, asked the same question a few years later, applying it to our early dalliances with night-time (mis)adventures.

Whether it's the illicit liaisons hinted at by Sheffield's elder statesman of pop or the raving epiphanies celebrated by Deller, those early nocturnal explorations are significant. Not only in how we go out but in terms of how we view ourselves and interact with the wider world.

Over the last 50 years, nightclubs have provided an important opportunity for those seeking entertainment after dark. For some, they're a place to let off serious steam. For others, they leave an imprint on their characters that's hard to remove. In the daytime, these spaces are unassuming and usually dormant as you trudge past them on the way to work. But as Friday night rears its head, they begin to stretch, yawn, then slowly open their jaws to usher in the night-time reveller. The rush of homing in on a club struggling to contain the bass thumping against its walls is only surpassed by the release of letting the sonics carry you over the threshold.

Once you're inside, you can block out the real world and let the music, sweat and vibe overwhelm you. For a brief, dazzling time, everything is here in this twilight zone, carried to and fro by taxis, ushered in and out by security guards, frantically smoking or cadging fags in the queue, necking drinks at the bar, doing deals in the shadows and being led by whatever bounces out of the speakers. As long as you're out of sight, anything goes and it's all scored by the musical furrow the DJs choose to plough. These spaces are exciting, full of energy and volume - and, since their inception, have been an integral part of our makeup, a refuge for music and entertainment alongside resistance and ideas.

My early dalliances with clubs were as a teenager in the mid-nineties. You'd often find me in the corners of the Roadhouse in Manchester near Piccadilly Gardens. We'd meet at the nearby Wetherspoons to imbibe some cheap lager, head to Newton Street, stumble down the stairs, pay Elbow's Guy Garvey (who often worked on the door at the time) to get in and sneak inside. We'd have to avoid the piss overflowing from the blocked toilets, then get involved at the bar, all the while crossing our fingers that anyone in a position of power wouldn't get wise to our age and refuse us a watery pint of John Smiths. If our geeky group weren't loitering awkwardly in the Roadhouse's dark nether regions, it would have been in the lager-drenched indie clubs dotted around Manchester's city centre with their endless soundtracks of Inspiral Carpets, Stone Roses and Oasis and messes of floppy-haired youths pawing at each other.

These places aren't eulogised, but for us, clubs like The Venue on Whitworth Street, 42's or Fifth Avenue on Princess Street were just as important as the Hacienda or Fabric may have been for others, allowing us a sneaky peek behind the velvet curtain of adult life. As infatuated as we were with clubs, it took us a while to learn the fleeting nature of these experiences. We'd often meet up in Manchester city centre in the daytime for record shopping stints with whatever dosh we could scrape together. When the money ran out, we'd hang around outside these venues waiting for something to happen. But nothing much ever did. It was only when the sun went down that things started to get interesting.

For many of us, that first club will be one of many we'll pass through. Some of us might experience a life-shaking Warehouse Project, Rage or Renaissance moment at an impressionable age. For others, it might strike later when we're not so wet behind the ears. In some lives, local clubs might be the only nocturnal space they visit. Maybe they're just places to get drunk in once the pubs have rung their bells for last orders. Those dedicated to the dancefloor will carry on raving throughout while others call time when they have responsibilities and 'real-life' butts in.

Just as we enjoy different stages of our clubbing lives, the venues and spaces where we dance often experience a significant number of existences too. The buildings that make up our towns and cities usually adapt to human needs and are moulded around how we live. Many clubs have been warehouses, shops, maybe a car garage, an abattoir or cutlery factory in past incarnations. While some of the most famous have been specifically designed, many physical spaces that often accommodate the music, dancers and lights of a club spill out of an accidental combination of factors - availability, money, necessity.

This reflects how towns and cities are built, particularly in the digital post-industrial era we're now navigating. Yet, whether they make up a venue on a market town high street or an abandoned building on the fringes of a city, the bricks and mortar that keep a club standing must be located somewhere. Or at least they did when nightlife as we know it first started. The spaces within those walls are also unique, which is why they're revered. This is where we get up close and personal with anonymous fellow patrons. We know nothing about them other than a shared appreciation for what's pumping out of the sound system.

Club culture often grows by chance from the random sparks of more marginalised groups coming together, perhaps people of colour or queer communities with lives lived outside the mainstream. The majority of clubs also run on the tightest of budgets. They are commercial entities, but only the most successful generate enough cash to crossover from underground to mainstream and grow outwards and upwards to subsume the space around them. Others that survive either need to build a dedicated audience to stay afloat or use other income streams to keep going alongside their events.

All this helps explain why so many of the greatest clubs are transient. We're all too aware of how money talks in urban settings, with cities usually marching to the beat of property developers rather than DJs. London, in particular, has shed dozens of nightclubs since the nineties, in large part due to the impact of the development of residential and commercial enterprises. This cull became so bloody Dutch architects OMA (who we'll later speak to) described the capital as "Disconecropolis" (a necropolis being "a city of the dead")[2] as part of their research into their now-cancelled renovation of Ministry of Sound. According to figures from the Mayor of London Sadiq Khan's office, the city lost more than 50% of its clubs between 2010 and 2016[3]. Statistics from the Night Time Industries Association (NTIA) published in August 2023 have subsequently revealed how 31% of clubs across the UK were forced to permanently close between June 2020 and June 2023[4].

As we travel across the country, taking in the story of the clubs and the people who made them happen in these pages, we'll hear what's required for spaces to thrive from venue owners, promoters, DJs and those who've built them. We'll also learn why certain clubs have endured and others have fallen by the wayside.

Venues range from big to small, polished, corporate, illicit or merely flirting with illegitimacy. And although many of our most heralded spaces have gone - Plastic People, Bagleys, Shelley's, the Wherehouse in Derby to name just a few - their importance still reverberates through us in our connections, clothes, and ways of thinking. It's important to acknowledge that some clubs exist only as commercial spaces to drink in. But many others are where lifelong journeys begin and lessons are learned. Certain places have a wider bearing on us, breathing life into social groups and letting communities connect. The sound system celebrated every year at Notting Hill stems from the Windrush generation bringing bass culture to the UK, particularly in London, Manchester, Birmingham, Huddersfield and Leeds. The spaces where this occurred were initially people's front rooms or basements, as blues dances, before the sounds of heavyweight dub and reggae headed outside to infiltrate community centres, pubs and more mainstream venues. Meanwhile, for the LGBTQIA+ communities, clubs are an integral pillar of queer culture, with venues like Dalston Superstore, the Joiners Arms or the Eagle in London playing a pivotal role in pulling people together.

Art and ideas come alive in the post-midnight hours, often taking a sidestep into mainstream culture. And as each of the UK's cities ripple with different attitudes and perspectives, so clubs beating within them add various rich shades of colour to civic life. As we saw during the Covid-19 lockdowns, our lives are quieter and considerably less exciting without them. Now in the wake of the pandemic, many of us who care about the future of the night are questioning exactly what nightclubs are. The romantic view is perhaps as a playground for youth, creativity, experimentation and innovation. But maybe they need to take on a greater, more functional purpose as well as offer a space to dance if they are to stick around and flourish in our changing city centres.

This book was first published at a watershed moment for club culture and the challenges it explored continue to persist. Initially, it was written at a time when many of these spaces were shut. Since then, a cost of living crisis has wrecked even greater havoc upon our nightlife, meaning the future for many clubs looks increasingly fraught. Amid this fractious landscape, we'll delve into the role of clubs and their relationships with the environment around them, how the cities and towns where many of these spaces call home have influenced how we dance and the music these scenes have birthed. We'll discover how they fit into a population that is becoming increasingly urbanised and whether this poses a threat or opportunity for the nightclubbers of tomorrow. We'll also argue why, in turbulent times, many of us need them more than ever.

Each of our own clubbing experiences are as different and as haphazard as the spaces themselves, taking place across a range of locations and time periods. While putting this together, I found so many stories that you could easily write a book on the night-time sounds of each city. So instead of offering a definitive text, we will jump onto some of the dancefloors I've been privy to via my own experiences and the voices of the people that made these scenes happen. We will explore how our cities and towns provided a platform for rave music to rush into during the eighties and nineties. We'll then examine what's happened since and how the fates of venues, promoters and electronic music entrepreneurs have been shaped by the changes that have permeated our lives - from urban regeneration and renewal to online music consumption and the arrival of the digital world.

This isn't an epitaph for the nightclub. Many of those I've interviewed have said that great clubs can change your life, as they have for me. This is a celebration and recognition of how special these places can be when the necessary factors for them to succeed come together. It also underlines how life-affirming clubs are when they continue to survive and thrive despite the countless adversities thrown their way. In one of the many interviews conducted for this project, Danielle Moore from Mancunian dance music outfit Crazy P tells me: "Clubs are like weeds; they will always find a way through." This book will get lost in those weeds and make sure there's still plenty of room for them to grow. And hopefully, continue to unexpectedly flower…

# PREFACE

## THE DEATH OF THE PARTY?

*"Ultimately, this is not a story of gay bars closing, but of cool places to go out being ruined by people who want to go to sleep in silence at 10.30pm on a Tuesday"[5].*

Alex Lawless and Aaron Wright (Knickerbocker)

Back in 2015, it felt like the writing was on the wall for nightclubs. At the time, I'd been living in Hackney with a bunch of mates for the past few years. When we weren't sitting in our kitchen, nailing cans of Holsten Pils and listening to Wham's *'Everything She Wants'* on repeat, we spent the first part of the decade falling out of our favourite clubs before witnessing their actual fall firsthand. Celebrated places like The End, Plastic People and Passing Clouds in Dalston were inspiring, late-night haunts that all sadly shut their doors. Other casualties, including Soho's Madame JoJo's and Cable near London Bridge, weren't regular spots for us but their untimely demise added to the clamour surrounding this contraction of London's nocturnal landscape.

Statistics released at the time demonstrated the stark reality of the nightlife crisis. In the ten years from 2005, the number of nightclubs in the UK halved, falling from 3,144 to 1,733[6]. In 2017, the Mayor of London's Office published similarly frightening numbers showing how the capital had lost more than half of its LGBTQIA+ clubs since 2006. This catastrophe came from a convergence of factors that combined to deliver a blow to the jugular of nightlife. London's population was growing rapidly, exceeding nine million by 2020 and up by nearly a million from 2010. This meant more and more people were living inside it, generating noise complaints and concerns about nightlife's perceived 'nuisance'. The stories of the challenges faced by nightclubs during this time were many; Ministry of Sound had to campaign hard in 2014 to ensure it would not be silenced by a new residential development. Dance Tunnel in Hackney became much-loved over the three years of its life-span but closed in 2016 due to the "licensing climate" in Hackney[7]. As the city's human density grew, property prices rocketed, with certain areas seeing the cost of housing up by 62% in the last decade[8]. For landlords leasing space to nightclubs, it made the idea of turning this into residential property or hiking up the rent much more appealing.

In 2016, London's flagship venue Fabric was one of the world's most beloved leftfield clubs but had been forced to close by the authorities following two tragic drug-related deaths. Only nine months earlier, Fabric was heralded as a "beacon of best practice" after operating without incident for the last few years[9]. Although it managed to reopen at the start of 2017 under intense scrutiny and new security processes, its near permanent closure was a bruising moment for club culture, revealing its vulnerability in a city where competing agendas – including from police and politicians, council planning and licensing departments, developers looking to profit from housing demand, and new residents angered by noise – continue to swirl. As Dan Beaumont from the Dalston Superstore told the BBC at the time: "As the pressure mounts on some of these institutions, it seems that clubs are pretty easy targets. As an operator [Fabric's closure] is terrifying and I think everyone is very nervous because it does set a very scary precedent"[10].

Led by Mayor Sadiq Khan, the authorities were spurred into action. A Night Czar was appointed, then a night tube connecting different parts of London was unveiled. Louder conversations and more forceful dialogues started up around the future of clubbing and its 'value', a loaded term that influential figures are still arguing over. That all this happened confirmed a couple of important things: that the night-time was at risk and it was deemed worth saving by policymakers. Fast forward several years and this worth has been articulated into the kinds of numbers the powers that be understand and appreciate. Figures from the Night Time Industries Association revealed how the night-time economy accounted for 1.6% of GDP (or £36.4 billion) and 425,000 jobs in 2019. Yet, at the time of writing, the picture is of an industry in freefall, with only around 960 nightclubs remaining in the UK[11]. Now, the challenges clubs continue to face increasingly hinge around their relationships with the towns and cities they call home. The reporting on nightlife's decline in the mid-2010s may have reframed how clubs are discussed and show how decisions made by government and local authorities directly impact where we go to dance. But thanks to the Covid-19 pandemic and the subsequent economic uncertainties it created, they are in greater danger of extinction than ever before.

Before we embark on our journey through UK nightlife, we need to define what a nightclub is and whether this has changed since its inception. If you quiz certain dance music lovers, they'll say "a red light, a basement and a feeling". Others describe it as "a safe haven for freaks"[12]. A nightclub could be a community or even a movement. In the past, it required four walls to house it, a sound system and a dancefloor. Traditionally, it's a physical place that needs to exist somewhere for the community surrounding it to gather. But since its inception in "the ballrooms and dancehalls of the late 19th and early

20th centuries, which blossomed into the jazz clubs, record hops, disc sessions and discothèques in the 1940s and 1950s youth culture explosion"[13], this idea has mutated into different shapes. These have been driven by the increased digitisation of our lives and behaviours as well as the ageing of the first generation of contemporary clubbers who started raving when the conception of acid house was a mere glint in Mr Fingers' eyes.

From orchestral spaces to food halls via music festivals, casinos and more, DJs are increasingly playing in new settings, including virtual worlds opened up by new ideas and technologies. Still, some clubbers believe that dance music starts and stops around the Second Summer of Love in 1988. As venerated DJ Graeme Park says of the Hacienda nights he continues to DJ: "There are a small percentage who always appear by the DJ box looking like they have the weight of the world on their shoulders. They're usually silent until they accidentally catch my eye. Then they'll say something like, 'Oh Parky, it's not the same anymore, is it?'" This sense of comforting nostalgia is more obvious in guitar music but you can see the effects within club culture as beats and bleeps begin to inhabit spaces traditionally associated with older generations. Hacienda Classical celebrated the 40th anniversary of the club in 2022 with a night of orchestral beats at the Royal Albert Hall, a sophisticated setting some distance from the sludgy, smoky nightclubs of the past. It shows how the club music sound has diversified and encroached upon different parts of our cultural consciousness. This fix may come via a concert hall while some ravers still like to cut loose in dirty basement clubs. Others view the nightclub as part of a larger ecosystem alongside music streaming, TikTok and more.

There may be new landscapes for dance music to traverse, but the relationship between city spaces and their club sounds has been important with certain locations associated with particular styles. Juke in Chicago. Bleep in Sheffield. Techno in Detroit. You can pin them on a map, at least until the internet made the world seem much smaller and blurred the distinctions between places. The stories and scenes we've uncovered challenge these perceptions to show how sonic realities in urban environments are more complicated than just one style or genre. They form from a knotty web, a unique confluence of chance encounters, connections and inspirations. Fortuitous meetings between entrepreneurial individuals, access to certain types of equipment or the availability of a particular record in one town - these are just some of the strands behind how a scene and its sound come together. The narrative surrounding the clubs of a city like Sheffield is usually all about one particular style, but there's always much more bubbling below the beats that rise to the surface. Different geographies also offer different environments for sounds to exist within. For example, a club located on top of a mountain in a cold country will sound different to a club in a hot country located in a basement. Tony Andrews, Founder of Funktion One and Head of Engineering and R&D, says how air pressure, temperature and humidity all impact how sound travels through air.

"I recall a number of Glastonburys where the bass became better defined and stronger as we hit dew point," he states. "At altitude, something quite intriguing happens to high frequencies which seem to become more transparent and dimensional."

Now, we're in a digital era where the space music inhabits is not just physical but in an intangible virtual environment. Yet, in our global world, scenes can still be localised as surviving clubs look to take root within their communities and offer more than a dancefloor to their patrons. Over the coming pages, we'll explore the relationship between space and sound and question whether location can still shape the tracks that emerge from a particular town or city. As the way we rave changes, we'll also ask if the nightclub is struggling to breathe in a crowded entertainment market. My book title not only nods to the Prodigy's rave anthem of the same name[14] but questions whether club culture is running 'out of space' both in terms of geography and shrinking attention spans. We'll see how innovative scenes, promoters and venues have risen to this challenge when there haven't been places to hear the music they want or spaces for their community to gather - and how they continue to do so in the face of ongoing troubles.

Back in 2007, when iconic Sheffield dance mecca Gatecrasher burned to the ground, the devoted 'Crasher kids' were described as looking for a "sense of meaningful belonging" from their beloved club, something which represented "not just an escape somewhere but an escape to somewhere better"[15]. Here, we're going to find out if club culture can still offer this release and respite. And, if it can, where this might now be...

# CHAPTER 1

## WENT OUT FOR THE WEEKEND, IT LASTED FOREVER...[16]

*"The best records of that time were like messages from different countries and cities - they were transmitted through the clubs and allowed you a window into what was going on elsewhere"[17].*

Neil Landstrumm

Scotland's appetite for rave is almost as legendary as its eye-watering enthusiasm for artery-clogging snacks.

From macaroni pies in vending machines[18] and deep-fried Mars bars in chippies to raw, panel-beating techno and never-ending after-parties, elements of the Scottish national psyche can tip towards the extreme. Or at least embody a passionate lust for wringing every drop from any situation.

Glasgow is Scotland's biggest city and enjoys notoriety as an epicentre for nightlife which only a few can rival[19]. Alongside other forward-thinking electronic music hubs such as Berlin or Barcelona, this infamy is propelled by a glut of brilliant clubs and record shops and a string of internationally loved producers and DJs all calling it home.

In the 2020s, Glasgow's population is 1.6 million and expanding. This makes it the fourth biggest in the UK, a size reflected in how it has been well served when it comes to clubs and live music venues. From the Arches (now reopened and known as New World) and the

Soundhaus in Finnieston to La Cheetah via the Berkeley Suite, warehouse and arts hub SWG3 and grungy bar, Nice N Sleazy, the city's late-night offerings are as varied as they are electrifying. But to trace Glasgow's enviable electronic music lineage, you need to go back to a time when it was known more for industry, manufacturing and trade than an unquenchable thirst for Buckfast and beats.

As the curtain fell on the 19th century, Glasgow's reputation as a hub of production was well established, forged in the white heat of an industrial revolution driven forward in the city by shipbuilding. The arrival of heavy industry was heralded by the opening of William Elder's famous Fairfield yard in 1864 around the River Clyde, an essential route for trade that weaves its way through Glasgow[20].

The subsequent population explosion saw its size swell from 84,000 in 1800 to 762,000 by 1901 as its revolution attracted hordes of workers, all keen to get a piece of the action[21]. The yards on the Clyde played an important role in ship production during this period, with workers surrounding the river responsible for almost a fifth of the manufacturing of the world's steamships[22]. The toil of this industry helped shape the city's economy here and around the Govan district of Glasgow.

If you trace the ebb and flow of the river to the south-east of the city, you run into the Glasgow Bridge (also known as Jamaica Bridge), a route connected to Jamaica Street and teeming with hustle and bustle. This part of town would have been where hands shook over rum and sugar, with the latter road name taken from the booming trade success with the West Indies during the back end of the 18th century. Alongside other avenues through the city, such as Buchanan and Ingram Street, Jamaica Bridge's name is derived from Glasgow's connections to slavery and its transatlantic trade, tethering the city to the people and pastimes of the British Empire's painful history[23]. If you imported goods in and out of Glasgow back then, chances are you would have stored it in a warehouse on Jamaica Street. As the century progressed, it became a centre for drapery, an industry that was almost as important as shipbuilding to the local economy. Historian Clare McDade has described how, by the mid-19th century, one in ten Glaswegians were employed in textiles[24].

It was during this evolutionary period that Glasgow earned its name as "the workshop of the world" and became known as the second city of the empire. This area would have seen many industrial changes as it grew in line with its rapid economic expansion. However, Glasgow entered a period of decline and unemployment in the wake of successive world wars. In contemporary times, Jamaica Street remains an active vein of Glasgow, although one where money is now briskly exchanged in the remnants of high street shops, chain hotels and fast food joints.

Typically, it's a street blurred by movement, lined with honking buses and trains running in and out of Glasgow Central station just around the corner on Gordon Street. But if you allow your eyes to cut through the buzz, zone in on the small doorway of 22 Jamaica Street, and follow a flight of slightly perilous stairs down into the basement, you'll find yourself transported to a different dimension. On most pre and post-pandemic Fridays, Saturdays and even Sunday nights, it'll be one where sweat drips from a low-hung ceiling onto a wild array of roaring waving arms and hands. They'll be moving to an electronic soundtrack propelled by a well-heeled sound system, specifically designed to pummel those in the room into submission.

Welcome to the Sub Club, one of the UK's smallest, rowdiest and hardest-working basement spaces. It has lorded over this small spot of Glasgow real estate for more than 30 years and is quite rightly revered among ravers and clubbers, despite only being capable of ramming 400 of them in at a time. While so many clubs and venues have faded away over recent years, the Sub Club has managed to fend off adversaries via a mixture of astute business acumen from current owner Mike Grieve and an on-point musical booking policy. The brilliant resident DJs, Harri Harrigan and Dominic Capello, are an essential part of the club's makeup and ongoing success, helming Saturday night's Subculture and laying claim to one of the longest-running residencies in clubbing history.

Throw in the eclectic, infamous Sunday nights previously hosted by fellow locals Optimo (DJs JD Twitch and JG Wilkes) and a loyally raucous crowd, powered by a love for chrome-hoofed house and techno, then its appeal is irresistible. Alongside record shop institution Rubadub and the long line of Glaswegian DJs, producers and nights from the likes of Slam and their influential Soma record label to the latest generation of talent, including Eclair Fifi, Jasper James, Nightwave and TAAHLIAH, "the Subbie" is one of the main reasons Glasgow is a must-play destination for dance music's best. Everyone from Carl Craig to Lil' Louis and Honey Dijon has rinsed the room from that dark booth.

Mike Grieve's life is thickly intertwined within the story of Scottish rave culture, a narrative that is closely aligned with the Sub Club he owns. Originally brought up in Glasgow, he cut his teeth in Aberdeen, a city roughly 150 miles away and one with an unlikely influence over those first vibrations of Scottish acid house.

"I was in Aberdeen around the late seventies and early eighties and that's when I first started kicking around with Harri Harrigan, who also lived up there at that time," he remembers. "We've been pals for a long, long time and used to go to a local club called The Venue. It had a typical indie disco repertoire, so playing the same music every week while putting on live bands."

"At the same time, we were starting to explore contemporary Black American music," he continues. "Hip-hop was appearing and we both loved reggae. Harri's first DJing experiences were as a reggae DJ. I helped him promote a night in Aberdeen back in the early eighties, then Harri moved back to Glasgow a few years later. He had started playing at a night called the Sub Club before there was even a venue with the same name."

After Harri returned to Glasgow, Mike started running a night called the Bang Club with fellow music obsessive Jim Rennie. This fresh sound of house, blending machine-made beats with strong melodies, was beginning to detonate in clubs up and down the UK. Killer tracks included *'The House Music Anthem'* by Marshall Jefferson, an early house music classic alongside Hamilton Bohannon's *'Let's Start II Dance Again'* and the upfront funk of Lyn Collins' *'Think (About It)'*.

"Around 1986, we started to buy a lot of this new music," Mike says. "One guy at a London shop said we were buying more house records in Aberdeen than they were in London at that time. Jim Rennie and I went on to open our own club called Fever in early 1989, which grew out of the Bang Club. This was a house music club right at the point when the whole ecstasy revolution happened."

Those early energy flashes in Aberdeen were an important driver behind dance music taking hold in Scotland, driven by strong connections not only with some of London's music retailers but with burgeoning scenes elsewhere. Mike and his crew used their network to access the latest US imports while magazines such as *Blues and Soul* and *Record Mirror* provided reference points, particularly when searching for the best incoming tracks.

"DJs submitted charts to those magazines all the time," he states. "Graeme Park was DJing in Nottingham and we would devour his selections. We hooked up with him when Fever opened and invited him to Aberdeen to play with us alongside our other resident DJ, Jacqui Morrison."

"Just as we opened Fever in 1989, HMV had opened a massive store on the main street in Aberdeen. The manager, who Jim had previously worked with in a Glasgow record shop, set up a dance music department, the only dedicated section at any of its stores across the UK."

While Mike was in Aberdeen, as the eighties progressed, Glasgow's nightlife was beginning to bubble over with different shades of club music. Stuart McMillan and Orde Meikle are legendary Scottish dance music duo Slam. With their early forays as DJs beginning during the decade, they went on to establish themselves as international stars and heavy hitters in electronic music, known as innovators and forward-thinkers with influence stretching well beyond the Scottish border. They were key players in Glasgow's sweaty embrace of dance music and worked with Harri on his return from Aberdeen.

"Funnily enough, two of the best nights in our formative years were in the same place as you'll find the Sub Club now," say Stuart and Orde. "In the mid-eighties, the venue was known as Lucifer's and Harri ran and played at a night on Fridays called Beatbox. The Saturday night was called Sub Club and run by Graham Wilson, then they renamed the venue after this in 1987. We also went to a place around the corner called Fury Murrys, where we did our first semi-regular night Black Market. That started the same year too."

From these beginnings, Slam grew in stature to become one of Glasgow's most beloved musical exports. As artists, DJs and label owners of Soma, they were responsible for releasing early tracks by French duo Daft Punk, co-founded the Riverside Festival and hosted the Slam Tent, originally at T in the Park, now a standalone event in its own right. Bangers such as *'Positive Education'* and *'Lifetimes'* have become rave classics and the duo continues to release, DJ and tour. They also ran their own venue in the form of the Arches, a hallowed clubbing space that sadly shut its doors in 2015 before reopening under a new name in December 2023[25]. When it comes to dance music, they've seen and done it all.

"Slam was the name of a club night we started up in July 1988 and by the end of that year, we had nights running Thursday through to Sunday, all packed with a completely new crowd of acid house devotees," the duo says. "We had Black Market at Fury Murrys, Joy at Sub Club on Fridays and Slam on Saturdays at Tin Pan Alley alongside Sundays at Sub Club, which had a few different names including Hustle. Three of these nights got into the top ten UK acid house nights out in the i-D magazine annual in 1988."

Mike Grieve, who was then still in Aberdeen, recalls some of the changes to nightlife as the twin pincers of ecstasy and house music began to grab popular culture by the scruff of the neck.

"When we planned to open Fever, we were still aiming to have a mix of programming - we'd play hip hop, soul, jazz, house music - all mixed together," he says. "Obviously, the music became more uptempo as the night wore on, so you'd be playing louder and faster. But when ecstasy really kicked off, things changed dramatically. By the summer of 1989, six months after we opened, the place was properly into house music and the programming reflected that."

Fever operated for a few years before the club night was forced to close and Mike decided to move back to Glasgow. After a stint managing a new bar in the city, he was asked to run the Sub Club in 1994 and has been at the beating heart of the venue ever since.

Long before Mike's return to Glasgow, and even before Slam's days of playing at the venue in its previous guise of Lucifer's, the

Sub Club has been through numerous musical incarnations, and it's a history Mike has dug into since he's been connected to the club. During the fifties and sixties, it was known as Le Cave[26], a 'speakeasy' after-hours jazz venue which, legend has it, saw many of the scene's luminaries, including Louis Armstrong and Ella Fitzgerald, performing after hosting live shows at bigger Glasgow venues, such as Green's Playhouse.

"Later in the sixties, the venue attracted artists like Lulu who sang there when the underground rock scene peaked," says Mike. "Maggie Bell from Stone the Crows, one of Scotland's greatest ever vocalists, performed with the original members of The Sensational Alex Harvey Band. It's got this history of live music alongside being a club. Then bizarrely, in the seventies, it became a dinner dance venue. Reo Stakis owned it and it was the original Jamaica Inn which spawned a chain of steakhouses under this name."

In its current guise as a cutting-edge party space, the Sub Club has attracted many house and techno legends over the years, with Chicago house king Derrick Carter, master at work Louis Vegas, and Detroit maestro Jeff Mills just some of the top talent to have graced the decks. But it is the residents' skills that have helped keep the club locked on the future and given it a reputation as a space any dedicated clubber must dance in. Optimo managed to run a brilliant Sunday night for an incredible 13 years[27], maintaining a left of centre booking policy and an aural aesthetic slung around post-punk, techno, dub and electronic experimentalism. From 1997 to 2010, they ensured Monday mornings would be a struggle for discerning ravers across Glasgow who would slump into work with only memories of the previous night to sustain them. Even more impressive are the achievements of Harri, who has been a Sub Club resident since 1990[28], firstly as part of Atlantis with Slam until 1994 before launching Subculture on the same Saturday night. Over the years, he's become revered by his peers, yet is still one of the most under-rated house and techno DJs around.

"In the late eighties and nineties, it seemed that everyone went out four times a week," Harri remembers. "I've played at the Sub Club pretty regularly since 1985, even before I was a resident. I don't remember a bad night. Some of my favourites are playing with my son [DJ Jasper James] when he'd just turned 18 and a six-hour back-to-back with Andrew Weatherall."

He lists tracks such as Mike Dunn's *'Magic Feet'*, Mr Fingers' *'Washing Machine'*, Lil Louis' *'French Kiss'* as Sub Club favourites from the depths of his record box, which he always returns to. Despite his lengthy association with the venue, he still gets a rush from playing in the space.

"I love Saturdays down there, I always have and the next one I play will probably be my favourite," Harri laughs. "My best nights blur into one lovely, verging-on religious experience with like-minded people. I love meeting clubbers who say it's their first time at the Sub Club and are blown away by the venue and the music. I always love that. I always remember one night when the captain of the Scottish football team was off his face and tried to order drinks at the cloakroom too."

Dr Sarah Lowndes is a writer, curator and lecturer who moved to Glasgow in 1993 to study. Now a Research Fellow at Norwich University of the Arts, she's written numerous books covering the creative scene, including *'Contemporary Artists Working Outside the City: Creative Retreat'* (2018), *'The DIY Movement in Art, Music and Publishing'* (2016), and *'Social Sculpture: The Rise of the Glasgow Art Scene'* (2010). Sarah became embroiled in nightlife as much as her studies and cites the Sub Club alongside the Arches, Slam's venue which opened in 1991 just around the corner under Glasgow Central station, as two of the city's most important clubbing destinations.

"I went out dancing with my friends at both, where you could feel the bass through your entire body," she remembers. "Detroit techno and Chicago house were the order of the day, played by visiting American DJs like Juan Atkins, Blake Baxter, Larry Heard (aka Mr Fingers) and Cajmere."

As a student, Sarah not only raved within these spaces but worked there too, behind the bar, as a flyerer and a promoter for Optimo in between classes. She believes there are distinct and intertwined aspects to Glasgow that have influenced the city's sound and its nightlife.

"One is the longstanding rivalry between Protestant and Catholic communities in the city, and the other is the city's dramatic periods of boom and bust," she explains. "Glasgow grew from a small town to a polluted, overcrowded metropolis in the space of a hundred years. By the late 19th century, the city's population had swelled enormously, mainly due to the massive influx of settlers displaced by the Highland Clearances and the Irish Potato Famine," Sarah says.

"The majority of the first Irish settlers were Catholic and worked mainly as sweated labour in the new industries - textiles, chemical and dyeing works - and as casual construction workers and dock labourers. The smaller community of Protestant Irish immigrant workers were more concentrated in the textile trades and later in shipbuilding and engineering."

In her book, *'Social Sculpture'*, Sarah notes the impact the arrival of these new communities had on opportunities for entertainment and socialising. By the 1930s, the city had more than 130 cinemas[29], then by 1946, there were 93 dance halls, almost "three times as many as London per head of population". While there was an expansion in such leisure and entertainment activities, the authorities have never been overly excited by the potential of Glasgow's night-time economy.

Since the industrial revolution and the city's population spike, there were ongoing tensions between those who loved to party and the temperance movements set against alcohol consumption. The latter was solidified in 1853 through the passing of the Forbes McKenzie Act into legislation[30]. Licensing laws were rigidly fixed between 8am and 11pm with Sunday closing and these draconian restrictions have since continued to be inflicted on the city.

In the seventies, Glasgow played host to live gigs from many of the biggest pop acts of the time, but a particularly raucous show from punks The Stranglers led to the council banning these kinds of bands from performing. The gig saw the crowd invade the stage and was likened to a 'mini riot' by one council member in attendance[31]. With these performances no longer allowed, any young punks wanting to go and watch the latest groups such as The Fall or The Clash had to travel to nearby Paisley[32]. A brief leniency seemed to come into place when Glasgow was awarded the Capital of Culture status in 1990 and shows how cultural creativity is allowed when managed by the powers-that-be. According to Slam, this let up came as a mixed blessing.

"We could suddenly get a 5am licence every weekend," the duo says. "There would still be [illegal] raves such as Desert Storm in old railway arches in remote parks but we had the most continental licensing in the UK with Manchester and London clubs closing much earlier."

"This really helped and beyond our weekly Saturdays at the Sub Club, we also did a series of big all-nighters, which again got licenced until 8am for up to 5,000 people[33]. But then the rave scene got commercial quickly and lots of undesirables got into it, so we went back underground in 1991 and back to clubs only."

Following this period, Slam discovered the Arches theatre underneath Glasgow's Central Station. Opening its doors at the start of the nineties, it became a multi-arts space with plays, restaurants and club nights all featuring among its programming until it lost its late licence in 2015. The midnight curfew imposed effectively meant its club nights could no longer take place.

"It was never one thing or the other," say Slam of the legendary space. "The gigs and clubs helped to fund the artistic pursuits and we ran parties there for 23 years until we had to close."

Strict rules surrounding licensing and curfews were very much a feature of Sarah's time in Glasgow during the nineties too. She describes how the licensing board introduced stringent measures for clubs, with no entry after midnight and everything done and dusted by 2am.

"This meant that the nights could be very compressed," she says. "Last orders at the pub at 11pm, rushing to get into the club before midnight, and then back out on the street within a few hours. In 1994, this was slightly relaxed - the entry cut-off was put back to 12.30am and chucking out time to 2.30am or 3am. Today, Glasgow clubs still have to close at 3am unless they are granted a special late licence. This means two things: there is an intensity, a sense of rushing to each evening ... and there are often after-parties for those not yet ready to go home."

Slam's DJing skills helped push their reputation far beyond Glasgow's city limits as acid house's blue touchpaper began to spark at the end of the eighties. Before their reputation as leading DJs blew up, the duo started travelling between various cities across the north of England, making connections and establishing new friendships to fan the flames of the nascent scene.

"We often went to Manchester in the late eighties and early nineties and developed a friendship with Jon DaSilva, then through him DJs like Graeme Park and Mike Pickering who were a little bit older," they say. "We would get the train down and go and hang out in the Dry Bar, the Eastern Bloc record shop and Joe Bloggs in the Arndale centre. Later the manager of Dry, Leroy Richardson, would organise coaches to come up to the big all-nighters we put on in Glasgow."

Manchester Hacienda DJ Jon DaSilva was not only the first guest they booked in Glasgow but one of the first to properly mix records together as well. Prior to this, much of the soundtrack had come from blending tracks but soon, Stu, Orde and Harri from the Sub Club would all be mixing records, joining house and techno together in one thrilling flow. Slam were then invited to play at the Hacienda at Jon's Hot night in Manchester.

"It took place every Wednesday with Mike Pickering and was such an eye-opener," they say. "It was on a much bigger scale to our parties in Glasgow, which had been capped at 500 people. Here, there were more than a thousand people losing it on a midweek night."

The pair's network continued to extend down the spine of the country. They befriended the likes of Nicky Holloway in London, who invited them to play at the Milk Bar, as well as Danny Rampling with his Pure night and Dave Beer of Back to Basics infamy in Leeds.

"I guess this was the start of the so-called Balearic Network up and down the UK. This ended up including The Bomb in Nottingham, Sugarsweet and later Shine in Belfast and Fever in Aberdeen. DJs including Andrew Weatherall, David Holmes and Justin Robertson would play most of these places regularly. We'd think nothing of jumping in a van and going from one end of the country to the other for a party, or if Slam were booked, there would be a crew coming with us."

Aside from inbound geographical connections, there were international relationships between Glasgow and other US cities such as Chicago and Detroit. Detroit native, DJ and producer Claude Young even went as far as moving to Glasgow, such was the synergy between the two cities[34]. This global network has continued to carry transmissions between these locations right up to the present day.

Sarah Lowndes says: "There was undoubtedly a resonance between the energy of Chicago and Detroit house and techno and the post-industrial struggles of Glasgow, and there were also local DJs and producers with equally strange monikers as their American counterparts."

"Harri at Atlantis, later renamed Subculture, Twitch of Pure, H'atch and J'Ilkes, who ran Knucklehead at the Art School, not to mention A-man and Panic of Tangent putting on raves on trains, boats and underground bunkers and mobile sound units like Desert Storm and Breach of the Peace."

Slam's own label, Soma, has underlined this international vision, releasing records from artists such as Daft Punk and Jesper Dahlback, who would go on to become dance music heroes. The label was behind the original release of the Daft Punk classic, *'Da Funk'*. And while the early dance music scene took off, independent guitar music has also been long-associated with the city via the home-grown talent of Postcard Records, Edywn Collins' Orange Juice, Teenage Fanclub and many more. A DIY ethos, which originated from punk, was shared by the key players, regardless of what kind of noise they were making. As Slam say, the prevalent attitude was one of energy and action. If there wasn't something to your tastes, then you'd get out there and turn it into a reality.

"If no one is making the music you like in your city, then start making it," they say. "Start a label, start a fanzine. We were influenced by our surroundings. The heavy industry was in decay and the hard-drinking, hard-working ethic was still there though equally a grungy creativity was emerging in the eighties and we were part of that…"

In contrast to the ostensibly grittier Glasgow, Scottish capital Edinburgh can initially appear as a tartan tourist trap. From the striking Parliamentary buildings to Arthur's Seat, the castle and the annual festival over August, much of the city seems picture perfect and is beloved of those seeking a Time Out-approved authentic Scottish experience. Edinburgh may know how to wear a kilt but does it know how to party? In a word, yes. Although its reputation for dance music isn't quite as hallowed as Glasgow, the city's cooler brother. Fred Deakin is a DJ, graphic designer, creative, academic and more, although many may know him as one half of experimental electronic duo Lemon Jelly. He was brought up in London before heading to Edinburgh to study in the mid-eighties. Back then, he encountered what he remembers as "a very eclectic and confident city".

"Edinburgh had a real swagger at the time. Maybe Glasgow is a more credible clubbing city now but that wasn't the case when I arrived," he explains.

After he landed in Scotland, Fred cites a whole host of important club nights that shaped him before he took the plunge and began throwing himself into promoting and DJing his own ventures.

"There was the Hoochie Coochie run by Allan Campbell," he recalls. "This was at Coasters in Tollcross, which was a four-floor mega disco. I saw bands like Teenage Fanclub, Primal Scream and A Certain Ratio there. I preferred Manifesto, though. This was a much cooler club that took place on a Sunday night where you'd hear proto-house, dance music somewhere between disco and house, go-go, hip hop, synth disco."

"There was also a great club called Hoover, run by Peter Ellen, which broke a lot of new ground," Fred continues. "Peter used to work behind the counter of Fopp Records and was one of the first people to play whatever he liked: mainly early, pre-rave explosion house music."

While an eager punter, Fred tasted his own success as a promoter, particularly through his night Thunderball. Held at the Assembly Rooms in the centre of Edinburgh towards the end of the eighties, the party regularly packed in 2,000 revellers while he also opted for experimental events such as early-nineties club Misery. The playlist was far more offbeat and complemented by "strange props like vacuum cleaners and chopped onions on the dancefloor"[35]. Fred views the nocturnal spirit of Edinburgh as more eclectic and funkier than other Scottish towns and cities. Yet when house music struck, party-goers weren't shy about getting fully embroiled.

"It's a lovely village, which can be a pro or a con depending on your point of view," he laughs. "But house music was a tsunami of culture we all got on board with. One of the guys from London Records came up to Edinburgh and gave me one of the first *'House Sounds of Chicago'* compilations. I played tracks off this at a Thunderball we held at Stirling Castle. Then when house music really hit, we did a club called Devil Mountain in the Fruitmarket Gallery with a very banging house room downstairs."

"House music was really hard for anyone to resist," he continues. "When we first started playing it, plenty of people would initially be like: 'What's this stuff all about?' Then a week later, you'd see them wearing a bandana, standing on a podium, doing the big fish, little fish, cardboard box."

Edinburgh-based producer and DJ Neil Landstrumm has been an exponent of underground bass and bleeps for over two decades, releasing techno LPs on labels like Tresor and Peacefrog before embarking on a more experimental sonic trajectory. Albums on Planet Mu and his own label, Scandinavia, have ricocheted through shards of grime, dubstep and other kinetic dancefloor styles.

"The most commonly held belief is that Edinburgh is quite insular and hides its light under a bushel," he laughs. "But that wasn't the experience I had at clubs like Pure or Sativa in the nineties. Glasgow has this reputation as a party city but in those early years, Edinburgh was where it was at."

Neil's musical mind was blown by catching the Happy Mondays as a teenager at Glasgow's SECC with the Hacienda's Mike Pickering as DJ support. Mike playing LFO proved to be a lightbulb moment which sent Neil down a rabbit hole of electronic records and music-making equipment.

"At first, I went out as a raver, but then I quite quickly wanted to know how these records were made, started meeting various people who told me which machines made which noise, then began hunting down these bits of gear in second-hand shops."

Pure is one of Edinburgh's underground clubbing success stories, a party that inspired a loyal and devoted crowd and, as Ray Philp says in a Red Bull Music Academy piece, left a "strong mark on a city notorious for being difficult to impress"[36].

Headed up by resident DJs Twitch and Brainstorm, the first incarnation of the night was hosted at The Venue and known as UFO. According to fellow resident DJ Carole Kelly, it began life in the early nineties amid the alternative indie scene but was forced to adopt a new guise due to football hooligans throwing regular wobblers.

"The casuals destroyed it on several occasions, so it was rebranded and opened as a members-only club," she recalls. "This was happening all over Edinburgh at the time, the casuals taxing all the pubs and clubs or threatening to smash them up. Becoming a members-only club did stop the violence but it calmed down everywhere after a few months of its opening. The dance scene became so large, it just seemed to drown the thugs out."

Pure was loved for its richly diverse playlist, which included new beat, metal and house, despite some perceptions of it as a straight-up techno night. But the club went much deeper with even its name flicking the V's at those who liked the sound of their events to stay in one lane. As Pure picked up pace and attracted a following, it began to be frequented by up-for-it and switched on ravers making the journey over from Glasgow.

"The connection between the cities was such that several of the Pure DJs and posse moved there after that, notably Twitch [who went on to set up Optimo]," says Carole. "The night was special because there was nothing else around like it at the time. It really shaped the dance scene at the time in Scotland."

"In fact, it felt like Andy [Brainstorm] brought dance music to Edinburgh in some ways, having visited his dad several times in Tenerife and discovered the Balearic scene. At the time, Edinburgh was still immersed in alternative, metal and hip hop music."

According to Neil Landstrumm, the night offered an essential education for Edinburgh's producers and punters alike, with plenty of electronic music pioneers descending on the party to play.

"Twitch and Brainstorm were the tastemakers; they introduced us to the music of Detroit, Chicago and Holland," he says. "We were really lucky in that they would book people like Aphex Twin and Orbital, Sabresonic, Underground Resistance, Andy Weatherall."

"One of the best stories I heard about Pure was when Shut Up and Dance played," Neil continues. "It was an amazing night, then this famous snooker player appeared with his manager after playing in Edinburgh. He was wandering around looking for cocaine, absolutely steaming. It doesn't get any weirder than that and that's what I loved about rave culture."

Carole says how most of her favourite nights at The Venue blur into one joyous whole as she was at the club so frequently. Pure and the club held such influence she even decided to buy her first flat as it was just around the corner.

"Pure was almost like my second home," she laughs. "In terms of standout moments, Derrick May playing whale sounds over the music was really emotive. But I loved it when our crew played too. That was what it was like; it made you feel like grown-up kids, just loving everyone, having fun and being so carefree."

Cast your mind back to the mid-nineties, and one of the most vital and abrasive pens of the time belonged to *'Trainspotting'* author Irvine Welsh, a writer Neil feels sharply dissected the contrasting lives of Edinburgh's dwellers and ne'er do wells. Alongside the glittering tourist attractions, a huge amount of hardship lay underneath the city's surface.

"Edinburgh was certainly an interesting mixture of people with posh students, then this football casual element too," he states. "For all its beauty and intellectual success, the city does have a very nasty underbelly of poverty and heroin addiction - and this was all part of the makeup of the rave scene too."

Neil believes that some of the initial rush created by nineties dance music culture has slowly drained away over the years, leaving it in a more sterilised form. Emerging out of the mass unemployment of the late eighties brought on by a restructuring of work and an economic recession, acid house culture seemed to promise a utopian, technicolour ideal but it's a vision that has been diminished.

"There was a whole social political element attached to dance music when it took off," he says. "You could see it in the lack of jobs in these cities which had lost their industries. There was something entrepreneurial about setting up the Blackburn raves, launching your own record label, getting off your arse and picking up the baton of punk culture."

"All you needed was the energy and enthusiasm to go to the studio to lay down some tracks and press the records," Neil continues. "Before you knew it, there would be record shops everywhere selling white labels - I loved all that. It was like a call and response between these different towns and cities. Since then, clubs have been slowly squeezed out of Edinburgh. The Venue that Pure used to be in has been turned into a gallery, while others have been sold to developers, mainly because of their prime locations in the city."

Fred Deakin has since left Scotland's capital but remembers how its centre is constrained by hills, castles and history. A sprawling metropolis like London has a more fluid geography and seemingly endless amount of space.

"I used to go out in Soho, then it would be Hoxton Square, then up to Dalston in east London," states Fred. "It keeps evolving but for other cities, space is more confined and doesn't have the opportunity to expand in the same way. In London, there always seems to be another stop on the tube."

Fred remembers combing every inch of Edinburgh, searching for new spaces in the forms of function rooms, cafes, halls. In fact, anywhere a sound system could be installed and a dancefloor rolled out.

"My entire reason for living back then was to find a space where I could put my nights on," he recalls. "The dream was always to find a venue and new territory to start running parties. We did it with the Fruitmarket and also La Belle Angele, which was a gallery originally. We were the first to use it for the club Wildlife but it later became a real fixture in the Edinburgh scene."

"At the same time, we found the council's nightlife policy frustrating. It could be very expansive in August during the Edinburgh Festival so tourists could party until they were blue in the face. Then when they had gone, people would have to go back to a normal life."

Despite now living elsewhere, Fred is still enthralled by Scotland's rhythm of life and the night-time spaces he occupied while living there. His *'Club Life'* show, hosted at the Edinburgh Festival in the summer of 2023, offered attendees a chance to immerse themselves in the best nights of the eighties and nineties[37]. "Emerging culture, mutations and alliances are made at two or three in the morning - and in your twenties, this time belongs to you," he says. "If you're in this space at that time of night, then you've earned your right to step into this community."

"One of the things Scotland has is a very keen sense of cultural identity. To a certain extent, other parts of the country follow London's lead but Scotland's culture is fiercely independent. That is very powerful and beguiling and why I fell in love with the country."

Until 2012, a shining beacon of that independent spirit could be found by heading to the west of Glasgow and the litter of warehouse spaces scattered around the north bank of the Clyde. Just outside the city centre, this is the former shipbuilding part of the city. It's an area that went into a slow yet terminal decline following the culmination of the Second World War, described as a "stagnant moat" during the 1960s[38], and a shadow of its former illustrious past. As with many cities across the north of England, the death of industry created an opportunity for nightlife to flourish, with abandoned factories and warehouses providing an environment for creatives to move in. One constant in the changing area was Bilslands' Bakery, a towering building visible for anyone coming into Glasgow from the south of the city. The bakery was set in motion in 1872[39], eventually employing hundreds of people and distributing bread not just all over Glasgow but Scotland too. The factory closed down in 1985 but only sat derelict temporarily with the Soundhaus, a band rehearsal space, music studio and venue, opening inside it in 1992. Manager and long-term promoter Lynn Macdonald remembers how the building was just up the street from the Daily Record building and in an industrial area surrounded by paint and material sellers.

"We were in Finnieston, so we were only located on the edge of the city centre," she explains. "The bakery was a big employer for years but I'd been working there for some time before I realised that my uncle used to work for them too. I used to run around that space when I was a wee kid."

The Soundhaus was a unique, multi-functional offering in Glasgow's nightlife. While it provided much-needed rehearsal and recording rooms for bands and musicians, after dark it functioned as a private members club.

"The licensing laws were often restrictive, meaning clubs would have to shut at 3am," Lynn explains. "As we were a members' club, we could stay open until 5 or 6am. It gave us a unique selling point. Even though we couldn't sell any booze after 3, people would still come as we were one of the last places open in town."

Some of the Soundhaus' most popular events veered towards the more experimental underbelly of electronic music, with the sounds of nights such as Monox, Pussypower and Chakra running the gauntlet from electro to darker acid and techno. But an unfortunate legislative change to the way private clubs operated meant the venue had to start shutting its doors earlier, denting its popularity.

"Around 2005, the rules changed. These used to allow you to be licensed until 2 or 3, then you could be open until whenever you wanted," Lynn recalls. "But they made it so you had to close half an hour after you stopped selling booze. It was the start of the decline for us."

Ultimately, Soundhaus' demise came at the hands of property developers who bought the building from the owners Lynn was renting it from. The speed at which the transaction went through meant they were unexpectedly booted out of the space at the beginning of 2012. But not without a huge party as a send-off to the venue.

"We went on until 11am the next day when we were leaving and drank the place dry," Lynn laughs. "We had tried to get along with the new owners, but every time we asked for something to be repaired, it just felt like it was too much of a bother for them. They said they would knock the building down as they supposedly wanted to use it for something, but it never happened and the land is still empty."

Despite the collapse of its industry, Glasgow's course has been one of reinvention, attracting greater investment through winning European Capital of Culture status in 1990, then hosting the Commonwealth Games in 2014[40]. A large student population has ensured a steady flow of new ideas and an ongoing audience with the time, energy and passion for continually getting under the skin of the city's clubs and live music culture. Glasgow has been a university city since 1451 and today is home to the largest student population in Scotland.

As Sarah Lowndes says: "In addition to Glasgow University, there are a further three universities (Glasgow Caledonian, Strathclyde University and the University of the West of Scotland). Glasgow is home to eight colleges, The Royal Conservatoire of Scotland and the Glasgow School of Art. It means that every autumn brings new waves of students to the city and they refresh the city's art and music scenes."

Andrew Fleming-Brown, aka Mutley, was born in Glasgow and went to study in Aberdeen before returning to the city after he'd finished his time at art school. He dipped his toes into event promotion, gradually getting into street postering and flyering, then came across an abandoned warehouse space in 2004, which set off ambitions to create a Glaswegian equivalent of New York's Museum of Modern Art[41]. Located on Eastvale Place, what would go on to become the SWG3 arts and music space is close to the Clyde but tucked away next to a railway line.

"Our little corner of Glasgow kind of felt like it was at the end of the world when we first moved here - which was perfect for illegal raves but not so great for transport links when putting on licensed live music," Mutley laughs. "But as we've developed and grown, the area has become a more connected location. The OVO Hydro Arena is close; there are now lots of great bars and restaurants nearby. We've grown up here and played a role in this regeneration. Glasgow is now finding a love for the Clyde and putting money in here. It shows how rivers are the lifeline of any city."

Back in 2009, more than £2 billion was committed to public and private investment in major regeneration projects to continue the makeover of this waterfront area[42]. Mutley has always had a long-term view for SWG3 too. Following its opening as an arts space with studio opportunities for creatives, he set about raising the requisite funds to buy the building around 2010. After accessing Creative Scotland funding and a brewer's loan from Tennent's[43], Mutley was able to open a music venue on the first floor in a space called the Warehouse. SWG3 has since continued to expand, securing the neighbouring site, previously known as the Clydeside Galvanisers, now simply called the Galvanizers. A huge yard outside has enabled the team to host a series of open-air gigs with performances from the likes of The xx and LCD Sound System.

"We bought the building, then the site next door, so we own the assets, the venue that it trades through," Mutley states. "We also have an arts charity and a big arts programme and this engages a lot with the community. We position ourselves as a cultural and a community asset."

Although the area is changing rapidly, Mutley believes SWG3's location and ownership of the space mean they should be able to fight their corner in the face of any encroaching regeneration. The venue's defences to change are, at this point, standing firm. Not only has it spearheaded the surrounding redevelopment, but it diversified its offering via corporate event production and studio space to shore up its resilience.

"We have big developments happening on either side of us but we're also hemmed in by two railway lines and they act as a barrier, both acoustically and in terms of people reaching us," he says.

Mutley also points out that there will always be potential issues with a venue of SWG3's size, especially when 2,000 Glaswegians are spilling into the streets at two in the morning. But ever since the city lost the Arches venue in 2015, the authorities are now keener than ever to protect the cultural jewels in their night-time economy.

"At SWG3, we have been lucky enough to receive significant investment from the Scottish government, which has been supported by the city council as well, to achieve some of our development plans. We certainly feel that there is more support for venues like ours now than there ever has been."

The addition of the 560 square metres Galvanizers area in 2017 has enabled SWG3 to play host to an array of events, from corporate dinners to late-night raves.

"The Galvanizers work really well for any production you want," says Mutley. "It's got great height, no columns, just raw brick and steel fabric, meaning the event opportunities are huge."

"A total moment was the Optimo 20 party we hosted in 2017, which was a massive rave they did with DJs the Blessed Madonna and Avalon Emerson on the bill," he remembers. "It was the first music event we'd done in this new space. You'd come in the doors of the venue, through a corridor, then into the Galvanizers and it would just blow people's minds. The programme Optimo put together was sensational; it was massive for all of us."

While many of Glasgow's original trendsetters are still leading the way, newer generations of Glaswegian players have sent the city's nightlife scurrying in numerous directions. The Numbers crew are among the most influential, a collective drawn together from the Wireblock, Dress 2 Sweat and Stuffrecords labels back in 2010, with members including Scottish party starter Jackmaster and DJ Spencer. They have taken on the baton of hosting eclectic and inspiring parties across many of the city's different spaces and Richard Chater is one of the multifaceted team, along with Rob 'Bobby Cleaver' Mordue and Neil 'Nelson' Morton. They bonded via a love of electronic records and 'going out, out'.

"Myself and Adam [Rodgers] had previously run a lot of parties with mates in Glasgow and at the same place [infamous Paisley institution] Club 69 was held," he explains. "Jack [Jackmaster] and Calum [Spencer] were both in their teens and working Saturdays in Rubadub and running a party called Seismic, which hosted the likes of Claude Young. Neil also was involved with Seismic and Rob was a big part of what we all did."

In 2003, the various members of what would become Numbers were at the Autechre edition of All Tomorrow's Parties in Camber Sands, taking inspiration from the Manchester's Skam Records room's visuals and similar eclectic sonics from the likes of LFO and Anthony' Shake' Shakir bouncing off the walls. At the time, the friends were all working on their own labels in Glasgow. Once they'd returned, recovered from the ravey weekend and made the connections between each other's ventures, they decided to cross these different beams. In this way, Glasgow's size certainly helps draw the like-minded together and provides the space for the cross-pollination of antics encapsulated by how Numbers formed.

"What I like about Glasgow is that the city is big, yet small enough to be the perfect environment for incubating ideas and forming friendships," he explains. "Unlike London, where getting from one side of the city to another is a bit of a mission, Glasgow is easy to navigate. In some cases, this can lead to a more communal energy, especially as clubs mostly finish at 3am and you usually congregate at someone's flat afterwards. This can be the ideal spot to share music, thoughts and take stock of what you've just heard in the club."

With Numbers' various members alternating between London and Glasgow, both places have cast influence on the label's attitude and ethos. But interestingly, many of the best artists whose music they've released - almost unclassifiable auteurs such as Hudson Mohawke, Rustie or the late, great SOPHIE - have all hailed from the Scottish city. The world-leading distribution set up from Rubadub means they can share music across the world without leaving their home town too.

"Glasgow has always been the place that allows us to look out to the wider world," explains Richard. "Rather than the stereotypical aspects of Glasgow - the weather, decline of heavy industry - we're inspired by the people around us, the city's deep connection to Black American music and its appetite for new sounds."

Glasgow may have hosted a plethora of successful and exciting clubs, but Richard points to the legendary Club 69, just outside the city in Paisley, as one of the most important. Hosted in the basement under the Koh-I-Noor restaurant, it's seen many of dance music's greats perform, attracted by the small capacity and low-key vibes.

"Some people have Plastic People or Berghain; we've got 69," laughs Richard. "It technically isn't in Glasgow but was at a venue formerly called Rocksy's Basement."

"The party was helmed by Rubadub's Martin McKay, Wilba, Barry and also Euan McGinnis. The vibe and the music was like nothing else in Glasgow. The music took in IDM, dub and reggae, house and always the maddest unheard Detroit shit from Drexciya, UR, 430 West to Erik Travis. You were either dancing like crazy or constantly running to the booth to find out what the record was."

The location of the venue, now known as Club 69, outside the main metropolis of Glasgow enabled the night to have a real mixture of attendees. The crowd ranged from randomers who had stumbled across the space to hardcore Rubadub devotees.

"There was no laddishness or snobbery, anyone was welcome and people really appreciated that," Richard explains. "For most of the time, there wasn't even any security."

Alongside his responsibilities with Numbers, Richard has worked at Rubadub since 2004. The influential shop has turned countless music heads onto electronic music of all shades and sounds since it opened in 1992. From vinyl and music technology to offering distribution for myriad different labels, it's been an important conduit for music to enter the city, then flow throughout the rest of the UK.

"It's where I discovered records from Underground Resistance, Metroplex, Drexciya, MMM, Basic Channel, Clone, Viewlexx, Skam, Sahko, Direct Beat, Dance Mania to name a few," says Richard. "Parallel to the vinyl and tech, there is a distribution company which started by first supplying stores with vinyl from Detroit now exclusively distributes labels such as Mood Hut, Inciensio/Proibito, Apron, Firecracker and Night Slugs as well a lot of labels from Glasgow including Numbers, Dixon Avenue Basement Jams, 12th Isle and many more. I'm a strong believer in the power of what a record shop can do. Rubadub is genuinely one of those places where you will be welcomed no matter what, given new music to discover, advice on DJing, producing, setting up a label or promoting."

Maya Medvesek, the Slovenia-born, now Glasgow-based artist better known as Nightwave, agrees that Rubadub has and continues to do a huge amount in breathing life into the city's clubbing scene, providing a space for it to congregate around.

"The Rubadub store is an institution," she says. "Not just for records and music gear but a place for the community to share and uplift each other."

Nightwave originally moved from Slovenia to London during the early noughties, where she spent a decade honing her bass music sound, a dizzyingly frenetic style which sees flacks of UK garage, grime, jungle and dubstep all vying for attention. Her music has definitely mutated thanks to her relocation to Glasgow.

"Since I've been in Glasgow, I dived deeper into techno waters, and inevitably the parties and general energy of this town influenced the tunes I make," she states. "I always think, 'How would this tune go down at the Subbie?' I make a lot of acid, electro and different takes on techno and it's definitely Glasgow's fault."

But, she adds, Glasgow's indelible impression on her musical style goes far beyond the techno stereotype the city is sometimes associated with. "There's certainly not a shortage of nights like this," she says. "But Glasgow is far more than that, the passion for music is omnipresent and it seems everyone you meet is in some way connected to it, either as a promoter, producer or a DJ."

Nightwave's musical output has been rapid over the last few years, with her styles evolving via releases for the likes of Hotflush and Unknown To The Unknown. She's enjoyed a BBC Radio 1 Residency, hosted her own nights and become an integral part of Glasgow's nocturnal scene. She believes that the city's tight-knit electronic music community is one united by a desire to not only make great music but do this by being themselves too. From purple, the more melodic subgenre of dubstep pushed by producer Rustie to the hazy, jazz-inflected electronics of Rebecca Vasmant and queer parties hosted by Bonzai Bonner, Glasgow's scene spans an exciting musical scope.

"There is definitely a distinct 'sound' that many explore but we also have masses of innovation and individuality," she says. "If you look at people like Rustie and Hudson Mohawke, they completely changed the game and started a whole new musical direction. The whole world is copying that sound, the biggest rappers want those beats and you hear the tracks in ads for huge global brands. All from Glasgow."

Compared with other cities synonymous with club culture, Glasgow's smaller geographical size certainly plays a part in uniting collaborators. The sense of community is close, with the various DJs, promoters and venue owners on hand to foster creativity and lift each other up. The Sub Club is a prime example of a space that has seen different generations of DJs, clubbers and even management remaining within its orbit for great lengths of time. Before Mike Grieve took on the lease and ownership, it was owned for some years by the MacCrimmon family[44]. Meanwhile, the club's resident Harri has passed on the baton to his son and internationally renowned DJ, Jasper James, who regularly plays there too.

Sarah Lowndes says: "The club's atmosphere and reputation have remained positive throughout the years, thanks in part to a door policy that has always stayed the same: strict but fair. The Sub Club even survived a fire in an adjacent building in 1999 that meant the club was closed until 2002 and had to rove around a number of temporary venues until it could return home."

The club itself is a hub of positivity, Sarah continues, citing the importance of Optimo's long-running night and association as another key axis around which ideas and innovation have spun.

"You can see the Sub Club as a confluence where lots of creative people could meet and influence each other at club nights, notably Optimo," she says. "Lots of the people who went to Optimo collaborated together on work projects, had important friendships, got together, and had children."

"In recent years, Twitch and Wilkes have run many fundraising club events to benefit food banks and other worthy causes," Sarah adds. "But to build communities and impact meaningfully on the local area, you need to be able to stay somewhere and grow. The Sub Club might be a bit of an exception to do this by staying where it is for so long."

Mike Grieve agrees that the friendships and trust between the key players at the Sub Club has not only led to its long life but forged a tight team and community around the residents, music and space. As a basement club, the intensity of the nights is also unforgettable. Whether you've watched any of the Boiler Room sessions online[45] or attended a raucous Sunday night session with Optimo, the small space acts as a catalyst in terms of ramping up vibe and atmosphere. With the dancefloor in the centre of the room, attention is all about the energy between the ravers and what pumps out of the speakers rather than on the DJ.

"The shape of the space is a classic shoebox with the dancefloor in the centre," says Mike. "We rebuilt the place in 2002 after the fire and those were the things we concentrated on maintaining from the original space - that the dancefloor was close to the DJ booth, so the intensity was created in the centre point of the club with the low ceiling. It's all about the energy and atmosphere that you can build."

Unsurprisingly, Slam's Stuart and Orde are firm believers in the power of the club to sustain communities and be beneficial for society in ways that go far beyond dancefloor release.

"A great club is a community of people who enjoy music, dancing and hanging out," the pair explain. "And there is an ecosystem that forms around it with a record shop, designers, clothing, artwork, graffiti, studios and music making, bars, an online community too."

Glasgow is known as a party place but its comparatively small centre brings the key players together who are all supportive of each other and their home. Slam and Optimo might be big-name DJs who regularly play all over the world but their commitment to the city extends to doing what they can to help those in need within their local communities. Slam have become involved with the Turn the Tables charity, a social enterprise initiative set up to help homeless people learn to DJ and make their own music. They also host an annual event called Soma Skool which features discussion panels with music industry experts and promoters, all aimed at inspiring the next generation of dance music professionals and showing how this local clubbing ecosystem can sustain itself.

"The pause offered by Covid-19 is our big chance to restart with the ideals and ideas of the early days of house music," the duo says. "These kinds of initiatives are important and you see the benefits. They show that electronic music is not just a hedonistic release, but provides a lifestyle and support network too."

# CHAPTER 2

## AN ODE TO PAST, PRESENT AN FUTURE MANCUNIAN "TEMPLES OF BACCHANALIAN EXCESS"[46]

*"I've played some shitholes in my time, but this takes the fucking biscuit"*[47].

Bernard Manning

Thomas De Quincey, opium-eater, Manchester Grammar school pupil and lauded essay writer and author, was one of the original hedonists of a city that has long had a reputation for being as infatuated with having it large as spinning poetic charms.

This lyrical love has been passed through generations: from the subversive verses of punk poet John Cooper Clarke and the wide-eyed scally excess of the Happy Mondays to today's tongue twister par excellence Aitch and the more soulful styles of IAMDDB. Intertwined within these words are a litany of artists and creatives who've helped set Manchester's night-time and passion for dancing alight: brilliant Black artists Marcel King, A Guy Called Gerald and breakdancing crew, Broken Glass, huge, life-changing guitar bands such as The Stone Roses and Oasis, a tuned-in LGBTQIA+ community alongside some of the best clubs and nights in the land. Then venues like Sankeys Soap, Antwerp Mansions, Soup and the White Hotel, then nights, including the Electric Chair and the Warehouse Project, underline Manchester's lust for good times.

While De Quincey passed away in 1859, if he had somehow returned during 1988's fateful Second Summer of Love that put a firecracker under youth culture, you might have found him on a podium in a club on Whitworth Street, wearing a bandana with a jaw doing cartwheels. His description of the effects of imbibing his favourite tipple would not have been out of place in the Hacienda that year: "I took it - and in an hour - oh, heavens! What a revulsion! What an upheaving, from its lowest depths, of inner spirit! What an apocalypse of the world within me! That my pains had vanished was now a trifle in my eyes: this negative effect was swallowed up in the immensity of those positive effects which had opened before me - in the abyss of divine enjoyment thus suddenly revealed"[48].

This "fondness of chemical exploration", as acid house veteran, DJ, artist, author and epitome of sartorial elegance Justin Robertson describes it, is a maxim to live by in Manchester, along with a 'work-hard play-hard' attitude. The city's love affair with parties stretches back to the turn of the 19th century in line with the great wave of industrial change which swept through the UK. Manchester's appetite for boozing and partying was spiralling back then, driven by a new wave of drinking halls and a workforce looking to let loose at night after toiling in the midst of industrial change by day. As with so many cities, this sudden injection of manufacturing and production brought huge structural changes to Manchester and attracted a new populace with a desperate urge to live life to the full. The city's size increase was rapid and dramatic. At the start of the 18th century, Manchester's population was less than 10,000. By the end of the century, this number had hit 700,000, with only London and Glasgow larger[49]. DJ, journalist and Mancunian commentator Dave Haslam says this passion for drinking, singing and making merry was directly linked to Manchester's surge in the number of people suddenly calling it home.

"When the city exploded during the late 18th and early 19th century, hundreds of people were arriving from rural Ireland, the British countryside and eastern Europe," he states. "But from sewage systems to housing, there was little in the way of infrastructure in place to cater for them. The factory workers and those in warehouses and the mills all needed somewhere to be entertained."

This new urban and hard-working society wasn't unique to Manchester. Other cities such as neighbouring Liverpool and Leeds, then further afield in Newcastle and Glasgow, all experienced a similar seismic shift. From this developed a new form of entertainment: the music hall.

"These were big places where people would meet and drink, get intoxicated, and watch all kinds of performances on stage," says Dave. "This idea of living for the weekend was born out of this culture - and ever since there has been an embedded history in the DNA of the population - you escape at the weekend. What happens over those two days is just, if not more, important than what happens in the rest of the week."

In Dave's book 'Manchester, England: The Story of the Pop Cult City', he highlights Ben Lang's Music Hall as one of the first and most popular places for revelry in the city. Located on Victoria Bridge at the top of Deansgate, Ben Lang's was a drinking den for Manchester's new working class, who you would find knocking back beers in this location during the 1840s and 1850s. It showcased music and comic entertainment to as many as 2,000 people despite a false alarm over a fire in 1868 that led to the death of more than 20 punters in the crush to escape[50].

Dave described how the venue showed "the first stirrings of a music hall circuit which would remain intact for decades, and an urban popular music culture in Manchester which can be traced from the very earliest days of the city right through its history, via nineteenth-century street life, jazz, the cinema and the 1960s, to standing in the rain at the front of the queue outside the Hacienda"[51].

From here, this appetite for enjoying itself was lodged inside the city's guts. Despite the ways our working lives have evolved, this sense of living to escape the dreariness of the 9-5 persists.

"Every generation thinks it is the first to discover staying up all night and intoxication and learning how music oils the wheels of life," laughs Dave. "But in fact, every previous generation has known that too, ever since Manchester started partying hard in the 19th century. Back then, various social commentators of the time would arrive in Manchester on a Friday night and would have to step over people lying in the gutter. The hunger for hedonism, entertainment and music is embedded in cities like Manchester."

Whereas Glasgow's fortunes were made in the shipping industry, Manchester's growth was based on cotton manufacturing, leading it to be dubbed 'Cottonopolis' during the latter end of the 19th century. With the city housing more than 50 mills[52], political novelist of the time and later British prime minister, Benjamin Disraeli, was moved enough by the city to write: "a Lancashire village has expanded into a mighty region of factories and warehouses. Yet, rightly understood, Manchester is as great a human exploit as Athens"[53].

However, the cotton industry's success did not last forever, with production peaking in the early 20th century[54], then steadily collapsing. This decline came from the disruption of the Great War in 1914, where keenly competitive overseas markets offered cheaper labour and more advanced production methods than the UK[55]. Cotton's slow fall from grace took place throughout the 20th century and was felt across the industrial heartlands of the north of England. But Manchester's downturn was perhaps the most severe. Jane Jacobs, a US-Canadian writer and expert on urban planning, described how in the sixties it was "the very symbol of a city in long and unremitting decline"[56].

While Manchester's industry and economy entered freefall during the fifties and sixties, important movements were bubbling, some of which would not only have a profound impact on the early days of what we now know as club culture but define Manchester's independent character, defiant spirit and economic future.

As one of the north-west's original DJing heroes, Greg Wilson is a selector who has lived through most of the arch of dance music's history since his career began in the mid-seventies. His musical life is a unique one: Greg enjoyed hugely popular residencies in the early eighties at Wigan Pier and Manchester's influential Legend, having first started out in his hometown of New Brighton on the Wirral in Merseyside[57]. He was one of the first DJs to mix records together in the UK and, in 1983, became the first 'dance music' specialist hired for a regular weekly session at Manchester's Haçienda. Greg quit DJing to focus on management and production in 1984, before returning to the nocturnal fray in 2003. Before his own DJing adventures, Greg cites the importance of Manchester clubs such as the Twisted Wheel and resident DJ Roger Eagle in creating a blueprint for today's nightlife.

"Eagle and Guy Stevens from The Scene in London were laying the foundations for the specialist approach I'd later be a part of, by importing Black American music and going to source the best records for their environments," says Greg.

"That the roots of UK club culture began with such aficionados should be to our eternal gratitude, along with Jamaican immigrants Count Suckle and Duke Vin, who played R&B to the Windrush generation," he continues. "US R&B was the original JA Sound System music before the island's own intoxicating sound emerged. Suckle was able to take this new sound of ska into the centre of London for his residency at The Roaring Twenties on Carnaby Street."

Roger Eagle's Twisted Wheel started life in 1963 on Manchester's Brazennose Street and saw him become an influential figure, playing a livewire mix of soul and R&B[58]. His all-night DJ sessions are credited with influencing the Northern Soul scene, which emerged there some years later. But he left the Twisted Wheel in 1966 following its Whitworth Street relocation, moving on to his psychedelic venture at Magic Village. Eagle then headed over to Liverpool to promote live concerts, including David Bowie and Led Zeppelin gigs at The Stadium boxing arena before he opened post-punk haunt Eric's. It was around this venue that many of the city's most eccentric and talented musicians, such as Julian Cope and Pete Burns, congregated.

"After 1971, the Black music scene in Manchester began to wane," explains Greg. "Then, later in the decade, the Ritz all-dayers started, initially as Northern Soul events. But as the disco and jazz-funk influences became stronger, mainly due to Ian Levine and Colin Curtis' more progressive approach at the Blackpool Mecca, featuring contemporary releases, this caused a schism on the Northern Soul scene."

In Manchester, these all-dayers began to attract a diverse jazz-funk leaning crowd with this sound becoming popular, thanks to DJs John Grant and Colin Curtis. They played a weekly funk night at Rafters, a club on Oxford Road which later became Jilly's, then the Music Box.

"Grant and Curtis were right at the top of the tree back then when it came to the specialist Black music scene I aspired to," Greg explains. "But they were more an inspiration than an influence and I always had my own ideas in this direction."

With all-dayers taking place throughout the seventies and early eighties, DJs would organise coaches from different venues across the region, bringing together various audiences, music lovers and spreading the word between towns.

"A lot of these events were held in old dance halls converted into discotheques, many owned by the Mecca organisation, who had venues nationwide," explains Greg. "In the north-west, the most important all-dayer of the late seventies was at The Ritz in Manchester, but during the early eighties, it was Clouds in Preston."

Of the key Mancunian clubs, The Reno and the Nile in Moss Side offered "rites of passage for the Black community" during the sixties and seventies, alongside the PSV/Russell Club, a venue famously used by Factory Records.

He says: "Their proximity to the city centre certainly had a bearing, as was the case in the rave era when the Kitchen, in Hulme's Charles Barry Crescent, became the prime afterparty location, just a short walk from the Haçienda."

This mix of young white and Black music lovers in the melting pot of Hulme was crucial in steering the direction of the sound of Manchester's club scene during the early eighties. Greg also highlights the importance of the Spin Inn on Cross Street and Mike Shaft's Soul show on Piccadilly Radio which supplied/featured all the latest releases.

"I've previously talked about what I refer to as 'the Black/white mix' in Manchester, which mainly resulted from white students and musicians moving into the Hulme crescents," he states. "It meant a young multicultural landscape emerged and impacted the wider city as ideas were exchanged and new influences gained. This brings to mind that famous quote by Tony Wilson, about Manchester kids having the best record collections – it was because of an open-mindedness with young people looking to explore outside the box, and Hulme was the main source of the melting pot. With the clubs, the radio and Spin Inn, Manchester had a healthy Black music underground with a deep legacy by the time DJs of my generation came along."

In the seventies and eighties, comedian Bernard Manning was at the epicentre of entertainment in the north-west. Notorious for racist and sexist gags, his act was at odds with the rapidly emerging multicultural Manchester remembered by Greg yet, when the Hacienda opened its doors on 21 May 1982, the comic's name was on the bill. It's not only his act that seemed archaic. The sticky carpets and crude humour of the Embassy Club on Rochdale Road where Manning could usually be found were part of a different, dying galaxy compared with the stark modernism of the Ben Kelly-designed Hacienda. On the club's opening evening, Bernard was so unimpressed by this new venue that he slagged it off on stage, handed his fee back and stormed off into the night amid a chorus of boos.

His turn couldn't have been a less auspicious beginning. But, Ben Kelly, the architect commissioned to create the space, believes booking Manning was all part of Factory impresario Tony Wilson's ambitions to get under the skin of the various punters and press in attendance and provoke some attention-grabbing headlines. If we want to romanticise the past, which Wilson would probably approve of, the moment seems pivotal. At the start of the eighties, the only places to go at night were coffee bars, dank basements and dress-coded old-fashioned clubs run by the likes of Manning and Peter Stringfellow. Although it took some time for the venue to find its feet, the unveiling of the Hacienda was the beginning of a future of contemporary design whose influence was to go far beyond nightclubs and seep out onto the streets, to embolden Mancunian hearts and minds. The brief appearance of the dated comic in the venue can be seen as a symbolic severing of old to new.

"I had never designed a nightclub before the Hacienda - and New Order and Factory Records as clients had never commissioned one," remembers Ben Kelly of the process behind developing Factory's venue. "We were all 100% naive in that respect but whenever I've worked on a project, I've always seen that as a strength rather than a weakness."

Kelly may not have envisioned a club like this before but he did have some design experience. He was behind the Howie Shop in London's Covent Garden, the first fashion and retail store that opened in the late seventies after the fruit and veg market had moved out[59].

"This was my first experience of building something with an end result," Ben says of the Howie store. "I was experimenting with new and interesting materials, particularly industrial kinds of materials and anything found out of context."

Ben was invited to take on the Hacienda project after working closely with Factory's designer Peter Saville on a number of the label's record sleeves. The pair produced artwork for Merseyside electro-pop outfit Orchestral Manoeuvres in the Dark, establishing a highly creative and effective working relationship. The venue's development began at the start of the eighties as Factory Records and the rest of the music world was rocked by the death of Joy Division's Ian Curtis. Despite the tragedy, the band gradually collected themselves and morphed into New Order, with guitarist Bernard Sumner taking on the role of frontman. A subsequent 1981 tour to the US proved to be a pivotal moment for both the group and the record label in finding their identity. Going out in New York exposed them and their manager Rob Gretton to the glamour, guttery glitz and electronic rhythms of the city's club scene, shaping their sound and planting the seed of an idea for a venue of their own.

"New Order were inspired by those New York clubs like Danceteria and they wanted their own version in Manchester," Ben states. "Creativity was running amok in New York back then in the late seventies and early eighties and exciting things were happening. After their tour, the band and their manager Rob Gretton went to Peter Saville, saying they had found some premises in central Manchester and wanted to design their own club. Peter visited the site, took one look at it and said no way but he knew someone who could help. That was me."

Ben journeyed up to Manchester from London on the train, then was taken on a tour of what had once been a yacht showroom in the city's centre on Whitworth Road by Tony Wilson and the rest of Factory Records entourage. At the end of the tour of the "dark, dank and dusty" space, he was offered the job of designing it as well as sleeve work with A Certain Ratio, another Mancunian punk-funk band on the label.

"I got the train back from Piccadilly Station with these two projects to work on, a big club and an album cover. I remember thinking that this was the most extraordinary thing imaginable," laughs Ben.

The building work of the physical space initially arrived without a fixed brief, specific budget and many sources of disagreement, particularly about the location of the stage. There were arguments with Rob Gretton but eventually, it was housed at the side rather than at one end of the building.

"I was very much in favour of avoiding placing the stage at the far end of the space. If that did happen, it could only be a venue and would lose the potential to be something more," Ben explains. "Ultimately, I always believe that this decision was behind the Hacienda's longevity and success - it became a hybrid - is it a bird, is it a plane, is it a club, is it a gig venue? It's all of those and none."

Even though the inside of the building resembled a "huge cathedral-like space," the Hacienda adhered to Factory's stark, modern aesthetic established by the record sleeves.

"Factory was Factory, and the history of its album covers was such that certain sleeves didn't even have band names on them," Ben explains. "Peter had set a template for doing things which were very unusual for mainstream record sleeves and the club was the first three-dimensional manifestation of a Factory product."

Rather than a glitzy, flashing sign outside shouting the venue's name, only a hand-carved plaque with 'Fac 51' etched on it gave any indication to what was going on within its walls. Ben also nodded to Tony Wilson's passions outside of music in the names bestowed on certain parts of the club.

"He was obsessed by cold war spies - so the main bar was called the Kim Philby bar, the cocktail bar was the Gay Traitor [which refers to Soviet spy and art historian, Anthony Blunt][60] and the bar on the balcony was Hicks, named after a code word used by spies," says Ben.

"There was a narrative which I wanted to physically unravel and reveal more of itself as you moved into the space," he continues. "From a small, unassuming entrance, you suddenly came out into this gigantic hall which had a grandeur and a scale previously not seen before. Ultimately, to me, it was like building a giant piece of sculpture or a 3-D painting."

Many of the most striking aspects of the club's interior came in the use of colour and found objects, in part inspired by Ben's love of French artist Marcel Duchamp and his use of unassuming, everyday objects in his creations.

"He had exhibited a urinal in a gallery in 1910 and I just loved that, and this notion of the found object," Ben says. "So we had cat's eyes in the floor. I had always been interested in using colour and I wasn't afraid of utilising that in the scheme. I used roadside bollards to filter people on and off the dancefloor. To me, the Hacienda was almost like a living art project."

The vast amount of cultural mythology hanging around the club is difficult to digest and perhaps unrivalled in dance music history. From films such as Michael Winterbottom's riotous *'24 Hour Party*

*People*' to books penned by almost anyone with a connection to the club, no matter how tenuous, there's a deluge of Hacienda content, stories, myths and legends to wade through. Still, the club's impact on both Manchester and the wider dance music world is hard to ignore. Back in 1990, Graham Stringer, the then leader of Manchester City Council, now Labour MP for Blackley and Boughton, highlighted the importance of the Hacienda to the city following the tragic death of 16-year-old Claire Leighton after she took an ecstasy pill. He wrote to the magistrates describing how the space had made "a significant contribution to active use of the city centre core"[61], even going as far as to say "the Hacienda was to Manchester what Michelangelo's *'David'* was to Florence"[62].

Manchester's reputation as a hub of exciting youth culture also led to a dramatic increase in the number of young people wanting to move there to study. In 1990 when the Hacienda was at the height of its success, the number of students applying for places in the city doubled[63]. Since then, this trend has been turned on its head with the University of Lancaster offering a master's course in music industry management and promotion based on the experiences of New Order bassist Peter Hook and his approach to running the venue[64].

DJ and producer Jon DaSilva was one of the residents at the club and ran the infamous Hot night. His initial experiences of dance music were in Preston, then Kent, where he hung out with Skint Records founder Damian Harris and first started DJing. On his return to the north-west, he recalls being surprised by the Hacienda's transformative effect on Manchester.

"Pre-Hacienda, the city was pretty grim, to be honest," Jon says. "The only pre-club places were the local pubs and the one around the corner was about the size of a postage stamp," he laughs. "There was no proliferation of music culture and bars like there is these days."

As Ben Kelly says, the venue stemmed from the vision of New Order manager Rob Gretton. He was determined to push the project from a dream into a reality and bring the New York experiences he and the band had to Manchester.

"I remember that Rob always felt like the Hacienda was the club that the city deserved as he was a proud Mancunian," Jon states. "In some ways, it was a complete transplant of what they'd seen in the US. But it definitely started a revolution and rethink in terms of club design and the ambitions surrounding them. The stained carpets, chicken in a basket and glitzy style clubs of old were history."

Jon's stint at the Hacienda helped him make a name for himself, alongside other DJs including Graeme Park, DJ Paulette, Mike Pickering and Justin Robertson. Justin came to the city as a student, attracted to Manchester by its glowing musical heritage and reputation. Growing up in the Home Counties, his decision to study philosophy in the city was driven more by his love for The Fall and Factory Records than a passion for Aristotle and Socrates.

"Before I studied, I'd travel to London to go and see bands, then get the last train home, so there wasn't too much clubbing going on," Justin remembers. "But when I got to Manchester, it was a real eye-opener. I'd always thought of myself as quite worldly-wise as I was going to gigs and drinking in pubs; all these things I thought were markers of maturity. But when I arrived in Manchester, I realised I was very naive and hadn't actually experienced the world at all."

Justin immersed himself and his love for music in the city and remembers a number of influential clubs that provided him with important lessons in his musical education.

"There was the Man Alive club where they would play go-go and funk, then there was the Gallery, the PSV in Hulme, the Venue, The International. You could go out almost every night," he remembers. "This was all pre-acid house and the energy of the city was fantastic back then. You'd get dressed up, go out and listen to this crazy music, it was really exciting, then acid house happened and it went completely bananas."

From Justin's memories, Manchester's musical backbone towards the end of the eighties was one made up of house music. In contrast, London was more funk-orientated in its musical tastes and sounds.

"The fashion magazines were very London-based," he says. "So you have this idea that everyone was listening to funk and rare groove, 1988 happened, then everyone suddenly started listening to house music," he explains.

"But in Manchester, the music was already there. It meant that the soundtrack didn't change too much but the cultural side to it - the fixtures and fittings that went with acid house - definitely did."

The use of new drugs, the adoption of the smiley face iconography, and even how people danced became a new kind of uniform for many clubbers of the day during this time.

"Ecstasy arrived with a bang and became popular, which was very exciting," Justin says. "I vividly remember this i-D Magazine night at the Hacienda and Mark Moore was up from London; he was playing house. Me and my mates had gone out dressed in our suits and these outrageous hats. We were going for quite a fashiony look but when we walked in, there were all these kids from London who were dressed in loose clothes, Converse trainers and baggy jeans. One kid came up to me and gave me a hug and a teddy bear. I was like, 'all right then, this is different'."

The freedom experienced in these spaces at the end of the eighties and start of the nineties came at a particular moment when civic fabric was tearing under the collapse of industry and the austerity measures of Tory rule. Clubs like the Hacienda spiked in popularity by offering ravers a release and much-needed sense of community spirit that the authorities had tried to crush.

"Our society was increasingly fragmented during the eighties," says Dave Haslam. "Tory party policy was aimed at destroying communities around factories and sport facilities, something clubs could offer. But it's also important to remember that not everyone saw them like this. For some people, music is just wallpaper and clubs are places to go get hammered. So there are two stories; one of commerciality and another of innovation where these spaces would act as catalysts for cultural activity."

The Hacienda's downward spiral amid a whirlwind of debt, gangs, drugs and violence during the nineties is well documented. But other clubs were of equal importance to the city's dance music scene when the fire of acid house began to rage untamed. Located on Oldham Road in Miles Platting in a former Bingo Hall, the Thunderdome is often talked about in hushed tones as offering an alternative to the podium-dancing of the Hacienda. Jay Wearden, a weekly resident DJ at the club, remembers how it started off as a rock venue before attracting Mike Pickering, Jon DaSilva, the Spinmasters, Steve Williams, Sasha and the Jam MCs to play.

"Alan Evans was the owner and had trouble with the Cheetham Hill gang," remembers Jay. "Alan wouldn't take any shit from anyone, and due to that, the gang shot the doors of the club off. They then told him if any of the DJs who'd played came back, they'd shoot them too. I heard about this and saw it as an opportunity. I was desperate to play in bigger venues, so on my return from Ibiza, I spent an afternoon calling them until they picked up the phone and agreed to take me on. I've never looked back."

According to Jay, the Thunderdome was one of the city's most exciting clubs of the time and has often been ignored by mainstream media, bedazzled by the Hacienda, Tony Wilson and the Factory Records legacy.

"There was no fighting, no aggression, we had Manchester City hooligans, Manchester United hooligans, all the different gangsters from across the city and never any trouble in there," he remembers. "It was an unbelievable place; people lived and breathed it. It was the real heart of dance music; people came for one reason. It helped change a generation and 30 plus years on, its effect on those people is still evident to see."

Suddi Raval is a music technology teacher with years of raving experience under his belt, a lifetime dedicated to the energy and sounds created by nightclubs. As a Mancunian, his formative dancing experiences were at the city's spaces, including the notorious Thunderdome.

"It was a complete contrast to the Hacienda. The vibes at their events were, at least initially, more 'peace and love' while the Thunderdome's crowd seemed far tougher," he says. "But the teenage me went every week. It was hard, it was heavy and rough but so intense and strangely addictive. At the Hacienda, you'd hear plenty of strings, pianos and vocals but the music at the Thunderdome was more trancy, hypnotic and darker. It fitted the vibe of the place. But I felt like I changed in the Thunderdome. It definitely impacted me. There are plenty of myths around the club too. Apparently, there were syringes in the corners of the club, which makes you think of people taking heroin - but they were injecting neat alcohol to get incredibly pissed. That's just getting pissed on another level."

One of the Hacienda's most pioneering events was Flesh, a legendary gay night that helped bring Manchester's queer scene to the fore. Launched in 1991 during an uncertain time for the club after various gang-related incidents, the night's inclusive midweek vibes aimed to keep the violence away. A strong ad-campaign with eye-popping slogans such as 'Queer as Fuck' and 'Practice makes Pervert' took queer culture out of the closet and onto the street[65]. DJ Paulette was one of the Flesh residents at a time when women, particularly Black women, were rarely seen behind the decks brandishing records. Her way into DJing was via a multitude of different avenues, from writing music, performing to dancing at clubs, including the Number One in the city centre.

"There was a DJ called Tim Lennox who was really inspiring," she remembers. "There weren't any women who were DJing at a level of having their own night back then in the late eighties. But his sets, featuring tracks by David Morales, Frankie Knuckles, Larry Heard, made me want to DJ. He became one of the main residents at Flesh and that's how I got involved."

Despite some notable opposition, Flesh heralded a rush of gay nights and venues springing up in Manchester. Reportedly, the Chief Constable at the time was anti-LGBTQIA+ alongside certain members of Manchester's city council[66]. Paulette remembers this hostile environment seeped onto the streets and was something to be understandably wary of when traversing the city.

"It wasn't that comfortable to walk around in town, late at night scantily dressed or in full drag without putting yourself at risk of being propositioned or aggressed," she says.

"So people used to get changed in nearby car parks before walking over to the club," Paulette continues. "In order to have the cooler and edgier parties, it meant putting them on in clubs that were situated on the unsavoury fringes. We learned to co-exist with other groups that were very opposite to us culturally, racially, politically and socially."

As the nineties progressed, the so-called 'Gunchester' of the late eighties changed to 'Gaychester' as the city's nightlife lit up and embraced the LGBTQIA+ community. The Gay Village, a hub for the community centred around Canal Street, turned a page on the nightlife narrative thanks to the emergence of several ostensibly queer bars, including Manto, which launched in 1991. The venue was designed by Benedict Smith Architects with large glass windows, allowing anyone walking past to peer inside. Before, most spaces catering for the city's gay community were hidden away from view. According to Jon Binnie's *'Cosmopolitan Urbanism'*, "the architectural design of Manto was seen as a queer visual statement of "we're here, we're queer – get used to it", and "a brick-and-mortar refusal to hide any more, or to remain underground and invisible"[67]. The influence of the bar and the changes it heralded were thrust onto mainstream TV screens via Channel 4's groundbreaking, *'Queer As Folk'*, a series that championed Manchester's buoyant gay culture. More than 30 years on and the city continues to hold its LGBTQIA+ community ever tighter, not only in its bars and nights like High Hoops and Kiss Me Again but in landmark events such as Homobloc, a celebratory queer clubbing utopia held at Mayfield Depot in the same space lorded over by The Warehouse Project.

In the wake of the house music explosion and the cultural revolution it sparked, investment began to pour into the city during the mid-nineties, with money reaching previously untouched areas. As Manchester pivoted around the excitement and confidence offered by its nightlife, council leaders responded by reimagining its potential via ambitious events programming, bids to host world events and investment in infrastructure. From the launch of the Metrolink tram in 1992, which connected the previously disparate satellite towns of Altrincham and Bury, to the re-energising of certain parts of the city such as the Castlefield Bowl in 1993, Manchester used the acid house period as a cultural protein shake to look beyond itself and formulate new international ambitions. The National Cycling Centre opened in Manchester in 1994 while the Bridgewater Hall, a new multi-million pound home to the Halle Orchestra, also started life that year too.

At the same time, in the mid-nineties, the prevalence of house music fragmented into a rainbow of sounds that the nightlife incorporated. Record label Grand Central and their flagship act Rae & Christian spun the city in a more hip hop direction. The Electric Chair, lorded over by DJ duo Luke Cowdrey and Justin Crawford, became known for their basement soul music, a euphoric mix of house, techno, disco and everything in between. Skam Records delved into the world of brain-expanding electronica, releasing music from Boards of Canada and Bola. Sankeys Soap and nights such as Bugged Out! and Tribal Gathering pushed things forward, alongside a litany of smaller yet no less exciting events and venues such as Robodisco or Planet K and the Roadhouse. Sankeys opened its doors in 1994 and at a crucial time for a city struggling to shake off the 'Gunchester' label.

"Sankeys Soap was the place that took things back underground after the Haçienda and allowed Manchester to resurrect again," said Slam's Stuart McMillan in an interview with FACT Magazine[68]. Located in what was a former soap factory in Beehive Mills, its home would have been where you would have previously found some of the most powerful cotton looms on earth, with the Ancoats district an epicentre of the textile trade. It was thanks to much of the industry and work that went on here which led to Manchester's becoming Cottonopolis and a massive contributor to the UK's economic good health.

When Sankeys opened its doors to clubbers, one of the key nights was Bugged Out! a house and techno club dedicated to showcasing the best in underground dance music. While Cream in Liverpool and Gatecrasher in Sheffield wanted to elevate the DJ to superstardom, Bugged Out! was intent on keeping things lowdown and dirty, with DJs including Dave Clarke, Slam, Daft Punk, Miss Kitten and Detroit supremo Jeff Mills all holding court during its tenure between 1994 and 1998. Emma Warren, acclaimed journalist and author of the books, *'Dance Your Way Home'* and *'Make Some Space'*, used to write as a contributor for monthly dance music bible, *Jockey Slut*. Run by Johnno [Burgess] and Paul Benney, the pair were also behind the Bugged Out! brand, meaning Emma had the opportunity to experience the raw machinations of the club night first hand.

"Ancoats, where Sankeys used to be, is now unrecognisable from what it used to be," she says of Bugged Out!'s past venue. "Back when Bugged Out! lived there pre-gentrification, there was nothing around - just some cabbies, an old pub and cafe, that was about it. The first time Jeff Mills came to play, he came in a cab with Johnno and when he saw Ancoats said: "Oh my god, this is just like Detroit". He felt this spatial kinship with us."

Since then, Emma has travelled to Detroit and experienced firsthand the similarities between the city and what Ancoats previously resembled before Manchester's shiny property developers moved in.

"The buildings in both places were almost identical," she says. "There was a literal geographic relationship between us in Manchester dealing with house and techno parties and the Detroit originators, and this relationship was created via the built environment. The situation for Black Americans in Detroit in a city which has been abandoned was different to ours in Manchester. But it definitely established a connection."

Balearic Mike is a revered DJ and record collector long associated with Manchester and his current home of Brighton. He remembers the past desolation of Ancoats and the surrounding area, now revitalised as the Northern Quarter. This part of the city, based around a maze of streets just north of Piccadilly Gardens, became a location for many pop cultural businesses during the late eighties, with the music-related Afflecks Palace, Eastern Bloc records and Dry Bar all finding homes there. Since then, an ever-increasing number of cafes, independent shops, restaurants and music venues have appeared, entering parts of the city previously seen as run-down and shady no-go zones for Mancunians.

"I started working in Vinyl Exchange in 1991 and the Northern Quarter was a total shit hole back then," Mike laughs. "But it's amazing now. Every corner has a deli, a coffee shop, clothes shops, microbreweries, loft living - it's like downtown Manhattan. Every time I return, something new has appeared."

"The whole area has regenerated out of these independent businesses," he continues. "I remember it was initially a real place for record shops, which were so important back in the nineties. Without them, DJs would have nowhere to hang out, buy records or chat with their peers to see what was going on in the scene."

While Mike partied during the arrival of acid house, it was in the post 'Madchester' world that his DJing had an impact as one of the selectors behind the Luvdup night. Alongside co-founders Adrian Gent and Mark van den Berg, the night began in a series of peculiar venues, including a Chinese restaurant in Chinatown and a gay bar near the coach station before calling the Venue on Whitworth Street home[69]. Amid the success of their club, Mike remembers this time in the mid-nineties as one of transition for the wider dance music narrative.

"The scene just kept getting bigger," he says. "And as it became more popular and more mainstream, it fragmented between those bigger clubs and the underground."

From those heady days, Mike has taken a step back from DJing, playing out less frequently and instead curating the inspiringly offbeat *'Down to the Sea and Back Again'* compilations with fellow acid house veteran Kelvin Andrews. He's now back in Brighton, a city where he went to art college before house music really kicked off.

"It's changed a great deal since I was a student and has become very band and gig-orientated," he says of the seaside town. "There are still great DJs and places to party - clubs like Patterns, for example - but there's a paucity of venues compared to other places."

He also cites the ethnic make-up of Brighton as being majorly different to the rich diversity of cultures he experienced while living in Manchester.

"When I first moved back to Brighton a few years ago, I was struck by how white the place is. In Manchester, it's far more ethnically diverse and that's reflected in the hip hop, dub and sound system culture you hear there."

In recent years, this diverse sense of independence and a DIY spirit has permeated to the heart of Mancunian nightlife. While more mainstream nights offer headline DJs in cavernous rooms in Manchester's underbelly, there's raw excitement fizzing in the leftfield names and talent embraced by underground clubs, DJs and promoters. Meat Free is an all female-led techno party and encapsulates this contemporary vision of the city's nightlife, one where preconceptions about what a night out in Manchester can be should be left at the door. First pulled together in 2013, the club is led by four DJs - Alice Woods, Steffi Allatt, Natasha Carter and Lucy Ironmonger - and was set up in response to the perceived male dominance of the scene.

"At that time in Manchester, there were no female-led techno parties that we knew of in the city. So we decided to start one," recalls Alice. "And although we didn't intentionally set out to be a 'female promoter', looking back, it was important that we did."

Since locking horns, Meat Free has found an appropriate home in Salford's gritty White Hotel, welcoming an inspired array of techno talent to its turntables. Big nights have included sessions with Thomas Heckmann, Ben Sims and Eris Drew. Alongside nearby club Hidden, this venue has proved to be an essential melting pot of techno sounds during the last few years.

"The space we currently occupy is a run-down car garage in Salford and has become one of the most incredible places to rave in the UK," says Alice. "I'd like to think it'll last forever but I have no doubt that it will one day become just another page in Manchester's story. Future generations will have their own White Hotel, just as others have had their own Hacienda. The spirit of a place and its people isn't in its bricks and mortar - so when one is lost, another will rise."

Meat Free is one of the reasons the city's techno scene is on fire, but Alice is keen to highlight the supportive nature of the community surrounding the music. It has successfully navigated the Covid-19 pandemic and continues to fly the flag for Manchester's late-night shenanigans. After parties have been hosted in the Derby Brewery Arms, an "old school boozer" located on the edges of Manchester's city centre and unlikely location for rave energy to pop and fizz[70].

"We're an industrial city, so those sounds naturally make their way into the music coming out," she says. "The attitude and ethos, though, are much more commonly shared values. Today's promoters are blazing a trail for inclusivity and diversity, and there's absolutely a sense of camaraderie in the scene. With everyone wanting everyone else to do well, we don't really have an ego on the dancefloor in Manchester and that makes for a stronger scene overall."

Alice mentions inclusivity as a pillar of the Meat Free ethos and the club has gone further than most in its aims to open up the dance. Under One Roof is an offshoot she runs, offering nights for adults with learning disabilities. The team behind it wanted to create a safe and welcoming environment for those who may have previously felt either uncomfortable or unable to attend regular club nights.

"The idea for it came from the extension of Meat Free's key value - bringing good music to more people than before by democratising dancefloors to be open and welcoming," explains Alice. "Starting out, I really had no idea what impact it would have, but I soon realised that there is so little access to the arts for this community that it is extremely important to put on. For many people coming, it may be their first ever night out despite being in their forties or older."

The event has taken off since its inception, travelling to other cities such as Glasgow and Liverpool while welcoming top DJ talents, including DJ Seinfeld and Optimo's JG Wilkes. All nights have featured less intense lighting, a lower capacity and a quieter volume of music to cater for attendees. The Under One Roof concept shows how clubs can create new areas of inclusivity and reimagine who these spaces are for. Opening up this community to everyone makes a different, more generous social vision possible.

"Clubbing is something many of us take for granted but is so out of reach for some," says Alice. "I hope that one day this night doesn't need to exist, though, as there is no reason for dance music lovers to be separated just because of their differing needs. More than many places, the dancefloor is where we should all be equal."

Meat Free's home at the White Hotel is a mere hop, skip and a jump away from Hidden, another important club for contemporary Manchester's music-loving community. Billed as "an award-winning music and arts playground", Hidden can be found in Downtex Mill, a brutal looking box of a building in a part of town close to the infamous Strangeways Prison. As uninviting as this location may seem, living slightly off the beaten track in an area so far relatively untouched by property developers stands the club in good stead for the future.

Anton Stevens is in charge of promotions and programming at Hidden and has spent the majority of his life involved in nightlife.

With his dad running his own venue and well-connected within the city's clubbing community, Anton had the opportunity to get up close and personal with some of Manchester's most important ventures at a young age.

"Tribal Gathering in 2003 was a precursor to The Warehouse Project. It took place in this old industrial estate on Ancoats which has since been turned into flats," he remembers. "It was for 10,000 people with DJs like Jeff Mills performing. I didn't really know any of the names playing but I remember being on the stage and looking at this endless sea of people losing themselves in the music. It was a big buzz, even though I'd be completely sober as a kid at these things, just feeding off the energy."

These formative experiences led to Anton working in various clubs and cities before he returned to Manchester to take on his current role as a director at Hidden. It's been a rewarding opportunity with the club now revered as one of the best the city offers. A combination of multiple spaces such as the Courtyard and Blue Room, a killer Neuron Pro Audio sound system and great bookings policy have made for regular sold-out events, with clubbers flocking in their droves. But where the Hacienda's location would now be considered in the centre of Manchester, Hidden, as its name suggests, is trickier to find. You might just stumble upon it, but it's unlikely unless you hang out in the slightly seedier side of town towards Cheetham Hill. Living out of sight in a more shadowy part of town has worked in the club's favour.

"As we're out of the way, it means we end up with a crowd of people who really want to be there," Anton explains. "They'll be really into what is happening, have done some online research and connected with us, perhaps by an artist, theme of the night or the music on offer. It means you end up with a like-minded crowd of people, which creates a great atmosphere in the space."

Anton also feels that for those coming to Hidden for the first time, the location outside the city centre lends an air of excitement to a night out. Travelling away from the bright lights of the Northern Quarter or Deansgate is a huge rush for anyone looking for something different from their late night experiences.

"Being off the beaten track definitely makes clubbers think they are going somewhere special, especially when taxi drivers aren't really sure where they're heading either," he states.

With bookings including big name players like Moodymann and Jeff Mills alongside local heroes Homoelectric, the Hidden team has also gone out of its way to give back to their surrounding community.

"Homelessness is an issue around us and we've tried to help out when we can," he says. "We've done some work with local charities like the Mad Dogs Homeless Project to try and help those around here going through a tough time."

Looking at Manchester's nightlife beyond Hidden, Anton says the urban landscape of abandoned industrial spaces has been well-placed to offer the city some brilliant venues and clubs for its population to party in. It's a story seen elsewhere but one Manchester has pulled off to fine effect.

"I remember coming into the city as a kid and heading up towards Ancoats and it would be full of empty buildings. Before they were transformed into flats, these outskirts were primed for different uses," he states.

The city has seen a huge change in the use of land and the relocation of homes into urban centres. Yet, Anton is still optimistic for Mancunians to continue their love affair with dancing despite the urban landscape's evolution. It's almost as if a lust for life, parties and music flows through the water supply.

"Even if it goes fully London in terms of gentrification, there's a spirit here which is synonymous with rave culture," he says. "Clubs are an essential part of the city's make-up. You can take away a building but the spirit will live on and people will always find a way to host a party, no matter how far away it might be."

DJ Paulette, a regular selector of house, disco and techno at various venues and clubs across the city and UK, is a passionate advocate for Hidden and its emphasis on the music rather than decor or DJ drinks tokens.

"Hidden is a perfect representation of Manchester's club culture and what it takes to put on a club night - the attitude, energy and environment is amazing," she says. "It's all about the music and the DJ booth is sacrosanct. But apart from that, there's no purple roped off area of VIP table service - it's all about the dancers, a dirty space and a fat-ass sound system."

Paulette also agrees with Anton that clubs have to think pragmatically about their relationship with their surroundings if they are to survive and thrive in today's modern world.

"You make being an outsider the actual selling point of your club in these industrial environments," she says. "The rents are so astronomical, it's very hard to have a club in a really central area. You have to head to the outskirts and believe in what you're doing: if you build it, then they will come."

Paulette has been DJing since the Hacienda days and spent time pushing her dancefloor wares in Paris and Ibiza. Despite stints living elsewhere, she feels a close connection with Manchester and holds a passion for new music that joins the dots between the ever-evolving diversity of nights and DJs the city has to offer.

"There's a real love here for all types of music, whether you're house, disco, tech-house, afrobeat, techno, grime or drill. There's room here for you to be whatever you're into. Music lovers are really into it and honest about it too," she says.

"DJs here are willing to take risks with their sets too; most of those I know will push it and play something that might not sit comfortably but will somehow make it work," Paulette continues. "I loved returning to the city to reconnect with that musical passion - it gives you the enthusiasm to develop and draw on your own musical energy."

The history of Islington Mill in Salford is strongly connected with the fortunes of Manchester and only a mile from Hidden and the White Hotel where Paulette regularly plays. Built in the 19th century to provide a space for the cotton manufacturers and distributors of the day, the building fell into decay during the city's industrial decline. Artist Bill Campbell began its reclamation by first taking on a space in the property in 1996, and now, more than 100 artists and groups call it home. Among them is the Partisan Collective, a DIY group that initially wanted to offer somewhere for people to come together and share ideas[71].

"To start off, it was a pop-up but this model struggled, so Partisan started looking for somewhere more permanent," says Sophie Hayter, the collective's Venue and Licensed Events Coordinator. "The concept was to have somewhere which could sustain itself financially and this is where the idea for the parties came from. The aim was to bring the party space and social space model together to create an entity which could support itself as a DIY co-op."

Partisan subsequently found a permanent base in Cheetham Hill in 2017, but the pandemic took its toll on the organisation. Backed into an increasingly tight financial corner as the lockdowns wore on, the group made the bold decision to move to a smaller location.

"We're now in a warehouse space behind the mill itself in a much smaller area to our previous home," says Sophie. "This decision was brought on by the pandemic and the uncertainty of whether we would be able to continue to be able to afford the costs of running somewhere bigger. It was also a move towards creating a wheelchair accessible space more quickly than planned in our previous home."

Moving to Islington Mill in November 2021, time has been spent plotting and filling their new offices with social justice and arts groups. The collective has also taken the time to invest in forming a close bond with Salford Council. With revenue streams decimated by the pandemic, the organisation leaned on funding to keep them going during the difficult months.

"Now that things have opened up, our previous financial model is returning - so, for example, we're looking at hosting events and using any profits to put back into the space," says Sophie.

The new location places Partisan in a slightly different part of Manchester but close to its city centre. One of the main differences for the collective is being surrounded by the cranes and apartments that now dominate the Mancunian skyline.

"There have been issues with noise from a club in the past and this is something that always has the potential to come up," Sophie states. "However, we hope we're perceived as a space for the community of Salford and Manchester. We're here to be useful rather than aggravate. We do a lot more than parties and that helps - we're much more than a club."

This is demonstrated by the rich variety of event programmes they offer. While parties with local hero Ruf Dug, German DJ Prosumer and the harder techno offerings of Objekt have all taken place under its roof, these are run to fund the space and help them connect with the communities that need them. From Queer Family Tea events to fundraisers and climate action groups, there's plenty of energy bouncing between activism and parties. No matter what takes place between their walls, the world around them is evolving.

"The changes in Manchester have happened quickly and it feels horrible like you're being encroached on," she says. "When I first moved here, one of the things I loved about it was the random wastelands in the city centre, but slowly that's ebbing away. If we can hold onto what's already here, protect it and keep reminding councils of how important it is, then maybe we have a chance against the developers."

While Hidden, Partisan and the White Hotel all offer a more DIY approach to club culture, the glossier yet still cutting edge programming of The Warehouse Project has attracted ravers from across the world since the mid-noughties. As befitting of its name, this seasonal event series has hosted big nights at exciting, cavernous spaces within the city. Initially starting life at the Boddingtons Brewery near Strangeways Prison in 2006, it spent many years at Store Street in a car park underneath Piccadilly Train Station, establishing itself as one of the UK's must-attend nights. Some of my highlights of partying there include a legendary show by Chic's Nile Rodgers with Johnny Marr of The Smiths joining him on stage. But like so many other buildings in the city, Store Street has a colourful history. During the Second World War, this area underneath Piccadilly Train Station was used as a huge air raid shelter capable of welcoming more than 1,000 people[72]. Fast forward to 2024 and The Warehouse Project has continued to grow and move between spaces, currently calling the Mayfield Depot home. This 10,000 capacity space was part of a £1 billion regeneration project from The Mayfield Partnership (consisting of representatives from Manchester City Council) and venue specialists Broadwick Venues and Vibration Group[73].

The Depot worked as Manchester's primary train station during the Second World War and onwards until eventually closing in 1960. It was then the main mail distribution centre for the Royal Mail before shutting in 1980 and remaining dormant until it recently reopened in 2019 as the city's now top entertainment destination. The gargantuan size makes it a flagship area for Manchester, offering events organisers the flexibility to host mega-raves as well as high-end culinary experiences. It's also home to Escape to Freight Island, a new restaurant concept from DJ duo, Luke Cowdrey and Justin Crawford who run other bars, including the Refuge and Volta in West Didsbury. Billed as a 'long forgotten freight depot from the city's industrial past, reimagined as a cultural space for our future'[74], it bulges with street food, colour and gallons of fancy cocktails. With DJs and live music embedded within its programming, this new form of entertainment zone caters for a variety of needs on a night out. As the team behind it says, it's yet another example of Manchester turning its grubby rail heritage into something more polished and gleaming. DJ Justin Robertson likens this reclaiming of old factories and derelict buildings to the way other groups move into parts of a town or city that have been left behind.

"Warehouses may have previously been places to store furniture or manufacture goods, but now they've transformed into these spaces for parties, temples of bacchanalian excess," he laughs. "This is similar to the ways in which skateboarders move into an abandoned part of the city, perhaps under a railway arch, and turn it into a skate park and hours of endless fun."

This interplay between urban renewal and decay certainly influences perceptions of what makes Manchester's music, something Justin agrees with as a producer, songwriter, and remixer.

"Your environment completely informs the kind of music you make as a songwriter and artist," he says. "Detroit is, of course, a great example of how techno is the futuristic sounds of the city's dying industrial scene. But the city and its industry are symbiotic; they both inform the other with the buildings taking on the energy of those who live and work in them. Then the bricks and mortar push back and inspire you too."

Justin left Manchester behind in 2003, now calling west London home but is still a regular DJ in the city. As a result of moving out and away from the people and the buildings, his art and music have taken on a slightly different hue.

"Now I have two dogs and go walking in the fields around Wormwood Scrubs every day, I feel like my music has definitely become more pastoral," he states. "But as cities become increasingly homogenised, this could lead to people wanting to kick back against this. Perhaps there was something about the uniformity of suburbia which led to people getting into punk and this could spur a similar reaction again."

In 2022, Manchester's Hacienda celebrated its 40th year and is still revered with events, exhibitions, books and much more still flowing through its legacy. The city's Museum of Science and Industry curated an exhibition dedicated to the club and Factory Records while the Hacienda Classical project continues to go from strength to strength.

"I've always said that the Hacienda will never die," laughs its designer Ben Kelly. "There are thousands of men of a similar age who still want to hang onto its memory and anything that is released or related to the club they want to be part of."

"Wherever I go in the world whether it's a bar, a beach or some hotel, if I'm chatting to someone, they ask me what I do and what I designed, I tell them and they'll say:- 'the Hacienda changed my life'," he continues. "I met my wife there, I met my husband there, I met my business partner there - it's unbelievable how global its influence has become."

Ben's involvement with Factory and the Hacienda will continue and it's clear that the club's legacy looks set to stretch on and on with further myths, legends and stories to add to the narrative surrounding it.

"Tony Wilson once said that every city needs its cathedral and he saw the Hacienda as fulfilling this," Ben explains. "You don't go to worship but to be a part of something. But if he was alive and could see how far this has gone, he'd be laughing his head off…"

# CHAPTER 3

## SCOUSE POWERHOUSING AND THE SECRET AGENTS OF CHANGE

*"You could just feel the whole place was soaked in e and sweat. It was like your team had scored the winning goal every couple of records"[75].*

Andy Carroll

There are very few religions that the denizens of Liverpool follow more fiercely than football. Indeed, most Scousers likely bleed red or blue depending on the team they support. If you scour the city's districts, from L1 to L40, then raving is perhaps the one passion that might come close to rivalling the intense energy football creates around local teams Liverpool and Everton. These twin-loves are captured in the city's late, great defender, Gary Ablett, with his first name one of the earliest rhyming slang terms for ecstasy tablets (Gary Ablett = Tablet - 'I had 25 Gary's last night'). It's a psychedelic line of thought that might appeal to KLF agitator Bill Drummond who, when managing Echo and the Bunnymen in the early eighties, ignored traditional travel plans and plotted the band's world tour based on a path of mystical ley lines stretching from Mathew Street in Liverpool's city centre to Iceland[76]. Like the city and its artistic community, it's slightly surreal, a little bit cosmic and totally befitting of a place which cherishes its own and a love of balls and beats as hard as possible. Out of all the UK's places, Liverpool's DNA is bound up in a tight double knot of musical mythology, thanks to a lengthy lineage of artists, venues and clubs stretching like an aural umbilical cord through the ages.

Liverpool's nocturnal roots can be traced back to its past as a port and a doorway for trade with the rest of the world. Indeed, it's the recent collision between Liverpool's old docks and industrial buildings, the hand-rubbing glee of developers and the ambitions of canny promoters and venue owners which have created such a kinetic breeding ground for nightclubs and music in the city. As with other towns and cities across England's northern tip, Liverpool's industrial past saw a period of huge change. As a 'Gateway to the Empire', its port "brought the city great wealth but depended on a large and unskilled workforce"[77], meaning there was a huge divide wedged between rich and poor.

During the 19th century, Liverpool's size rapidly increased in part thanks to the sheer volume of traffic and trade which passed through it. At the start of the century, 40% of the world's trade went via Liverpool and its prestige and status is reflected in the architectural beauty of the Albert Dock. Much of the wealth came out of the transatlantic slave trade[78], which was the engine room of the city's economy until the practice was abolished in 1807. The existing waterside buildings show how rich the city became: the Three Graces consists of the imposing Royal Liver Building, The Cunard Building and the striking Port of Liverpool Building all looming over the Mersey on Liverpool's Pier Head.

Located near Liverpool's waterfront was Eric's, a club closely associated with the spiky roots of Liverpool's post-punk scene. The venue could be found on Mathew Street and has followed the nearby Cavern, where an embryonic Beatles cut their teeth, into our musical folklore. After establishing successful and influential nights at the Twisted Wheel in Manchester and the Stadium in Liverpool, Roger Eagle, along with Pete Fulwell and Ken Testi[79], opened Eric's in 1976, just in time for punk to bring its guitar-based squall from London to its stage. Young upstarts at the time including The Clash, the Sex Pistols, The Stranglers and The Damned all performed while it became a hang out for a generation of star-spangled homegrown stars - Pete Burns, Julian Cope from the Teardrop Explodes, various members of Frankie Goes To Hollywood and Ian McCulloch from Echo and the Bunnymen.

Jayne Casey, then a member of Liverpool punks Big in Japan, remembers what the city's nightlife was like during the latter half of the seventies. Her love of music and powers of making creative magic happen has seen her shape every stage of the city's cultural metamorphosis. But when she first started venturing out after dark, Liverpool's nightlife existed in the shadow of the male-dominated world of industry born from the port. Her clubbing story begins as a teenager who ran away from home.

"I left at 14. It was only to New Brighton on the other side of the Mersey but it meant I was in a club at that age and managed to experience the glam rock period," she says. "Funnily enough, years later, the guy who owned that club also owned the building Eric's was in. He couldn't believe how young I was when I first visited."

Looking back at the riot of guitars and excitement Eric's ushered into Liverpool, Jayne believes the venue was at the centre of a big bang that transformed the city's old-fashioned outlook on art and musical anarchy.

"When we hit the scene as young punks, the city was a closed place," she remembers. "The docks employed thousands of men so on a Friday night, they would go out in big gangs, meaning the streets were quite heavy."

"It was a very narrow culture; they worked together, lived together, then we turned up. It was our presence, bravery, and ability to stand up to their sexism and racism which changed Liverpool.

When I look back on all the changes I've experienced, I think this was the most important, this influence that one young person has on another when one is brave enough to fight for something. We were the first generation to say we don't want to work at the docks, we want to go to art school."

The influence of these self-made bands and musicians who hung out, went out with each other and made a glorious racket together not only transformed Liverpool but the rest of the UK too. Throughout the eighties, the impact of Echo and the Bunnymen, Pete Wylie, Julian Cope, Frankie Goes to Hollywood, Bill Drummond, Jayne herself went far beyond the city centre limits. They were tangled up in number one hits, amazing music and a willingness to embrace and show off their identities. The effects of what they did more than 30 years ago is still rippling through us today.

"We changed people's lives by being brave," says Jayne. "That's the biggest cultural shift I've seen music, fashion and attitude bring to a city - they can really alter young people on the street. It's not about regenerating a city in terms of building and property. It's about regenerating people's hearts and that's what I've got from music and culture. I'm so glad to have experienced that."

Initially seen as outsiders in Liverpool, the Eric's crowd had their fair share of trouble to contend with. Frankie Goes To Hollywood frontman Holly Johnson received plenty of abuse over his sexuality, even at home from his father Eric. In his biography, *'Bone in My Flute'* (a title taken from the slang term for an erection), Holly describes how his dad, a merchant seaman, went ballistic when he asked for a Babycham one Christmas: "That's a fucking tart's drink! No fucking son of mine's gonna have a fucking Babycham!"[80] Jayne says that despite the abuse, this gang of "queers and weirdos" set the standard for subsequent generations to aspire to.

"The punks who they battered went on to become really famous," she says. "This was the period of Pete Burns and Frankie Goes to Hollywood when the freaks were on Top of the Pops. The city became more open as a result. Even though some people might have been homophobic and they didn't like queers and weirdos, these were their own queers and weirdos."

Their success came during the eighties, a bleak period for Liverpool when it was blighted with austerity, destitution and upheaval. Employment was hard to come by, with 80,000 Liverpudlians losing their jobs between 1972 and 1982 as the docks closed[81]. David Alton, MP for Mossley Hill told Parliament: "The picture is bleak and depressing ... Imagine life in a city where one in five people are on the dole, where half the people in some districts are without a job and where young people face a lifetime without employment."[82] Jayne believes it was the creatives who kept the lights of the city on during those strained, tumultuous times.

"We kept things going", she states. "In every interview we ever did, we spoke about Liverpool. It felt like we carried the city with us during those years and that massively mellowed the culture out - then after that came dance music."

Prior to the coming together of the Eric's scene, one of the biggest Liverpool success stories of the seventies was the Black R&B and soul of local group, The Real Thing. Chris Amoo was singer and songwriter with the band that formed in the inner city area of Toxteth in 1972. They went on to become the biggest selling Black outfit of the decade thanks to the irresistible pop hits of *'You To Me Are Everything'* and *'Can You Feel the Force?'*

"When we started, we were just teenagers and our world was Toxteth," says Chris of the band's formative years. "Our youth club at Stanley House used to have these big events where all the Black community from Birmingham and Sheffield would attend and we'd manage to bunk our way in there."

"A fantastic venue called the Sink opened on Hardman Street when we were about 16. It didn't sell alcohol. It was a cafe upstairs in the day, then at night, there would be a discotheque in the basement. It was the one place where all the Black guys from Toxteth would be allowed in."

As the band's reputation grew, they began playing at an increasing number of venues in Liverpool's city centre. Chris remembers how if they hadn't been performing, then they wouldn't have been allowed through the door.

"It wasn't until we started playing in these places and our faces became known that we would be let in," says Chris. "At that age, if you went with your friends, you'd be turned away."

The Timepiece club in Fleet Street, "where Toxteth met the north end of town", was an important venue for the group and the city's Black community.

"Les Spaine was the DJ there and it was very safe and very vibey," says Chris. "This is where you'd hear all the latest R&B, soul and funk. I took *'You to Me Are Everything'* in there for its first play as a white label. It filled the floor without even being released as a single."

While the band were undoubtedly made in Toxteth, they looked further afield to Black America for musical inspiration. But their track *'Children of the Ghetto'*, with lyrics about *"Runnin' wild and free / In the concrete jungle / Filled with misery"*, is about Liverpool 8, an area of the city between their home and the docks.

"We weren't influenced by the music of Liverpool but your city is what makes you," says Chris. "It has a vibe about it and is so inspiring no matter what style you pursue. We were very fortunate as we grew up in a community in Toxteth and it influenced how we wrote, especially when we heard music by Marvin Gaye or Curtis Mayfield coming out of America. These artists made us socially aware of what was around us and how to bring that to our music."

DJ Greg Wilson, a purveyor of fine electro-funk, disco and more, is originally from Merseyside, although his success is synonymous with Manchester. Despite their proximity, he says that the music scenes of the two cities were very different.

"Liverpool was ahead of the curve in the early/mid-seventies when DJ Les Spaine held court at The Timepiece and The Pun beforehand," Greg says. "But then Les went to London to work for Motown in 1977 and there was nobody able to replace his formidable presence. The late seventies was more about Manchester and DJs like Mike Shaft, Colin Curtis and John Grant."

1981's Toxteth riots amplified many of the city's divisions and the already racist door policies on clubs in Liverpool's centre. The arrest of Leroy Cooper sparked off nine days of clashes between locals and the authorities, with 70 buildings destroyed, 500 people arrested and up to £11 million of damage caused[83].

"Liverpool was not going to encourage groups of Black lads into city centre clubs," says Greg. "The riots were used as an excuse to discourage the type of Black-led scene developing less than 40 miles away. What was encouraged in Manchester was stifled in Liverpool."

Journalist, music industry entrepreneur and Liverpool's Head of UNESCO City of Music Kevin McManus agrees. He describes how Liverpool's Black community has been left out of the standard take on the city's musical story.

"Looking back, what I'm conscious of now when compared with other cities is how the Black community should have been writ large in this," he explains. "But it wasn't the case, and the mixing between the Black and white communities was slow to happen due to how the city was back then. Outside of acts like The Real Thing and The Christians, there hasn't been much mainstream musical success from the Black community. You'd never see many Black faces in the city centre clubs due to the institutional racism that was part of the city."

Kevin's life has long been interlaced within the Scouse music scene. He worked initially as a Liverpudlian journalist for magazines like i-D, The Face, NME and Mixmag, reporting from dance music's frontline as acid house broke in the late eighties and nineties. With DJ Dave Seaman in charge as editor, bleary-eyed staff wouldn't enter the office until late afternoon to pick over the bones of the night before in their copy. But Kevin was a prominent voice at the magazine, one of the few contributors who was a writer first and foremost. Since then, he has researched various music scenes and been a powerful figure in setting up the Baltic Creative initiative, a development company aimed at supporting the city's vibrant independent sector within the Baltic Triangle. He believes there's a unique party spirit embedded within Liverpool's inhabitants, which gives its nightlife an unparalleled energy and attitude.

"You go out on Saturday and you don't give a fuck about Sunday, Monday or Tuesday," he laughs. "My wife was exactly the same as me when I first met her. She'd just been paid and had 200 quid in her pocket. So when we went out on a Friday, we'd think nothing of blasting the lot on whatever we needed to get us through the night."

DJ Andy Carroll is an influential selector in Liverpool's dance music history, enjoying a career that has seen him play at every important club the city has offered. A lifelong music fan, his events and gigs have run from the eighties to the present day and take in legendary nights and venues such as The State, Quadrant Park and, of course, Cream. As with Jayne Casey and so many other peers who broke bread for Liverpool's music, his formative musical experiences were at Eric's.

"The streets were a bit rougher than they are now, so if you looked a bit different, then you could be set upon," he remembers of those febrile times. "It meant you often had to put a big coat on to cover what you were wearing. I tried to turn this negative into a positive and used it as a massive opportunity to hide cans of cheap lager in the lining of my jacket."

Andy's tastes were formed via a musical family alongside his experiences at Eric's watching punk outfits like the Ramones blast through their three-chord anthems. His older brother used to visit Wigan Casino for an injection of Northern Soul, while Andy himself acquired an eclectic record collection via local institution, Probe Records.

"The scene at Eric's was a huge influence," he says. "It was through going there that I met people like Geoff from Probe, Roger Eagle, Jayne Casey, Pete Burns who were all making this big statement about how to live. Just follow your dreams, get out there and have a go. If I hadn't gone to Eric's, then I wouldn't have started putting bands on or contacting agents. It was massively important for me."

Andy went on to work in a local record shop and DJ in and around the city, growing his music tastes and reputation. When acid house first began to break out into a sweat, he and his friend Mike Knowler were DJs at The State, a club based on Dale Street.

"We were residents there from 1984 until 1989," he says. "We'd already been playing alternative indie bands, then Mike went to New York in 1986 to the New Music Seminar, heard acid house and brought back an enthusiasm for this new kind of dance music. I loved the punk ethic but I could see the same energy in acid house too. All you had to do was bring the right attitude and anyone could be at the party - it was all about how you wore yourself."

The State Ballroom, where the two first bonded as DJs, was originally a restaurant hosting tea dances in the thirties and forties. According to Andy, at the time of his residency with Mike, it was the biggest club in Liverpool's city centre.

"It was quite unusual as it had coloured, leaded glass windows and marble frescos in the wall," he explains. "It was the first club in the city with a laser disco. We had all sorts of things going for us without even realising it. Me and Mike would do an hour on the decks, then an hour on the lasers and lights. You'd have to be a lighting engineer and a DJ, that's what you got paid to do."

Andy would DJ at the club on consecutive nights from Thursday until Monday, a residency he describes as "the most intense and longest" he's ever had. Acid house increasingly thrust itself to the fore of his sets but this was coming from record foraging jaunts to shops outside Liverpool.

"The city wasn't massively well set up for records," he states. "You could get imports or go to Manchester or even Hot Waxx in Warrington. No one would think to go there as it was a bit off the beaten track. There were other places like Eastern Bloc and the Spinn Inn in Manchester too. But in those days, you had to hunt down music and if you wanted the edge over other DJs, then you didn't go where they went."

Even when 3Beat Records opened up on Wood Street as Liverpool's go-to hub for vinyl dance tracks in 1989, Andy continued to cast his net further afield for dancefloor gems unmined by his peers.

"If you did go to 3Beat, then you'd make sure you'd get there before anyone else," he says. "We did support them but I didn't shop there too much. If I'd got all my records from them, then we wouldn't have had the edge on the other DJs in the city."

The ongoing adoption of house at The State was a natural fit for Andy and his accomplice Mike Knowler, who were always thirsty to get their hands on the latest records and sounds. Before those fledgling house tracks, they played plenty of hip hop and electro.

"I loved it all," Andy remembers. "But house was a complete revolution which changed everything. It created the concept of the guest

DJ, increased wages, and brought the nation onto the dancefloor. I loved that happening and got a career out of it. Before acid house, I'm not sure how long I would have remained a pro DJ. It was only when it kicked off that wages suddenly rocketed."

While Andy believes that young people have always sought out exciting ways of getting loaded and having a great time, the arrival of this new style of dance music was like nothing else to previously have hit Liverpool or the rest of the UK.

"Youth in time immemorial have always been seeking pleasure wherever they could," he says. "But with acid house, it was like someone pulled a big switch on the whole country and overnight, everyone just wanted an e."

Quadrant Park was the next big event to take Liverpool's infatuation with nightclubs to a higher level. Located in a warehouse in Bootle, north of the city centre, the dock road where it could be found highlighted how the place was in a state of flux during the 1990s. By the middle of the decade, the dock entrances near Seaforth were reportedly overrun with protesting workers who had lost their jobs[84]. At Quadrant Park, located a few miles away, a rave was going on and searing the minds of the city's younger generation. While the Cavern, Eric's and Cream are globally renowned spaces that make up different chapters in Liverpool's musical heritage, Quadrant Park is often overlooked. It had a similar impact in terms of welcoming dance music to the city but the building has since been demolished and turned into a waste collection centre. Andy describes the club as an old-fashioned venue complete "with sticky carpets". But thanks to his DJ partner Mike Knowler, it was transformed into a destination for club lovers. Mike balanced his passion for music and DJing with work as a lecturer at the nearby Hugh Baird college in Bootle.

"Mike's students wanted a Christmas party and they were all State heads," says Andy on how they found the venue. "So he organised this club in Bootle near the college, which turned out to be Quadrant Park. Mike did the first few nights there; demand went well, it became a regular night and I became involved alongside James Barton and John Kelly. We started bringing in guests, international DJs like Laurent Garnier and Frankie Bones."

Kevin McManus hails from Bootle and says how incongruous it seemed for a night in the area to attract people from across the country to dance in a rundown warehouse.

"Quadrant Park was bizarre as Bootle is a pretty undesirable place to be," he says. "I'm from there and love it but have to be honest. But the club night took off and was huge."

He remembers how Liverpool felt "a bit slower" when it came to dance music getting a hold. Other towns and cities were more open to this new form of electronic music.

"There were still some amazing nights like 8 Orgasms run by Peter Coyle from local band, the Lotus Eaters," says Kevin. "This was at a club called Macmillans. There was also the Underground Club which James Barton, who went on to run Cream, had a hand in."

Jayne Casey remembers the huge rip Quadrant Park made in Liverpool's existing nightlife. She took Paul Rutherford from Frankie Goes To Hollywood to witness the first ecstasy rush that gripped the dancers.

"I remember ringing up Paul and saying: 'Paul, you've got to come into town - the scallies have discovered ecstasy and they're all loved up'," she says. "So we went and he walked onto the dancefloor with a t-shirt with 'Queer as Fuck' on the front. It was full of 1,000 scallies who gave him so much love. When we walked home, we felt triumphant. We'd done this whole journey with the city and now thought that culture here was changing. It started to come during punk, then in the post-punk Liverpool success story years. Dance music blew away the last vestiges of white working-class male elitism."

Quadrant Park was perfectly in tune with the acid house epiphany coursing through the veins of the UK and suddenly ravers were descending on Bootle from all corners. A loophole in council licensing laws meant that the space could host one of the UK's first legal all-nighters while it also featured the Pavilion, a popular basement space below the main dancefloor. The location on the outskirts of Liverpool played a significant role in its popularity too.

"It was easy to come off the motorway and reach the club by car and there was a big car park," Andy Carroll explains. "It couldn't have happened in the city centre as we had coaches full of people arriving from everywhere. When people ask me what's my most amazing clubbing experience ever, I've been blessed with many, DJing in places Cream, Manumission and Space. They all come close but Quadrant Park was so unreal. When it comes down to it, nothing could beat it."

When the club shut its doors in early 1992, other spaces were quick to pick up the mantle and capitalise on this new thirst for raving. James Barton had been a resident at Quadrant Park and tried his hand at various ventures before landing on what would become Cream at Nation in Wolstenholme Square. Jayne Casey became heavily involved in the club on opening but it wasn't new musical territory. Electronic sounds have permeated her musical endeavours since the early days of Big in Japan.

"I've always been a futurist, so as soon as I heard acid house, I was blown away," says Jayne. "But I had previously made music that was more industrial and electronic with my band Pink Industry. It was pre-digital but created these futuristic sounds by experimenting with tape."

The influence of Jayne's innovative group, which featured a rolling cast of musicians and released several albums and EPs, can be heard and felt in mixes and selections from many discerning DJs, including Andrew Weatherall and Sasha. Newer musicians and artists such as

Mancunian post-punk act Lonelady have adopted a similarly experimental, DIY approach to synths, beats and bleeps.

"When Quadrant Park closed, James Barton wanted to bring that culture into the city centre," Jayne says of Cream's origins. "Up to that point, dance music was still illicit and took place in fields or somewhere on the fringes of the city."

Part of Jayne's role at Cream when it opened in 1992 at Nation was to oversee this transition and manage how dance music moved from a semi-illegal pursuit to complying with the rules of the local authorities and government.

"There was a massive cultural shift needed for dance music to move into Liverpool's centre," says Jayne. "This meant it was under more observation from the police and needed to be carefully navigated. It was a difficult move for it to become a legal culture."

Andy Carroll was instrumental in the launch of Cream, having previously partnered with James on different musical ventures, including DJing at The State and managing rave act K-Klass.

"I met James at The State as he was a regular and he was a natural entrepreneur," says Andy. "But Cream was about forging ahead with new energies and sounds. With all our experience and combined efforts, what started as a club for like-minded friends and family, it turned into this phenomenon."

When Cream first opened, Jayne's concern was navigating drug use in the club. Rather than ignoring the issue, she introduced first-aid rooms and on-site doctors to acknowledge the presence of chemicals and make the space safer for ravers.

"It's part of the culture and there was no point in denying it," she says. "So we decided to be open and take a different strategy to other venues. It meant we were targeted by the police and they wanted to close us down due to the number of ambulances we'd called. But we weren't prepared to let kids die."

The club fought on, defined the careers of dance music greats like Paul Oakenfold and Carl Cox and became a multi-million pound business entity in the process. Cream may have left its physical space behind in 2002[85] but this was part of a deliberate ambition to focus on other creative outlets rather than a weekly night. The festival Creamfields launched in 1998 and went on to unveil different versions in Spain, Chile and Brazil, with the brand acquired by Live Nation in 2012 in a six-figure deal[86]. Its propellor logo is one of dance music's most distinctive, while James Barton has been recognised as one of the most important influencers in electronic music by Rolling Stone Magazine[87] and named as a Citizen of Honour in Liverpool in 2017[88]. Andy Carroll looks back fondly on the early years of the club, believing it captured a zeitgeist that may never be repeated.

"I think people still have great nights out but I'm not sure if anything as spectacular will occur again," he says. "Everything is instant these days with the way the internet and media are. Nothing has the chance to bubble and gain momentum organically. Cream was a once in a lifetime collision of circumstances."

"It's such a fabulous success story," says Jayne. "I go to the Cream office now and it's all the kids who used to work there for me now running it."

The journey from the underground to the mainstream has been a hard one for club culture and a battle Jayne continues to fight alongside fellow musicians, artists and cultural curators. She remembers speaking at a past conference with European leaders alongside Factory Records' Tony Wilson about the importance of the night-time economy. It's telling that the message of her speech about recognising the value of artistic endeavours still rings true today.

"I got up at this conference and said how the biggest challenge for a modern city is to accept culture as it is when it exists, warts and all, rather than just looking to capitalise on it as a heritage product," she says of this tense relationship.

"With a city like Liverpool, it's held up as this beacon of culture but the city never understood the significance of the Cavern in its day. The authorities' lack of understanding led to the original club being knocked down."

Over the last decade, the most recent part of Liverpool's creative narrative has been written by the emergence of the Baltic Triangle, a redeveloped area in the city full of musicians, bars and venues all jostling for space.

Located just south of the city centre, it was previously occupied by industrial warehouse spaces and takes its name from the numerous businesses previously located there that would trade with Baltic countries such as Sweden, Russia and Norway[89]. The area also houses a Scandinavian Church on Park Lane, built in the 1860s with the Grade II-listed building described as one of the most striking buildings in the whole of Liverpool. Mainly full of rundown spaces and a little way off the beaten track, it was classically undesirable and ripe for regeneration.

"Jayne Casey initiated the concept of establishing a creative quarter for the Baltic Triangle when she was at the Liverpool Biennial Festival and came up with the term 'Independents District'," says Kevin. "I headed up Merseyside ACME, the UK's first specialist creative industries support agency. We were part of the council essentially but operated quite independently. I carried on speaking to Jayne about the area and was in a position where I could bring public money in."

To take the vision of the Baltic forward, ACME commissioned several pieces of research over a two-year period. Beginning in 2006, the aim was to prove that there would be sufficient demand for creative spaces from businesses. This was followed by a business case, then a costed plan was drawn up, which formed the basis for a bid for public funding. The city council was supportive, as were the Arts Council and Liverpool Vision, another organisation connected with the council.

"When I was growing up, Liverpool wasn't the nicest place to live," says Kevin McManus. "But over time, things have started to change. I was involved in the team that wrote the capital of culture bid and it marked a moment when we all started looking at Liverpool differently. It also shifted how the rest of the country and the world saw the city too. Perceptions changed because suddenly we were in the media across the world with lots of positive stories about us and what was happening here."

A successful bid for public funding of £4.5 million (including money from the EU) allowed for the purchase of almost 4,000 square metres of industrial warehouse space, which was owned by the North West Development Agency[90]. The funding also covered refurbishment costs and revenue support for the new company established to manage the buildings on behalf of the creative and digital community in the city. The Baltic Creative Community Interest Company (CIC) was set up by Kevin and a manager and board were quickly recruited to run the operation.

These old warehouse spaces were converted into office spaces appropriate for creative businesses. The success of Baltic Creative CIC and the neighbouring Elevator buildings has fostered a creative community featuring hundreds of diverse and innovative organisations, making the Baltic Triangle a desirable area for people to live, work, and socialise within.

"The idea was to counter that problem of creative people in clubs and spaces getting forced further afield by spiralling rents," says

Kevin. "We wanted to offer an alternative investment model to help protect their interests."

"Jayne's District club is there and was one of the first movers to recognise the potential of what is now known as the Baltic Triangle. Even though it's ten minutes from the city centre, people weren't used to going out there, so it was slow going at the start. Since then, it's boomed. 24 Kitchen Street and Camp and Furnace are just some of the venues to call it home and we've made a conscious effort to try and take it forward organically."

Kevin was a major player in setting up and leading this new vision but ten years later, these venues they sought to protect are competing with developers such as Brickland, a company behind a 200-home project which is proving to be a headache for the 24 Kitchen Street club.

"Venues are now having to fight for space due to residential developments taking off," sighs Kevin. "It's become a cool area, which in some ways is a pain in the arse for the creatives who have called it home."

24 Kitchen Street has been locked in an ongoing fight with nearby developers building residential flats on a neighbouring car park on Blundell Street[91]. In 2019, the city council voted to adopt the Agent of Change policy to ensure more weight was given to music venues in cases such as this. Agent of Change ensures that any property developers looking to build near a music venue are responsible for ensuring that noise does not affect the building's occupants.

24 Kitchen Street is a 400 capacity space in the Baltic Triangle and a hub for underground DJs, live acts and cutting-edge artists. Co-founder Saad Shaffi had a lifetime of experience in nightlife before becoming involved with his business partner Ioan Roberts. He initially helped Ioan run the bar before taking on a wider role in steering the club's direction.

"Ioan used to put on nights while he was at university, then he came across Kitchen Street as it was being sold," Saad says on the sourcing of the space. "When we started, we were using temporary event notices before eventually getting a proper licence. People would be buzzing when they'd come here as some thought it was an illegal rave. It meant the rule breakers and trendsetters wanted to be here. We're close to the city centre but we're something a bit different to the bar culture and booze crawl you get elsewhere."

The team behind Kitchen Street has certain advantages in operating as they own the building themselves. Unlike many other clubs, they are not at the mercy of a landlord who might try to hike rents up and put pressure on their financial margins.

"We won't be pushed out in that respect but we do have issues with planning developments around us," says Saad. "As a property owner, I can also see why businesses move on from here. I've noticed some which aren't part of nightlife head elsewhere and set up somewhere less expensive."

Highlights in the 24 Kitchen Street events programme are many. Liverpool DJ Mele runs his own riotous Club Bad label parties here while Hamburg's electro-techno selector par excellence Helena Hauff is a regular guest. Elsewhere, jazz producer and multi-instrumentalist Kamaal Williams has played a brilliant live show with DJ Stingray, also bringing his militant mix of techno and booty bass to the dancefloor. Despite booking talent of such calibre, Saad says Liverpool's location can often make attracting big names a challenge.

"Artists and DJs do tours and Liverpool can be left out of the schedule," he says. "Manchester is easier to access as the transport links are more connected. Liverpool is the last stop destination on the train - you have to be coming here rather than passing through. We cut ourselves off from our closest neighbours due to a lack of transport links, so it's sometimes more challenging to be more experimental than other cities."

"I love Kitchen Street and how they responded to the Covid-19 restrictions," says Sonic Yootha DJ and promoter Ian Usher. The party, billed as "a dislocated disco for homos, fauxmos, gender-blenders & part-time Brendas"[92], is one of the venue's most popular and has built up a steady head of steam since launching in 2015. "They made their own garden bar outside, trained staff and external promoters like us with gender intelligence courses. It was of huge concern when they were under threat from these apartments being built on top of them. We can't just plonk our night anywhere. Kitchen Street is our home and the venue is an intrinsic part of what makes it."

Run by a collection of DJs and party starters led by Ian, at first Sonic Yootha struggled to find its place in Liverpool's nightlife, initially taking in a brief stint at the nearby Camp and Furnace. The night itself sparked into life from Ian regularly posting his favourite musical picks on Facebook. The management at Camp and Furnace noticed the online excitement his selections were generating and asked if he would be interested in bringing it offline and into reality at their venue.

"Ian Richards at Camp and Furnace introduced me to John Aggy and Tracey Wilder to chat about the music we liked," he says. "We bonded over everything from Sandy Shaw to Rihanna and the B52s, and just thought let's give it a go."

But the eclecticism of the venture initially confused rather than delighted. After three poorly attended events, Camp and Furnace requested they wrap it up, leaving Sonic Yootha homeless.

"I went to collect my records and, as I was walking back home, the door to Kitchen Street was open," Ian recalls. "I'd never been but I'd heard about it, so I went in and met the team. I told them I had this night but I wasn't sure what it was - it's gay but not gay - it's for older people but everyone is welcome. Thankfully, they were very open-minded and gave us a shot."

The location has proved to be a space where the night can thrive, adding an extra frisson of excitement to the Baltic Triangle's cultural offering.

"We love being in the Baltic with all of these venues and brilliant spaces," Ian explains. "Everyone has each other's backs and helps to support and promote each other. It feels like there's a real family vibe."

This community ethos is at the heart of Sonic Yootha alongside being an anything-goes party put together in the spirit of DIY late night happenings. The soundtrack, which ranges from hi-NRG to pop curveballs, is all about inspired selections rather than technical mixing.

"It's the eclectic nature which is appealing," Ian explains." It's more like a jukebox, so we'll play The Smiths, then follow it up with A Guy Called Gerald. It shouldn't work but it does."

The club stems from a lifetime of going out for Ian. When he was younger, he used to make the journey over to Manchester to dance at the Hacienda. He remembers how Liverpool's vibes and late night offering contrasted sharply with its neighbours.

"Liverpool didn't really have the thing that I needed back then," Ian remembers. "It felt moody and dangerous. But the first time I went to the Hacienda, you can imagine, my head just fell off. This was high-end design like nothing I'd ever been to before in Liverpool. The Hacienda was this wonderland. Quadrant Park was a snooker club."

Liverpool's gay scene has been long-associated with Garlands, a club which opened in 1993 at a time when many saw the city's queer spaces as "seedy, underground and unable to offer anything as fresh and exciting as Manchester"[93]. And while its reputation has spread far and wide over more than two decades of parties, the club has passed in recent years, leaving the baton to be picked up, albeit in a more alternative fashion, by Sonic Yootha. It now feels as if it's in safe hands with the party hailed as "the club night that saved Liverpool's gay scene"[94]. Their notoriety hit such heights that queen of pop Kylie Minogue even invited them on her tour.

"We'd been asked to play at Pikes in Ibiza and were like 'fucking hell, this is unreal' as we were making this shit up as we went along," laughs Ian. "They'd flown us over and we were at the pool bar where Wham filmed *'Club Tropicana'*. It came on the news that Aretha Franklin had just died. Then, we got this text from a mate of mine who works with Kylie that she had heard about us and checked us out. It was a very strange day."

A few days later, life became even more surreal after Ian received the call asking for Sonic Yootha to join Kylie on an arena tour that took them and their musical selections across the UK and Europe.

"It was one of those pinch-me moments where we couldn't believe our little night ended up opening arenas for one of the biggest pop stars in the world," he says.

Despite Ian and his gang travelling across Europe, it's back in their home in the Baltic Triangle where they continue to build their reputation. Clubbers now come from as far away as Reykjavik to dance, while some regulars live in London.

"When London comes to you, then you know you're doing something right," says Ian. "But some people travel from Newcastle and Edinburgh too. Some have moved their lives to be closer to the night and the city via the friends they've made in our club."

The night's crowd makes the Sonic Yootha events so special, with a huge range of ages on the dancefloor. If you feel like you don't fit in anywhere else, then Sonic Yootha will welcome you with open arms.

"Initially, it was just old farts like us but we're now getting this younger generation too, so the club has evolved," says Ian. "We'll have more indie sets earlier, then techno at 3am. But there are few places where 70-year-olds and 18-year-olds can all party together - it's very special."

One of the city's biggest homegrown talents in recent years is DJ and producer Mele. Another selector who runs his Club Bad nights at 24 Kitchen Street and works out of a studio in the Baltic Triangle, he is closely affiliated with Liverpool but also part of a global house sound pushed by Simon Dunmore's Defected Records. Killer tracks like *'Groove La Afrika'* or *'The Latin Track'* are often percussive, internationally flavoured and find homes in the sets of big names like Diplo and Solomun. Despite this global traction, Mele's musical roots are firmly based in Liverpool.

"Quadrant Park and all these legendary clubs definitely informed me," he says. "I got into music via my uncle who gave me this compilation of old acid house records and it was this that made me really want to start DJing and producing. I remember the first club I tried to go to was Nation where they used to do Cream to see David Guetta."

"All my mates were going, I had a fake ID as I was only 16 and spent two hours queuing to get in," he continues. "I used to read Mixmag religiously and had this vision of what the club might look like inside but they kicked me out of the queue as soon as I arrived at the door."

Chibuku Shake Shake is an important and eclectic club in Liverpool's nightlife history and one Mele cites as an early obsession and inspiration. Started above a pub around the year 2000, the night's exploits are most associated with the Arts Club.

"My experiences at the Masque, what is now called the Arts Club, at Chibuku completely changed my life," Mele says. "You'd have dubstep titans Skream and Benga in one room, Mo' Wax's James Lavelle in another and indie band the Klaxons in a third. I was always into lots of different music but it helped me realise that I was getting inspiration from these varied sources."

As his music career took off, Mele upped sticks and moved down to London to get stuck into the industry around 2011[95]. But during the past few years, he chose to pull the plug on life in the capital and return to Merseyside. Being back in Liverpool has helped him rekindle a creativity he feared he almost lost when living down south.

"It felt like an entire weight was lifted after I came back and I was able to make music again," he says of the impact of his return. "There was a period in London when I only made three tunes in a year as I wasn't really vibing in the studio. Then when I got back here, it felt like the pressure was off and I felt freer to just be the artist I wanted to be. I felt much more settled."

Now firmly back on home turf, Mele is taking stock of a burgeoning career as a DJ and producer and a Liverpool club scene in a state of ongoing flux. He cites Kitchen Street, Meraki and Invisible Wind Factory as important current spaces, while the 3Beat Record Shop has been an ongoing source of electronic music influence and inspiration.

"Historically, Liverpool has always had this strong relationship with dance music," he says. "When I was in school, it would be Scouse house and happy hardcore. Scousers are definitely drawn to harder, bouncier music."

Mele is also optimistic about the future of Liverpool's scene, thanks in no small part to the power of the web in making our worlds more connected and inspiring younger generations to get involved in the city's dance music scene.

"Now, it's a lot easier to be a DJ, and that's not a bad thing," he laughs. "When I was 15 as I started going to clubs, if I found out someone was making records and they were from the same place as me, I'd be amazed. Now, because of the internet, and more access to music and DJ software, the crowds are getting younger as people get into it younger. It's incredible here alongside this strong network of creative people."

Across the River Mersey opposite Liverpool, you'll find the so-called Paradise Peninsula of the Wirral, a sleepier and leafier relation often bundled up in the shadow of the big city. But the so-called 'oblong of dreams'[96] (coined by cult Wirral band Half-Man-Half-Biscuit) has its own character-filled vein of musical success stories. With a population of more than 300,000[97], it's a smaller place and full of contrasts with coasts and countryside sitting next to smoky, belching areas of industry. This sense of geographical juxtaposition is reflected in the musical diversity of its artists, from the electronic pop of Orchestral Manoeuvres in the Dark to the melancholy of former Coral guitarist turned solo artist Bill Ryder-Jones. The town of Birkenhead was once known as the 'New York of Europe'[98] thanks to the shipbuilding industry it is famous for. Oddly, Birkenhead Park inspired American landscape architect Frederick Law Olmsted to come up with the blueprint for Central Park in New York[99]. But in recent years, it is more known for its decline and some of the poorest areas in the country in Rock Ferry and Bidston[100]. Emerging from this backdrop is Future Yard, a new gig venue that opened up in 2019 as a one-off festival. It now operates as a fully-fledged space for live music, aiming to provide the Wirral's eclectic scene somewhere to go as well as a new stop in the diaries of touring acts. Chris Torpey, co-founder of Future Yard and previously editor-in-chief of local pink music paper Bido Lito!, feels that these often overlooked areas like Birkenhead can provide the perfect space for creativity and culture to thrive.

"It's now in the suburbs or those places deemed unattractive that clubs will pop up," he says. "There was Smithdown Social to the south of the city, then we're here in Birkenhead. It's in these repurposed areas which are either cheaper to live in or have been forgotten about; these are the avenues for creativity to come out. City centres aren't necessarily the places for music-making. They're now places to shop and go to the cinema."

Future Yard has hosted various events/parties in its short lifespan. From the initial festival with Anna Calvi and Bill Ryder-Jones performing, its programming is decidedly left of centre and aimed at championing emerging talent. Alongside a cafe and restaurant, the venue also commissioned the Leftbank Soundtrack, an "animated music walk [which] is the result of a collaboration between music and place"[101]. Each of the featured artists is from the Wirral and was asked to come up with a piece of music as a response to particular locations around Birkenhead, including the art deco Ventilation Tower and the Woodside Ferry Terminal. Alongside She Drew the Gun's Louisa Roach and Bill Ryder-Jones, electronic producer Matthew Barnes, who works as artist Forest Swords, was among the contributors to this new score for the area. Born in Birkenhead, Matthew grew up in West Kirby, an idyllic, sunny town on the coast with views over north Wales. Since studying in Liverpool, he's flitted between the northwest and London with touring and performance commitments taking his contemporary version of electronica - ranging from ambient sound design to dubbed out techno - all over the world. Matthew's clubbing experiences began during the mid-2000s when he started his studies and remembers how the nightlife of the time was beginning to reflect the less tribal way music was consumed.

"The internet made music borderless and easy to access, so when we'd be hanging out with friends, we'd be listening to everything from dubstep to seventies post-punk to afrobeat, anything that made your head fall off," he explains. "My favourite club was Korova, a venue owned by the band Ladytron. On a normal Friday, you'd go and see a DIY punk band play downstairs to 50 people and then head upstairs for the rest of the night and dance to Aphex Twin, ESG, Fela Kuti. Hive, which booked a lot of glitchy electronica, and Chibuku, which booked eclectic clubbing sounds from Jeff Mills to John Peel, were also really formative experiences. I can pretty clearly trace the line from all these nights to the type of music I ended up making."

Matt's musical career as Forest Swords has been characterised by embracing experimentation. His stunning *'Compassion'* album from 2017 dazzled critics and music lovers alike but he also provided the soundtrack for *'Ghosts of Sugar Land'*, a Sundance-winning Netflix documentary. *'PYLON'* was a structure of lights and cymbals at Birkenhead's Priory that could be programmed to respond to the environment. It's an innovative and self-motivated spirit of adventure reflected across Liverpool's musical community.

"It's a working-class city with infrastructure chronically underfunded for years," says Matt. "It has meant the people here don't seek permission to do things or wait for something to happen; they just decide to do it because nobody else is going to. Those opportunities are becoming fewer and fewer now but the spirit is still there."

This DIY attitude persists alongside a deep-seated passion for making the most of any opportunity to escape from the working week. As with other poorer cities such as Berlin and Sheffield, there's an emphasis on letting off serious amounts of steam when Friday night hits

"When you work hard all week doing a crap job, the weekend is the only outlet you have, and so going out becomes an extremely important bit of the fabric of your life," says Matt. "That's often reflected back in the music that gets played out."

As Forest Swords, Matt's music has inhabited an array of different environments, settings he believes are integral to the kinds of sounds he's sculpted from them. He feels that this is down to the locations available and how the "spaces that are used for clubs have a conversation with the music played within it".

"Everything feeds back on itself in that respect," he explains. "I could never imagine listening to jazz in Berghain or ambient music in Cream. So the more industrial cities generally have tougher sounds associated with them because those kick drums and the sonics of techno or house just hits harder and differently in old factories, warehouses and office blocks. Practically, those buildings aren't engineered properly for sound and so the more aggressive and minimal music bounces and reflects around the walls in a more satisfying way."

Alongside its current crop of diverse musical talent, Liverpool has long-been associated as the home of melody with bands like the Beatles, the La's, and the Teardrop Explodes chasing this spirit of song through the city. Although Matt doesn't feel this is a defining influence on younger generations of artists, there are still unavoidable reverberations within the city. With the Fab Four using so much of Liverpool's landscape to inform their music, walking through the city means visions of the band come into focus on every street corner.

"Even the weirdest noise music or heaviest Scouse house stuff here has a very strong melodic through-line to it all, which is an echo of all the sixties, seventies and eighties Mersey beat pop that still gets played locally on the radio, in pubs, or is floating around your parents' house," he says. "Those faint echoes of local musical heritage appearing in forward-thinking club spaces are really important. Taking the past and rewiring it is the foundation of most electronic music."

While our past can inform the future in this very localised musical sense, Future Yard's Chris Torpey feels that the way in which people go out and dance has significantly changed during the last 20 years, partly thanks to the impact of social media on how we perceive and portray ourselves.

"Historically, the most important thing about a club night was to be there and in the moment. There was a hedonistic element too but maybe it felt purer," he says. "Now, a club is sometimes more of a thing to be seen at rather than for the pure music heads."

Amid the changing ways in which ravers now approach the club, nights themselves have morphed. Cream started life as a traditional club night that now no longer has a weekly event but is more alive than ever thanks to special one-off events, compilations and other activities pushing the brand forward in exciting new ways.

"Cream has utilised the central docks in Liverpool for its Steelyard events, these huge, all-day parties," says Chris. "Other nights such as Circus and Chibuku Shake Shake have used these spaces too. It's all about repurposing the industrial past and reusing them. The impermanence is also attractive. As an event, it will take place and disappear, so there's a sense of jeopardy for attendees and a genuine fear of missing out."

For city centre clubs, Chris says that they need to go beyond music to provide an all-round entertainment experience and really understand their offering and legal rights.

"When you see a venue like Kitchen Street with its own programming and own community, to continue, they have to become experts in planning legislation, noise levels and soundproofing," he explains.

Matt agrees that this might be the only answer for these spaces if they are to give themselves the best chance of operating successfully in the long term. Going further out of the city centre is not necessarily an option for those businesses looking to build a loyal community around them.

"I would love people to look towards smaller towns or the commuter belt, but it's tied into things like infrastructure and transport," he says. "Nobody wants to go to a club 45 minutes away if you can't get home properly after midnight."

With these pressures on promoters to act within the law, this has the potential for braver party starters to look outside of nightclubs to host their ventures.

"I think we'll probably see an upsurge in unregulated private clubs, unofficial clubs, temporary pop-up raves, or stuff out in the countryside like the nineties," Matt explains. "Basically anywhere that might be available for a weekend, rather than somewhere permanent. During the pandemic, we already saw that there's an appetite for this sort of thing and the fact that cities are actively making it harder for clubbing spaces to exist long term means these sorts of things might flourish."

Jayne Casey is scathing about how artists and creatives are treated by cities. Her involvement as a pioneering figure in the launch of the Baltic Triangle was driven by a desire to prevent culture from being forced out.

"The way the authorities often treat culture is that it becomes second class for anyone who has the cash to buy a flat in town," she says. "Ownership of property by creatives is, therefore, key to survival."

Jayne's model for activity in the Baltic Triangle has helped new enterprises spring up. Bongo's Bingo, events company Boss Nights and Sonic Yootha are three international success stories to emerge from the area. Meanwhile, in 2021 as the first tentative post-lockdown steps were taken, the cultural focus was once again on Liverpool with the first live music event trials held in the city. First up was Yousef's Circus club night while a gig from Stockport indie band Blossoms took place on a Sunday afternoon in Sefton Park. As local artist Zuzu said on stage, "this was one small step for Scousers" and a massive leap forward for the live music and clubbing community. The vibe at the gig was similar to the madness you might experience at the Stonebridge bar on the opening Thursday afternoon of Glastonbury. At the same time, Liverpool has seen some setbacks. From a spate of homophobic attacks in the city centre to losing its UNESCO heritage status due to the impact of ongoing development to the Victorian docks and the "irreversible loss" it has wrought on its historical value. Despite these challenges, Jayne is upbeat about what happens next and sees light in unexpected corners. As far as she is concerned, change is coming and if you aren't on board, then you're part of the problem.

"There is a new future forming around us," she says. "At my venue, District, we consider every aspect of our customer experience. We have signs up to discourage any hate speech; our staff are trained in mental health and can help anyone who is struggling. There are thugs out there but they are fighting the final battle that they have already lost. The creativity I'm seeing in the queer movement is fascinating and the openness is coming out in music and footballers. I've lived through these changes as a young girl and struggled in clubs surrounded by guys, on stages where you were defined by four men and a guitar. But culture is moving forward now and it's exciting to see."

# CHAPTER 4

## SYNTHS, STEEL, KLANG AND BASSBINS IN THE PEOPLE'S REPUBLIC OF SOUTH YORKSHIRE

*"We all fucking hated Thatcher but she inadvertently created a landscape that allowed culture to evolve"[102].*

Stephen Mallinder (Cabaret Voltaire)

You could see the smoke wafting out of Sheffield from the train.

We were crawling back to the Steel City on a brain dead Monday afternoon. The weekend had been a large one. A Saturday night of DJing at our ill-attended club night, then a Sunday having our minds blown by Daft Punk in a park somewhere near Leeds. Frazzled after a post-rave night spent writhing on our mate Joe's wooden floor, if the French robots pitching their pyramid in a park in Yorkshire felt like a dream, then the reality of witnessing the mighty clubbing behemoth Gatecrasher burning added a surreal edge to our collective lag, particularly as the bar we'd played at on the Saturday was just a few corners away.

Previously, the black plumes might have emanated from Sheffield's industrial centre in the Don Valley, but by 2007, most of these factories and chimneys had long gone. Rather than steel, Gatecrasher's iconic brand was one of the main reasons Sheffield was on the map, creating a devoted army of day-glo 'Crasher kids who not only danced within the city but pumped their dosh into its local economy too. Alongside Cream, Sundissential, and Ministry of Sound,

Gatecrasher was part of the wave of superclubs to dominate British nightlife during the nineties and had done a huge amount to put a little swagger into the walk of the place it called home. The club had attracted thousands of ravers, then students and businesses, and given Sheffield plenty to shout about, something many would say the city has never excelled at when it comes to its achievements. Gatecrasher's ubiquity was all-consuming, so this strange, burnt ending we were witnessing seemed like more of a whimper than a snarl. As Stacey Sampson wrote for Vice: "You would've had to come through the nineties with your eyes shut and a pair of earplugs on to have not been aware of the iconic Gatecrasher."[103]

But for a club whose life is so intertwined with the city, Gatecrasher wasn't actually born on Sheffield's streets. Instead, it began in Birmingham, only moving beyond the city limits in the mid-nineties. The club night roamed between Sheffield venues such as the Arches on the Wicker and the Leadmill near the train station, before finding a home in what was the Republic club on Matilda Street in Sheffield's city centre in 1996 (although it was known as Gatecrasher One at the point of its untimely demise). Part of the reason Gatecrasher's lion found its roar in South Yorkshire was due to the iconic branding developed by Ian Anderson and The Designers Republic. His creative agency had been collaborating with various bands, clubs and record labels such as Warp Records since the mid-eighties but it was with Gatecrasher where their success went up several notches. Ian worked on the *'Disco-Tech'* compilation sleeve as well as the branding for Gatecrasher's huge Millennium show in the Don Valley Stadium with their iconic *'It Will Always Be With You'* slogan in 1999. From this event, the relationship exploded, almost as much as the pupils of a 'Crasher kid on a Saturday evening.

"The *'Disco-Tech'* album design came after our first night at Gatecrasher," says Ian. "We'd witnessed all the flashing lights and glow sticks, then were outside a pub the next day when an ambulance went past. That's where the look for the compilation came from. The stripes, the colours and the punk look of the 'Crasher kids all collided."

Ian believes the brand, which went on to become a global dance music movement running events worldwide, was successful in Sheffield for similar reasons to the adoption and adoration of Motown and Northern Soul in the city.

"It was mass audience participation," he says. "Although the music was of its time, as with previous dance music scenes, this was about escaping the drudgery of the working week, dressing up and letting loose on a Saturday night."

Many of the most iconic ideas to come from the Designers Republic, as well as their work with Gatecrasher, are rooted in South Yorkshire. Ian may originally hail from Croydon outside of London, but his designs have toyed with a sense of place, at times speaking a global language, at others, being hyper-local, dubbing Sheffield 'North of Nowhere' and 'SoYo'.

"All our peers were London-based and they seemed to be offended that we'd be anywhere else," he explains. "We'd get asked what the best thing about London was and we'd say the train back to Sheffield." As the Designers Republic website proclaims, "it doesn't matter where you're from, it's where you're at"[104].

Despite countless albums, festivals and sold-out parties, the Gatecrasher brand came to a chaotic end in Birmingham in 2015 some years after the demise of its flagship venue. Watching it burn to the ground in Sheffield wasn't how anyone thought it would go. Many came to the wreckage in the days after the fire to lay flowers and pay their respects, mourned like a lost family member by its devoted, fluorescent crowd. Now the space, known as the Gatecrasher Apartments[105], is home to students at the nearby Sheffield Hallam University and is another chapter in the neverending story of nightlife giving way to property. It's a transition we've witnessed numerous times over but for Sheffield, this homogenisation of its city centre is just the latest in a series of tumultuous periods of change.

The face of Sheffield has evolved beyond all recognition during the last 50 years, with the development of the city's terrain reflected in an ongoing cultural shift around how its population works and plays. Its reputation as a hub for industry came through stainless steel production as cutlery has been manufactured in Sheffield since the 13th century[106], with Harry Brearley developing what was widely regarded as the first 'rustless' or stainless steel in the Brown-Firth Research labs in 1913. This was at the height of the industrial revolution that tore through the economies of many cities at the time, transforming the lives of the UK population as workers moved into urban hubs looking for work. This fuelled a massive growth in Sheffield's population that expanded from 60,000 in 1801 to a peak of more than half a million by the 1950s[107]. However, due to greater competition from cheaper, overseas imports, the heavy engineering industries the city was known for nosedived into decline during the sixties. With the city's economy almost entirely dependent on steel, it was dealt a hammer blow when this sector began to collapse. Between 1971 and 2008, the manufacturing sector in Sheffield declined by 74%, shedding 120,000 jobs with thousands more lost across the rest of the South Yorkshire sub-region[108].

Many of the musicians, producers and DJs to emerge from the Steel City during the eighties were born just prior to the industry's fall from grace. Writers Ron Wright and John Schofield explore this very evident influence in their book, '*How Industry and Electronic*

*Music Forged Sheffield's Sonic identity*'[109], describing how the sound of the drop hammer from the city's steel forges left an indelible imprint on the minds of these young artists. Martyn Ware, a founding member of electronic pop auteurs such as the Human League and Heaven 17, has previously referred to the stomp of the forges as "the heartbeat of the city"[110]. His father worked in the steelworks while his mother in a factory and was brought up with these industrial sounds lodged deep within him.

The Human League, Heaven 17 and Cabaret Voltaire were the much-documented purveyors of the industrial funk that Sheffield is so well-known for. This aural psycho-geography associated with the city is something that continues to occupy, inspire and fill the music and mind of Cabaret Voltaire's Stephen Mallinder.

"You could say this early electronic music represents the sound of the city but in some ways, it's also very futuristic," he explains. "We're connected with the industry and steel and that kind of past, yet at the same time, the sounds were sonars and bleeps which went into outer space and into the future."

Cabaret Voltaire, which included the late, great Richard H. Kirk and Chris Watson alongside Stephen, formed in 1973 and took their name from a nightclub in Zürich, Switzerland, which artists from the Dada movement attended. As with other cities witnessing the decline of industry, the spaces that these factories previously occupied created a vacuum sucking in artists and musicians looking to find somewhere to flex their creative muscles.

"There were all of these abandoned workshops and Little Mesters spaces [workshops belonging to craftspeople]," Stephen says. "The key was in us being able to inhabit them as we went through this phase of deindustrialisation in the late seventies and eighties. The other element was the Youth Training Schemes and the dole. People were able to build little music futures for themselves."

Cabaret Voltaire's musical experiments blended DIY electronica with a punk squall to great, confrontational effect. Pre-digital, they began to piece musical collages together through tape machines, homemade sounds and whatever else they could source. Stephen remembers that the city's clubs held an initial attraction for him and Richard as their musical tastes began to roughly take shape.

"We grew up drinking underage in the soul and ska clubs," he states. "We'd come from this club, dancefloor kind of background, then we began to make music as we got more into art. We didn't particularly want to be in a band as we didn't have instruments. Our inspirations were mavericks like Brian Eno, William Burroughs, and the Velvet Underground."

Stephen remembers Sheffield venues like the Broadway and the Merry England would play music. But as much of it was outside their tastes, the members of Cabaret Voltaire instead focused more on their own musical adventures.

"We withdrew from this world into our attic where no one knew what we were doing," he says. "Which was messing around and experimenting with sounds and tape players. That was our early embryonic phase, moving from being kids around town into kids experimenting in an attic."

The Western Works is an old industrial building closely associated with this gang of electronic dissonance lovers. In the mid-seventies, they opted to leave their base and head to the second floor of this space on Portobello Road in the centre of Sheffield. The band initially shared this with another punk band before the other group split, allowing the Cabs to take over ownership of both rooms. It "was unusual for a band to have their own studio in those days" and proved a popular haunt for other emerging music makers[111]. Acts such as fellow-Sheffielders the Human League and Manchester's New Order utilised the space as somewhere to record and experiment.

"It was a great place to hang out with mates and mess with tunes," says Stephen. "Back then in the late seventies, the pubs would shut at 10.30pm, so we were always in there working and experimenting and, to be honest, listening to music and watching obscure films on VHS."

Within 12 months of the trio setting up shop in the works, Cabaret Voltaire's musical ambitions had begun to ascend and make ripples within the industry outside of their headquarters. They signed a deal with Rough Trade in 1978 and began putting together the tracks which would become their debut album, *'Mix Up'*[112].

"Myself and Rich paid ourselves the equivalent of whatever the dole was back then," says Stephen. "We didn't want to go on it as we didn't need the hassle. That's how it started, recording and building it into a 16 track studio. We left Western Works around 1986/1987 after someone broke in through the roof and we had to find another space."

The Cabs' involvement in the fledgling post-punk scene meant they took the seemingly somewhat dubious accolade of being the first band to ever take to the stage of Manchester's Hacienda.

"We played the Saturday and there was no fucker there as the party had been on the Friday and everyone had got completely trashed," Stephen laughs. "It was a members-only club in the early days, so you had to be signed up and have a card with your membership; it was like joining the library."

"We played the Hacienda to about six people. It always sounded shit but it really sounded shit with only six people in there. Tony Wilson didn't think that one through and we totally copped it."

As with so many other British cities, Sheffield in the eighties endured a decade of discomfort under Tory rule as it struggled to cope with the closures of the steel plants and factories. In his research paper *'Sheffield Is Not Sexy'*, Stephen refers to places like Sheffield as "once the engine room of the nation's manufacturing hegemony"[113]. But this was the city of the past, not the one which struggled to stay upright as its economy buckled.

Richard Hardcastle, known as DJ Solid State, is one of Sheffield's longest-serving purveyors of house and disco and began his nocturnal excursions during this transitional period. Releasing music on his own All Out War, Society and Toko Records, he's had a foot on the dancefloor during every phase of the city's modern clubbing story and continues to DJ today. Richard played guitar and drum machine in two local industrial funk bands inspired by the Cabs, Chakk and Hula. The music he was making in 1985 already had accidental parallels with later house and techno in the equipment and approach, which became much more deliberate through 1986 and 1987.

"There was a massively long comedown from punk and trying to be weird and dour was what many people did by default," he says. "Goths were rife. The indie bands of that time were pretty shite, on the whole, except perhaps The Jesus and Mary Chain, The Smiths, Killing Joke and a few other honourable exceptions. The golden era of Sheffield music was over and there was generally quite a negative, edgy atmosphere. It's something you could probably say about the country as a whole in the Thatcher era, with all the unemployment and general social unrest."

According to Solid, clubs such as the Leadmill and the Limit on West Street in the mid-eighties in Sheffield played an intriguing mixture of Cabaret Voltaire, Glenn Miller and James Brown, even if the DJs would spin the same tracks at the same point every night.

"To pep things up, I would hassle DJs for 400 Blows' *'Movin'*, A Certain Ratio's *'Sounds Like Something Dirty'*, *'You've Got the Power'* by Win, *'Sensoria'* by Cabaret Voltaire, *'Fever Car'* and *'Get the Habit'* by Hula, *'Let The Music Play'* by Shannon and *'You're the One for Me'* by D-Train," he says. "But the crowds were as bad as the DJs and they fed off each other, creating a downward spiral of complacency that meant, sooner or later, something else HAD to happen. And eventually, it did, when Jive Turkey started in November 1985."

Inspired by some of the early Chicago house records they'd heard at the Jive Turkey night, Richard and his friend Dave Thompson tried articulating their own version of this sound but using electric guitars and bass. Their track - known as *'The Spiral'* - was long forgotten but was clearly inspired by the primitive, rhythmic tracks they'd been exposed to.

"We had no idea what they were, but we really liked the Chicago records and quickly realised it was a very easy formula to copy - just a one-bar bassline and lead riff over a Roland drum machine, with loads of handclaps," he says. "When I listened back a few years ago and remembered the thought processes and intentions, it was very obviously the Chicago house records we'd copied, although we fucked it up by using electric guitar and bass."

Before this house music sound landed, Solid remembers how there were many insurmountable barriers for young kids wanting to make dance music. But Chicago house music's arrival massively moved the needle along.

"Prior to house music, you needed shit-hot, funky musicians, great programming skills and very expensive gear alongside super-strong, soulful vocalists," he explains. "The Chicago tracks appeared and blew that idea to pieces and opened up possibilities that seemed game-changing. You can absolutely hear it in the repetition and simplicity of our track, *'The Spiral'*."

Solid started investing in dance music records towards the end of the eighties and began promoting his own Kangeroo night with a bunch of like-minded mates. At the time, Jive Turkey, helmed by DJs

Winston Hazel and Parrot, led the way in Sheffield, though its musical policy was less house and more funk, jazz-soul and Black music. The night, which started in the mid-eighties at a club called Mona Lisa's on Charter Square above a restaurant, has clocked up much in the way of column inches for its forward-thinking music policy and influence[114]. It called the City Hall home for a period before heading back to its original venue, where it kept punters moving until 1992. The diversity of the crowd and the DJs made for an inclusive dancefloor at a time when the wider world was anything but. Resident Winston Hazel continues to be a powerful force as a club DJ and producer in Sheffield and was one of the Forgemasters who released the first track on Warp Records, *'Track With No Name'*. Its influence stretches on and on.

"Our premise with Jive Turkey was that anybody could get in and you could do whatever the fuck you wanted," says DJ Parrot in an interview with the Red Bull Music Academy[115]. "But hopefully, once you got in there, even if you weren't aware of the records we were playing, maybe you'd be... It's a terrible word, but... educated into liking them."

Cabaret Voltaire's members were regulars at the night, a club which Stephen says kicked open the door on the next chapter of Sheffield's electronic history.

"Many of the DJs and producers who came out of Jive Turkey - people like DJ Pipes, Parrot and Rob Gordon and Winston Hazel - they acted as a bridge between our electronic music and this new generation of Black and white kids coming through. The club scene really took off from there," explains Stephen.

Jive Turkey's success combined with several other key, complementary factors gradually exposed Sheffield's underground music scene to a wider audience. Set up in 1985, FON Studios (standing for 'Fuck Off Nazis' after a piece of local graffiti[116]) was launched by local punk-funk outfit Chakk after receiving an advance when they signed with the major label RCA. In his book, *'How Soon Is Now? The Madmen and Mavericks Who Made Independent Music 1975-2005'*, author Richard King describes the studio as connecting "the dystopian futurism of the Sheffield of Cabaret Voltaire and Human League and the city's next generation of bands like Hula and Chakk"[117]. The impressive facilities certainly attracted similarly impressive artists to record there, including Ian McCulloch, David Bowie, Yazz, Erasure, James, and Altern-8. But while it encouraged non-Sheffield acts to visit the city, FON was also vital in nurturing what would become the team behind the legendary electronic label Warp Records. Both founder Steve Beckett and Rob Mitchell had played in local indie bands before being asked to work at FON's record shop and they drafted in Jive Turkey resident DJ Winston Hazel as their dance music buyer. Winston told Resident Advisor: "Word got out from the nights we were running at the time that we were playing a lot of techno and house. People started to bring music into the shop for us to hear. FON was the shop in Sheffield for dance music imports and it had a reputation all over the north [of England]."[118]

In the spring of 1989, Winston Hazel's friend Rob Gordon, a rising star as part of the FON Force production team alongside Chakk's Mark Brydon, celebrated a big pay cheque for work on Yazz's debut album by buying some equipment for his home studio. Winston went round to collaborate and the resulting track, the otherworldly bleeps and bass of *'Track With No Name'*, was the first slice of music to come out on what would become Warp Records. From there, the imprint released vital electronic tracks from Nightmares on Wax, LFO, Tricky Disco and many more, trail-blazing a rich seam of innovative, sometimes intelligent, dance music.

Ian Anderson from the Designers Republic played a significant role in sculpting Warp's visual aesthetic. While Rob Gordon and

Winston Hazel were taking care of beats at FON Studios, Ian handled the eye-catching look and feel of their records, flyers and other promotional assets. Ian's route into design work in Sheffield was via gigging and hanging out on the local music scene before managing local band Person to Person during the eighties. The group signed to Epic Records and worked with the System, an influential production duo from New York. Alongside managing the nuts and bolts of their fledgling career, Ian also crafted the artwork for their records, including various logos and other visual elements.

"The Designers Republic started by accident, really. It was based on this artwork for Person to Person," he explains. "As the band was folding, I was getting more and more requests to come up with artwork based on what I'd done for them rather than requests from artists asking me to manage them."

Ian gravitated towards Steve Beckett and Rob Mitchell at Warp via Sheffield's music scene as their social circles overlapped. The beginning of Warp's visual identity came part by chance, part through their organic collaboration.

"We were just creating graphics in and around Sheffield and some of it was in dance music," he explains. "I knew Steve and Rob who set Warp up already and they asked us to start doing artwork after we did some flyers for them. It wasn't really a commission as we already knew each other; it was more about helping them out as mates. When they started, they were just selling records out of the back of cars. It wasn't planned but we ended up growing together. Obviously, there was something about what we did and how we worked and it just clicked."

Chantal Passamonte moved to Sheffield to work with Warp as a press officer in the mid-nineties. Her journey with the label saw her leaving the role to sign to Warp as an artist in her own right known as Mira Calix. Tragically, during the writing of this book, Chantal sadly passed away but her influence and legacy with Warp and as a creative is a powerful one. As Warp Records said, "Mira was not only a hugely talented artist and composer, she was also a beautiful, caring human who touched the lives of everyone who had the honour of working with her"[119].

"I was initially living in London working for various labels, a record shop, running a fanzine and events with a collective called Open Mind," she recalled when I interviewed her. "I was in direct contact with Warp Records and when I heard their press officer had left, I applied for the job along with around 400 people. I was thrilled to land it, which meant moving to Sheffield where they originated from and were based at the time."

As has been well-documented, the first Warp releases continued the legacy of Cabaret Voltaire and Human League's pioneering electronic experiments, initially with Yorkshire acts such as LFO and Nightmares on Wax. By the time Chantal joined, the label was beginning to look further afield for talent, working with an increasingly diverse, geographically disparate collection of artists including Aphex Twin, Autechre and Boards of Canada. Although she felt that the label's sound has become more global over time, the early Warp releases from artists based in Sheffield and Leeds shared an affinity with "bleeps and bass".

"A Leeds-based band called Unique 3 was part of that original crew which included DJs and producers, and it's what Warp was born out of," she said. "Many of those first records from the Forgemasters and Nightmares On Wax shared this distinct dancefloor sound - Casio tone bleeps, minimal, mid-tempo, heavy sub-bass. That stripped-down sound did go on to influence a load of subsequent genres of dance music. You can see the connection to dubstep and grime, and drum & bass and started as a response to what was coming out of Chicago and Detroit."

While she was a publicist for Warp until the mid to late nineties, Chantal was then signed by the label as Mira Calix and pursued her own unique line of abstract and electronic music. Over numerous records, sound installations and performances, her music was always born in response to the environment around her.

"I've spent just over a decade living in a very rural environment, which has been a source of endless field recordings," said Chantal. "I've often made beats out of the sounds of twigs and rocks recorded on daily walks and it has certainly led to my music being full of pastoral melodies. But my first album was written on a busy Sheffield street. The constant passing of buses was the undertone of everything I wrote."

While Warp was beginning to carve out its own take on dance music, sometimes in ways which were impossible to dance to, elsewhere in the city, Sheffield started moving to the beat of house music in a big way. As the whole country simultaneously began to throw shapes, Solid State remembers it as a perfect mix of energy, great music and a new appetite for recreational drug use.

"It helped bring on board a lot of youngsters," he recalls. "But it felt like Sheffield was a couple of years behind the 'E Culture' you read about and saw on TV. It wasn't an influence for ages. Then when it did eventually arrive, it killed off some nights, the main one being Jive Turkey, where it had all started."

A particularly memorable evening where this cultural shift towards ecstasy was highlighted went down when Spinmasters (also known as the 808 State DJs) played at the Leadmill back in 1990.

"As you can imagine, it was wall-to-wall curtains, ponytails and Joe Bloggs," says Solid. "Some of the punters looked no more than 14 or 15. But the main shock to me was that the cosy and familiar

Leadmill suddenly resembled a war zone. There were bodies everywhere; kids were literally just passing out on their feet, completely bombed on pills... That, or dancing like complete lunatics with little or no sense of timing. This scene wasn't about an appreciation of Black music; it was all about 'losing it' and it jarred massively with what Sheffield's indigenous house scene considered itself to be about. A real schism was about to happen."

He remembers several key venues in the city back then, including the Palais, the City Hall Ballroom, which played host to hardcore nights like Creation, as well as the Limit on West Street, a club night informed by ravier sounds.

"Wherever you turned, the Manchester model was prevailing and by 1991, Jive Turkey was dying on its feet," says Solid. "Quite rightly - if suicidally - for a club built on zero compromise, they didn't reach out one iota to the student/young raver market that was flooding the other clubs. The attitude was that the Palais and others catered for that crowd – and they were welcome to them."

The Palais, located on London Road, is an iconic Sheffield club that has enjoyed many different incarnations. Previously, the Locarno, it became the Music Factory, then later Bed (which was managed by Gatecrasher) before lying derelict. Now it's open again but as a Sainsbury's, selling bread and milk to hungover students who live in this part of town. But back in the nineties, it was down to the vision of one Mancunian that the Palais became synonymous with the arrival of house music.

Anwar Akhtar grew up in Hulme, Moss Side in Manchester as a working-class Pakistani kid and now lives in south London, operating as a cultural producer within the worlds of arts and media. He initially made his mark on the capital as director of the team who brought the creative institution Rich Mix arts centre to life in east London back in 2006. Anwar led business development and delivery of the £26 million project before going on to head up The Samosa, a digital media news, culture and publishing project, focusing on Britain, South Asia, the Pakistani Diaspora, the politics of identity and human rights. He was also producer of Dara, the first South Asian History play at the National Theatre in 2015 about the Moghul struggles to control India and the producer/presenter of the documentary film, *'Pakistan's Best Kept Secret: Lahore Museum'*.

Anwar's time in Sheffield helped give him the skills and experience to succeed in London, but the confidence and eyes for an opportunity were something he already had when he landed in South Yorkshire. He drove the Palais forward, then pushed for the creation of the Republic, the futuristic city centre club that went on to house, then become Gatecrasher One and transformed Sheffield into a clubbing mecca.

"The PSV in Hulme was what turned me onto the magic of club culture," he remembers. "It was a brilliant mix of Manchester ruffians, dope heads, scallies and beautiful people, all races. It was counter-culture at its best."

This space, previously known as the Russell Club, alongside formative dalliances with the Hacienda and the reggae culture of his native Moss Side left a big impression on Anwar and his musical tastes. But there were a range of reasons he left to study in Sheffield. The city's relative proximity, love of football, record labels such as Warp Records, club nights like Jive Turkey alongside the diversity and socialist politics coursing through its arteries all pulled him away from Manchester.

"Sheffield is such a Labour city as well as an anti-racist place too, and this really resonated with me and my own views and politics. There was a lot of emphasis and respect surrounding Black music history, too," he says. "But when I arrived in 1988 as a nineteen-year-old fresher, it seemed like there was a divergence between what was happening for newcomers like me and for Sheffielders. I kept myself to the university/student club nights at first but then started going to the nights with the likes of Winston Hazel and Parrot. Others would travel further afield to Nottingham, clubs like the Garage or Venus."

It was drinking in pubs on Abbeydale Road, such as the Broadfield Tavern, on the south of the city near leafy Nether Edge, that led Anwar and friends to begin hosting house parties in the neighbourhood, although initially, these were illicit affairs. After the boozer closed its doors, they would carry on the party at one of the large student houses around the corner.

"We had hundreds of people there at the first party we hosted," says Anwar. "Then, we did it again a week later and the same number showed up. The next month it was like the Notting Hill Carnival with people spread out across the entire road. The police had to close it down, but it gave me a bigger idea to speak to the nearby club about putting on proper nights there given how many students and locals were turning up at the house parties."

Anwar convinced the management of the Locarno, later named the Palais, a club located further down Abbeydale Road towards the city centre from the Broadfield, to allow him and his social circle to start hosting events off the back of this unexpected house party success.

"We worked out a deal and on the first Thursday, 2,000 people turned up," he laughs. "They asked us if we could do it again - we got 2,000 again - why don't you have a go on Friday? Saturday? Nights like the Blow Out, Jam Factory, Compulsion all came from this. The club itself had a reputation among Sheffielders as being a place for bruisers but it worked out for us. We were lucky to be in the right place at the right time."

Anwar and his team of friends and music lovers began promoting events as dance music gripped the UK in 1989 and the start of their nights that summer heralded the arrival of ecstasy in Sheffield.

Simon Manders, also known as DJ Green, met Anwar at university and joined him on his musical mission to bring Hacienda-style raving to Sheffield.

"Sheffield had its own thing going on with Winston and Parrot," he says. "But I brought in more rave music, European and US tracks. We would play more piano and the happy side of house rather than rave - that was Friday night at the Palais."

Simon remembers how the Palais events attracted out of towners as well as those local Sheffield ravers. Dancers living in the satellite towns would get in their cars and drive to the party.

"We sucked up a lot of people from small suburban towns like Wakefield and Morley, Chesterfield, Matlock, Derby, those sorts of areas too," he says. "We definitely put people's noses out of joint by playing this Manchester house sound rather than Sheffield's homegrown form of dance music."

Despite the Palais bringing a different form of club culture into Sheffield's nightlife, Green says that the DJs weren't allowed to become the stars of the club.

"There was no way anyone would let you become too big for your boots," he explains. "At [another legendary Sheffield club night] Occasions, the DJs were in a closet at the back of a tiny broom cupboard. At the Palais, we'd be right at the back of the stage while there was this sunken dancefloor. All these people dancing would be facing each other and it really worked well."

But as with so many clubs, the initial rush of excitement and craziness surrounding their venture became all-consuming. By the summer of 1992, Anwar and Green had decided to call it quits on the Palais and move on to something less chaotic and demanding.

"It quickly turned into this monster that needed constant feeding," says Anwar. "The venue hire went up, so we had to do more nights and charge more on the door. I remember one night just before I was about to start my DJ set, looking outside the front door, there were about 500 people in this queue stretching round the block. The club was already full to capacity, and the manager was frantically emptying an adjoining room, so we could get everyone in. It was great fun, from Shades of Rhythm playing a legendary set with 1,500 people singing along at the Jam Factory and queues all the way down London Road. So suddenly, there was this momentum around constantly booking artists, people like Sasha and Dave Seaman. It was brilliant but unrelenting for more than four years."

After Green left at the end of the Palais, he parted ways with dance music for more than twenty years.

"Drugs and violence got ahead of us," he says. "There were battles with bouncers on the dancefloor, we also had a really horrendous time with [football hooligan gang] the Blades Business Crew - we barred them but that was their local club as it was at the end of London Road."

While Sheffield's industrial sounds sonically infiltrated the music of the first wave of artists, DJs and producers to emerge during the eighties, a wave of decisions were made by the authorities wanting to accommodate the burgeoning music scene. When local acts started collecting national acclaim, members of the city council responded by lobbying for more space for these captains of musical industry to flourish. The result was the establishment of the Cultural Industries Quarter (CIQ), an area near Sheffield's train station dedicated to the city's creative sector[120]. This officially started life in 1981 with the opening of the Leadmill as a live music venue with an alcohol licence the following year, a music space financed by the authorities and a home for many legendary live gigs and raves down the years[121]. The

CIQ gradually came together during the mid-eighties as the council looked to pull the city's economy up by its bootstraps following the industrial collapse. Matthew Conduit worked closely with the council in formulating its strategy around reversing the downward spiral. Initially, he was drawn to Sheffield to study fine art, then opened the Untitled Gallery on Paternoster Row in 1988 when the city was still reeling from the steel industry's crisis.

"You've got to remember that in the mid-eighties when policy around creative industries was being fought for, Sheffield was on its knees," he says. "The Don Valley was like a wasteland, steel plants were shutting and Thatcher was in power. It couldn't have been much worse."

Back then, thanks to the vision of Paul Skelton, Head of Sheffield City Council's new Cultural Industries team, which eventually included Matthew, the authorities acknowledged that it needed a strategy to support the creative surge. It was in this sector where things were beginning to bubble with Sheffield Independent Film winning a franchise with Channel 4, the synth-pop of the Human League hitting the charts, and the cock rock of Def Leppard taking on stadiums alongside the opening of FON Studios. The challenge was to keep this talent within the city rather than let it escape to London. The opening of Red Tape Studios in 1986 was a big step for Sheffield and the CIQ to solve this problem. As the first ever municipal-owned facility of its kind, it not only offered recording services for artists but provided a wide range of training courses on sound engineering and music technology for unemployed young locals too.

"I was involved with the council at the time and Phil Oakey from the Human League was pushing the debate among others," says Matthew. "They didn't want to go to London to record and instead preferred to stay in Sheffield. I became involved in meetings with the council and chamber of commerce as they happened to own this street of empty buildings where the Untitled Gallery and the Workstation would eventually open."

Two years after Red Tape set up shop, the Audio Visual Enterprise Centre launched, featuring specialist recording facilities and space for FON, Axis 24 track recording, Sheffield Independent Film and the Untitled Gallery, now known as the Site Gallery. This coincided with the formal publication of the CIQ Mission Statement and Outline Plan in 1988, giving the venture greater cohesion and strategy. Still, despite the hard work which had gone into pushing this forward, Matthew was initially overwhelmed when his venture began.

"I remember sitting on the wall outside the gallery a few days before we opened and just thinking 'Fuck, what have we done'," he says. "There was just no one around there, it was dead. A lot of the surrounding buildings were either shut down or empty. It was a whole chunk of the city which had been largely ignored for years, which is why we spotted this great opportunity to move into it."

Despite these misgivings, the CIQ gradually attracted support and began to see regeneration with the opening of the Workstation in 1993, a space dedicated to the creative industries and the Showroom Cinema in 1995. Within this climate of creativity and overhauling Sheffield's identity, Anwar Akhtar's visions for a new club slotted in.

After some time out to focus on his studies, in between books and classes, Anwar would spend his days roaming around Sheffield's city centre, acquainting himself with its different areas and rundown spaces.

"I used to like having a spliff and walking around, listening to music and looking at buildings, the nooks and crannies of the city," he says. "Sheffield has this brilliant mix of civic architecture, the City

Hall, Town Hall, Ruskin Gallery, Crucible Theatre and all the industrial buildings. It all gets a little bit *'Blade Runner'*. That was my way of relaxing - but I'd always be exploring the quieter parts."

At this point in the early nineties, Anwar believes Sheffield's nighttime economy was restricted and missing out on some of the benefits reaped by other cities. He wasn't alone and began contemplating a new venture through his social circle and connections he'd forged within the local authorities and business world.

"The licensing laws represented a significant obstacle," he remembers. "You had to prove the need for a new nightclub. From the licensing perspective, it was quite obscure stuff you had to demonstrate, including the idea that liquor consumption wasn't the road to damnation. Manchester had all these issues too, which is why they had a club night called Temperance Club at the Hacienda, but the laws there had changed a decade before. Sheffield hadn't and we had to really fight to prove there was a need and an audience there."

Matthew Conduit and Paul Skelton's vision of a new city and economic reality very much chimed with Anwar's ambitions and they pushed local leaders to take action.

"Paul and Matthew told the then Sheffield City Council Leader, David Blunkett, that something had to be done to save Sheffield's economy, which was blighted by the loss of steel manufacturing," he says. "This could take the form of a knowledge economy and cultural services and really help the city move forward."

"That's what led to the bus station becoming the Showroom Cinema, the Workstation, the Site Gallery, and the Republic was very much about putting club culture into that mix. That process was already happening - but what we didn't have was a licensed large nightclub venue to complement it."

The derelict former Roper and Wreaks steelworks on Matilda Street was found via a connection through financial experts PwC and the seed of an idea about a new venue and club began to take root. Working with a team including Matthew and Paul alongside PwC representatives, ideas began to form about the potential space. This would be more than a club but somewhere offering daytime work and office areas to creative companies and startups alongside rehearsal spaces for bands. The aesthetic was very much embedded in Sheffield's industrial past while simultaneously looking to the city's next phase.

"It was all about Sheffield's heritage, its steelworks and its politics," Anwar explains. "I loved the city as much as I loved Manchester and by that time, the Hacienda had gone. But I always loved the idea of an underground disco - of having an alternative space, nodding to the Loft and the warehouse scene."

The Republic eventually opened to great fanfare in 1995 after a protracted legal battle to get the licence, becoming the first new club to arrive in the city for more than a decade. Its many original design features included a giant industrial crane that hung above the dancefloor. Despite the achievement of getting through the courts and opening up, Anwar's tenure as leader of the Republic was all too brief.

"I was 25 and trying to do too much amid this crazy maelstrom," he laughs. "One minute, I was walking into PwC with an idea and wanting to raise a million having found the perfect building. The next minute I had a phone call saying we've raised the money, you can buy the building, the council will support the new liquor licence as part of its night-time economy development plans - can you sign the business plan off in three months for bank approval? Ultimately, we just couldn't hold it together financially and there was a lot of pressure on me."

With Anwar out, it took its sale to Gatecrasher to turn the Republic into one of the most successful venues of the era. After a £1.5 million refurbishment, the club reopened as Gatecrasher One in 2003[122].

"For Gatecrasher, it was a huge opportunity," says Anwar. "The architecture was magnificent and it was a venue which arrived with 2,000 capacity. But I was already on my way out. I'd booked my train ticket."

Anwar headed down to London, where he found himself heading up the creation of a new cultural space in London's East End. Rich Mix, located on Bethnal Green Road, features three cinemas alongside performance and exhibition spaces and opened in 2006.

"So much of what happened in Sheffield was played out in my work at Rich Mix," he says. "Some of the mistakes previously made, we managed to avoid. So not allowing any single investor or funder to have majority control, locking in a wider range of arts and cultural programming and not just banging club nights. We created partnerships with other cultural organisations and educational partners, which is the basic tool kit of running cultural institutions."

"After I'd finished working on Rich Mix when I was 35, I told myself that's it, I'm not doing another building project," he says. "I've done three, I'm not doing another and I've managed to stick to it so far. I went off to explore Pakistan, where my parents had come from and make films and theatre."

Gatecrasher is a central space in Sheffield's clubbing story off which so many other ventures ricochet. Before the club found its home at the Republic, one of its first ports of call in Sheffield was at the Arches. Located on the Wicker, on the cusp of the city centre, the space was part of a railway viaduct more than 600 yards long and named after the road which passes under its main arch. Originally built in 1848 to offer an extension to the railway, it has been described as an "outstanding example of monumental early railway architecture"[123].

Those who toiled on it probably didn't realise how it would provide the perfect rave cave for some of the most ludicrous parties the city has ever seen. The Arches at 9-11 Walker Street was the home to many legendary nights from Gatecrasher and techno club Remedy to dance music's harder, more feral side in the form of Headcharge and Planet Zogg. Sheffield promoter and DJ Alan Deadman helped establish Headcharge towards the end of the nineties with fellow music promoter Jamie Smith. The pair met after Alan was asked to programme a stage for a festival on Devonshire Green organised by students from Sheffield Hallam.

"Jamie had a stage representing a *'Made In Sheffield'* band compilation album he had put together as a charitable project," says Alan. "Interestingly, another element on Devonshire Green was the Curfew Sound System, a crew who had built this reputation for hosting outdoor raves."

The pair started chatting and decided to collaborate, drawing on Alan's love of dub and Jamie's wealth of local contacts and involvement in the techno scene.

"Jamie told me about the Arches which had just reopened," says Alan. "He had been involved in putting on nights there including Livemind in the Arches during its first incarnation."

"He came up with the name Headcharge which is a kind of reworking of Livemind and suggested we try to create an indoor rave vibe," Alan continues. "So he booked the acts for the downstairs space at the Arches, with advice from the DJs. I took on the upstairs room, mostly programming eight hours of DJs with some live music sessions, drawing on my world music contacts."

Headcharge managed to create an inclusive yet eclectic musical world that formed a close-knit community around it. The club was split between two rooms of colourful rave - downstairs acid techno and hard trance raged while upstairs was more eclectic with sounds taking in everything from world music to breaks and beyond. Both spaces were connected via two corridors, one inside and another on the outside. On paper, this sounds simple to navigate, but when in the moment, pummelled by music, vibes and everything else one had imbibed, you could get lost, both mentally and metaphorically, for what felt like days. Emma Webster first ventured to Sheffield to study in 1998 and joined the Headcharge family in 2001, playing an integral role in helping the club operate.

"The Arches was the perfect venue for Headcharge and it was in the perfect location," she says. "It was just far enough out of town that you had to make the effort to get there, meaning that the venue was very unlikely to get random walk-ups who might not 'get it'. It was also far enough out of town that we were pretty much left alone."

The industrial, musty feel, alongside the hard music policy and location meant that the Headcharge crowd was incredibly tight. Those who knew held the experience of going down to this part of town close to their chests. Located near Pitsmoor, Alan describes how the all-nighter attracted a diverse mix of "climbers, outdoor ravers, hunt saboteurs and people who had been trained in circus arts at Sheffield's Circus School".

"It was beyond the city 'bounds' and on the edge of Pitsmoor, which students were officially advised to avoid," Alan explains. "Pitsmoor had a large Afro-Caribbean population with accompanying 'blues nights' such as Donkeyman's, and also had a strong 'alternative' community. A lot of our crowd came from that area. The space itself also played a part. I can still feel and hear that warm wall of chat and music that hit you as you walked up the steps to the top corridor."

Emma went to almost every event Headcharge hosted for six years, describing how discovering the club on Halloween back in 1998 felt like "finding home". She lists the energy, bouncy techno, and trance of acts like Lab 4 and Headcharge's own resident band OS1 as loud, neon-coloured highlights.

"I remember one night where a whole load of 'Crasher kids turned up in matching Cyberdog gear including fluffy legwarmers, glowsticks, and spiky neon hair," she says. "Most of them didn't last the whole night but a small number started coming regularly, just without the matching gear!"

"I also remember one night finding my newish boyfriend (now husband) sitting on the stairs at the back of the downstairs room with his head in his hands. He was apparently wondering how and why his girlfriend could love this - I thought banging, he thought dreadful."

"Resistance is futile" is the clarion call surrounding Planet Zogg, a "hyperdelic trance" party that also found a loyal crowd at the Arches. Beginning life in a "dodgy biker" bar[124] in Sheffield in 2000 by resident DJs and promoters Greg and Dill Zogg, the pair were inspired by raves they'd experienced during the nineties - such as Brixton's legendary trance night Escape From Samsara - and mixed it up with cosmic visuals in a friendly and fun environment. Their night was born at a time when the various threads of Sheffield's alternative counter-culture seemed united.

"If there was a cause and a good musical line-up, then the club would be full of very alternative people," says Greg. "The city's music scene was very cooperative and everyone would get involved, meaning you'd get this real variety of DJs and musical styles playing on the same night."

Planet Zogg orbited the small bar for a year before upping sticks and heading to the Arches, chasing a bigger space which the pair could truly make their own.

"We did our first birthday there, which was a step up in terms of capacity but the venue had the vibe we wanted," says Greg. "The

Arches was so raw and exciting and allowed us to fill it with our own sound production and decor."

The Arches was the second home for Planet Zogg. Since then, it has taken its otherworldly mix of trance, breaks and techno to various clubs and venues within the city over its 20-year history. Greg and Dill threw free parties over a number of summers in the Plug, an ambitious three-room club located on Matilda Street which opened its doors in 2005. Other spaces have included the Adelphi, a club venue on the city's outskirts in Attercliffe and its current home at Yellow Arch Studios in Neepsend, a recording facility turned venue. Zogg is still going strong, although Greg and Dill have reduced the number of events they do over a year. But their production values and attention to detail have never been more on point.

"These last few years at Yellow Arch have been amazing," says Greg. "The professionalism and vibe is wicked, the buildings are great too and you can rave without the sludge forming on your shoes like it used to at the Arches."

Yellow Arch, located on Burton Road in Neepsend, enjoyed a former life as a nuts and bolts factory for the shipping industry but has been a musical location since 1997. Local stars including Jarvis Cocker and Richard Hawley have graced its studios while its current incarnation as a venue started in 2015.

"Heading to Yellow Arch felt like a great move," says Greg of their decision to call it home. "It was on everyone's radar and a very vibrant spot. But the increase in the number of bars, cafes and craft beer places around them in nearby Kelham Island has been dramatic in recent years. They've done brilliantly to keep going."

Kelham Island certainly nods vigorously to Sheffield's industrial heritage. This part of the city is a man-made island, the result of the development of a channel to carry water from the River Don to the Town Corn Mill, and originally stuffed full of factories and industry to power the machines used there. The remains of the workshops and steelworks have since been transformed into a rich array of flats, independent shops, cafes and restaurants. When I lived in Sheffield, Kelham Island featured one pub usually frequented by old men, so from a distance, its revival seems surprising. But while this part of the city offers a glossier take on Sheffield's heritage, there are still underground rumblings joining dots with the industrial funk of its past. Hope Works is a nearby warehouse space and former gun factory run by local DJ Lo Shea, a self-proclaimed "warehousing agitator, rave maker, connector, facilitator, planner and instigator"[125]. Home to the exceptionally well-programmed No Bounds Festival, it features forward-thinking electronic outsiders like Space Afrika, Batu and Ben UFO and continues pushing a musical narrative which is never too far removed from the city's industrial past.

Dan Sumner is Sheffield-based and founder of Pretty Pretty Good, a club night specialising in bleeding-edge house and techno, which went on to become a UK-wide venture. Now working directly with various venues in Sheffield, including Dryad Works, Foundry, Peddler Warehouse and Signal, among others, he cites Hope Works as one of the city's best spaces to open in recent memory.

"Seeing the likes of Jeff Mills, Ben Klock, Floating Points, Martyn, Karenn and more back in 2013/2014, in an industrial warehouse space in Sheffield, was pretty special," he says. "The DIY vibe of the venue (and it really was very DIY back then, too) was something that resonated with me. Around this time, I started to think about organising my own parties for the first time."

Pretty Pretty Good was inspired directly by Dan's experiences in spaces such as Hope Works and The Tuesday Club, a leftfield programmer of underground electronic music based out of Sheffield's University since 1998. When Dan first moved to the city back in 2010, the line-ups for the weekly night were focused around bass music with headline DJs including Loefah, Jackmaster, Skream and more

"Everything started with The Tuesday Club for me," says Dan. "The Foundry (the venue that houses the night within the Students' Union) was much rougher around the edges back then and was actually pretty dark and dingy before the big refurbishment. Seeing the likes of Ben UFO and Joy Orbison play in that kind of space really changed things for me."

Dan's Pretty Pretty Good began at the Harley in 2015, a pub-turned club and gig venue located minutes from the University of Sheffield on Glossop Road. The motivation to begin the night with Sheffield producer Yak (John Randall) came from the absence of their favourite acts from Sheffield's nocturnal scene.

"There were a load of artists we wanted to see here who just weren't getting booked, so we thought we'd book them ourselves," he states. "It really was as simple as that and we never intended for it to be more than a small party."

From a Thursday night in April, with a focus on quality event production from brilliant resident DJs to lights, the night's popularity quickly blew up, bringing students and locals together on the dancefloor via an astute booking policy. Dan helped expand and grow the promotions company with events at other venues across the UK, including London's Corsica Studios, Wire in Leeds and Manchester's Soup.

"We caught the bug from that very first event at the Harley," Dan says. "We didn't run our second party until September of 2015, selling the venue out with 350 tickets on the Monday of 'Freshers' Week'. Then for our third party in November, we did our first party at Hope Works, bringing Hunee back to Sheffield with the Thrillhouse guys. After three years of doing it at university alongside my studies, I went and ran it as a full-time job. It was quite a ride."

As with so many other cities, Sheffield's nightlife has seen countless clubs and ventures succeed and fall. Scuba was an inspirational home for left of centre house music during the noughties at the Fez Club on Charter Square, while Remedy would be downstairs at Po Na Na, welcoming tougher acts such as Slam or Dave Clarke, the so-called 'Baron of Techno'. C90 was a more experimental night that started during the mid-noughties, doffing its cap to Warp Records' glitches and bass explorations. The event took it in turns to roam around Sheffield's spaces while hosting artists as weird and as wonderful as DJ Scotch Egg and The Bug. Around 2007, we witnessed the latter decimate the sound system of The Corporation, usually a rock venue, in a thick fog of dry ice so dense you could barely see your hands or limbs. These nights have all contributed to the rich story of what has happened after dark in Sheffield but few have cultivated their own separate myth such as the notorious club Niche and its armoury of thick, almost rubbery basslines.

The doors of Niche were first opened in 1992 by Steve and Mick Baxendale and the club's name is synonymous with the sound of bassline. Alongside the bouncy, hyperactive music, the club had a reputation for drama, gangsters and trouble. As Daniel Dylan Wray wrote for the Red Bull Music Academy, for many of us living in the city during the noughties, "it became the haunted house at the end of the road that all the kids talked about"[126]. The club, which featured DJs Jamie Duggan, Shaun 'Banger' Scott and Andy Spoof, played a unique form of speed garage that morphed and mutated via a fusion of sugary female top lines and snarling basslines. Big Ang was among the music makers fueling this scene with her production and beats.

"A chance night out on a Monday in Rotherham allowed me my first taste of the style many refer to as "Niche" with reference to the nightclub," she says. "I do remember Shaun 'Banger' Scott and it was a good set. I found out about the rest through friends who had already discovered this style of music. It's generally a fusion of speed garage, organ and piano house, bassline, with house, jungle, drum & bass and UK garage influences, and hints towards the old skool rave and Italian house."

In London, garage was one of the dominant genres of nineties clubs led by producers like the Artful Dodger, DJ Zinc and MJ Cole. But in Sheffield and around other spots of the north, it was bassline that paved the way thanks in part to the loyal crowd around the club and the ingenuity of many of the DJs. Niche's Steve Baxendale has described in a past interview how "the DJs asked if they could take the vocals out of the speed garage (pitched vocals, particularly female singers were a central point of the sound) and the house and just thump up the bass a bit"[127]. Elsewhere, DJs would also re-record different versions of popular tracks to bring the bassline to the fore, helping to evolve the so-called 'Niche' sound.

"I think things just grow naturally when a group of people not only want to buy and play a genre, which people may not have realised was a genre at the time, but want to make it, and to listen to it," says Big Ang of the tight community around the club and the music.

"Down south was all about deep house, UK garage ... up north we did have very lovely house nights, hard house, trance, drum & bass ... but something just a bit special in the early days got a lot of people up here hooked."

The stories surrounding the club are the stuff of legend. The numerous police raids on Niche's venue on Sydney Street, the stabbing of Mick Baxendale outside the club, the global dominance of the sound and how it sparked other genres, including Bhangra Niche, a fusion of two ostensibly far removed musical worlds.

Alex Deadman, a Sheffield DJ, journalist and promoter who previously interviewed Steve Baxendale as well as hosted his own nights such as Junglist Alliance, says that Niche's scene, musical style and brand was driven by the club itself.

"It became really unique when Sheffield artists started getting on it and coming up with their own versions of these garage tunes," he says. "Local MCs would put vocals on them and give them to other DJs and it spiralled from there."

"But once the Baxendale brothers saw this popularity spike, they asserted ownership of the sound. They could see this market was about to explode and they wanted to make sure that the Niche brand was at the helm as a new genre emerged."

As Steve says in his interview with Alex, changing the style of the tracks "led to a change from a predominantly white crowd to a predominantly black crowd. Bassline music was evolving. London never had bassline music as we had it here; they had the grime. It was our DJs at Niche that created that sound."[128]

After its home on Sydney Street was closed down in 2005 following a massive police raid[129], Niche went on to inhabit Club Vibe on Charter Square and the sound peaked with T2's big track *"Heartbroken"* reaching number two in the UK Singles Chart in 2007. A Ministry of Sound compilation followed but since then, Niche's dominance surrounding the genre has retreated, especially after Steve Baxendale left the city.

Following the closure of the club, other Sheffield labels such as Off Me Nut have become known for bassline during the 2010s while producer and DJ, Toddla T, who has enjoyed huge success as a host on BBC Radio 1 and BBC 1Xtra, took on board elements of the sound in his own productions. Toddla's music was born out of bleep, then shaped by a residency alongside Winston Hazel and DJ Pipes at club night Kabal, a nomadic entity that would take place in found spaces across the city. From their infamous all-nighters at the Ebenezer Chapel in Walkley (which was student flats at the time of the party but still had an altar where the decks could sit) to a former abattoir near the site of Gatecrasher, their mix of bashment, hip hop and bugged out dub and bass continues to inspire. Now living in London, Toddla's music thrums with those early influences, although his production style has morphed to include music with rappers Aitch and Ireland's Kneecap.

"You're a product of your environment whether you like to admit it or not," he says. "When you leave a location, certain things are going to stay there but my sound has definitely changed."

As an emerging producer, Toddla was influenced by those in his immediate circle of mates, all bubbling on the kind of music thrown down at Kabal, Scuba or Niche. Through his peers and mentors, he could gauge what was acceptable and what would work as a track or in a DJ set.

"When you leave somewhere, you then need to look to different people for inspiration," he states. "Sheffield was where I learned my craft, so I will always reference those individuals. But I've always wanted my music to evolve rather than just being stuck in a particular place. Certain people like you to stay the same but I'm into moving forward. I realise that sounds wanky but I want to evolve and I get as much inspiration from younger artists as older people nowadays."

The influence of the internet has meant that inspiration can arrive from anywhere, heading far beyond geography and a city's boundaries. Music makers are now in a position where their phones can connect them with any type of sound, meaning that musical differences generated via location are harder to discern.

"Everything has become more unified in terms of the sonic sound of music across the board because of the internet," says Toddla. "A lot of production now isn't as distinctive as it was and it's tougher to tell if a beat is British, Jamaican, African or American."

"That being said, you can't just wipe the roots and foundation of each area overnight. Sheffield with the bass and bleep, Jamaica with reggae and dancehall. They will still be at the source of these place's sounds, even though we're more connected through technology."

Sheffield record label Society's tag line of 'Like the Past, Love the Future' encapsulates the energy and aesthetic surrounding Sheffield trio, the Adelphi Music Factory. Purveyors of contemporary house music pumpers, their name combines two of the city's most venerated nightclubs, the Adelphi located on Vicarage Road in Attercliffe and the Music Factory, previously the Palais and later known as Bed.

"These two clubs obviously spawned our name and a lot of our tracks take their titles from famous Sheffield club nights or venues," they say, "Rise, Love To Be, Jive Turkey, Uprising, Cuba and NY Sushi at The Unit was brilliant. We've got a real affinity for Yellow Arch as we used to work in the studio and rehearsed there in previous bands. It's now also a great live/club space. We played our debut gig at the venue and the atmosphere was electric."

The group has been picking up plenty of acclaim over the past few years with serious props levelled at them from tastemakers such as Disclosure, Annie Mac, and the Blessed Madonna. Their sound is big-room house music, perfect for soundtracking BBC Radio 1 on a Friday night or booming between Manchester's cavernous Warehouse Project walls. They may have enjoyed national success, but the trio attributes their outlook and musicality to the city they grew up in and still call home.

"Sheffield has had a big impact on us, both culturally and musically," says the group. "It seems a common theme with Sheffield artists that they aren't shy of showing what a massive inspiration the Steel City has been. Despite massively punching above its weight musically and being one of the biggest cities in the UK, Sheffield always seems a bit of an unsung hero. People who've lived here bang on about it, and anyone who visits says how amazing it is, but somehow it's a bit below the UK's cultural radar. Hometown pride and the British love of the underdog make people in the know shout about it."

While they acknowledge the importance of Warp Records, Adelphi Music Factory also feel it's time to create new electronic music stories and go beyond the "long musical shadows of the past". Sheffield's current musical scene can play a defining role in pointing the city onwards.

"Most of the successful Sheffield nights have had a DIY feel which is in keeping with the city's reputation as the world's biggest village," they say. "Even glossy affairs like Gatecrasher started down and dirty at The Arches. It's something we've tried to recreate with our shows back in Sheffield, get all our friends down, lots of giveaways to everyone who comes. We want to make it feel like a house party."

The city's record shops have also shaped their music and production style, independents like the Store on Division Street, Area 39, Underground Records and Dance Records on Abbeydale Road.

"Cool Wax in Orchard Square used to have some great US house and techno too," they say. "We remember walking in there one day and Kenny Dope was behind the counter. These shops were more than just a place where you bought music. They were a community, a meeting place and our musical education."

If you cast your eyes and ears across Sheffield's contemporary nightclub scene, then there are still plenty of opportunities to dance and party the night away. Its musical ecosystem goes far beyond the Sheffield bleep and bass title often so unceremoniously pinned upon it.

"The idea of place has collapsed in a sense," says Stephen Mallinder. "When you think about dubstep and grime, there's still a connection to place. But on a larger scale, the ways in which we consume music has been stretched and I'd argue that the specifics of place have become diminished. Having said that, all of the little scenes that exist still depend on the local clubs and spaces."

Now, numerous local scenes - from Tottenham to south Manchester and beyond - function in isolation with the different threads uniting these musical networks back underground and out of sight.

"It doesn't mean they don't exist. It just means they're not quite as visible or as connected with the wider culture," Stephen states.

Pretty Pretty Good's Dan Sumner has noticed how changes in student behaviour have impacted the city's nightlife in recent years. Hikes in tuition fees and a growing interest in healthier lifestyle choices means more young people are inclined to look elsewhere for their kicks outside dancing all night in nightclubs. Combined with the devastation wrought by Covid-19 and the ongoing economic decline, the clubbing community stands on an uncertain if potentially thrilling precipice. Whether the landing is catastrophic or graceful remains to be seen.

"A city like Sheffield has been particularly hard hit because the students form such a large percentage of the nightlife market," he explains. "The students who are at university now have essentially had two years where they weren't allowed to go to clubs, so they just haven't explored and found the warehouse and grassroots venues slightly further out. That said, there are a lot of good signs in Sheffield and I hope that over the next couple of years, the nightlife scene will continue to grow."

Some of Sheffield's best loved club nights have always taken place out of the spotlight in more mysterious places. From my experiences in the old industrial works or at the Arches, the occasional rum goings-on in the city's fingernails offer the most enthralling nighttime escapades.

"You have to know where to look for great nights in Sheffield," agrees Solid State. "As a promoter, there's a lot of luck involved in getting the right venue at the right time and usually this isn't in the main clubs. I think that's always been true. There has always been a healthy undercurrent of spaces, off the radar and where the real exciting musical ventures happen."

Because of this, Sheffield hasn't always been a destination for clubbers and attracted them in the same way that Manchester or even Nottingham have been able to.

"Gatecrasher certainly put Sheffield on the map," Solid says. "But although we've never had a shortage of good nights, a lot of cities seem to be better at shouting about their nightlife and get way more famous nationally. People in Sheffield either aren't as well connected, or maybe they just aren't as bothered. All the weird or interesting stuff won't be found in a guide. This might be true everywhere to a certain extent - but it's definitely true in Sheffield."

# CHAPTER 5

## IN THE 0121 / BRUM, CITY OF ALMOST A THOUSAND SOUNDS

*"Birmingham's sound is an eclectic melting pot of post-industrial culture"*[130].

Lai Power

*"There's a heaviness and an intensity - but also a sense of humour - that's how I would sum up a lot of what comes out of Birmingham"*[131].

Tony Child (Surgeon)

Birmingham's cultural and creative identities are as thickly entangled as the routes and roads zig-zagging over each other in the nearby Spaghetti Junction. The notorious Gravelly Hill Interchange on the M6 located in the second city has been giving drivers headaches since it was unveiled to great fanfare back in 1972. Initially, it was heralded as an engineering triumph thanks to its bold design and the close connections it forged inside the UK's national motorway network following the construction of the M1, M5 and M6 routes. The £10 million multi-lane highway's impact on the city provided "one in six Birmingham residents with work - over 30,000 at Longbridge", according to reports[132] and made the Guinness Book of World Records, as "the most complex interchange on the British road system"[133].

Despite the economic benefits and futuristic vision surrounding the development, the junction also became something to laugh and poke. Comedian Ken Dodd dubbed it the eighth wonder of the world because "once you're in you wonder how you'll get out"[134]. The anarchic artist and pop music troublemaker Bill Drummond described it more cryptically as "the entrance to the underworld"[135].

The most populous city in the Midlands (with 1.2 million residents at the last count in 2021) has certainly been prone to a pisstake over its lifetime[136]. Its geographical location in the heart of the country has somehow led to this sprawling beast of a place often being overlooked in narratives exploring the UK's musical creativity. Instead of being celebrated, histories are replaced by impressions of Ozzy Osbourne shouting for his wife Sharon. As it's neither north or south, for some it's a place you pass through on a journey to another, supposedly better location. For others, rather than cultural aesthetics, it's a retail destination with the stark gleam of the Bullring pulling them in.

"Brummies are humble and self-effacing, we've always been the butt of jokes for our accents, people saying that we're thick and all the rest of it," says Adam Regan, DJ, promoter of Leftfoot and co-owner of the Hare & Hounds pub in Kings Heath. "Outside Brum, there's this sometimes negative perception - but then once they come here, they love it."

Doris Woo, better known in dance music circles as the brilliantly named DJ Bus Replacement Service, is a selector who dons a Kim Jong-Un mask to smash out DJ sets veering from gabba to crunching pop edits. She married iconic UK techno producer Surgeon (Tony Child) in 2002 following long-distance dating between Birmingham and New York for a couple of years. Although now living outside the city, the couple have often been associated with the tougher, grittier side of Birmingham nightlife.

"Birmingham's club culture is unlikely to be regarded as a cultural asset in the same way as Berlin's," she says of the city's nocturnal scene. "This is at least partly due to deep-rooted snobbery against anything that's not so-called 'high art'."

Mo Jones (also known as DJ Mistress Mo), founder of the city's old school rave night Flashback, and co-founder of TicketSellers and Eventree, agrees that doomy connotations surrounding Birmingham and its identity are hard to shake off.

"If you're cool, it seems you go to Sheffield, Leeds or Manchester," Mo says. "I always think that's a bit sad. Brummies have always been very self-deprecating, it's hard to be proud of yourself here. The Commonwealth Games did give the city life in 2022 but now the council has gone bust. So we're back to thinking we live in a shit place without any money."

Perceptions of Birmingham have certainly tended to veer towards the negative. As Robert Shore wrote in the Guardian, "the Midlands has an image problem. And that problem, essentially, is that it doesn't have an image"[137]. In the novel *'Emma'*, published in 1815, Jane Austen penned: "They came from Birmingham, which is not a place to promise much, you know, Mr Weston"[138]. Authors Jon Bounds, Jon Hickman and Danny Smith felt they had to go as far as publishing a book entitled *'Birmingham: It's Not Shit'* in 2022 to prove the naysayers wrong[139]. Tory minister Helen Wheeler referred to the city as "godawful"[140] while the local authority unfortunately compounded these perceptions by declaring itself bankrupt in September 2023[141]. Still, the city's narrative is also evolving in the face of such stigma. The 2022 Commonwealth Games gave the local economy a significant boost, with over half the economic impact (£453.7 million) benefiting local businesses and communities[142]. The controversial HS2 project will eventually make it to the city and is expected to bring investment and opportunities along with it.

Scratch at the city's skin of shops and brutal architecture, you'll find an energy pumping through the streets of Birmingham, driven in part by what some have described as its "superpower" - its diversity[143]. The 2021 census revealed how 51% of the population are people of colour, more than any other city of its size[144]. Like so many other British cities, its ethnic make-up was shaped by the migration of people from the Commonwealth countries during the fifties and sixties. This led to Afro-Caribbean and South Asian communities forming all over the city, particularly in wards such as Handsworth, where the proportion of ethnic minority residents amounts to 88%[145]. From within this population, it's unsurprising that many different musical styles have sprung forth - which is perhaps also why its musical and clubbing personality is challenging to define.

A rich musical history features plenty of sounds and styles for the city to be proud of. At the tail end of the sixties, the template of early rock and roll was amplified by the success of the first metal bands, Black Sabbath and Judas Priest. The narrative veered from the synth pop of Duran Duran and the smoky alternative world of the Mermaid pub in Sparkhill, to the glam house of Miss Moneypenny's and much more. Birmingham scenes often seem to be straining at diametrically opposed poles. They may veer wildly in sound and style - the New Romantics, Bhangra culture, the more extreme sounds of Godflesh, reggae and dub of Musical Youth and ska of The Beat - yet geographical energy and creativity binds them.

"In Brum, you can link Black Sabbath to the more industrial techno of artists like Surgeon and Regis," Adam says. "But you also have the dub sound systems influencing Steel Pulse and UB40, an underground reggae scene that became pop music, a Bhangra scene with this huge Asian community, grime artists coming out of the city. There's so much variety here that it doesn't give Brum an identity in the same way as Bristol or Manchester."

Writing in her book, *'The Economies of Cities'* in 1972, New York urbanist Jane Jacobs champions Birmingham as a city of the future when comparing efficiencies with Manchester. While Manchester's economy was driven by cotton mills, Birmingham's prosperity was more disparate, a "muddle of oddments" as Jacob describes. Then, when the mills went into decline, it was Birmingham's "great, confused economic laboratory" that kept the lights on, arguably a fitting description for how its disjointed creative scene has evolved and grown[146]. Neil Spragg, aka Sir Real, DJ at legendary techno night House of God and producer/sound designer, believes that a lack of spotlight has allowed Birmingham's nightlife to grow wildly without being watered down by hype or attention. The conflicting narratives, artists, sounds and styles have allowed for a unique music culture to ferment, however irregular and erratic commentators and journalists may see it.

"The city has been largely ignored by the music media since forever, and I think this helps promote a distinct lack of ego in many of the people involved in making and promoting music in the city," he says. "The attitude has been influenced by that, a kind of understated 'fuck them all' that comes from the Brummie underdog nature."

Leading the way in trying to navigate these numerous, overlapping musical histories is the Birmingham Music Archive (BMA)[147]. This online resource was launched to scoop up the different strands formulating Birmingham's story into a more coherent whole. Founder Jez Collins has explored various nooks and crannies of Birmingham's cultural life with an enduring love for the sounds that course through the city's veins. From an Irish family, his life has been rooted in music, young ears filled with folk music and feet moved by ceilidhs.

"I'm 55 this year and have always been in and around Birmingham artists - my identity and politics have been formed through music," he says.

Having worked in bars, academia and recording studios alongside facilitating opportunities for young people, Jez's work under the BMA banner aims to underline Birmingham's contribution to the UK's creative character. His efforts have stemmed from a sense of frustration that Birmingham was being overlooked and left out of national cultural conversations despite its many influential artists and sounds.

"I have this 20/30 years of work around Birmingham and have always asked why the music press don't ever talk about the city," Jez says. "Regis and Surgeon developed this fierce electronic sound. They were inspired by Mick Harris from Napalm Death, so this scene of grindcore, anarcho, political, DIY energy. Mick was interested in the avant garde, started fusing this love for experimenting with his love for Black Sabbath alongside the industrial heritage of the city. This background, this fusion of noises and influences would give rise to a form of techno that would become known as the Birmingham techno sound which is huge internationally - but barely recognised within the city, or indeed in the UK. Birmingham is constantly written out of the Shoom and Hacienda dominating narratives when it comes to the rave culture explosion."

It was out of this that the BMA came to life and aimed to go deeper in celebrating the city's artists. Jez has succeeded in turning negative perceptions into a positive energy, creating installations, films, and broadcast media, culminating in 2023's Rave Ukraine, a simultaneous party held in Liverpool and Kyiv as part of the Eurovision Song Contest. The BMA's Que Club exhibition was hosted in Birmingham and London and put together to document the infamous club and Grade-II listed building that has been a battleground for so many raves and parties. As the city's sounds expanded, so has the urban landscape surrounding clubs, becoming glossier and taller with older venues and buildings repurposed or knocked down. Digbeth has long been a nightlife hub for the city yet has recently been a building site for the much-vaunted HS2 project.

"When it came to development in the city centre, I have started challenging the council and developers," Jez says. "If you want to build here, I can't stop you but do you understand the history and importance of that building to different people and communities? How can you reflect this and incorporate it into your designs, how can you keep that connection to our musical culture?"

The BMA's roots can be traced back to the eighties and the pubs and music venues where Jez cut his teeth. One such pub, the Mermaid, might be the antithesis of regeneration, an unruly space that existed outside of any urban planner's dream. At the time, Jez was into post-punk, goth, psychobilly, bands like Spear of Destiny and this ramshackle boozer, alongside other pubs like the Barrel Organ, provided subcultures somewhere to hang out and grow. Dilapidated, and hosting a cross-section of the city's society, the rickety stage and room welcomed early incarnations of influential bands like Napalm Death.

"You'd have this anarcho hardcore crowd on a Saturday night, psychedelia on a Thursday, then perhaps more psychobilly sounds on a Friday," Jez recalls. "It was a strange pub in a big Irish/Asian area. Lots of Sikhs would be drinking downstairs and you'd be in this grotty room above listening to weird music - it was an important cultural space, a lot of the musicians, promoters and audience would emerge in the techno and rave scene that was developing at the time."

Located in Sparkhill, to the south of Birmingham, the Mermaid's building has housed a pub for some time. It changed into a curry house towards the end of the nineties, then suffered severe damage due to a fire and is now open again as Farro's grill-house. Today's visitors would be oblivious to its importance for anarcho-punks and hunt saboteurs as "somewhere to gather within the sprawl, somewhere to play, somewhere to organise, somewhere to bond and share ideas and somewhere to find your own community"[148]. The pub was just one ingredient in an eclectic Birmingham scene.

"In the eighties and nineties, you'd have big clubs like the Hummingbird, what is now the Forum, this hosted the Hipnoziz and Snapper Club house nights," says Jez. "Then the next night Nirvana might play followed by Gregory Isaacs, followed by the Menagerie indie nights. There would be reggae and heavy dub nights over at the Monte Carlo in Handsworth which was where I was properly introduced to Black music, in their basement bar with their huge sound system. Or you could go to the Mermaid and see an early incarnation of Napalm Death playing. You'd flit between these places and these scenes, and be exposed to so much different music on any given night. No one would care what you looked like, or what you dressed like."

Dance music of all shapes has sprung out of Birmingham throughout its musical history. Various strands of techno have appeared from producers such as Rebekah and Female alongside speaker-rattling jungle, drum & bass, bassline, and grime with artists ranging from Mike Skinner and The Streets to Lady Leshurr all feeding into the city's musical personality. With so many sounds swirling around Birmingham, the city has provided creatives with the vital space to evolve, including, in an unlikely turn of events, pioneering music producers from far further afield.

"One of my bugbears around techno history is how it came into the UK via Neil Rushton here in Birmingham," Jez says. "Neil compiled the seminal '*Techno! The New Dance Sound of Detroit*' album, the first time techno was used to name what is now a worldwide movement, but this often gets missed in the standard retelling - and there were lots of other styles of dance music going on in the city too. Gatecrasher started in Birmingham, Sundissential, the dance music scene would run the whole gamut, from glitzy superclubs to really underground, DIY-type spaces."

Network Records' entrepreneurial founder Neil Rushton used the city as an unlikely platform for many of Detroit techno's artists to beam their music into countries and dancefloors around the world - and had a defining influence as a conduit for Kevin Saunderson, Inner City and the rush of this new generation of musical talent. He was initially a lover of Northern Soul, journalist and record collector who turned his passion and hobby into an unlikely profession.

"As a teenager I was obsessed with soul music and got heavily involved in the Northern Soul scene," Neil says. "I DJed, promoted huge all-dayers with over 3,000 attendances featuring live acts including Sylvester, Brass Construction, Players Association, Crown Heights Affair, Al Hudson & The Soul Partners."

"I was trained as a newspaper reporter and was the first staff writer when Black Echoes was launched in 1976. I imported records and from that set up a record label Inferno and that was a kind of apprenticeship for when we set up Kool Kat Records which morphed into Network."

Rumblings of the UK's nascent electronic music scene and Network took hold in the incongruous town of Burntwood, located near Lichfield where Samuel Johnson, author of the first dictionary was born[149]. A low-key wine bar called No 7's became a key space for early rave transmissions.

"One of my best friends Pat Ward was a resident DJ there and he was one of my two partners in Kool Kat," says Neil. "Pat invited Neil Macey to DJ there every Thursday and this little wine bar in a small Staffordshire town became rave central. One of those Thursday night sessions was where I met Mark Archer and that led to us signing Nexus 21 who later became Altern-8."

It was in 1987 that Neil first became aware of what he describes as "Detroit house records" - later known as techno although at the time no one else was calling it that. These records were arriving as imports with Neil attributing his curiosity in them down to his obsession with past generations of Detroit soul artists. It was hearing Rhythim Is Rhythim's *The Dance* that galvanised him into picking up the phone and calling the number scratched on the record label.

"Derrick May answered the phone and we got on like a house on fire," says Neil. "I invited him to come over to the UK over Christmas 1987. None of us had any money and we asked Derrick to bring over 50 or 100 copies of *Strings Of Life* so we could sell them and put the takings toward his air fare!"

Neil subsequently started working with Derrick May, arranging for him to work on three remixes while he was in the UK - Bang The Party's *Release Your Body*, Two Men, A Trumpet And A Drum Machine's *I'm Tired Of Being Pushed Around* and T-Cut-F's *House Reaction*. The artist asked Neil to manage him although his music didn't immediately make a positive impression on everyone.

"I took Derrick to a meeting at 4th & Broadway/Island Records as I thought it would be the perfect label for him," Neil recalls. "But to my amazement a legendary A&R man said he didn't 'get' *Strings Of Life*. I was astonished and vowed there and then never ever to go to another record label and seek their approval on how good a recording or an artist is."

Early in January 1988 after Derrick had gone back to Detroit, Neil delivered Derrick's remix of T-Cut-F's *House Reaction* to Mick Clark at 10. Mick loved it and after the 4th & Broadway experience, Neil's alternative plan was to compile and licence to Virgin an album of Detroit house tracks. Other music industry manoeuvres fell into place around this central ambition.

"Right before going to Detroit to put the compilation together, I was lucky enough to sort out a very lucrative licensing deal with Pete Tong at FFRR for a Kevin Saunderson track," Neil explains. "Almost as soon as I landed there we agreed I would also manage Kevin. The album came out great on an underground level but the great bonus of course was that *'Big Fun'* by Inner City was on the album. That led to Inner City becoming the biggest house group in the world. I got John Mostyn on board to co-manage Inner City, Kevin, Derrick and Juan Atkins."

While the music embraced Afrofuturism - "a cultural and familial context in which Black people work together to build speculative futures" - and sought to envision an other-worldly tomorrow[150], Network's Birmingham location also influenced the attitude of the label. Their base in the city exposed some of the Detroit artists to some of the city's musicians as well as industry movers and shakers.

"We were very conscious that we were not part of the London-centric music scene," says Neil of Network's location. "We didn't want to be part of it and were very pro-Birmingham and anti the London establishment. We were very good at PR and consciously built up that image. It was a little bit like smoke and mirrors because we got very good at being paid money from the London music biz too."

Neil's friendship with John Mostyn, manager of The Beat, Fine Young Cannibals and Alison Moyet, helped him get to grips with the intricacies of music publishing and the best ways to work with major record labels. Together, the pair co-managed Inner City, Kevin Saunderson, Derrick May and Juan Atkins. Kevin also married Ann Nanton from Birmingham and she became a musical collaborator.

"The Detroit guys were in Birmingham all the time," Neil says. "John was working with Ocean Colour Scene at the same time.

He had the office upstairs and we were downstairs and I can vividly remember the band chatting away. I would not say there was anything in Birmingham's musical DNA that we inherited, but we certainly liked being based there."

In UK techno circles, few producers, DJs and artists are as revered and, in some ways, as feared as Tony Child, aka Surgeon. Operating since the tail end of the eighties, initially out of Birmingham with a love for improvisation and hardware, his take on electronic dance music is as abrasive and mind-melting as it is obscure and off-kilter. From his early *'Surgeon'* EP to 2023 album *'Crash Recoil'*, his music has bent the original techno blueprint into a series of idiosyncratic contortions.

Surgeon's roots in electronic music are wrapped around a punk DIY attitude and anarchic streak that lurks beneath a demur exterior when we speak. He grew up in a village outside Northampton before moving to Birmingham in 1989 to attend Sandwell College for an audiovisual design course where he was able to flex his creative muscles in sound as well as photography, TV and radio. Hailing from a small place where his musical passions were deemed niche, moving to a bigger city expanded his horizons and social circle. He met likeminded individuals attuned to similar wonky musical persuasions.

"When I moved to Brum, there were loads of people into all sorts of odd music, it really broadened my musical palette," he says. "It was amazing to hear so many different things I'd never heard. It was in Brum where I heard Faust for the first time, they were a really important band for me."

Among these new-found friends was Mick Harris, a fellow music lover and creative, and their coming together proved to be a pivotal moment. As the drummer of Napalm Death in the late eighties, he invented the term 'grindcore' and connected Surgeon with fellow techno producer Regis, helping kickstart Downwards Records. Surgeon initially bonded with Mick over a love for Coil, Basic Channel and Mike Leigh films.

"He influenced me in two ways - one really key moment was when he bought me the double CD of Miles Davies' *'Bitches Brew'*," he says. "He would do that, buy important music and give it to me. It took me 15 years to understand that album, it was way over my head at the time. He also had a small studio at his house, which was basically a cupboard. He let me use it on my own, which was great as I had very little access to any equipment after the course and no money either. I had to borrow gear and would carry what I could round to his place. The first EP that featured *'Magneze'* was recorded at Mick's house."

Surgeon's way of working on his own productions has been informed by those around him and a DIY-approach to learn new ways of making music while doing. At college, he rebelled against the tutors' more formal approach to creativity, eventually dropping out from the course.

'When I started out you couldn't just go on YouTube and look something up," Surgeon says. "Instead, you'd hear a sound, ask how it was made, and try and figure out how to produce it. I look back and see the value in having basic equipment and having to be really inventive in how I used it. I know some younger producers create amazing music on laptops with all these pieces of software available but for me, it really helps to have limitations."

His career as Surgeon speaks for itself. A mighty discography features plentiful albums, remixes and collaborations, released through his own labels Counterbalance and Dynamic Tension alongside established imprints, such as the much-loved Soma and Tresor. A relentless DJing schedule has taken him all over the world, yet this globe-trotting career was born out of Birmingham. It was the city that first offered him a playground for his musical activities and introduced him to defining connections, fresh sounds and influences. These days, he resides outside of Brum and is slightly sceptical about the idea that moving from the countryside to a big urban municipality suddenly led to the harsh and abrasive techno he was known for.

"It's not quite as literal for me," he says. "Birmingham has a wonderfully diverse sound - even when you think about the history of metal - Black Sabbath, Napalm Death. From the outside, it might seem heavy and intense but from living here, I've always recognised the very self-deprecating sense of humour."

Surgeon was in Birmingham when the cork came off the bottle of dance music culture at the end of the eighties and early nineties. As for so many, it was a powerful and influential force that had a significant impact on his life.

"You saw dance music in the pop charts and on the TV, it really smashed through into the mainstream, without the mainstream wanting it to be there," he says. "I've since travelled a lot and seen how revered British dance music is in other countries, it's so well regarded. However, here it's seen by the authorities as something to stamp out, it's seen as this dodgy, dirty world - they'd much rather have nice, expensive flats instead."

House of God, the Birmingham night Surgeon has been associated with as a resident DJ, has operated as a defiant beacon of counter culture and at the grubbier end of the musical spectrum. It might be one of most confrontational, yet playfully eclectic techno nights in the country. With the tagline 'Brum as fuck', the night is still doing its thing some 30 years after this group of self-proclaimed misfits first bonded over a love for ferocious music and placing their tongues in their collective cheeks. Steered by a group of mates, main organiser Chris Wishart and founding residents Paul 'Damage' Bailey and Neil

'Sir Real' Spragg alongside Surgeon, House of God has been on a freewheeling ride through Birmingham nightclubs big and small ever since.

Sir Real remembers punk, new wave and prog musical influences swarming within the night's DNA, often not heard in traditional clubs but other slightly more illicit spaces.

"The (dance) parties that we enjoyed were some of the early hardcore raves that largely played the UK sound of the time - breakbeat hardcore and early jungle, but mostly it was house parties that we and friends were throwing, playing early rave and Belgian techno, and UK stuff like Orbital," he says. "There wasn't really any club in Birmingham at the time covering that sort of sound."

It was a trip outside the Midlands that cemented their desire to put on their own events. The group visited Holland and it was experiencing rave culture here that helped them zone in on the kind of music they wanted to play and type of night they wanted to host.

"House of God really came together after many of us visited Holland to work 'the bulbs'," he says. "That was where we first experienced proper raves playing all the music that we had heard only bits of in the UK. We resolved to put on our own proper parties as soon as we got back."

Surgeon's connection with the group came through playing in a band with Neil called 'Blim'. He then met House of God founder Chris at a sparsely attended Birmingham club night called Bedlam.

"There weren't many people there and the DJ played *'Didgeridoo'* by Aphex Twin and me and Chris were the only people to madly dance to it," he laughs. "We loved the song so much. We were just a group of mates who loved techno but we had our 30th birthday in March 2023 - somehow we're still alive."

From these disparate influences, House of God has ploughed its own musical furrow, with various Birmingham venues and spaces hosting their musical deviancy. Clubs like the Dance Factory, the Institute, the Que Club, the Rainbow Rooms, Subway City and the aptly named Satan's Paradise have all welcomed them.

"I think the majority of moves between venues were mostly dictated by necessity or circumstance," says Sir Real. "If you ask most House of God attendees of any 'vintage', they will express a lot of fondness for our first 'proper' venue, the Dance Factory, which was a very grubby and industrial space behind (and part of) the Digbeth Institute."

"We did numerous gigs in the much bigger main building over the years, but the Dance Factory was a filthy sweat-hole, and suited us and the music down to the ground! Que Club shows were also pretty special, huge and with spectacular (and weird) production. Subway City is now the Tunnel Club and has been our regular home for years now though, and has a great vibe, similar to the Dance Factory in many ways. Satan's Paradise was a pretty seedy club in Balsall Heath, an area local to where most of us (and our social circle) lived, but it had a very weird and not always entirely pleasant atmosphere (unrelated to our crowd), and I think most people were happy that we only did a few gigs there."

DJ Bus Replacement Service has been a regular raver at House of God over the years. She cites the Tunnel Club in the Jewellery Quarter as her favourite of the spaces the night happened upon.

"It's been the home of House of God for more years than not now," she says. "It had a lot more character when it was more predominantly a gay club kitted out with playrooms. House of God's overlord Chris Wishart gave me and Surgeon a tour during the day and we found a prosthetic ear in the corner of one of the caged rooms."

Surgeon can remember the very first home at Birmingham university at a venue called Berlins which is no more. On the night, the DJs played everything from "weird dub" to the industrial thrum of the Revolting Cocks.

"The Dance Factory was crazy too, the energy and the noise," he says. "You would start to mix the next track in and the roar from the crowd was so loud, you couldn't hear anything. It was insane, very anarchic and lawless, the security staff would stay on the door, there was no trouble, they would leave us to our own devices inside. There were all kinds of things going on, people fucking everywhere, it was wild."

"Things are much safer now and I agree with the ideas of safe spaces," Surgeon continues. 'Back then with House of God, it was a place for the outsiders, the weirdos, the rejects, the queer community, anyone who didn't fit, could come together at our nights. It was really diverse and policed itself - if you were an arsehole, you wouldn't be there - the music was so extreme you wouldn't want to be there unless you were a weirdo."

DJ and promoter Mo Jones' raving roots can be traced back to the dawn of acid house culture. During those early days, geography was something she and countless other electronic dance music lovers had to get to grips with and navigate their way through to find the source of the party. Her older self looks back in some disbelief at the optimism of her endeavours to track down a great time.

"You never really considered how crazy it was back then," she says. "I had a little orange mini Metro with four gears, there was obviously no sat nav or mobile. Two weeks prior you'd have arranged to meet your mates, so you'd set off in the hope that they would have stuck to the plan like you. I missed Castlemorton due to concentrating on my A Levels. But then when I landed at uni in Birmingham, SL2 did a live PA at our Freshers Fair and I immediately fell in with loads of ravers who were doing parties at the time. It was brilliant."

Memorable nights have been many for Mo, with her passion for promoting and party organising taking off while studying at university. Having organised a leavers party at school, she took these experiences and hosted her own night in the early nineties.

"We organised a club night with Digs and Woosh from Nottingham's DiY in Berlin's Bar in the Guild," Mo says. "Everyone laughed at us as we were in our first year but we did it, sold 400 tickets and it turned out to be a brilliant party. Then the first Flashback event happened a few years later in 1996."

The night has taken place at various Birmingham spaces including the Medicine Bar and welcomed some of dance music's bassiest DJs, MCs and producers. Mickey Finn, Kenny Ken and Randall have been among the selectors to play hardcore, jungle, drum & bass and more to a loyal and devoted crowd which still gets together to party (if somewhat more sporadically) to this day.

"We didn't do a stand-alone Flashback party for eight years, then we returned in 2022 at the Mill, a club which has since become XOYO," says Mo. "We waited to find somewhere that would suit our crowd, many of whom are over 45, and it worked perfectly with the different rooms and outside space."

"I had so many messages afterwards saying what an amazing night it was, how those who attended felt revitalised - and that is the point of Flashback, sustaining this sense of community which I think is vital for our generation. This is my family, it sounds a bit corny, but I still feel like that."

While Flashback's community are still on the dancefloor, Mo sees the challenges facing venues in the city, particularly when so much money is tied up in the real estate in its centre. She wants venues to exist, to offer spaces for the next generation to discover new sounds, ideas and experiences.

"I feel very passionately about celebrating small city venues," says Mo. "What are my kids going to do? I don't want them to only go to big corporate events, I want them to go to the grungy small spots that become an integral part of your life. The best bits of nightlife happen when you get together with your mates in these small spaces, this is where excitement bubbles and pops."

"I used to love the Custard Factory, the Medicine Bar that had a pool in the middle," Mo continues. "They'd sometimes drain it and that would be mad, you'd be raving in it and had to watch out to avoid getting green pond life all over you."

Located in Digbeth in the city centre, Birmingham's infamous Custard Factory was built by Alfie Bird to produce what would become Bird's Custard at the start of the 20th century. He was a chemist with a wife who was allergic to eggs and came up with the idea for his eggless powder so she could still eat desserts. It was through serving the food to other guests that he realised its commercial possibilities[151]. Little did Alfie know when he was tinkering with powders that his factory would have another life as a centre for Birmingham clubs during the nineties and 2000s. The Medicine Bar, with its notorious pool loved by Mo and so many other clubbers who visited, was an integral party space in the city. Adam Regan at the Hare & Hounds played an influential role in the Medicine's bar launch and subsequent establishment.

"Around 1994, my girlfriend's brother and his best mate opened the Medicine Bar in Islington in London," he says. "I was student poor so I'd get a bus with my records to the motorway outside Nottingham, then hitchhike my way there and DJ for the weekend. I'd stay above the bar and had some great times, DJing alongside people like Richard Fearless, Norman Cook, Jon Carter. I was going to move down, then they decided to open one in Birmingham in the Custard Factory."

Adam joined the new venue as assistant manager, then became manager and spent years booking DJs and artists including Nightmares on Wax, LTJ Bukem and Fabio during what he refers to as a "really eclectic era" for Birmingham's music.

"In Brum in the mid-nineties, there was Moneypenny's, Gatecrasher, this party called Wobble, so a lot of house nights," he says. "Everyone was dressing up and I kind of dabbled in that a little as I used to DJ for Moneypenny's and Chuff Chuff. But I preferred the more eclectic attitude of a night like the Electric Chair in Manchester and things in London like Gilles Peterson's nights - we were trying to do parties like that."

DJ, broadcaster and influencer Bobby Friction originally hails from London but has made his home in Birmingham thanks to the twists and turns his life and musical career have taken. He was a key figure in the Asian underground explosion of the nineties and 2000s and helped build the Asian Network in Birmingham alongside broadcasting with Nihal on Radio 1. In the club world, Bobby began DJing at the Blue Note in Hoxton Square during the nineties as the Asian Underground sound - a mix of traditional South Asian styles blended with Western music - exploded before heading to play at Shaanti in Birmingham. This club was hosted in a few small venues in the city before finding a more suitable home at the Medicine Bar.

"When Shaanti hit Brum, it was like a bomb going off as people had heard about the Asian Underground in London - but it hadn't moved outside yet," he says. "There were all these artistic people, those who are a bit different, South Asian goths, radicals and alternatives, all in Birmingham, all ready for a night like this, that's why it worked."

Bobby cut his DJing teeth in London's East End, initially becoming known as a regular party goer at the Blue Note before being asked to step behind the decks as a DJ. He sees cultural differences between Birmingham and elsewhere with the music he played in the Midlands touching a musical nerve that many other cities never found.

"Musically, things were different in Birmingham," says Bobby. "In London, you would never get Bhangra in the Asian Underground club nights. Bhangra was played with hip hop, it was a bit more working class for the second generation South Asian. In Brum, you could drop the Asian underground stuff and people would love it and see it as radical. If you dropped a Bhangra track, people would love that too and lose their shit - that's something that never happened in London."

The first Shaanti nights that took place were "kind of empty but full of joy" according to Bobby. But when he returned to the Custard Factory towards 2001 to play again, he found that the party had morphed into a warehouse rave.

"I clearly remember walking into the first room in the club and just going 'Fuck me, how has this grown into this?'," he says. "It never got to those levels in London, no matter how famous the DJs were. I could also tell that the class structure was much wider in Birmingham, my heart was beating faster, the adrenaline was high, Bhangra fans dancing to drum & bass, drum & bass heads dancing to Bhangra - that never happened in London, it took a few years in Brum and it was a joy to behold."

"What was amazing about Shaanti was how when you walked in, you'd get students, partying with local artists," he continues. "It was a very rare time when every tribe of South Asian kid under 30 would be raving together. It was the second summer of love for South Asians without any class differences."

In 2005 Bobby moved to Birmingham to host his show on the Asian Network where the station was based and has been involved in broadcasts ever since. Even though he has lived in Birmingham for over 15 years, he often gets asked about why he stayed in the city.

"Wherever I went, people would ask me why I would be stuck in Birmingham. But it's amazing, the people are amazing, I married a girl from West Brom, my kids have been brought up here," Bobby states. "I really love the city but feel like it has suffered from an insecurity about its identity especially in the mid-noughties."

He remembers the golden era of Shaanti at the Custard Factory fading during that period. Now the Asian music scene is still prominent in Birmingham but has entered different types of spaces within the city.

"After the Custard Factory finished, the Asian music scene is definitely still around but it's not underground, it's more housed in venues like the Arcadian," Bobby says. "Asian music has never stopped being played in Brum, it's just moved from creative spaces into more commercial spaces."

Alongside the Custard Factory, the Que Club is one of Birmingham's most striking and memorable club venues. Manchester may have had the Hacienda and Liverpool had Cream, but arguably the Que Club was just as iconic and far more beautiful to behold - if not quite as well known outside of Birmingham. The club could be found in the city centre on Corporation Street inside a striking red terracotta facade Grade II-listed Methodist Hall and featured multiple rooms pumping out lights, lasers, noise and mind-blowing music. While the venue was open between 1989 and 2017, a vast array of talents performed within the hallowed space, including Daft Punk who chose to release recordings from the club as their *'Alive 1997'* album[152]. The amphitheatre hosted an array of different parties - Bubble Club, Quest, Dance Trance, Amnesia, and Third Eye among them. One of the jewels in the crown of nights at the Que Club was Atomic Jam and Chris Finke was a resident DJ at the night. He was first booked to play the Atomic Jam party at the end of the year 2000 and vividly remembers the club's winding corridors and gothic architecture making it an astonishing space to be in.

"I was always surprised that there weren't more accidents - even when it's empty, it's hard to navigate the steps going up to the top," Chris says. "But you add in whatever people were on and it's a miracle no one was hurt. Behind the stage, there was this huge church organ. I used to wonder what it would have been like if someone had hooked it up for a live PA, it would have been incredible. The assembly hall would have the births, deaths and marriage certificates listed on the walls, they would still have the signs on them as it was such a historical building. If people were smashed, they'd come across these doors and just be really confused. "

There were plenty of incongruous elements that made the Que Club so special. From the building's grandiose architecture to the up for it crowd, the night had unique traits that DJs would struggle to find elsewhere.

"Anywhere north of Northampton, people would go far crazier than in the south at a party," says Chris. "Birmingham people at Atomic Jam were almost excessively aggressive, they'd be really going for it at 3am and still no one would fall down those stairs."

"At one of the last parties, Marcel Fengler from Berghain played and when he walked in, he was just like 'I can't believe this is in England, this is unreal'," he recalls. "It was so crazy that he couldn't understand how it existed here. I thought that was so cool, especially coming from someone who is a resident at the techno kingdom that is Berghain. Atomic Jam was the opposite of that, I used to call it the anti-Berghain."

The strain of dance music that filled the Que Club at Atomic Jam would usually be techno in the main room, a drum & bass room and third space where electro would be played, often by a DJ who would play a main room set too. There was a sense of freedom to the club experienced by DJs that Chris feels was unique.

"DJs used to love playing Atomic Jam as they knew they could get away with being more interesting than some other areas of the country and delve into different parts of their record box," Chris says. "Dave Clarke was kind of the unofficial resident who played all the time. DJ Rush, when he was a huge name, did a full live show with live vocals. People often say that was one of the most legendary shows we ever did."

In recent years, Birmingham's wheels of nightlife have been spinning in numerous directions. In 2023, XOYO opened up a "sister space" in Birmingham after lording it up in Old Street in Shoreditch for some years, taking over what was previously known as the Mill[153]. Food and events business BOXPARK announced they will open a huge new site in Birmingham in 2025 in Digbeth's Floodgate Street Arches space as part of a 15 year-lease[154]. The 17,000 square foot space will be transformed into a food hall and events destination which management say will allow "independent traders to thrive". The Rainbow, a pub, music venue and club with a long history re-opened in 2021 after a £750,000 makeover following its licence being revoked[155].

Ostensibly, these openings are in contrast to the NTIA figures showing that one-third of UK nightclubs closed by the end of 2022[156]. Yet, development work in the city's cultural hub of Digbeth has led to cultural spaces being edged further out of its centre into new territories. Producer and DJ Emily Jones, who records and plays out as Echo Juliet, initially came to Birmingham to study, then went on to work in the arts and release her own music. She currently lives in the city and is cautious about the future direction of nightlife in terms of location.

"Digbeth Dining Club have launched their own Hockley Social Club as there's more space there, some empty warehouses," she says. "It's more awkward to get to and begs the question of how far you can push people out. Birmingham certainly feels like a very young city in some ways - but also perhaps lacks those with the interest or disposable income to invest in this local creative economy."

According to the BMA's Jez Collins, Digbeth has long been a cultural epicentre of the city but the work around HS2 has had a significant impact. Advocates of the development have shouted about the economic benefits of the project, how it will offer more jobs, enhanced transport and "a £6.2 billion increase in economic output per year"[157]. At the same time, with greater investment comes higher property prices - a report from JLL predicts that average property prices are set to grow by 4.9% per year in the next five years - an increase of 27% by 2026 - and is a trend that could force club owners and cultural spaces to the fringes[158].

"There is a lot of investment and development currently happening in Digbeth, partly because of HS2 and the proximity to the city centre so Digbeth is changing," he says. "You speak to developers and they have bottom lines to stick to - it means you have to get creative in how you talk to them about culture. We try to explain how if you do this and put more money here, then you're able to maintain a community, people will be invested, will want to stay longer and it may make it more desirable to others - it creates longevity."

Emily is part of the Selextorhood Collective, a community group set up to champion underrepresented minorities in DJ line ups and electronic talent. Driven by an ethos that centres around anyone typically excluded from dance music production, Selextorhood is challenging music industry stereotypes and calling for more opportunities for women and gender minority DJs and producers.

"Selextorhood is an amazing group of people coming together and sharing opportunities," Emily says. "It's been really powerful in helping people develop things for themselves and see what's possible, and the way people have jumped on board and engaged has been brilliant too."

"When Selextorhood started, there was a real lack of representation in line-ups in Birmingham and that has improved massively. There are still some promoters that don't care - but generally that has become better and it's interesting to see what Selextorhood's mission is now that these changes have started to impact - so thinking about those who have been marginalised in other ways - non-binary, trans, there are a whole bunch of intersectional issues that we're looking at which has been great."

DJ and artist Lai Power is a fellow member of Selextorhood and chief architect behind the club night, Energy Flow, held at Artefact in Stirchley - another rapidly gentrifying neighbourhood. Their party has been called "the best night in Birmingham that doesn't have 'house' or 'god' in the name," by DJ Bus Replacement Service[159].

"Birmingham's sound is best expressed as a melting pot of its constituent cultures," Lai says. "Everything from reggae to UK garage to punk to Bollywood. We have an underrated musical history that still echoes through the present."

"We don't respect posturing or shallowness here. You'll get respect and admiration if you are true to yourself and serving the people rather than your own ego. There is an overriding open mindedness too. If you dropped a ska record in the middle of a techno set, everyone would still go nuts dancing."

Lai cites issues with Birmingham City Council as having put nightlife in a stranglehold that it is struggling to escape. An ongoing lack of support for arts and culture has starved the nocturnal landscape of the funding it needs to develop and grow while the arts and culture departments "are basically non-existent". The programming surrounding the Commonwealth Games in 2022 was a rare beacon of positivity and an example of how the local authority and cultural scenes can engage effectively with each other when required.

"It was programmed by a skilled team and there was no censorship that took place to my knowledge so arts practitioners were able to freely explore the topics of the games and the city and the UK more widely," Lai says. "Sadly, even this scarce celebration of our city left a sour taste when it emerged that Birmingham City Council was essentially bankrupt soon after the event."

Lai joined Selextorhood during the Covid-19 lockdowns when they decided that DJing was something they wanted to pursue. Prior to accessing the community, they struggled to find a sound for their electronic music productions but the group's support has been invaluable in helping shape their musical identity.

"There's a bunch of really talented women and trans/non-binary folks in the group that have so many skills that I don't have and are willing to teach and nurture talent in a super caring ecosystem," they say. "I've learned so much from them and have hopefully been able to help others with the things that I am good at. This reciprocal mutual aid is a really beautiful and powerful thing."

Inspired by their experiences in Selextorhood, Lai has now started their own Energy Flow collective featuring Dee`Cleo, DJ Forgets and Sexy Roy. Their cosmic dance parties take place in more underground spaces in Birmingham including Artefact and Pan-Pan.

"We're influenced by the legacy of parties such as David Mancuso's Loft, Nicky Siano's Gallery and the Paradise Garage which situated the dancefloor as a space of connection, liberation and counterculture," Lai explains. "We mostly book our friends who happen to be a lot of DJs from Selextorhood plus people we meet on our travels through the UK dance music underground."

DJ and producer Emily Jones may call Birmingham home but feels her style of dance music - influenced by classical and more obscure electronic textures - is out of time with what's currently rumbling in the city after dark.

"If you want to be a regular local DJ, it sometimes feels like you need to play bass music, house or disco," she says. "For me, I only really play at the Hare & Hounds or Cafe Artum. It feels like there is genuine diversity in the scene but no one sound or style approaching critical mass."

Still, Emily's DJing often takes her to play in other cities such as Bristol or Newcastle while her work with the Rhythm Section International collective means she's engaged with a vibrant musical community in south-east London. Clubs like Colour Factory and Peckham Audio alongside audiophile bars Moko and Jumbi have offered worthy homes for her own music and DJ sets.

"My music is electronic, influenced by garage, broken beats and deep house," she says. "There aren't too many spaces in Birmingham where I can play these kinds of sounds. In fact, a lot of what I'm doing is outside of Birmingham, so it really suits me that the city is where it is - it means I can get to everywhere from here."

Adam Regan at the Hare & Hounds in Kings Heath has been promoting his Leftfoot nights on and off for more than twenty years. Started with Richard Whittingham in January 2000, their first event was with the legendary Keb Darge before Moodyman, Mr Scruff and Gilles Peterson all followed in his footsteps.

"We got into this nice pattern of booking people we loved and they could just play what they wanted," Adam explains. "It was great and a vibrant period for Brum - there was a great hip hop night called Substance, Capsule started then, you had people like Procession doing drum & bass, Procreation doing deep house, everyone would go to each others' nights. It felt like an alternative to the mainstream club scene in Birmingham, it was much more than just one style of music."

In 2005, Adam was running the Different Drummer label with DJ Dick and put together a label compilation with Richard Dorfmeister who selected his favourite tunes for a mix. The release proved to be one of their most popular, shifting 25,000 copies. Sadly, with more releases ready to go to continue the momentum, disaster struck when their German distributor went AWOL.

"Eventually, we found out that they'd gone under like a lot of distributors did at the time but unfortunately owed us £150,000 or more," Adam says. "In 2006 this was a lot of money, it would have set us up for the next five years with the label. I'd just had my first daughter - and within 18 months we had three kids as we then had twins."

With activity beginning to slow down at the Medicine Bar, Adam ended up teaching for a couple of years to support his family. Struggling to find enjoyment in the classroom, he started looking for other opportunities, then learned that the lease at the Hare & Hounds in Kings Heath was coming up.

"It was a famous old pub, very much like a Wetherspoons back then, full of old fellas slowly drinking themselves to death amid a thick plume of smoke with fruit machines and racing on the TV all the time," he laughs. "It was a real mix of wrong 'uns, old men, and locals, an old school, traditional, and very rough pub. Kings Heath was different to how it is now too, it was a bit of a gamble but we put a business plan together."

Adam and his team managed to secure the boozer with bold ambitions to reimagine the space as a live venue and club. By 2009, they were well established with two rooms meaning they were able to host a variety of events, from Dave Clarke banging it out on a Friday to welcoming a jazz band to their stage the following evening.

"We now have a reputation for great production as we've always invested in sound and light, even though essentially these are two rooms above a Grade-II Victorian listed pub," says Adam. "At first it was a hard sell to agents as we're outside the city centre and it's a boozer but now we're known for production quality."

"We had Laurent Garnier here for the first time at the beginning of 2023, he loved it so much that he really wants to come back. It's great to get these DJs who often play to huge crowds wanting to do these intimate gigs."

Kings Heath is where the Hare & Hounds calls home and is located several miles south of Birmingham's centre. The area has significantly changed since Adam took on the pub and now calls a natural wine bar, pizza joint and several craft beer places its neighbours.

"It's like one of those areas in London, it will never fully gentrify," he says. "It has changed and the Hare has played a part in this. But the high street is still very mixed, full of charity shops and betting shops. There are some pockets that are more expensive but it's got a real vibe and can be pretty wild with some mad shit going on."

"We had a Pride event on York Road for 2000-3000 people on the street over the summer with Self Esteem performing. We've got great things going on, artisan markets, festivals, it's become a popular area because of the entertainment and hospitality and we're definitely part of that change."

Adam is optimistic for the future of the city's nightlife thanks to his own kids inheriting his passion for electronic music. His son and daughter both love house and disco and are part of a group exploring soulful sounds he can connect with.

"My son has DJed with me at the Queen's Heath Pride afterparty so I see this new generation coming through," he says. "Lab 11 tends to do tech-house and bass house and garage. The Mill, which has turned into XOYO, is programmed by Pete Jordan from Weird Science, Cafe Artum is part of the Hockley Social Space - they did a We Out Here launch with Wookie, Steve Cobby - there seem to be more of these little spots that are similar to us trying to do friendly party vibe with great sound."

James Stammer is one of the younger generation of promoters bringing musical energy and talent to the city. His Genesis Collective started during the Covid-19 lockdowns and have since welcomed DJs including Girls Don't Sync, Interplanetary Criminal and Skeptic for upfront nights of UK garage and bassline. Their venture has also taken them all over the city including spaces like the Hare & Hounds and XOYO.

"Birmingham does come under undue criticism," he says. "It's almost a bit of a meme with some other snobby people. But I think that's what makes what goes on inside the city more hardcore and the ravers and scene more community focussed and committed. When something catches on it becomes the fabric of the city, not just a sound or genre."

James' first parties were held in basements and kitchens in the city before migrating to the industrial space of the Tunnel Club. Having built a following during the pandemic, they hosted their first official party on the day that restrictions ended.

"The buzz from pulling off a rave of that scale and energy after 18 months of lockdown was something I'll never forget, nor replicate, and it felt like we had genuinely given people a night and space they would never forget," he says. "All of our early raves at Tunnel Club had a great vibe, the space is really underground and it did feel like another world," he continues. "The club goes back to the nineties, so I always felt like the energy from the decades of its existence was stored in the walls of that place."

The city's perspective of nightlife certainly seems to be changing. Despite the council's misfortunes, there are now three official nightlife champions working to support it. Lyle Bignon was appointed as Birmingham's Night Time Economy Ambassador and one of 30 across the UK in 2023[160]. The previous year Lawrence Barton, the Festival Director for Birmingham Pride, was named Birmingham's first Night-Time Economy Champion[161] while restaurateur Alex Claridge was given the role of Night-Time Economy Advisor in the same year[162]. The "huge gap in knowledge of the night-time economy", identified by the BMA's Jez Collins in a report in 2018 at least seems to have been acknowledged by the authorities and efforts are being made to close it with these appointments[163]. With 40% of Birmingham's population under 25 and supposedly the youngest major city in Europe, there are huge potential opportunities for change[164].

Jez envisions a different view of city living as generations shift and is optimistic that this will hopefully open up opportunities for nightlife to succeed rather than be chastised.

"If you go to Paris or Barcelona, you can leave your Airbnb and be in a bar or nightclub within seconds," he explains. "Historically the UK has been about moving people out of city centres - but because of the shortage of housing, and how this has led to depopulated city centres, we want people to move back in."

"The situation hasn't matured enough and over the next 10/15 years, we'll see less of these issues as it becomes the accepted norm that city centres are full of life and noise. Generations will tick over, younger people will become more accustomed to this."

Genesis Collective's James Stammer is looking forward to nightlife's future wherever that might be. As a relatively new promoter in Birmingham, he says it's hard to say nightlife as a concept is on its knees when a huge 15,000 capacity club like Drumsheds can open up in London. But a venue like Drumsheds and rave culture are both riding a volatile sea of changing tastes and trends today's tumultuous world provides.

"Raving, in my opinion, is a concept where like-minded people come together in a shared space to enjoy a shared passion for music, while also experiencing new music and ideas," he says. "This could be in a dingy club in Digbeth, a field in Wales or someone's kitchen with a portable speaker at 6am. Raving won't die, it will take different forms, as it always has done."

"The narrative spun by the media has always been anti-nightlife, from the newspapers claiming acid house raves were the crime centres of the world, to nowadays where a similar narrative is still spun by out of touch journalists. I think that's a good thing though, raving should feel anti-establishment, underground and naughty - the second it loses that feeling, it loses touch with its roots."

# CHAPTER 6

## CLOSE ENCOUNTERS OF THE REMOTE KIND: DANCING AT THE EDGE OF THE WORLD

*"People talk about Berlin as the home of techno but Morley had even better line-ups and DJs. All the provincial towns were like super feeders in getting the club scene going"*[165].

Mick Wilson

If you've heard of Todmorden, a small market town nestled somewhere in the rural crevices between Lancashire and Yorkshire, it might have more to do with its reputation for little green men and flying saucers than late night excursions into house music.

Since the eighties, UFO sightings have been the main reason behind Todmorden's notoriety. Newspaper reports from the time tell a seemingly tall tale of how local man Zigmund Adamski left home in June 1980 to visit the shops, only to be found dead five days later, his body lying prostrate atop a pile of coal[166]. No one could explain what happened to him. Then one of the policemen called to the scene also experienced his own out of this world experience less than five months later. Under hypnosis, one PC Alan Godfrey, told a story about being kept on board a UFO, then given a physical probe by two non-human beings[167]. Alongside these extraterrestrial goings-on, the towering Stoodley Pike Monument on the nearby Pennine Way, plus plenty of character-filled local boozers and eccentric shops selling curios, Todmorden is as much *'Twin Peaks'* as it is the BBC's

*'League of Gentlemen'*, some of which was fittingly filmed there.

On first appearance, the town seems pleasant and picturesque. Manchester is over 20 miles away; Rochdale, where I spent my teens, about ten. Back then, my folks would often drag my sister and me to Todmorden and its more bohemian cousin Hebden Bridge on a Sunday for a day of walks, secondhand book shops and sandwiches in the family car as the rain endlessly sloshed down, drenching everything around us. These days, Todmorden is billed as "an ideal base for walking, cycling, horse riding and bird-watching"[168]. But despite the genteel setting, back in the mid-nineties, there were rumblings of something going on after dark destined to attract a different type of tourist.

Out in the Sticks was a night held at Todmorden's Blue Note club and led by DJ, promoter and record shop owner Russell Malland. It earned no end of infamy, not only for being geographically remote but also by enticing some of dance music's top talent to dig out their A-Zs to track down the party.

"I originally knew Todmorden from passing through on car journeys when I was looking for a house in the late eighties," remembers Russell. "In the early nineties, I ended up living in Lees just outside Oldham but worked in Manchester. I had a record shop in the Corn Exchange called Manchester Underground a few doors down from the Konspiracy nightclub."

At the time, Russell was a DJ in Manchester at the Hacienda, warming up for Mike Pickering on Fridays, then at Oz in Blackpool on Saturdays and Shelley's in Stoke on Trent. Then in 1994, Russell departed the Hacienda due to the "uncontrollable rise" in gang activity. He was left looking for more DJing gigs, which unexpectedly came through some of the record diggers visiting his shop.

"I used to have a couple of old Northern Soul heads come in to buy soul and jazz," Russell explains. "One was a builder, the other an accountant. They had bought a three-storey building in Todmorden and put a club in the basement with two other floors as function rooms. They wanted a place where they could go out and listen to music they liked. It was originally a jazz club, hence being called the Blue Note."

Russell found they were looking for DJs for their Saturday nights and passed them a tape of his most recent house mix. The pair liked it and asked him to pay them a visit.

"I said I'd have a drive over to scope out the place. But three times I said I'd go and didn't," he says. "I finally did drive over from Oldham and went the long way round because I wasn't sure where it was. On the way up the road to Todmorden, which seemed to have taken ages, I thought to myself: 'this place is out in the sticks'. I had a lightbulb moment and the name of the night before I'd even seen the club."

Out In The Sticks started in 1994 with Russell and fellow resident Craig Edwards working hard to try and attract a crowd "back when super clubs ruled and trance was king". Although it took some months to get things off the ground, once they had secured an audience of loyal punters willing to make the journey, they worked on growing their crowd by booking a who's who of house music greats. Joey Negro, CJ Mackintosh, Full Intention, Jazz-N-Groove, Deep Swing, Graeme Park and Knee Deep all played in Todmorden as a result. It was thanks to Russell's shop and reputation he'd built via DJing at the Hacienda that compelled them to make the journey and risk getting lost on the AO633.

"We initially attracted a crowd through flyering all the shops we could in Manchester and Leeds," he says. "Myself and Craig would do this every month, offering guest lists to any staff in the shops who would take the fliers. We'd hand them cassettes with the previous week's recordings too and make tapes for the punters as they came into the club."

"Before Out In The Sticks, Todmorden was a sleepy backwater town in the hills," continues Russell. "But the night attracted clubbers from all over the country with people travelling up from Brighton and down from Carlisle on a regular basis. It mostly brought in people from the satellite towns around West Yorkshire and Lancashire as well as Manchester and Leeds."

While the crowd was initially made up of outsiders willing to make a pilgrimage, slowly but surely, Todmorden's residents began to dip their toes into its mix of US vocal house and garage, a combination rarely heard anywhere else at the time. Russell's job at the record shop meant he had access to some of the freshest imports and promos, fueling what he reckons to be more than 450 nights over nine years.

"The club had a massive influence on the younger locals," he says. "This was their first clubbing experience and Out In The Sticks was one of the most upfront house music clubs in the country through the late nineties and early noughties. These kids were spoiled and a few went on to become successful DJs and producers in their own right. So, I guess it did have a positive effect on the community."

Graeme Park's name has long been associated with the Hacienda but it was in Nottingham where he enjoyed formative years as a DJ and music fan. Having been brought up in Scotland, he played in several bands during the post-punk era before heading to the city during the early eighties. Here, he ended up working in local shop Selectadisc Records and was put in charge of the second hand and singles department, which was on the same floor as the owner's office.

"Brian Selby was the owner of Selectadisc. He bought the Adlib Club in Nottingham, decided to rename it the Garage and told me I was going to be DJing," laughs Graeme. "He didn't ask me - he just told me as he liked what I used to play in the shop."

Initially, when Graeme started out behind the decks in 1984, he was playing a mix of indie, new wave, electronic music alongside disco, funk and soul picked up from his day job. Throw in the likes of the Human League, New Order and 12-inch mixes of ABC and Orange Juice and his bag was broad enough to impress many other switched on music lovers alongside the Selectadisc manager.

"My sets were directly informed by working in the shop," he explains. "Plus, my tastes were very eclectic, which is why I took to DJing so much. As a teenager in those days, you were very tribal but I was across everything. I loved *'I Feel Love'* by Donna Summer but all my punk friends couldn't understand it."

Graeme's early DJing days involved "playing anything and everything, then mixing it all up" but were increasingly influenced by the music arriving at Selectadisc. From the classic hip hop of Big Daddy Kane to the up-front electro of Arthur Baker and Afrika Bambaataa, he soaked up every sound that came his way, including some of the earliest house music records to reach UK shores.

"Through the record shop, I got my hands on very early 12 inches from Chicago, and techno from Detroit," Graeme remembers. "It was the most amazing thing I'd heard since punk rock and by '86, then '87, it was really beginning to take over."

Graeme remembers his move towards more electronic beats as a DJ alienated some of his regular crowd at the Garage. Still, the floodgates of acid house had been opened and were impossible to stop.

"Some people would get really annoyed and ask why I wasn't playing Talking Heads," he says. "But there was no time as there were all these other amazing sounds. For everyone who complained, there were more people coming to the night and it suddenly went crazy towards the latter end of the eighties. I started DJing all over Leicester, Sheffield, Birmingham, Coventry and Derby."

Graeme believes it was very much down to the network of record shops that lit the touchpaper and set ablaze a dance music inferno across the Midlands and northern towns.

"Back then, every city had several different shops," he remembers. "In Nottingham, there were three Selectadiscs. If I was travelling somewhere to DJ, then I'd always make sure I arrived early so I could hit up the local record shop. They might have something I'd never heard before."

In the early eighties, the British government's austerity measures and the associated high unemployment (where the numbers signing on topped two million in 1981[169]) meant that the UK faced a challenging period. Overall government expenditure as a percentage of GDP fell from 49.7% in 1975-6 to 38.9% in 1988-9 as the country, led by Margaret Thatcher, cut state spending[170]. Graeme feels this backdrop of an economy locked in a downward spiral led to the increased popularity of club music, especially in those towns and cities struggling to find their feet amid all the decline.

"In the mid to late eighties, many of these places were pretty grim," Graeme says. "If you look at somewhere like Liverpool now, it's a modern, well-designed city but it used to be that you'd always feel on edge walking around its centre. The combination of a Thatcher government, poverty and ecstasy meant that the north and the Midlands totally embraced house music."

Harry Harrison and his DiY Collective were born out of Nottingham but all their core members were originally from outside the city. Harry and Pete Birch (DJ Woosh) had been regulars at the Hacienda in the early days of acid house and at the Garage/Kool Kat to hear Graeme Park DJ.

"From 1988 onwards, we'd travel across the UK to hear DJs like Andy Weatherall and Sasha," Harry says. "We went to some of the late Orbital raves in '89 but having paid silly money to get stuck on a motorway for five hours, we just decided to do it ourselves."

Back at the end of the eighties, Harry remembers the clubbing scene as "very cliquey and fashion-orientated". The DiY ethos was to go beyond these different tribes and bring everyone together around house music. The collective took their musical props from their experiences at free parties alongside what they'd heard in legal clubs.

"As DiY, we managed to unite the different clans," he says. "By around 1992-1993 we had crusties, students, fashionistas, football lads and punks all coming to our events and dancing together. Whether it was clubs, raves at the Marcus Garvey centre or free parties, I think our lasting legacy was to dissolve the boundaries between these different factions. We also brought the energy of free parties and festivals into clubs and all-nighters and tried to recreate that mind-blowing synergy by utilising much bigger sound systems, crazy lighting and wild décor."

DiY's influence indirectly shaped the early musical world of Nottingham born and bred DJ and promoter Luka Wigflex. His older sister used to go out on a Friday and not return until Sunday evening, spending the weekend raving at events including DiY's infamous parties. His own clubbing experiences first came some years later at Nottingham club, the Bomb.

"When I first started going out, we used to go to these pound a pint type clubs," says Lukas. "One weekend we couldn't get in so we were walking around town and I saw my brother's mate working on the door at the Bomb. We asked him to let us in - he did, it was a drum & bass night and I caught the bug."

He continues: "The Bomb was a fucking insane little club and set the template for what I look for in a clubbing experience now. Intimate, great sound, minimal, stripped-back lighting and a low ceiling. It was a right little sweatbox."

Lukas' adventures in promoting his own parties began in 2006 when he found Nottingham's nightlife to be lacking in musical vibe and excitement. He made his *'Wigflex 2000'* mixtape, then landed a weekly residency at a bar in the city centre where they'd serve punters 2-4-1 pizzas and have Super Mario Kart playing on a big screen.

"The crowd was just mates who would hang out together all the time," Lukas says. "This was when I was a hip hop style DJ who also played breaks and tech house. We started putting on parties after that, just with residents and charging people 99p to get in."

Without the stress of having headline DJs or needing to liaise with agents over booking fees, Lukas remembers these nights as some "of the most fun, best times ever". Although Wigflex has expanded over the years to include festivals, all-nighters and host events around the UK, the emphasis on the vibe and the party remains the same.

"There's never been any kind of strategy or plan behind Wigflex," he says. "It's always been about having fun, a good bag of records and letting it do its thing. We've been lucky to go on for this long - and maybe that's why we're still doing it."

As the party has grown, the sound of Wigflex has also expanded into something they've dubbed as "rude boy techno". With the city's central geographical location, Lukas has been able to absorb influence from all around.

"My sound has probably changed as I've gotten older," he says. "But it's still got to be a bit fucked up, psychedelic, a bit proggy like James Holden. Growing up in Notts meant I was influenced by the ruder, shuffly stuff coming from London as well as the bleeps from Sheffield. Living in the centre of the country exposes you to a total melting pot of ideas and styles."

Lukas has seen clubbing behaviours significantly change over the lifetime of his party. Rather than using the dancefloor as somewhere to escape the pressures of the working week, it's currently a challenge for punters to earn enough for them to be able to go out.

"The cost of living crisis has really hit people hard," he says. "It's difficult, if you do parties everything is costing you so much due to fees around artists and venues. It's challenging to put anything of merit on that people want to come to and not charge 10/15 quid a ticket - the numbers just don't add up."

Over its lifetime, Wigflex has never had a regular home in Nottingham. Instead its nomadic nature has led it to warehouses, kebab shops, basements and more, moving into spaces to party whenever they can.

"The shared ethos among promoters is very DiY," says Lukas. "We're always on the lookout for new spaces and like to make nights happen, and do it whether we get the recognition or not."

"One of my favourite recent parties was at an art gallery with Jorg Kuning playing. Honestly, it was the best atmosphere we'd had in fucking years. I think these events have to happen outside of the major cities as there's just not lots going on in regional places. This party has made me realise how important it is to do it and we're gonna keep pushing."

As a city known as the home of the British automobile industry, Coventry played an unlikely but important role in the spread of acid house in the UK[171]. In 2021, the city was European Capital of Culture, a title at odds with its reputation of "grimy decline" earned during the mid-eighties[172]. Coventry's most famous musical sons, The Specials, captured the economic doom permeating the country in their landmark chart-topper, *'Ghost Town'*, a song which could have been about any number of recession-blighted places of the time. Mick Wilson, a music-lover, journalist, and now editor at DJ Magazine, was a resident DJ at the Eclipse, a venue that opened in 1990 and acted as a driving force in turning locals onto euphoric beats. As a Coventry kid, his early clubbing experiences were spent in regional towns and cities where he strove to find something more musically stimulating than the prevalence of the "Ritzy kinds of clubs".

"We used to go to clubs like the Black Orchid in Nottingham," he says. "The places we went to would have soul and funk nights, and we'd get coaches from Coventry all over the Midlands to go out. So to towns and cities like Leicester, Birmingham, and Derby too."

"More mainstream clubs would be open every night of the week, then, when they got to Wednesday or Thursday, they would experiment with a dance night. The rest of the weekend would be more cheesy, offering free entry to girls or free bottles of sparkling wine to entice people in."

Alongside these nights, entertainment in the form of roller discos played an important part in furthering Mick's musical education, even offering him opportunities to enjoy initial forays into playing records in front of people.

"These events were like the precursors to raves and you'd hear remixes, imports, acid house and dance music," he says. "I started when I was 14, making tapes, then I began playing at roller discos which is where all the kids went on Fridays and Saturdays. Because I had a certain collection of records, I'd play a half-hour of dance music, then I got asked to start doing my own night."

Echoing Graeme Park's take on Nottingham, Mick emphasises how record shops underpinned Coventry's local scene. From indie retailers to chains such as HMV and Virgin, the import section proved to be a goldmine for discovering new music and shaping his sound as a fledgling DJ.

"Musically, they had literally everything and anything. But there were important shops in Birmingham and Leamington," he states. "You'd be following the white label man between these places. You'd know the day he'd arrive, so you'd make sure you were there soon after to get hold of whatever he'd sold."

"Back then, you'd become known as the person from that city with a certain sound, or you'd be known for having particular records," Mick continues. "In those days, there would only be three DJs in the city. You'd be a rare breed, whereas now there are probably ten DJs just living on your street."

From collecting and playing records, Mick's profile in Coventry steadily increased and he began to get asked to play at different illegal parties and on pirate radio. While he cut his teeth on these adventures, it was at the Eclipse, a club located on Lower Food Street in what was formerly a bingo hall, where he really made his name. The multi-floor venue was opened by entrepreneurs Stuart Reid and Barry Edwards in 1990 and was transformed into a mecca of acid house, spilling over with air horns, poppers and the smell of Vicks. Mick was involved with the club from the very beginning as one of the few local DJs with any technical knowledge and the appropriate gear to tackle a club setting.

"No one knew much about equipment or sound systems when they were opening up," he recalls. "I had Technics decks and was asked to bring them as they only had these crap decks on the first night. I brought my equipment, my records and started playing. From then on, we were slotted in to do these parties."

From its early days, the venue's popularity blew up. Clubbers descended on the town to party and established Coventry "at the epicentre of electronic dance music and rave culture", as Chenine Bhathena, creative director of Coventry City of Culture, has said[173].

"People would really follow the scene once it took off," says Mick. "We'd have people coming from as far afield as Europe to the Eclipse."

While the club was a hit with ravers on the dancefloor, it also managed to lure some of the biggest names in dance music to Coventry to play sets alongside Mick and his DJ partner Mick Parks who

DJed together as Parks and Wilson. Part of the Eclipse's appeal was the late licence which dramatically changed how people would treat their nights out.

"The owners managed to get this 24-hour licence as the authorities and the police didn't really understand what was going on, especially as there wasn't any alcohol involved," says Mick.

"We had Moby, the Prodigy, DJs like Kevin Saunderson and Laurent Garnier, all these legendary names coming to Coventry," he continues. "At the same time, it started impacting people's behaviour. Suddenly we were dancing all night and the club scene was never the same again. All the provincial towns had clubs like ours and were super-feeders in getting the fledgling dance scene going."

As the name suggests, Coalville is a former industrial mining town located in Leicestershire just off the M1 motorway. Of all the hotbeds of electronic music and club culture, this is one of the most unexpected, although it took off in the mid-nineties after acid house peaked in other parts of the country. It's known for many things but not necessarily dance music. At the town's Palitoy factory, Action Man, Star Wars and Care Bears figures were first manufactured. Before dance music arrived, Coalville's nightlife was more associated with a bingo hall, a working mens' club, some old pubs and a chip shop rather than "a succession of repetitive beats"[174].

Passion, a club night established in the town, continues to make people dance, even after more than 25 years of parties. Hosted at Coalville club the Emporium, the night began in 1995 and, according to resident Jason Kinch (aka JFK), was a slow-burning success. The venue has a long entertainment history, having hosted music events since the turn of the century. During the Second World War, it took on a different guise, with its basement transformed into a temporary morgue due to its low temperature, perfect for preserving human bodies. Before DJing, Jason was a clubber and spent nights partying at Venus in Nottingham, Progress in Derby and Moneypenny's in Birmingham.

"Passion became a success by accident, really," he remembers. "Back then, the club was called Crystals and I was asked to be the dance music specialist on their commercial night. We did Passion as a one-off event to test the water with a whole night of dance music with the legendary DJ Todd Terry. It was a huge success and we then moved on to book DJs like Alex P, Brandon Block, Jeremy Healy and Judge Jules."

Coalville's location, some two hours drive from London, meant Passion used "the middle of nowhere, the centre of everywhere" as a tagline. Its proximity to the motorway made it part of the so-called 'Golden Triangle' for canny DJs looking to maximise profitability from a night of playing.

"Judge Jules quickly cottoned onto the fact that because our licence was 9 while 2, everyone would come to the club early," Jason says. "We'd regularly have a queue around the block of thousands of people waiting to get in from the very start."

"It meant a DJ like Jules could drive up the M1 from London and be playing by 10.30pm. He'd do an early set with us, then get to Progress in Derby within 30/40 minutes, do a set there, then onto Sheffield to play another set there. Our location played a real part in attracting great talent to play."

Coalville's geography also fed into the crowds Passion lured with clubbers from towns like Northampton, Peterborough, Rugby and Lincoln all making the journey to its dancefloor.

"Places like Birmingham and Coventry had their own scenes going on and we knew we couldn't compete with them," says Jason.

"In the mid-nineties, people would travel; they would jump in the car and drive from party to party. But when DJs did arrive, they would often be shocked by Coalville itself. It doesn't have the look or feel of a major city centre."

Alex P and Brandon Block were among the first big names to venture to Passion to play. Apparently, they very nearly turned around and left when they first arrived.

"When you drive in, you might think: 'Crikey, is this where the party is?'" laughs Jason. "Alex and Brandon were about to leave but then they saw the venue and this huge queue of people dressed in day-glow gear. When you walk in, the club itself is like a Tardis and just expands into this energised rave cave."

"A lot of DJs tell a similar story," he continues. "When it became more trance-led, we'd have DJs like Paul Van Dyke who would say: 'You've booked me to play a club next door to a chicken shop?' But this is what makes the history of the place so fun."

The club has experienced some serious exposure from the dance music media, stories that have all fed into its mythology. Big-name DJs Seb Fontaine and Steve Lawler both played live Essential Mixes on Radio 1 from inside the club around 2000 and 2001, something that may have been commonplace for an established club like Cream but was mind-blowing for the Emporium. Passion and the club it called home not only had a positive effect on the dance music community but did much to transform perceptions of Coalville itself. The local economy was a direct beneficiary, with other bars springing up to cater for the hoards of people visiting every Friday and Saturday night.

"One headline in the local newspaper referred to it as 'Coolville' which was a revelation," Jason explains. "As a former mining town, it was somewhere you would have probably avoided on a night out for fear of getting in a fight. But its popularity endured and even when the recession hit during the mid-noughties, we still had people coming to dance."

"Now we're almost 30 years on, we're still a legendary spot. I always said we were like Wimbledon in the Premier League, in the middle of nowhere competing with the likes of Gatecrasher, Slinky and Cream."

The club night and its audience may have aged, but Passion continues to run, throwing a handful of events each year to its enduringly loyal crowd. Jason believes part of its long-term success lies in how it provides a welcoming, safe space for ravers of all generations. They're invited to leave any problems at the door and shake off the working week on the dancefloor.

"It's a very working-class area, people graft for their money, then as soon as Saturday comes, they want that release," he states. "It means the atmosphere is just unreal. You come in from the main entrance and you can feel the energy as you walk in. It opens up into this big auditorium; everyone comes running in and goes berserk."

The sense of community around Passion now unites different age groups with parents wanting to introduce their kids to the magic of the Emporium. The number of parties has streamlined to reflect the lifestyle changes in the demographic of attendees.

"We always do the first Saturday in January as it's usually the last weekend before people go back to work," Jason says. "Most of our crowd don't do NYE as they can't get babysitters, so we do a cheap party on this weekend instead and it always sells out."

"We don't host as many parties as we used to but then those who have been with us since the start don't go out as often. Some might be in their later years but once a clubber, you're always a clubber - it's a way of life now."

While Coalville had Passion and Coventry had the Eclipse, there were other important club nights and venues across the Midlands, including Progress at Derby and Renaissance, which started in Mansfield before becoming a huge global brand. Not to be outdone, new-town Milton Keynes also had its own share of killer clubs and spaces. Built during the sixties to alleviate housing shortages in the capital with an Act of Parliament in 1967[175], it may initially seem lacking in cultural capital but, thanks in part to local DJ and producer 'Evil' Eddie Richards, it has an influential role in UK dance music history. In July 1989, i-D Magazine ran a feature on *'The House Sound of Milton Keynes'*, underlining how the scene had grown to equal that of any London suburb.

"Three years ago, the house sound of Chicago blasted out of the Windy City for the first time. One year ago, the Summer of Love nurtured the house sound of London. Now acid house has gone suburban and Milton Keynes is preparing for its first major warehouse party…"[176] Eddie's Sunday party, the Outer Limits, was active for a year between 1989 and 1990 and an important night for the town. Hosted at Rayzels in Bletchley just south of the town centre, Eddie's guests included DJs like Todd Terry and Jeff Mills, who he convinced to play sets at the club. Before the Outer Limits, Eddie was a resident at the Camden Palace, but his most influential early musical years were spent in Milton Keynes. He initially started a mobile disco that he'd take to youth clubs, then began running a night at a bikers' pub called the Starting Gate around 1981 using the same set-up.

"It was a real mix of people who were thrown together in Milton Keynes," Eddie remembers. "My night seemed to unite all these misfits. I was playing music like post-punk bands, Killing Joke, the B52s and it became really popular."

The various waifs and strays who had moved to the new-town used Eddie's club as a place to gather and forge new friendships. They attended alongside the bikers who traditionally drank there, meaning he benefited from two very different crowds.

"The bikers would be at one end of the pub and everyone who had just moved would be at the other," remembers Eddie. "But this latter group really influenced me, encouraging me to go and dig for more post-punk tunes I otherwise wouldn't have heard of."

From these beginnings, Eddie was turned onto an array of new tunes and artists and told to go and check out the London club Heaven for its brilliant music policy. He duly visited and was blown away by the soundtrack, particularly impressed by resident Ian Levine who was skilled enough to mix records together.

"I had no idea that this scene existed but I got talking to one of the DJs who turned out to be Colin Faver," says Eddie. "I invited him to come up to Milton Keynes to play at the Starting Gate; he agreed and played a very similar set to the kind of music I was playing back then."

It meant when Camden Palace opened in London in the early eighties with Rusty Egan and Steve Strange acting as hosts, Eddie had done enough to impress Colin and was asked to join the club as a DJ.

"All of a sudden, I went from being a nothing in Milton Keynes to playing records in this really popular London party frequented by stars like Madonna and Grace Jones," he laughs.

Eddie never looked back, honing his mixing skills, DJing and running parties between the capital and his hometown. As he played, his musical style expanded to take in more exuberant Hi-NRG alongside early electro and indie post-punk. It was at the latter end of the eighties that Eddie called time on his gigs at the Camden Palace before he once again found himself in the right place at the right time as London's warehouse party scene took off.

"I started doing this party called RIP at Clink Street with Kid Fashion and Mr C, then bookings for bigger parties started landing," says Eddie. "I was asked to play at Sunrise, which was one of the biggest raves of its day, by [organiser] Tony Colston-Hayter, who lived in Milton Keynes too."

"I was doing the same Camden Palace kind of indie and Hi-NRG set in this club in the town. Tony came in and told me he had this idea where we wouldn't have to worry about commercial clubs or wearing a suit jacket to get in or getting any hassle from the bouncers. He put this proposal together for what would be the massive Sunrise raves with my name on it as the music coordinator. So I had to pick DJs like Carl Cox and I was the main DJ. When that kicked off, the clubs were suddenly empty and the fields were full."

As Eddie's DJing stepped up, he inadvertently found himself in the charts with his reworking of 'Acid Man' by Jack Frost and the Circle Jerks almost landing on Top of the Pops (TOTP). The track was one of the first acid tracks to appear in the UK and stemmed from an off-the-cuff conversation with Colin Faver about extending the original[177].

"I was complaining that the song was too short and Colin said I should do something about it," says Eddie. "So I went home, added some samples with my tape machine and reel to reel and it ended up in the charts. But then the BBC banned the word 'acid' so I never made it onto TOTP. Still, it was a crazy time where everything I did just seemed to fall into place."

As acid house's clamour became unavoidable, Eddie enjoyed success outside of Milton Keynes but still wanted to contribute to his local scene. This is where the idea for his Outer Limits party started life and he opened its doors in 1989.

"The night was deliberately small but by then I could attract people from all over to attend," he explains. "It was packed and I booked all the DJs myself. I had just started this agency called Dynamics and was representing everyone from Richie Hawtin to Louie Vega."

When the big UK raves began happening, many US DJs found out and wanted to get booked to play at them. As there wasn't already an existing agency, Eddie seized the opportunity and started bringing them over, helping to fill his parties with stellar international talent.

"I'd be getting calls from Jeff Mills saying: 'Hi, I'm Jeff Mills from Underground Resistance - can you get us bookings?' I ended up repping all these megastars, brought them over and a lot would play at this little club in Milton Keynes."

"Looking back, it's all a bit mad but I've always come back here," Eddie continues. "This is where I live and it has shaped me but it was a key place for dance music. If something was going on, then you'd have loads of people from Milton Keynes attending as they would be so clued up. People in London would laugh about it. It's that weird place with the concrete cows and loads of roundabouts but actually, it was on a level with Manchester, Leeds and Liverpool in terms of knowledgeable kids."

Mick Wilson agrees that the UK's clubbing clout came from many of the smaller, more random places that contributed to the country's reputation as one of the biggest exponents of dance music.

"It all started in these smaller cities and towns," he laughs. "The Orbit was one of the world's leading techno clubs but you'd find it in Morley, this little village outside of Leeds."

"People would talk about Berlin as the home of techno but the Orbit had even better line-ups and DJs. Who would have thought that a place like Coalville would have an amazing club? Or somewhere like Stoke-on-Trent would have a brilliant venue like Shelley's?"

Stoke has long been a weekend destination for dancers and one of the original homes of Northern Soul during the early seventies at The Torch[178]. But during the eighties and nineties, it would be Shelley's and Golden at the Void that sent clubbers flocking to the town. Local masked rave crew Altern-8 filmed the video for their track *'Activ-8 (Come With Me)'* in the car park of Shelley's in September 1991 after the venue had shut. DJ Justin Robertson remembers his diary was full of bookings taking him to play in many clubs found in smaller, more offbeat locations.

"Some of the best nights would definitely be in places like Blackpool, even Shrewsbury and little scenes would develop around them," he explains.

Justin was brought up in the small town of Chalfont St Peter in Buckinghamshire outside London. When acid house broke, he received a call from a close friend who talked him through some unexpected Christmas plans.

"When I first left, there was this quaint pub with Tudor beams in the centre of the village," he remembers. "My mate rang and said: 'We'll meet at this pub, you can get e's in there, then we'll go up to this farm to see Weatherall'. I couldn't believe it. Before, this was a spot for ploughmans' lunches where one of the blokes who starred in *'The Professionals'* used to drink. But when acid house landed, almost everywhere became a club and centre of experimentation."

While towns dotted across the waistband of the UK fostered the acid house scene in the eighties and nineties, present-day club culture has sought out new spaces to grow into. One of them is the town of Margate, located almost 80 miles from London on the Kent coast and often held up as the epitome of the great British seaside. From kiss me quick hats to sticks of dentist-scaring rock, optimistic sun-seekers have been descending on this part of Thanet to soak up thrills and spills since the 18th century.

The first town to offer visitors "fully developed bathing machines with modesty hoods"[179] and one of the world's first sea-bathing hospitals, Margate is credited as kick-starting this British love affair with the coast, a romance that endures to this day. Cheap rail fares and proximity to the capital made sure the town became a beloved seaside destination for those looking for respite from more densely populated parts of the UK. But its reputation as a domestic tourist hub was decimated with the arrival of cheap foreign holidays towards the end of the 20th century. Despite much of the town reportedly becoming a dumping ground for the rehousing of London's poor and vulnerable during this period[180], its decline has since been stalled and put in reverse with regeneration spearheaded by the opening of the Turner Contemporary Gallery in 2011. The glittering retro pastiche of amusement park Dreamland reopened in 2015 alongside a heap of independent bars and restaurants. A flood of creatives has swiftly followed, drawn to the fresh air and access to cheaper property. Combine this with ongoing investment through the Live Margate Housing Scheme[181] and 2021's Town Investment Plan, a revival appears to be on track. DJ, record label manager and now pub-owner Matt Walsh has lived much of his life between the coast and the city. Originally hailing from Clacton-on-Sea on the Essex peninsula, he now calls Margate home, running various music ventures and co-owning the Tap Room pub in Cliftonville. Matt is one of many creatives to have left a life in London behind to take inspiration from the sea and artistic community the town now fosters. Before moving to the capital, much of his formative clubbing experiences were initially in his hometown.

"Clacton-on-Sea was a big rave town when I was growing up; there was this place on the pier called Oscars which was a bit scary for a kid like me when I first started going out," he says. "It was all jungle and drum & bass and attracted lots of Londoners for nights out."

After a stint spent studying in Nottingham, Matt started to get the bug for electronic music with his university mates and began travelling around the UK to rave at big festival events, including Homelands, Sundissential and Gatecrasher. His tastes took him to dance to sets from more leftfield DJs playing in the smaller tents rather than the bigger headline acts.

"At Homelands, I'd always piss off and go and watch Ivan Smagghe or Craig Richards play," he says. "There was an amazing club in Nottingham called The Bomb, which was the first proper small club I'd been to. Craig and Lee Burridge used to do their Tyrant night there and I loved it: deep, melodic house, lots of acid."

Despite these influential experiences, it wasn't until after university that he discovered the sounds and DJs who would blend his twin loves for beats and guitars. At a chance night out at Fabric in London, he witnessed the genre-splicing magic of DJ Erol Alkan and found the seam of dance music he was longing for.

"I just caught him by accident and was blown away," remembers Matt. "He played Beyonce, then Oasis' *'Live Forever'*, and this was in a club which was supposedly all about house and techno." Matt ended up moving to London in 2003, then started hanging out at Erol's influential night Trash at The End, immersing himself in the scene and becoming friends with many of the associated bands and DJs.

"I was just this kid putting my face about," he says. "Erol was young and cool. He would stand on the decks wearing a Batman t-shirt when he played. These were the things I liked about my rock stars but I'd never seen DJs play like this."

Drawing inspiration from these late-night experiences, Matt gradually started his own musical ventures in both Colchester and London. He began to run nights at T Bar in Shoreditch, landing an important support slot with Montreal's electronic sensation Tiga for Bugged Out! on a Monday night. At the gig, many of the dancers Matt impressed consisted of influential industry movers and shakers all enjoying a night out after their weekends of work.

"I became that guy who played before Tiga, which led to Bugged Out! asking me to be their resident when they were running parties at The End in central London," he remembers. "I was the last DJ to play a record [the Kerrier District remix of Black Devil Disco Club's *'Timing, Forget the Timing'*] at the club before it was shut down."

The decision to leave this all behind and move to Margate came at a point when Matt felt like parts of the capital's creative soul and nightlife excitement were draining away alongside skyrocketing property prices. Since 2010, they have risen by three-quarters over the decade, an average increase of £204,400 per home, though the majority of the growth came before 2016[182].

"We ended up here by accident really," he says of the decision to head to the seaside. "We'd done the classic thing of spending a huge amount of money on a small flat in Hackney. We just wanted to live in a cool place and spent five years there."

"But everything was changing a lot, I was having to travel further to see mates, the community in east London was different, places were closing, [influential gay pub] the George and Dragon was shutting, a lot of gay clubs closed. It all seemed expensive, stale and uninteresting."

A failed holiday to Ibiza led to Matt and his girlfriend, now wife, returning to the UK earlier than planned. Fed up with how they'd not managed to escape on their trip, they saw a friend was offering up a place in Margate and went to stay. When they arrived, they found that many of their friends were DJing and partying at an event at the Dreamland amusement park.

"Before we went, I thought it might end up being like Clacton," says Matt. "But we really loved it; it had the same feel as east London did when I first moved there. All of these people in a small area, who were either into art or music and creating this community. That's how Shoreditch felt, then Dalston did some years after. People we knew like producers and DJs Hannah Holland and Ghost Culture were coming as they could afford a house with a garden or rent a studio for next to nothing compared with London."

Like Matt, fellow DJ and producer Hannah Holland made a name for herself in east London but has since found a home by the sea in Margate too. She says: "A dedication to DIY, alternative culture, community and creativity is what binds the town's shared ethos together." Both Hannah and Matt agree on the importance of the Margate Arts Club in giving the creative scene a focal point and clubbing venue.

Artist Luke Vandenberg is founder of the venue alongside his wife Amy Redmond. Amy co-created the infamous queer collective Sink the Pink, the "genderfucking" melting pot of creatives, drag artists and dancers who have gone from house parties to performing at festivals across the world. According to Luke, the Margate Arts Club was set up in 2013 as a reaction to the lack of safe, nightlife spaces in the town.

"Everyone I knew had had some sort of incident when going into a local bar, pub or nightclub," he says. "From builders working on the club to young artists, they would tell me stories about how they got into some unrequested conflict and I got into some myself. I thought it was essential to set up a venue that my friends, creative community, local music scene, LGBTQIA+ community could access, have a night out, listen to a great sound system and dance without any fear of violence, misogyny, homophobia or racism."

Initially, the club only opened for their immediate circle of friends but has organically grown, more "out of necessity for the community than as a business".

"We started by having pot-luck dinners, playing records on a vintage JBL cinema sound system and having a dance in a disused shop and our living room," says Luke when talking of the venture's early days. "But as time went on, more and more people from the local scene heard about our gatherings; they would come, knock on our door and ask if they could join us. It grew from there."

"One of the weirdest moments was when someone turned up in the middle of the night and said: 'Hi, I've come all the way from Paris to see what you do'. It was quite amazing to know word of the club had reached Europe."

The emphasis on facilitating a sense of community around the space is at the heart of how the Margate Arts Centre operates. Located on the high street of Northdown Road, the centre doesn't advertise a programme and only runs a handful of events each month. Anyone wanting to enter needs to ring the doorbell to be let in, meaning you could walk past and be totally oblivious to what was going on inside.

"Most of the nights are put on by people living in the town," Luke says. "We predominantly work with local artists, creatives and DJs, some who are born in the area. Others have travelled from outside of London, Europe or the world to make Margate their home."

"We try to champion our community and because of that, we've cultivated a real grassroots scene. Instead of travelling or moving up to London, they have been able to stay in their hometown and grow."

As part of the venue's ethos, it has a zero-tolerance policy to misogyny, homophobia and racism, a golden rule etched into its code of conduct to ensure the space is as safe and as welcoming for guests as possible.

"Luckily, it is extremely rare that we ever need to act on it, but we feel it's super important to provide a set of guidelines for a safe, respectful party," Luke states. "Ultimately, we just want a home for people to dance and listen to great music. This should be done with love for each other with a similar mindset and goal."

Matt feels that the growth of this new sense of creativity, which he, alongside Luke, Hannah and many others, are cultivating, is changing the dynamics in Margate. It means locals now have a good reason to remain in the town rather than head off to the bright lights of London with its pricier rents and lack of space.

"There has become this increasingly well-established scene down here now, "says Matt. "If young people are looking for opportunities in arts or music, then Margate is now another option for them instead of London as the capital has become so unaffordable. For some people in their fifties and sixties who live here, if they have a child aged 20, who is engaged with the scene and no longer wants to move to London, then that's interesting to see."

Margate Radio has been a catalyst in uniting the local music community. Set up by Paul Camo, a DJ with online broadcaster NTS, it has helped bring the various colourful strands that make up Margate's nightlife together.

"It runs online every weekend and has gelled people of all ages, ethnicities, and genders together," says Matt. "When I first started DJing here, I was just playing to 40-year-olds like me but that has now changed. There are now kids and twenty-somethings properly raving, which is brilliant."

The size of Margate, in particular Cliftonville, where Matt calls home, is part of its charm, with a population of around 65,000[183]. This area, situated to the east of the town centre, is full of big Victorian homes that used to accommodate poor and vulnerable people who had been rehoused from all over the country. While previously a hopelessly deprived area, life is coming back to this part of town, thanks to this new, creative and welcoming community.

"The support you get from people here is really positive," says Matt. "Everyone wants to spend their money with you and support you, it's a really positive thing and something I've not experienced before. You can pop around to someone's house for a cup of tea without messaging them beforehand. If this was in London, you'd have to arrange it three weeks in advance."

Bill Brewster, DJ and dance music author of books including *'Last Night a DJ Saved My Life'*, says that the high cost of living in London is driving musicians and artists to other towns along the south coast. The likes of Ramsgate, Rye and Hastings are the beneficiaries with their own vibrant music scenes now appearing.

"One of the best places I've played at recently is the Marina Fountain in St Leonards on Sea, a mile from Hastings on the south coast," says Bill. "The atmosphere was amazing, so this is a definite upside. Many of these seaside towns badly need some regeneration, too, as someone who grew up in one can testify."

"When I first started throwing parties and DJing, you could live on a very small budget in London and do creative things - but now I don't see how a 20-year-old kid who wanted to do a party or become a journalist could afford it."

Sitting on the bucolic south coast in St Leonards, the Marina Fountain is as unlikely a destination as any for a rave, being a small boozer located outside the seaside town of Hastings. However, over recent years, Rupert Walton and business partner Jess Scarratt have welcomed some of the best DJs and producers - from Radioactive Man and Andrew Weatherall to Nancy Noise and Manfredas.

"I've always said that we're in the hospitality business so the first rule is to be hospitable," says Rupert of the pub's appeal to these discerning selectors. "The day before, these artists might have been in a portakabin with a warm pack of Carling, they'll play, then spend the rest of their night at a Holiday Inn."

"Making people feel at home goes a long way particularly when they might be wondering why they're playing to a hundred people in St Leonards after headlining a festival."

Bill Brewster was among the first DJs to be tempted to play, then Jess' connections with Heavenly Records led to Andrew Weatherall coming to the coast for a Saturday session. He had such a good time that he returned the next day to host an all-dayer of dub and reggae selections before cranking up the bpms as dark fell.

"I couldn't believe it was happening when Andrew played," says Rupert. "We have a pub here and Weatherall is in the back blasting out chugging rave. It was fucking amazing."

Rupert is originally from St Leonards, then moved to London for work before coming back to his hometown. With property prices spiralling, it's a route many have taken, carrying the sparks they've found in the capital to ignite cultural energy in cheaper areas along the coast.

"Many of our regulars used to party in London," says Rupert. "Now they're in Hastings and have kids, they're like holy shit, I can't believe Optimo are DJing in that pub down the road. If we were to host a weekly night like this, there aren't enough local babysitters to go around."

There's certainly a sharp juxtaposition between the pub setting and the energetic, hedonistic soundtrack, but Rupert has relished creating memories for locals to enjoy.

"When I was a teenager, I remember having these lock-ins, drinking shots of these horrible rums at local pubs - these were the kinds of moments I originally thought I would be making," he says. "Then further down the line, we've got some of the best DJs coming here. I love the idea of walking down a calm sea front, it's all quiet, then you walk into a pub and in the back room, there's Greg Wilson or Craig Richards DJing."

Sadly, the Marina Fountain's time in offering this seaside rave escape comes to an end in May 2024, partly due to the financial climate's impact on the business and the landlord's lack of support for the team to sign a new lease. Rupert is philosophical and has learned to live with what's happened.

"I guess all parties have to end sometime," he says. "You hear of so many amazing venues, club nights and moments in time that were the be all and end all. But that's what they were, just moments in time. You had to be there, you had to experience it and you've got the memories to take with you. Good things are transient - enjoy them while you've got 'em and move on to the next."

While Todmorden's Blue Note club shut its doors in 2003, the town continues to be a destination for music and late night revelry, thanks to the Golden Lion pub. This distinctive boozer, located on Fielden Square in the centre of town, was opened in 2015 by proprietors Matthanee Nilavongse, better known to regulars as Gig, and Richard Walker, aka Waka. Over the last few years, the pair have forged a unique ethos and musical aura around the venue via a leftfield booking policy and love of the weird. DJs Andrew Weatherall, A Guy Called Gerald and Leftfield have all graced the decks while the venue hosts events ranging from the local UFO club to sound healing sessions. Gee, who has experience running the 3 Wise Monkeys bar in the town, says that Todmorden has inspired her to want to make a positive impact.

"When I first came to Todmorden, it felt like a very white conservative village with little in the way of culture going on," she says. "But because it felt so dated, it's really given me the enthusiasm to try and make a difference."

The bookings for the events programme has stemmed from the pair's networks with Waka's connections from his days on the road following the original free party collectives, bridging the gap between crews like DiY Sound System and Hawkwind. The pair often establish personal relationships with those who do and come and perform at the pub, sometimes heading to parties in Ibiza, Italy or Paris just to meet someone to ask them to play. Louis Sweeting is a manager, in-house engineer and event runner at the Golden Lion and plays an important role in helping parties go smoothly. His experience has seen him embroiled in Manchester's clubs before heading to Todmorden and helping coordinate the Golden Lion Sounds label.

"The first few releases have showcased acts like WH Lung and Working Men's Club," Louis says of the label. "The latter have played here a few times and have really developed over their series of gigs. Fostering a local scene is really important and we like to think we're part of that."

Throughout history, the town's character is defined by defiance, running from the Chartists and their working class movement of the 19th century to local groups such as urban gardeners Incredible Edible. This alternative outlook is an energy that the pub looks to tap into.

"One of the main things artists that perform here have in common is a dedication to their art, the courage to stand by what they say, a rebellious spirit and a strong heart," Louis says.

"We're located between Leeds and Manchester but offer a world away from the pressures of urban environments. The hills and open space, as well as the venue, provide a different atmosphere, which is an attraction for upcoming and established artists. They can come to try something different, to showcase new material, to play up close with the audience."

While the pub is flourishing, operations have had their challenges, particularly due to Todmorden being hit by the floods of 2015[184]. Covid-19 has, of course, been an issue too and event programming aims to tread a fine balance in catering to the needs of the locals yet still offering wild and ambitious parties.

"Having the wider community and all these groups use the space gives the opportunity for lots of crossover and communication between those who might not have talked otherwise," explains Louis. "Giving the space for the sparks of creativity and new ideas to take place is a pleasure."

Fittingly, Russell Marland's Out In The Sticks night has now returned and found a home at the Golden Lion. Excitement in his DJ sets and events has returned and is stronger than ever.

"When the Blue Note sold in 2003, I thought that was the end but after a few years on ice, there still seemed to be an appetite for us to play records," he states. "We started up again maybe three times a year but the venues we used never seemed right at the time until eventually we tried the Golden Lion and it felt like we were home."

The opening of the pub has certainly had a huge impact on the fortunes of Todmorden, with bars and restaurants setting up and ushering a new influx of out-of-towners all looking to make their mark.

"The Blue Note was bought, refurbed and became a typical small-town nightclub," Russell says. "Decent nightlife in Todmorden was dead and the town was full of charity shops and rough pubs. The Golden Lion changed that. That pub is a beacon of light in the town and has put Todmorden on the map for good."

With more events now planned at the pub, Russell is pleased that Out In The Sticks has endured, living a new life still in the fringes but with a dedicated crowd wanting to continue the merry dance.

"It wasn't about making money," he says of his enduring motivation to keep the night going. "It was all about letting others hear this amazing music I was fortunate enough to get hold of through the record shop. It really was that simple. How did it shape me? I became a more confident DJ and trusted my instincts when it came to choosing records. I had the crowd in the palm of my hand. They trusted my choices and I trusted that they would like what I played. These nights are special moments in time."

# CHAPTER 7

## 'I CAN SEE CLEARLY NOW MY BRAIN HAS GONE' / RAW RAVE VIBES UP INSIDE THE NETHER REGIONS OF THE UK

*"Nightclubs were shite. They were the epitome of everything we were opposed to. We believed you should be able to party for as long as you wanted to, that anybody should be able to attend, and no one should tell you how to dance or dress"[185].*

Tommy Smith

"You'd be listening to pirate radio and going to petrol stations looking for the party. You'd end up hearing the thump of the sound system from miles away, and somehow you found your way there … everyone is buzzed by the time you arrive. Then you walk into this field and see anything from 10 to 50,000 people, all having this same epiphany, this goodwill and energy pulsating through them, this sea of people dancing."

Jungle legend DJ Rap is recollecting the wide-eyed magic of the big outdoor raves of the late eighties. Dance music had already found its way into an array of spaces during the decade, from clubs to derelict warehouses before deviating into the fields.

"You walk in and know this is your religion, what you've been waiting for your whole life. You know it's special," she says.

The first documented outdoor acid rave is believed to have been chartered by the infamous Boy's Own collective in 1988 (rumour has it that a teenage Norman Cook – aka Fatboy Slim – fell for the charms of house music during one of their parties[186]). The fanzine, dubbed "the original village newspaper of the London acid house scene"[187], was led by Terry Farley, Cymon Eckel, and Andrew Weatherall and hosted this event in East Grinstead. Rather than a noisy intrusion into the pastoral idyll as portrayed in the hysterical press, many landowners were, in fact, keen to provide fields for ravers to dance. In his book *The Lark Ascending*, Richard King suggests how the nature of these illicit pastimes and the cash-in-hand deals struck to secure the spaces for parties were "second nature to anyone earning a living in agriculture, for whom a new style of overnight parties presented further opportunity"[188].

A year later, as acid house fever sent shivers up and down the spine of the UK, it must have felt like anything was possible. Mind-expanding ecstasy culture collided with a prickly political climate as the travelling community and free party people came together to create a wave of huge outdoor raves. It swept the nation from the late 1980s to the early 1990s until the passing of the Criminal Justice and Public Order Act in 1994, a piece of legislation that gave the authorities extra powers to curb these kinds of events[189].

Even before this, it had been a bumpy ride for dancers and event organisers. In the West Country, despite being badly bruised by Thatcher's attempts to destroy their lifestyle at the Battle of the Beanfield in 1985, members of the travelling community such as Circus Warp, Circus Normal and the Free Party People had the know-how, spaces and infrastructure to enable amazing free events under the stars. Various raves such as Energy and Back to the Future began popping up all over London and around the M25, the motorway encircling the capital. But as acid house peaked in 1989, by 1990 the authorities and media were vilifying organisers and ravers and a squat party scene began to loosely form. Traditional nightclubs might have been more expensive for punters and had door policies to contend with but these alternative events offered a more welcoming, underground attitude. Such spaces could also usher in more experimental and uncompromising musical policies compared with the more commercial vibes heard in the clubs. In the free party, you could play anything and be whoever you wanted to be.

Spiral Tribe is one of the most well-known names associated with the free party rave scene. This crew brought a different energy into the post-acid house world, with their roots in more alternative counter-culture. Their militant, black-clad look came from a different place to the gurning smiley, offering a grittier take on the big London parties such as Sunrise or Genesis 88. Debbie Griffith was one of the collective's founding members, joining after experiencing an epiphany in the great outdoors during 1989.

"I went to my first rave that summer, Sunrise at Santa Pod, and it was like a spiritual awakening for me; it felt like it was what I had been looking for all my life," she says. "The music was fantastic, like an evolution of the soul that I'd always loved with a dance beat. Thousands of people from all walks of life and ethnic backgrounds, the smiling faces and friendliness of the ravers. It was so different from the vibe of most of the nightclubs I'd been used to during the eighties."

Debbie's summer of 1989 was spent chasing similar parties around the British countryside with varying degrees of success. Then in 1990, the UK's party culture changed as the authorities passed the Entertainment (increased Penalties) Act[190], also known as the Acid House Bill. This legislation insisted on fines of up to £20,000 for anyone caught out hosting illegal raves or parties.

"Most of 1990 was filled with frustrated attempts on a Saturday night to find a rave," Debbie explains. "It was such a contrast to the previous year when we really thought the world was changing, coincidentally the same year as the Berlin Wall came down. For us, house music was the trigger for these world-changing events."

It was amid this backdrop of parties, music and upheaval that Debbie first met the other members of the Spiral Tribe collective - Simone Trevelyan, Mark and Zander Harrison. Her soon-to-be colleagues were squatting in a "a massive old school house" in northwest London, not far from where Debbie lived.

"In the beginning of 1991, we went to Amsterdam to put on a party, then when we came back to London we found a small abandoned nightclub just round the corner from our squat in Westbourne Park," says Debbie. "These were the very first Spiral Tribe events, where we charged a fiver in and invited our friends to come and DJ."

"We'd just bought our first sound system from a friend and were keen to use it as much as possible. When this venue got busted, people would come up with other places we could squat and party."

It was during the early months of 1991 that Spiral Tribe first began bringing their rig to events hosted outside London squats. They expanded their reach to take in free festivals, connecting with fellow travellers and sound systems.

"This was new to us as even though we were squatting venues and charging minimum entry, it opened up a new world of revolutionary possibilities," explains Debbie. "This was especially so when we travelled abroad and started partying in Paris, for example, where the raves were very expensive."

As with the first waves of rave culture that emerged in the eighties, Debbie believes that the underground scene came out of years of a Margaret Thatcher government, a kickback to the mass unemployment and the wrecking ball the then prime minister had taken to society[191].

"The bringing together of so many people from such different backgrounds was a huge threat to the government, which is why they clamped down so hard on it," says Debbie. "The Acid House Bill to start with and then the Criminal Justice and Public Order Bill. I think it seemed to us that this was a massive time of change with huge potential for transformation and the music illustrated that."

"Be there, all weekend, hardcore" was the rallying call surrounding the Castlemorton Common Festival, a week-long outdoors party organised during a hot and sticky Bank Holiday weekend in May 1992[192]. It was left on an answering machine that party-goers called to find out the details of what would go down as one of the most tumultuous events in the history of the UK's topsy turvy relationship with rave. The party spiralled out of control, attracting more than 30,000 revellers and resulted in a £4 million trial of the organisers, with the government ultimately delivering a hammer blow to the outdoor rave scene with its 1994 legislation. As Simon Reynolds notes in his book, *'Energy Flash'*, "during the five days of its existence, Castlemorton would inspire questions in Parliament, make the front page of every newspaper in England and incite nationwide panic about the whereabouts of the next destination on the crusty itinerary"[193].

The event saw huge numbers of revellers, ravers and sound systems bring their rigs to Castlemorton in the Malvern Hills in Worcestershire. Among them was the DiY Sound System, a party-loving crew that came together in inner-city Nottingham during the summer of 1989, although core members Pete Woosh, Rick and Harry Harrison were all from Greater Manchester. Their trail of inspiration can be traced back to the Hacienda and festivals such as Pickup Bank and Glastonbury.

"We were involved in the free party movement from the start as we had a foot in both camps - the free festival scene and the acid house scene," says Harry. "You could say that DiY's mission was always to unite these two very different historical strands, to unite disco with Stonehenge."

It was a meeting with some travellers in Glastonbury's free field in June 1990 which sparked off a weekly pilgrimage from Nottingham to the south-west of England to play music and party.

"They supplied the marquee, generator and sound system and we supplied the decks and records," says Harry. "The chemicals we supplied jointly. From then on, we travelled down to the south-west nearly every weekend to organise parties or DJ at free festivals. We then invested in our own PA in 1991 just in time for the huge free festival rave/rave crossover of 1991/92, which effectively ended at Castlemorton."

DiY managed to plough its own unique path through a range of different dance music ventures. Club nights and all-nighters in Nottingham, Derbyshire, across the UK and further afield were all rinsed while they poured their love for club culture into their own music and productions.

"We always refused to be pigeonholed," explains Harry. "From 1992, we started producing music, did an album for Warp Records and set up our own studio and label."

Despite the crackdown in the wake of Castlemorton, the sound system, the parties and the DiY reputation somehow managed to keep pushing the envelope forward, throwing hundreds of events, even going as far as being dubbed "culturally, the most dangerous people in the UK" at Manchester's In the City music conference. This was due to their egalitarian commitments and "unspoken ideology of liberation through fun"[194]. Location fed directly into the vibes of the DiY events, particularly as nowhere seemed out of bounds as a place to set up their equipment, play music and get well and truly on it.

"Over the years, we threw parties in every place imaginable," says Harry. "Remote Scottish lochs, car parks, drainage tunnels, disused airfields, gyms, boats, quarries recording studios, islands in addition to the traditional clubs and marquees."

The sound and feel of an outdoor event was certainly different to one contained within the four walls of a conventional club. At one raucous DiY Sound System event, there were people complaining about the sound of the bass up to ten miles away.

"Outdoor parties were far less manic, you could just wander outside and look at the stars," Harry says. "We found our locations through many means; perhaps a sympathetic traveller's site, perhaps a phone call offering some land. By 1992 DiY had contacts everywhere and local promoters were very keen to get us to their location. Often we would just drive round Derbyshire and look for somewhere suitable. We had everything we needed for a three-day party so we could arrive at 10pm, get going by 10.30 and be off and away by 8am. Proper acid house."

The influence of Castlemorton on the sound systems in attendance was significant. Ten different party crews, including Bedlam and Circus Normal alongside Nottingham's DiY[195], all represented at the event. While DiY continued to operate in the UK afterwards Spiral Tribe headed to Europe to embrace a freer existence away from this unwelcome media spotlight. Many of their core members were hauled in front of a judge after Castlemorton on public order offences but were later acquitted. The move to Europe by some of the group was part of an aim to leave this behind and rave without restrictions. Their departure from the UK certainly had an influence on their sound, explains Spiral Tribe's Debbie Griffith.

"In 1991, the music was still mainly house-based with some techno and breakbeat creeping in, very diverse but full of a dark promise," she says. "Then '92 brought more breakbeats and the beginnings of what became jungle and happy hardcore, and then when we arrived in Europe, we found our sound – pure, glistening, gleaming silver techno. From R&S in Belgium especially and many other German record labels and, of course, Detroit, the originators of the pure techno sound."

Spiral Tribe joined other expats who had fled the UK to embrace the freedom offered by our European neighbours. Joe Rush and his Mutoid Waste Company were a collective of ravers, sculptors, and creative pranksters who had left the UK before Castlemorton. As much performance art, street theatre as party hosts, Mutoid Waste fed off the refuse left behind in cities to create their elaborate events and installations. As Nik Turner of Hawkwind says in the 2021 film celebrating Joe, *I Am A Mutoid*: "They mutate everything, they try to mutate the world."[196]

Originally firing into life during the early eighties, the inspiration for their artistic vision came from Joe's time spent travelling with the Peace Convoy, a caravan of ramshackle vehicles that drove between Windsor and Glastonbury with many of the participants stalwarts of the free party scene.

"I realised that although this was very well-intentioned, this convoy wasn't having a party that people could be included in but was having a party on top of people," says Joe. "I thought we could do something more entertaining that would really turn people on, so I left and started the Mutoid Waste Company in London in 1984."

The company was born out of the scrap they sourced within the capital and bonded through their time together in squats and a shared love for a life lived out of the mainstream. Joe spent his early creative years working on set design and learning all the skills of prop and model making, beginning to construct his mutoid sculptures from stacks of leftover motorbike parts.

Initially, his gang would put on parades down Portobello Road in west London, resembling "extras from Mad Max" and driving "mutated motorbikes and flat-bed trucks from which flames rose into the sky to soundtracks of snarling guitar and dub reggae"[197]. This blend of anarchic creativity and street theatre continued to evolve until the group began to host parties in derelict properties where they would show off their salvaged art and bizarre, ruined constructions.

"We'd just use whatever we found, whatever we could drag into these spaces to create these dystopian worlds for people to party in," says Joe. "Back then, there wasn't a great push to develop in London, so there was plenty of space. We'd find somewhere and squat it, which would give us three months before they would serve an eviction order on us. We'd use this time to build sets, artwork and host parties before it was time to hit the road again."

This use of London's abandoned buildings and warehouses occurred ahead of the late eighties rave explosion. In 1986, the Mutoid Waste Company took over the abandoned bus depot in King's Cross and began to host events and parties. The following year they went to Glastonbury and built Carhenge, a Stonehenge memorial constructed from scrapped cars. It would only be a couple of years later that Joe and his merry band decided to abandon the UK, sick of being chased and fighting against the authorities.

"We were public enemy number one," laughs Joe. "So we went on a tour of mainland Europe where we were more welcome. In the UK, the police were constantly after us, always trying to confiscate our sculptures."

The company went to Amsterdam, Barcelona, Italy and Berlin, where they created some of their most striking works, including an "8m high chicken on wheels out of a Volkswagen Beetle, a motorbike with a tractor wheel on the front, an aeroplane out of a car trailer"[198]. Setting up in West Berlin during the summer of 1989, they hosted parties and built huge sculptures and installations. Then when the

Berlin Wall came down in November that year, they foraged through old military equipment and abandoned weaponry for inspiration.

"We had the run of it when the Berlin Wall fell and we went into the east of Berlin," explains Joe. "It had been under Communist repression for years but it was also the biggest scrap pile on the planet. We ended up nicking tanks, fighter planes and building stuff with that."

In the intervening years, Joe's work has found a wider audience and his reputation as an outsider has softened. The Mutoid Waste Company's creations are now the stuff of Glastonbury legend ("I get to do the big rock and roll style sculptures there which I really like," he says) while they have been increasingly embraced by mainstream culture. In 2021, his work was on show at Fulham Town Hall in London as part of an exhibition called *Art in the Age of Now* while their aesthetic saw him invited to art direct and perform in the closing ceremony of the 2012 Paralympic Games. Still, Joe rankles at being seen as closer to an establishment that has historically always been against him.

"We used to be really lucky when we did events in warehouses with people climbing on the roof. There would be open fires and electrical cables sticking out of walls," he says. "We managed to get away with it without killing anyone but we've become more health and safety aware with risk assessments. The only way to survive is to play them at their own game."

The closing ceremony's display of mutant automobiles is burnt into many memories and was the finale of an amazing London summer in what seems a more optimistic world than the one we're in now, hammered by Brexit, Covid-19 and rocketing costs. The irony of receiving such a global platform to represent the UK despite being chased from these shores 20 years earlier is not lost on Joe.

"All the music, staging, art direction, it came out of rave and festival culture," he says. "We're no longer these scruffy types in sheds, we're a world class act but we're still not appreciated for it. Everything we've done has been in spite of this country rather than because of it."

"When we got to Europe, we saw how they looked after their shows and their artistic people. In this country, all that happened was we got chased by the fucking police, battered at the Beanfield and smashed to pieces at warehouse parties. Then years later, they realise they actually need us."

"The papers were publishing headlines like 'Half Naked Girls in Acid House Frenzy'. You couldn't buy this publicity and the number of people attending our parties doubled in a week."

Blackburn party organiser Tommy Smith is recalling the madness of an underground rave scene often lost in acid house folklore, dwarfed by the monolithic presence of Manchester's Hacienda mythology. But some of what went down 30 miles away in Blackburn at the end of the eighties is just, if not more, important in the telling of the rave story of co-opting space. Tommy is a Glaswegian who had family connections with the town and was originally in Berlin with a theatre group when dance music culture erupted. Stories of the powers of raving and ecstasy were gradually filtering through to him and he firmly embraced it when he returned in 1988.

"I had this epiphany with a capital 'E'," Tommy laughs. "But I had come back to the UK to see what all these parties were about. Everyone was talking about being loved up and how things had changed. There were some people who I knew had been fierce enemies when I left England, but now they would be in the same house hugging each other. I thought that was some pretty weird shit."

Alongside his partner-in-parties Tony Creft, Tommy was a key operator in the organisation of the many legendary events that took place in and around the abandoned mills surrounding Blackburn. Whitehead Street was an important part of the town for this movement with an "unlikely row of terraced houses" acting as a nerve centre and eventual battleground. Tommy, alongside other Scots, lived in squats on the street while the first events he ran were above a bar called Crackers owned by "legendary drag queen, Clitheroe Kate".

"It was licensed for about 50/60 people, but we managed to cram in 250," remembers Tommy. "It was then that it felt like something was happening, this sense of energy, positivity, the sweaty bodies, it was all going on. You could feel that these big changes were afoot and we took it from there."

With the press getting wind of the events and churning out accusatory headlines in a bid to spark moral outrage and shut them down, their histrionics instead acted as a promotional catalyst and the numbers of attendees began to double each week. Tommy even appeared on TV's Granada Reports where he defended the acid house movement, declaring himself to be "high on hope".

"We'd started in small shops, then small industrial units around Blackburn," he says of the initial parties. "Thatcher had been finishing off the mills, so there were plenty to choose from. Now it would be hard to break a building but back then, there were loads available and the police were slow on the uptake too. It was all word of mouth; the local press were working in our favour. People would read about it and feel like they were missing out on something. You knew if we were having a party, then we would have it; there was nobody who could stop us."

Much of the impetus for hosting events was driven by ambitions to democratise the emerging dance music culture and make it more open and inclusive. This extended into making the parties free for anyone with a dole card or who simply could not afford it.

"I was coming at this from a political background," explains Tommy. "'Can you Feel it?' was the war cry but ours was 'Can you Afford it?'

We were seeing things further south at events where it was costing 20 quid to get in, then it would be even more for your pills. You shouldn't have to pay a subscription fee or ask for permission to party. That's why nightclubs were the enemy; they were the epitome of everything we were opposed to. They took place in this controlled environment, licensed, they told you when to stop dancing and get out of the door."

After 18 chaotic months, these illicit parties eventually came to a head and the authorities muscled in heavily on the scene to close it down. The Love Decade party, held in Gildersome, south of Leeds, in July of 1990 is seen by Tommy and others as the end of the northern acid house scene. The event culminated in one of the UK's biggest mass arrests with 836 party people cuffed and held in various police stations across Yorkshire. Tommy had his own troubles back in Blackburn as Salford gangs tried to intimidate them.

"They came and kidnapped us, took us to the basement of the Hacienda and said you're working for us now," he says. "It was serious shit and the first time I'd seen a gun. But it now feels good to be vindicated with some of the attention our story is getting. As Blackburn was considered by some to be a bit of a backwater shit hole, these events were kind of written out of the story. But the trail leads back to the town, the people can have some sort of pride in something, it's good for those involved, the organisers and those who raved."

Suddi Raval was among many of the attendees at the infamous Blackburn raves. Before he made his way out of Manchester and to the empty mills, he would spend his nights going to what he describes as "the worst clubs in the world with sticky carpets, neon lights and terrible music". A chance encounter in the street had a transformative effect on his social life, opening a doorway to the acid house euphoria he never knew he needed.

"I was walking down the street in my hometown of Ashton-under-Lyne wearing 'rave wear'," Suddi recalls. "This guy Kelvin saw me, stopped me and asked if I was into acid house and what clubs I went to. He was surprised to hear I didn't really go to any. He said: "You need to go to the Hacienda and the Blackburn raves warehouse parties." I said: "I'd love to but I wouldn't know how." We exchanged numbers, and he said he'd take me. He was true to his word and it completely changed my life."

As for so many of those coming of age at the time, 1989 was a massive year for Suddi as well as the nascent rave scene. He recalls how the events in Blackburn scaled up quickly in a matter of weeks as the hysterical press whipped up a hurricane of hype around them.

"Initially, it felt like a secret, then I saw it grow from a couple of thousand people to the biggest parties with 10,000," says Suddi. "I felt so lucky to have the Hacienda, the Thunderdome and Blackburn on my doorstep. The guys behind the Blackburn events were incredible. Breaking into warehouses, then evading the police and all the risks that go with that. At the time, I didn't fully appreciate what they were putting on the line."

Suddi became utterly entangled in the wave of rave the UK was surfing and formed the electronic group Together in 1990 with collaborator Jon Donaghy. Their aim was to release music they wanted to hear played in the Hacienda. Taking its name from the organisers of the Blackburn parties, Together's track *'Hardcore Uproar'* uses crowd noises samples recorded from what would be one of the last illegal events held.

"It all came crashing to a sudden halt when they raided this huge party in Nelson [a small town to the east of Blackburn]," says Suddi. "That was it but we had managed to record at this last ever event. Its notoriety really helped the success of the track."

*'Hardcore Uproar'* reached number 12 in the UK singles chart but while its life lived on, the Blackburn parties and Hardcore Uproar crew who inspired it were no more.

London's harder-edged acid techno scene has used the capital's derelict buildings as a breeding ground to spawn rough-shod, fast-paced musical bangers for more than 25 years. Taking in elements of early trance, squelching acid and relentless bpms, this propulsive subgenre of dance music hits like nothing else. Chris Liberator, DJ, producer and founder of influential label, Stay up Forever, is one of the scene's defining figures, having run underground parties and brutalised his 303 in the studio since the early nineties.

"We always used to say there's an alternative history of dance music," he laughs. "There's this Mixmag-approved narrative of clubs and Ibiza, then this more underground story which runs parallel but is often overlooked. From the early nineties onwards, there was just an intense amount of free parties and squat parties. This was in London but also across the country. Every city would have something like this that played this kind of harder music."

Academic Stéphane Sadoux agrees. Trained as a town planner, he lived in England in the late 1990s and early 2000s where he threw himself into the city's underground dance music scene. His subsequent research into nightlife culture (conducted after alarming stats were released about London losing over half its nightclubs during an eight-year period[199]) was released in 2016 and combined his academic life and passion for raving. Stéphane's findings have been featured in *'Electronic Cities: Music, Policies and Space in the 21st Century'* a book edited by Sebastien Darchen, John Wilsteed and Damien Charrieras. In his chapter, Stéphane explores London's underground acid techno nights, a scene which mostly lived, breathed and danced in illegal venues.

"The harder side of nightlife has largely been ignored or not treated with the gravitas it deserves in the majority of academic literature," he says of his research. "I felt it was important to ground research in experience rather than merely relying on second-hand accounts and data. The idea was to show that there were two different strands to the history of electronic music. The mainstream, licensed clubs under threat from regeneration and the squat party scene where ravers danced outside these licensed venues."

Stéphane's work is one of a number of recent attempts to return to these times and document what occurred in this underbelly out of the media's glare. As an instigator behind the acid techno and free party movement, Chris Liberator is one of the defining figures whose musical passions were ignited during punk. As his tastes evolved, Chris experimented in various different bands as he sought to track down his musical identity. He absorbed everything from the industrial funk of Sheffield's Cabaret Voltaire to the heavy dub of Adrian Sherwood and his On-U Sound, taking on the drums for anarcho-punk outfit Hagar the Womb. He remembers how when acid house first emerged in the late eighties, it didn't really touch the sides.

"I didn't get into it. It was too soft and commercial for me," Chris says. "I was looking for a harder kind of sound, combining the punk scene and squat scene. When I met the other Liberators around 1991, rave music seemed to have caught up with this - from Belgian techno to Underground Resistance in Detroit and Al Jourgensen in Ministry."

Chris and his fellow Liberators, Aaron and Julian, all came from the punk and free party music scenes, influences that helped define the tougher sonics they chased.

"We were used to crusty punks and never felt comfortable hanging out with rave kids wearing Fila," laughs Chris. "When we got together as the Liberators, we wanted to do these harder raves in an environment which felt like our own, which is why we used houses and punk squats. We were used to this scene and knew how to take buildings."

The Liberators started hosting events in 1991 around the same time as Spiral Tribe and a slew of other crews born out of the punk scene began to operate. The shared attitude was anti-establishment, with a collective desire to play and rave to music that writhed around outside the mainstream. Between 1991 and 1993, the alternative dance scene mushroomed with the Castlemorton weekend its peak.

"The mid-nineties was the heyday for squat parties in London," says Chris. "We would play an event in Europe, then come back and go straight to the squat party as it would still be going on a Sunday afternoon. You'd have all these techno tourists who'd come to London for a year or a few months and they would help fuel the scene too."

Living outside the already established clubbing world, where venues relied on punters staying and spending money, meant they could be both more open in who they welcomed and the music that they played.

"Those early squat parties, like the Bedlam parties, this was when gabba started in 1991, 1992 and it was in these raw spaces that you'd hear it," explains Chris. "I remember bouncing around in this warehouse to gabba one morning and everyone was really out of it. You could play bizarre broken beat or mental fucking acid records, whatever you wanted. If you were playing in a commercial club, then you'd be in danger of alienating punters and losing the venue money. The first paid gig we did was with Megadog and they asked us to avoid the faster sound. But then, in the squat party, we could be as experimental as we liked."

Stéphane's research highlights how squatting was in particular made possible by Section 6 of the Criminal Law Act 1977[200]. This stipulated that it was illegal to use violence to enter a building where inhabitants oppose entry. Squatters who lived in abandoned buildings also benefited from the support of the Squatter Advisory

Service. The law on their side helped fan the flames of a music scene that went beyond parties to offer a totally alternative way of life.

"Many of these acid techno parties were originally hosted in abandoned warehouses around Hackney," says Stéphane. "You can really hear this in Dynamo City's iconic track *'One Night in Hackney'*, which tells the "story of a young man who visited London for the first time". This kind of music somehow reflected the ambiance of the locations where they would be played – extreme, dark and filthy."

"But I'm not sure anyone deliberately produced dance music to sound like this," he continues. "It was more to do with their attitude and the gear available. For many of the scene's key players I spoke with, this music does represent London. But as a community of people rather than a place."

"If you compare this with Detroit and DJs like Derrick May and Juan Atkins, their vision was a way of getting their machines talking and singing at a time in the city when the factories were crumbling. It was very much anchored in the place and history of the city rather than the people."

Producer D.A.V.E. The Drummer is another key player in the acid techno scene and a close musical confidante of Chris Liberator and Stay Up Forever. Rather than punk, his route into the scene was via the travelling community, a lifestyle he embraced as a teenager after leaving home. D.A.V.E. initially met many like-minded people at the punk Harp Club in New Cross, south London.

"I started off in the squatting scene in London with some mates of mine and ended up in a band called Back to the Planet," he states. "The first squats I lived in offered a much more "hippy" environment, and I discovered music like Ozric Tentacles and Gong, dub reggae and smoked hashish for the first time."

"During this period, I found out more about the travelling scene and this subculture of people living in buses on the road. I had this realisation that I was part of a generation of young people who were looking for something different. We liked the idea of freedom, the culture, ideals and political edge."

The Dole House was a squatted unemployment benefit office in Peckham, south London, which opened up around 1989. It was squatted by the Dole House Crew, who started hosting regular weekend parties and after his jaunts on the road, D.A.V.E. returned to London to move into the building. Here, he enjoyed his first taste of the rave scene by helping organise the events.

"I used to book bands for the hall upstairs, work on the bar, clean and help with the sound crew while we had rave DJs in the room downstairs," he says.

D.A.V.E.'s band Back to the Planet were regular performers in the space and had been touted by the music industry for success. Many of the acts who played live noticed the impact of rave's arrival on how the dynamics of events now tipped in favour of DJs rather than live performers.

"At the free festivals, the live bands and old travelling stages were now found in the corner of the site," he remembers. "The main area would be a rave with someone like Spiral Tribe, who had a Quadraphonic sound system, DJs and everyone was out of their heads on pills."

The uniting of the travellers with this new rave generation was integral to the free party scene's rapid evolution during the summer of 1989. The colliding of these two different worlds was like a stick of dynamite going off underneath the fledgling rave scene.

"Acid house just exploded and massively infiltrated the travelling scene," D.A.V.E recalls. "It was a way for these guys to do parties. The ravers knew how to get hold of drugs and DJs and sound systems, the travellers knew how to take sites, they were quite organised in this way. If you had the key rave people and the key travelling people talking, then you'd have yourself a party."

Back to the Planet ended up signing a deal with major label London Records, made a series of albums and singles, including '*Mind and Soul Collaborators*' and '*Teenage Turtles*'. D.A.V.E. prudently used his share of the advance from the deal to invest in some equipment meaning when the band eventually fell out and split up, he was in a position to carry on making his own music. A subsequent chance meeting with local character John Deranged then led to the development of the Punishment Farm studio space above the latter's pub in Deptford, south London. It was through John that D.A.V.E. ended up meeting and collaborating with Chris Liberator with the resulting track, '*Spectrum*', released by indie label Bag in 1995[201].

"I liked playing around with sounds and the more technical side whereas Chris was more conceptual in his approach," says D.A.V.E. of their creative partnership. "I really enjoyed having the input of a regular well-known DJ and we came up with our first track, '*Spectrum*'. Colin Dale played it on his show on Kiss FM and dedicated it to Dave Angel on his birthday. We were made up."

Following this success, D.A.V.E.'s continued to make acid techno as a response to the parties he began attending. To plug himself deeper into this world, he started frequenting more free raves and nights at places like Club 414 in Brixton to check out how DJs like Chris, Laurie Immersion and Gizelle 'Rebel Yelle' would play out his music.

"You would have to have certain elements in place to make these tracks work: good sound, a nice thumping kick drum, simple rhythms, great 303 pattern, an interesting sample and all at the right tempo," he explains. "We were working at around 145 bpm at the time and it was really important to maintain this if tracks were to work on a dancefloor."

While he was embracing the sound and scene, D.A.V.E. also decided to up the ante and take on the challenge of playing live. His slightly risky approach to live performance was to take most of his studio hardware and set it up in squat parties.

"I was turning up at squats full of loonies with all my precious gear," he laughs. "Someone off their head would come along and pick up my sampler and say "shall I take this to the stage?" "No, you fucking won't. Put it down"."

Alongside the Liberators' Stay Up Forever label, Cluster, Routemaster and Smitten were also at the core of the mostly London-based acid techno sound. D.A.V.E. says that he and the Liberators loved labels such as Hardfloor and Phuture Wax but "often these records didn't quite do it for us, it would be too slow or cheesy so we did our version and acid techno became the name we used to describe it".

"We wanted hard 303s mixed with Belgian rave and German acid trance, with an uplifting sound but also dark and hard enough to represent the punk influences of our history," he explains of the scene's origins. "It was almost like artists like the Liberators knew what they wanted but couldn't buy it so had to make it themselves. When it came to our own music, we wanted to establish that it was punky; it had its own attitude and direction. This was a very conscious decision; we wanted people to know 'this is who we are'. That's why vocals started to sneak into the records; we wanted to show we were from London."

The London that the scene first inhabited and grew out of is very different to what the city now looks like. The Liberators' Stay Up Forever HQ is in Tottenham Hale, an area that has been transformed over the last 20 years. Gone are the abandoned buildings where you could party until Monday night. Now the skyline is increasingly overshadowed by flats, many whose prices are as high and unobtainable as the new buildings themselves.

"You can really see how the city is changing," says Chris Liberator. "Someone I know just bought a warehouse flat in London for some crazy amount of money. About 20 years ago, we squatted in the same building."

"Back in the day, we'd be doing parties every week in London and you'd get away with it," he continues. "We'd have 3,000 people in a car park just off Tottenham Court Road near Centrepoint. People would be coming to work and we'd still be out fucking raving. London was a squattable city and people knew what they were doing with the law on their side. It was a phenomenon."

Stay Up Forever's spiritual home in contemporary times is FOLD, an artist-led, community-driven nightclub and creative space located in Canning Town. Chris sees clubs setting up in these industrial, derelict areas as the future, although he's aware of how quickly a place can change when nightlife enters and enhances it.

"Places like FOLD are far enough away from where people currently live, they look cool and it feels special when you're heading there," he says. "They can build up their own crowd through the artists they book and the space they create."

"But these areas eventually get squeezed. Hackney Wick used to be a centre for squat parties until the Olympics and *'One Night in Hackney'* was based on that, you'd always end up somewhere amazing if you went there. But I've seen what happens before. Canning Town was one of the least desirable places in London - but you probably won't be able to afford flats there in a few years."

D.A.V.E. believes that despite the acid techno scene's growth, many of the core attitudes surrounding it have remained as it continues to operate on its own rebellious terms.

"It has always been very independent and anarchic," he explains. "It won't turn anyone into multi-millionaires but that's not what we want. At the same time, as an independent label, you need to be able to crunch the numbers for it to work. People need to get paid if we're going to run our lifestyles in this way."

While the Stay Up Forever label continues to release music, host parties and keep its community engaged, D.A.V.E. feels that the free party scene has always been a tough world to survive, never mind thrive, within.

"When I started squatting, I was a really troubled teenager, I had some difficult times at home and at school, I ran away, ended up in this scene and didn't know what the fuck was going on," he recalls.

"I made some pretty weird decisions but I was lucky to land on my feet a few times to get to where I am now. I suffered with drugs and alcohol really badly. I'm completely sober now and have been for two years, but I do largely feel like a massive amount of my life has gone down the tube. There's quite a legacy of music, but I could have done more. Still, you know, you can't live like that."

Although D.A.V.E. is several steps removed from today's free party scene, he sees positives and negatives to the direction some of the emerging conversations surrounding it are taking.

"I do see arguments and trouble online but also good positive things," he says. "As much as I don't feel particularly connected to it, I wish it was more inclusive; people should look to a more utopian reason for doing it as opposed to just wanting to go out and get fucked. There is this whole 'hate the police' thing. I get it, of course, I get it. I grew up with the Battle of the Beanfield on my doorstep, but the truth is, you don't get anywhere with this attitude. There needs to be a dialogue."

Alongside D.A.V.E., Gizelle 'Rebel Yelle' is a close affiliate of the Stay Up Forever stable. Her musical adventures began unfolding during the heady days of acid house in the late eighties before her tastes morphed and she became embroiled with harder, more underground sounds.

"The free party scene in London wouldn't have been anything without being able to take over empty spaces," she says. "It provided a raw environment to play with and the rundown ugliness of a lot of the buildings was actually their beauty. They provided the perfect places for underground parties."

Initially, Gizelle began playing funk and soul in a bar in Deptford around 1987/1988, inspired by London's rare groove scene. She'd progressed from pulling pints to playing records after the previous DJ had suddenly left without any warning. At the same time, she'd begun to hear about the new acid house parties and eventually went to one with a group of mates. From the moment Gizelle stepped in, she was hooked.

"The music, the vibe, the lights, the smoke, the people ... it was such a pleasurable sensory overload for me," she says of her first experiences in house music culture. "I was happy just dancing in my own little world to start with. Someone came up to me once while I was dancing and asked me what I'd taken. I was like... "nothing" - he looked at me as if I was crazy, but the music and atmosphere energised me and my musical tastes changed overnight. No more rare groove. Enter acid house and Balearic."

Gizelle became a dedicated night owl and spent many evenings at some of London's most important clubs as dance music went off in a massive way. From Rage at Heaven to DJs like Paul Oakenfold and Nancy Noise, she fully immersed herself in this exciting new electronic world. Clink Street, located at the back of London Bridge with DJs Mr C, Shock Sound System and 'Evil' Eddie Richards, took this to the next level.

"You walk around there now, it's all cafes, bars and restaurants but back then it was very different," she says of the area. "It was in the back streets of London with this Victorian, Dickensesque-vibe. Inside and outside Clink Street studios, it would be heaving with ravers trying to find a way in. And they would, through windows, by climbing up drain pipes, just any way they could. I remember someone walking in with a copy of Time Out under their arm pretending to be a music journalist."

As the club scene evolved and became more commercialised in the early nineties, Gizelle's musical tastes began to point her in a different direction to more underground beats. She would head down to Brighton for the Positive Sounds and dance to DJ Harvey, DJ Chocci and Roy the Roach at the Zap Club. After the club shut at 1am, the crowd would reassemble on the nearby beach and party until the sun came up. Gizelle then became involved in an all-women community radio broadcasting project called Brazen Radio, where she met the female crew from the Zero Gravity Collective. This led to her meeting Caro 'Sexy Rubber Soul', then the Liberator DJs and Stay Up Forever.

"Caro from the Zero Gravity Collective invited me to play at their second birthday party at a small venue around Hackney/Stoke Newington," she says. "It had loads of different rooms with their collective DJs playing all kinds of music. I felt like I had come home, as the atmosphere was so inviting. These people seemed so radical, creative and open-minded."

During this period of the mid-to-late nineties, there seemed to be a glut of large warehouse type spaces which free party organisers could really make their own. A barrage of colourful backdrops, lights and camouflage netting were just some of the elements needed to create "a very special space and atmosphere".

"Those days in and around the Hackney area were all about self-expression," Gizelle explains. "The crews would find these interesting old venues, put up the backdrops, bring in smoke machines, camo netting, rainbow lighting and literally transform their space by responding to these environments. Painted colourful psychedelic backdrops were a big thing in the nineties. You could be anywhere, but when you saw these signature backdrops, you'd know you were in the right party. These decorations were a massive part of each party crew's identity."

Tyson Street Studios in Dalston in east London was an old factory venue split across multiple floors and a significant destination for late-night thrill-seekers. It was at an event here that Gizelle first met Lawrie Immersion, who then invited her to play at Cooltan in Brixton, a squatted dole office.

"I loved playing the squats," says Gizelle. "There is this raw edge you get from DJing in that environment, and it was so damn exciting. I felt like I had to rise to the challenge when playing these parties. Hats off to these guys who cracked these buildings open every weekend. You would have a small crew who would focus on finding a building for the weekend, opening it up, squatting it and then the sound system crew would come in and set up ready for a weekend of raving in a very loud fashion."

An old Qasar building near Turnpike Lane, where the famous laser tag game was played, had a sloping floor and was squatted with parties going on for months. These illicit events "felt like being in a live video game". All of these grimy places fed into and inspired Gizelle's music productions and her DJ sets.

"These spaces were so exciting to play music in and inspired a lot of music productions from the Stay Up Forever collective and also other acid techno record labels such as Smitten and Routemaster," she says. "I produced for the Stay Up Forever label under the guise 'Rebel Yelle'. All the parties and interactions inspired me when writing music for the dancefloor."

"Let me prepare your body bags, I mean beds…" was the final email I received from the PR before we headed off to Bang Face back in 2008, the club night turned gonzo rave music festival and natural descendant of the original free party scene. As derelict properties have become harder to come by and clubs tamed by a sense of po-faced, sometimes overbearing security, this self-proclaimed "neo-rave armageddon" has offered an alternative outlet for those wanting to party hard in more recent years. Rather than abandoned buildings, Bang Face has squatted in traditional clubs, adopting an attitude and aesthetic where anything goes. Attracting a devoted, international crowd, ever since its inception in 2003, it's become one of the most vibrant and passionate subcultural events in the dance music calendar[202].

Taking place in some of the Butlins or Pontins seaside resorts littered across the UK coastline, the Bang Face Weekender is an extension of the night, a three-day blow-out of epic proportions, marrying surreal humour with a serious line-up of dance music heavyweights. The loyal fanbase, dubbed the Bang Face Hard Crew, completely capture the insane vibe. Of the three weekends I've been to as a journalist[203], no one really goes to bed but the majority carry a sign, an inflatable and wear fancy dress. From 'Tonight Matthew I'm Going to Be a Fucking Twat' to 'Hungry and Chalet Less - Spare 10 pence for Meow-Meow', the messages brandished by the Hard Crew capture the "mix of nineties rave vibe meets art college idiot" founder James Gurney was aiming for. His first nights out were spent in London at clubs like the Camden Palace, Turnmills and the Astoria as rave was blowing up in the UK.

"I've got loads of fragmented memories of going out, a real mix of excitement, wonder and discovery," he says. "The sounds, the colours, the people were just mind-blowing. One of my earliest and clearest memories was standing up on a balcony transfixed by a giant green laser making passes above the dancefloor and cutting through the dry ice. I've no idea how long I stood there but I remember saying to my mate, 'this is like something out of Star Wars'."

James' own ventures into promoting began as his career as a freelance animator and designer picked up. While his paid work became increasingly serious, he decided to vent his more unhinged side through DJing and running parties.

"I craved the buzz of putting on art shows and music events and reconnected with some mates from art college and we did a few things together," he explains. "I started playing really mixed up sets of all my favourite genres from the nineties and they seemed to be going down really well, so it all snowballed from there. Bang Face was just a silly thing I came up with at the time; it was more of a wind up than anything."

Bang Face's first nights were in 2003 at Public Life in Shoreditch[204], an old underground toilet capable of only squeezing in 100 people. James was searching for another home by the third free night as the event's popularity grew. His search for the perfect space took in several different venues before settling on the "industrial warehouse maze" that is Electrowerkz in Angel. Spread over three floors, the venue gave the Bang Face team the opportunity to truly let their hair down and expand their creative remit through various rave and electronic music styles.

"There were no strict rules, as long as it had the rave spirit and the Hard Crew were down with it that was cool," James explains. "We'd have live acid and techno shows on tables set up on the dancefloor, rave legends performing for the first time since the early nineties, plus the new wave of bass driven artists, breakcore was really blowing up and giving that manic energy to the scene which was incredible."

Artists ranging from rave legends Altern-8 and the Countryside Alliance to Venetian Snares, Leftfield and family-friendly entertainer Dave Benson Philips have all featured amid a chaotic soundtrack running from jungle to breakcore. The incongruous setting of the holiday park for the Bang Face Weekender adds another level of energy and plain weirdness to the event itself. Some of the chalets I've frequented have played host to events such as the Ketamine Olympics while the availability of leisure activities including go-karting, a swimming pool (once memorably referred to as "ecstasy soup" when full of Hard Crew bouncing around) and amusement arcades contrast sharply with the musical hardness on the line-up. James had experienced weekenders as a clubber before Bang Face started and vibed off the sense of community created by staying onsite for a few days.

"There's a long history of soul then rave weekenders being hosted off season in the holiday parks, so I always knew it would be a great fit for us," he says.

"The venues are set up for the heyday of cabaret and ballroom dancing, so they're perfect. I do like that juxtaposition of raving and seaside resorts, the idea that rave finds a way to exist and pops up in the gaps where opportunities arise. So much of life is about control and order and when you go to a rave, it's a chance to shake all that off and have fun."

The crowd and community following Bang Face are undoubtedly one of the most up for it. Any pretensions are left at the door with the Hard Crew's lust for life, Buckfast and staying up forever, possibly unmatched by any other club crowd. The lack of barriers between those who party and those who put on or play is a key element of the Bang Face experience. You're as likely to be up in the chalet with Altern-8 at 8am on Sunday talking nonsense as chasing your jaw with John Frusciante from the Red Hot Chili Peppers.

"It's definitely the Hard Crew that have driven and evolved the music styles at Bang Face," laughs James. "It's always been a multi-genre event featuring all the different flavours of rave. I love the idea that things change throughout the night and take you on an adventure or journey. Rather than being influenced by what's around you it's more like connecting to what's in your imagination. Like a fantasy or an alternate reality that we can escape to once in a while."

Looking beyond the power of Bang Face and the spirit of the free party continues elsewhere within our cities too. While the Covid-19 lockdowns saw a flare-up of illegal raves in various fields and parks across the UK, other events have taken place in community-owned spaces as private parties. Mailing lists and social media play a key part in building and communicating with a crowd looking for an alternative way of dancing. Across the country, there are pockets of small, dedicated groups pooling resources and ideas and manoeuvring into positions of power in this ongoing struggle to keep and retain spaces. The Rising Sun Collective has been based in south London out of an old pub somewhere between Peckham and New Cross since 2015. Initially, this group of former students at Goldsmiths rented the building as somewhere to record, create, rehearse and party without bothering the neighbours. The former pub was previously let to the collective but now they have ambitions to take on ownership.

"We got lucky and came across this old semi-converted pub in the local estate agent's window," says Scott Bowley from the group on how they tracked down the old boozer. "The building was clearly in need of a fair amount of TLC. There were huge chunks of flooring missing and the carpets and curtains were pretty grim from years of tobacco smoke but we could see the huge potential and instantly fell in love with the place."

The group spent months couch-surfing and waiting patiently for the building to be spruced up enough to be habitable. But when they did move in, they quickly adapted it to their needs. The idea to share the building with others came naturally through pooling their musical resources and the sheer scale of the available space.

"We started inviting friends along to jam in the studio and generally hang out then I guess the word got out that if we dig your creative practice and you're a nice person, this is a place you can come to do your thing," Scott explains. "Before we knew it, we were organising everything from life drawing sessions to full-on underground gigs."

For bands, artists and party promoters, the unique setting gives them the freedom and independence they wouldn't traditionally be able to access without a bottomless budget. Rather than being driven by profit, creatives are given the space and opportunity to let themselves loose on their ideas without any financial inhibitions.

"We've had bands come and rehearse in the basement when they were starting out and then when they're ready, play gigs in the same space," states Scott. "They can take their time to set up over a few days, decorate the space and generally get as comfortable as possible. It's a very different experience from what you'd get at any typical gig venue."

Their events programme has ranged from experimental art-rockers Black Midi taking up a residency to a Boiler Room session with AJ Tracey to film screenings for the Official Nicholas Cage Appreciation society of Peckham and a giant Risk tournament. They've also run a notorious stream of parties. When the collective first moved in, word of their raves spread as far as the Evening Standard, which featured the space in their 'What to do in South East London' guide.

"We started throwing fairly regular house parties almost as soon as we took on the building and word got out pretty quick," laughs Scott. "I remember just a couple of months after moving in, we completely lost control at one of the parties. There were over 300 people in the house and nobody could even move, yet more people kept trying to push their way through the door. After that, we built a little curtained entrance area and started hiring security to man the door who would check everyone was on the list before letting them in."

Recently, the Rising Sun Collective has set about trying to raise enough funds to take ownership of the building after they received notice that it was to be put on the market to sell. After taking advice from architect friend Ed Holloway from BEEP Studio, they decided that establishing their own housing co-op could be an effective way of bringing it under community ownership.

"We wanted to avoid the all too familiar scenario of a cultural space being ripped apart to be turned into luxury apartments," says Scott. "It took us a few months to get to the point where we could put in an offer on the house that the landlord would take seriously and we were very lucky that nobody came in and put in a better offer."

Eventually, they were able to strike a deal thanks to a mortgage in principle letter from the Ecology Building Society and a loan in principle letter from Co-operative and Community Finance. They are currently looking to raise further funds via a community share offer[205].

"Basically anyone can lend the housing co-op money for an agreed fixed term and earn up to 3% p.a. on their investment," Scott explains. "Then, at the end of the term, they get their full amount back on top of the interest. So it's a way that people can support a cultural institution like ours and maybe even make a bit more money on their savings."

The housing crisis in London demonstrates why this co-op model could be the answer. Local Government Association research from 2021[206] has shown how a quarter of a million Londoners are on waiting lists for council houses, with one in ten households waiting for five years or more due to what has been described as a "chronic shortage" of affordable property. In the capital, house prices increased by 62%

between 2010 and 2020. With average deposits almost £110,000 in London, these kinds of sums are well beyond the means of many[207].

"When you take profit out of the equation, there really isn't any need for housing to be anywhere near as expensive as it is in London," argues Scott. "And that's what housing co-ops do. They take all the profit out of the equation, so the property is fully governed by those who live there. The rent can be set at a price that just covers the cost of utilities and general maintenance."

Although community ownership looks like a way forward for both illicit and legal party ventures, some of the originators of the free party scene are unsure about the future of raving outside traditionally co-opted spaces. Regardless, during tough periods, the need for coming together to dance and move is an insatiable one, says Spiral Tribe's Debbie Griffith.

"In times of uncertainty, raving can really bring people together, especially young people who've had a really tough time during Covid-19," she states. "They need to believe in a future. Raving at least for a short period of time enables a connection, spiritual if you like, that gives access to other ways of perceiving and coping with this reality."

Blackburn rave organiser Tommy Smith agrees that the younger generation is up against it with "the current government and the greed and the sleaze", although an underground movement as powerful as that which took off at the end of the eighties might be hard to replicate. Social media and our instantaneous, always-on technology-obsessed world have changed how we live, communicate and engage with each other and the authorities.

"It feels like we are going backwards as a country," Tommy says. "And an underground movement would be tougher now. At the same time, everything is similar in terms of the dissatisfaction amid the political landscape. It just needs someone to come along and throw a match on it like we did."

But whether this revolution comes from dance music or rave culture is difficult to calculate. The world has moved on in the last 30 years and this form of cultural expression is so ubiquitous, it would take some drastic sea-change in our behaviours for it to head underground once again. DiY's Harry Harrison is uncertain about the power of clubs to offer radical innovation or the deep-rooted sense of community in the same way it did in the past. At the same time, an insurgency in our towns and cities could still be en route.

"We were blown away the first time we went to parties and clubs in San Francisco in the early nineties and saw that the clubbers would bring food and supplies for the homeless, the promoters collecting it all for local charities," he says. "But perhaps the location of future youth rebellion lies not around music but around some radical new technology or idea. At that point, the youth may stick two fingers up at us elderly ravers. Quite right too."

# CHAPTER 8

## THE ONLY GOOD SYSTEM IS A SOUND SYSTEM

> *"In the womb, all you can hear is bass through the veins of your mother. Once you're born, there's something inherently comforting about this sound every time you hear it again"* [208]
>
> Paul Huxtable (aka Axis Sound System)

Can you feel it in your chest? In your guts? Does it make your bones rattle?

Whichever way it hits you, the wobble of sound system bass is one of the pillars at the foundation of what we define as UK club culture. Both sonically and culturally, it's a force to be reckoned with as its weight reverberates through the years.

Sound systems originated in the roots reggae and dub music brought to the UK by those who arrived from Caribbean countries, known as the Windrush generation, after the end of the Second World War. Ever since, their influence has been felt within a wide range of bass-heavy music, with these disparate sounds united by the dancefloor. From the "ground zero"[209] of jungle breakbeats first thrown down at Rage at London's Heaven in Charing Cross by Fabio and Grooverider to the speaker-crushing pressure of Croydon dubstep via Rinse FM's fusion of garage, UK funky and grime - you can hear the sound system's fingerprints all over many of today's UK clubs, DJs and electronic styles.

Those initial UK bass moves came from the Jamaicans who landed during the fifties and sixties to help rebuild the UK's infrastructure in the wake of two climatic and deadly World Wars. The majority made the journey, initially "encouraged by poor economic conditions at home and a shortage of labour in Britain"[210]. From 1948 until 1962 and before the Commonwealth Immigrants Act curtailed this free movement, more than 100,000 people from the Caribbean made the journey across the Atlantic. For entertainment, this new population started to gather around speakers set up in houses and basements for so-called blues dances where attendees would pay an entrance fee on the door. It was in the slipstream of the mass migration of Windrush that led to London's spaces "becoming racialised", explains Caspar Melville, Senior Lecturer in Global Creative & Cultural Industries at the School of Oriental and African Studies and author of *'It's a London Thing'*, an account of the Black music culture that emerged in the capital during the latter half of the 20th century.

"Specific official and unofficial forms of racism - from landlords who would not let to Black tenants, to discriminatory employment practices, to the way the police regulated Black movement through stop and search (the so-called sus law), through the over policing of Black leisure venues, all had the effect of creating Black' colonies' in areas like Notting Hill and Brixton," Caspar says.

These areas allowed Black Londoners to find work, security and support networks, but also "a hidden, semi-autonomous, and laterally linked dance music scene around reggae sound systems".

Caspar continues: "These would take place predominantly in unofficial or unlicensed venues as the Black presence in official nightclubs was severely attenuated by racist door policies and quotas. Sound systems colonised squats, private houses at these blues parties, municipal buildings like Wandsworth Town Hall, youth clubs (like Shepherds in Brixton), church halls and turned them into dance halls and night clubs."

Among some of the most prominent sound systems to emerge from this nascent scene include Lloyd Coxsone's Sir Coxsone Outernational Sound System[211]. Lloyd first plugged in and blasted off in London during the latter end of the sixties, while Jah Shaka, Channel One and the Saxon Studio International were other legendary outfits that began fine-tuning their speakers at the same time. As Caspar says, this form of musical expression had to seek its own corners in UK towns and cities, an underground sound run by marginalised groups. Although some systems had towering bass muscles and threatening-looking speakers fighting their corner, their unwieldy physical presence and volume created challenges when finding suitable locations to place their dances.

Dr Julian Henriques, an academic and sound system expert from Goldsmiths, University of London, has written and researched extensively around the scene. "We usually think about places and spaces generating sound but sound also generates space and that is a very important and special thing for people to share and enjoy," he says of the physical sensations the sound system creates.

The communal aspect of the sound system and the safe space it created for this new Black British population came from its roots in the Caribbean. It offered many members of this populace a mode of expression to establish their identities in a strange new world. Those in the dance were reminded of home by the reggae and dub echoing around them.

"It's one thing hearing a sound system in a club," says Julian. "But when you hear where these sound systems come from, in downtown Kingston, you realise that the space and time they generate is the only thing that offers any respite from a ghetto situation with very little in the way of available opportunities."

"The achievement this represents is magnificent, that this grassroots culture, repurposing these commercial amplifiers and remodelling and rewiring them, can generate this amazing shared experience. That's not unique to a sound system, that happens in a good rave or club too but in this setting, there's no element of live musical performance; it's purely phonographic."

Since their inception, traditional sound systems have been operated by a crew including a selector and MC and made up of speakers stacked on top of each other. Julian's research suggests that the sound system goes beyond these tangible components, describing it as "a unique apparatus, a musical medium, technological instrument and a social and cultural institution"[212]. The music it channels, the bass and striking imagery of the monolithic speakers have all infiltrated our culture conscience, captured imaginations and left lasting impressions on minds and ears. Journalist, author and sound system owner Lloyd Bradley describes how this new culture inspired the first DIY efforts in the UK's music scene when it landed in the sixties and seventies.

"The big difference sound system culture made was introducing a DIY ethic to the scene," he states. "Initially, this was through necessity – as in Jamaica where it was born – sound systems had a viable economic platform to support the comparatively cottage industry record business it created, and allowed it to remain underground where it pleased itself and its immediate audience in a far more focussed and direct way than the mainstream. Such self-containedness allowed creativity to blossom without the pressures of having to reach as large an audience as possible."

Sound systems were originally part of the Black community but spread to influence white youth culture during the seventies thanks to the adoption of ska and reggae by mods. This baton was passed between different players in London's music scene, with the likes of DJ Don Letts bringing these scenes together by selecting reggae records alongside punk favourites at the iconic Roxy in Covent Garden[213]. But in much of London during this period, Black people were unwelcome in white nightclubs. So instead, they opted to party in adapted spaces. These wouldn't be located in the undergrowth of the city's landscape. Instead, you'd find them in more mundane settings usually associated with traditional daily activities and behaviours. According to 2021's Dance Can't Nice exhibition at the Horniman Museum in south London, much of the music culture's primordial soup was stirred in "the bedrooms, barbers, churches and living rooms that are home to Black music genres"[214]. The exhibition describes how a "West Indian living room from the 1970s onwards would have been the original dancefloor, a place of pride where music education and celebration collide".

Writer, academic and music industry professional Julia Toppin has a history of going out dancing, working with record labels and as a Music Business Lecturer at the University of Westminster. Her work led to a thesis for her MA on women in drum & bass - *'They're Not in It Like the Man Dem*[215] - with her interests taking her deep into Black music and culture, gender, jungle and more.

"As a kid, I'd always be at parties in people's houses," she says. "My aunt used to live in Elephant and Castle and it felt like she was permanently hosting a party. She'd move the whole flat around to accommodate the speakers."

The city of London certainly enabled a rich variety of sound system styles to emerge; Lovers rock, soul, disco, old school reggae and more. Lloyd Bradley remembers how they rubbed up against each other across an interconnected urban landscape, conducive to the forging of musical networks.

"Even in the seventies, London had pretty decent transport, meaning getting around was easy," explains Lloyd. "When we got cars, there weren't so many that parking was a problem when you got to where you were going - even in Soho. The good thing about this was it kept different areas in touch with each other and people from all over the capital knew each other. My lot from Hornsey and Wood Green would go to parties in Tooting or Barons Court or Bromley, and people from all over would come to ours."

Lloyd continues: "A significant amount of empty properties in London - houses, flats and industrial premises - meant it was relatively easy for sound systems to find somewhere to play without licensing constraints and at maximum profitability. This provided a template for the warehouse party and rave scenes of the 1990s."

Numerous fragments of club music can be traced back to the initial big bang of this sound system scene. Among these sounds are live pirate radio, leftfield broadcasters and myriad online communities that continue to bind music makers, promoters and fans together. It adds up to an independence of spirit instilled in subsequent generations by those original sound system operators and the Black music entrepreneurs who fought to be heard.

"Yes, many clubs had racist door policies, but so what?" Lloyd explains. "As long as I've been raving – since the late sixties – there's always been Black clubs and sound system dances that, to me anyway, seemed like much more fun."

"We knew the clubs which weren't going to let us in and gave them the swerve, so we never felt we were missing out on anything. In fact, the majority of us would treat those Black kids who actually wanted to go to those clubs with no small degree of contempt for it."

DJ, broadcaster and Good Times Sound System operator Norman Jay, has been DJing since he was eight-years-old[216]. Born in west London, he initially soaked up his parents' ska and jazz record collections before heading out to London's West End. Norman's musical life has been closely associated with the Notting Hill Carnival and the soul and disco stompers of Good Times, which debuted at the street party in 1980. Around this time, Norman also began to dabble in promoting warehouse parties, taking advantage of the city's many derelict and abandoned buildings.

"I'd just come back from New York where I felt like I'd seen the future in electro and hip hop," he states. "I got really into these sounds and loved it, although we didn't have much of that in the UK yet. It meant when I'd try and go out to clubs, I'd be bored as I wasn't hearing the music I was searching for. The main creative outlet for me in terms of playing music was at carnival. I started doing warehouse parties in the early eighties too."

Back then, the Black party scene Norman knew was scattered between flats and houses in different parts of west London, including Chiswick and Shepherd's Bush. His warehouse events, billed as Shake and Fingerpop, were an attempt to take advantage of these empty industrial spaces and populate them with the rare groove he'd become known for on the Kiss FM shows he'd started in 1985[217].

"I needed to hook up with some white partners to organise these events, as if I'd tried to do this on my own, it would have been a non-starter," Norman remembers. "So I worked with some white mates who I'd become really close to - a young Judge Jules and Mark Rayner. These middle-class white kids were from Hampstead and Highgate; they did parties with us Black working-class kids - and they instantly went off. We introduced them to a new culture; they introduced us to a whole new crowd of people who were digging our music. It was a symbiotic marriage that really worked."

These parties took place at various illicit venues across London during the eighties. New Year's Eve in 1985 saw Norman take over a carpet warehouse in Acton while another party led to an empty school being utilised for lessons in raving[218]. Casper Melville says that the innovative behaviour of Norman and Soul II Soul's Jazzie B and his parties at the Africa Centre in Covent Garden set a fresh course for the direction of London's nightlife at that time.

"Throughout this period there were, of course, official licensed nightclubs, especially in Soho, and on every high street," he states. "Many of these were significant, and some, like Columbo's on Carnaby Street and the Wag Club on Wardour Street, hosted Black music and Black crowds, but these spaces were always subject to regulation, racial door quotas, changes in management and music policy. They could not always keep up with the rapidly changing music tastes of the audience, so nothing was permanent."

Norman's sets incorporated a broad range of styles, genres, and musical artists at the warehouse events in the darker, more illicit corners of the city. The diversity of sound was reflected in the crowd of dancers all brought together to party under one roof.

"The soundtrack was always Black music, but then I'd bring my punk mates, those who were into football, dress-up, mods and more," he says. "I had an interest in all these subcultures and was able to unite them by mixing up the music. I'd play James Brown next to Paul Weller, mixed with The Clash, early Chicago house and Detroit techno. I broke down all those man-made clubbing constructs."

These parties pre-empted the arrival of house music in the mainstream towards the latter end of the eighties. But when house music did arrive, then take off, the rush was unstoppable and had a decisive impact on Norman's events.

"House music had huge cultural importance but it heralded the death knell for rare groove," says Norman. "Still, in some ways, acid house was the best thing that happened to our scene. It took the spotlight off us and we were able to go back underground again."

"My buzz was getting away with doing parties without the police scuppering them," he continues. "The warehouse idea came out of the frustration for a lot of people of colour and Black kids getting knocked back from certain places in the West End. There was this unspoken racism on the door and I just thought, 'fuck you'."

DJ and producer Ashley Beedle's mother came to the UK from Barbados in 1960[219]. He remembers growing up in Harrow in northwest London among a population of Greeks, Irish and Asian kids.

"We had a plethora of clubs, including the Bird's Nest in South Harrow," he recalls of his early years going out. "They used to run lunchtime sessions. There wouldn't be any alcohol, so we'd have to sneak it in ourselves. The music was amazing; we'd hear tracks like George McRae's *'Rock Your Baby'* and early reggae."

Ashley's parents were armed with what he remembers as an "incredible record collection". This family upbringing, alongside his mother's friends who loved reggae, ska, soul and funk, meant the musical "touch paper had been lit at a very early age". As soon as he was exposed to clubs, Ashley fell in love with the sense of community they created.

"Club culture as we know it comes from the early sixties in the UK," he says. "This mixes damn good music, great friends and drugs. It's an amazing combination. I look back with extreme happiness and fondness as I'm still here doing what I do because of what happened back then. The past has always been part of my future."

Ashley's early escapades as a selector rather than a dancer came to life when he met brothers Dean and Stanley Zepherin at the start of the eighties[220]. After reportedly bumping into each other at parties across west London, the pair invited Ashley to check out the sound system they had inherited.

"Back then, there were plenty of reggae dances taking place around where I grew up," he says. "But we wanted to have fun and hang out with girls. Many of these dances back then were very male-dominated."

The Shock Sound System, initially sketched out by the Zepherins, grew from this idea to push the music beyond reggae to incorporate jazz-funk, disco and soul.

"After I met them, the next thing I knew, we were suddenly organising our own system," laughs Ashley. "The idea was we were gonna come out and shock people with our sound. Initially, we were doing house parties, but then Stan managed to get us a slot at the Notting Hill Carnival. That was amazing and a big change for us, we were in a place called Powis Square, right in its centre. When we started, hip hop and rare groove were prevalent. But we got caught up in early house music and were the first to play it at carnival. Once that happened, it went mental."

While the stories and myths surrounding Balearic night Shoom are plastered all over acid house history, the RIP parties at the nearby Clink Street on London's South Bank are less well-documented and offered a harder musical sound when they kicked off in 1988. Ashley and the Shock Sound System were responsible for hosting the back room while Mr C, 'Evil' Eddie Richards and Kid Batchelor manned the front.

"That's where we honed our craft as DJs, learned how to play to a crowd and select the right records," says Ashley. "Our crowd ran from posh kids to gangsters. Everyone partied together and we'd go on forever. We'd get some crossover with Shoom, too, so people like Mark Moore and Boy George would be there at certain points."

Ashley and the Zepherin brothers also held down a residency at a club on Cold Harbour Lane in Brixton and would head there to play once the dust on Clink Street's dancefloor had settled.

"We'd go down and our warm-up guys were Jumping Jack Frost and Bryan Gee," he says. "They'd be playing Masters at Work records at the wrong speed. It was here where we first heard this initial evolution of what would become jungle and breakbeat coming out of house music. I'd go to Rage at Heaven in Charing Cross and see Fabio and Grooverider, which was really exciting too."

Rage began at Heaven in Charing Cross in 1988 and welcomed dancers and party people every Thursday night. Its influence in terms of the music - a breakbeat laden take on the acid house sound that was beginning to take off across the UK - alongside an eclectic, up for it crowd, touched the lives of many who would leave the dancefloor and go on to become influential producers and DJs. Goldie and Carl Cox were among those to have attained a higher state of consciousness at the club.

"Rage was one of those club events like The Trip at the Astoria, Love at the Wag and Spectrum at Heaven that defined that revolutionary era in the late 1980s/early 1990s when popular culture changed," says Mark Ellicott, Heaven's General Manager between 2009 and 2022.

"If the amphetamine-fuelled fury of punk ten years earlier had been about bile and a nihilistic contempt for the status quo, then this new movement was its flip side," he continues. "The eighties weren't an easy decade for many. Thatcher's government was a grim experience for those who lost their jobs or who had to contend with her government's many prejudices. Hence, I guess, the need for a hedonistic response. A "well, fuck it, let's just party and dance" approach."

Rage initially started with DJs such as Danny Rampling, Trevor Fung and Colin Faver in the big main room with Fabio and Grooverider playing their take on Detroit and Belgian techno upstairs. But such was the potency of their sets and innovative DJing style, the pair were soon moved into the bigger space.

"As time went on, the music they were playing morphed into something new - breakbeats and something which eventually got labelled 'jungle'," says Mark. "It's remembered today because in many ways it broke into new territory that at that point was previously unexplored. I used to come to Rage myself as a newcomer to London back in 1988/9 and remember marvelling at the peaceful co-existence of hip hop heads, techno heads, drag queens and just the plain curious in attendance. There isn't anything remotely like it now."

Metalheadz' DJ Storm describes how Rage at Heaven was one of the key clubs in her dance music initiation. As a co-founder of the label alongside Goldie and her late DJ partner Kemistry, she's played an important and ongoing role in pushing the drum & bass scene forward. It was through Kemi's London friends that Storm ended up at a Rage night.

"I remember when we first went to Rage, you had to get a membership form, complete it, get your photo taken too," she says. "By the time we got into the club, it was the last hour and a half and we heard this DJ called Grooverider. We loved it and started chatting to some other people in the club who told us to get down earlier next time to check out his partner Fabio. At the time, we called this mix of acid house and techno hardcore."

The eclectic sounds Fabio and Grooverider brought together became a deep well of inspiration for Storm and Kemistry. Energised by their visits to Rage, the pair decided to immerse themselves in this rapidly emerging jungle sound.

"Fabio was a house DJ, Grooverider was a techno DJ and they just started mixing the genres together," she says. "The other DJs said you couldn't do it. But we were so impressed, we'd rush to the record shop to try and find out the names of the tunes they'd been playing. We'd try and sing them to the guy in the shop."

From this point in the late eighties, DJ Storm and Kemistry became obsessed with records and raving and started getting to grips with the art of DJing. They met Goldie in the early nineties and took him to Rage to witness Fabio and Grooverider in full flow.

"He didn't quite get it the first time, then we went again and he did," recalls DJ Storm of those fateful nights out. "He was like: 'Right, I want to make this music, you play it, we'll have a record label, we'll have a club, I can do design, we'll have merch, the whole package'. Goldie really spurred us on to be more forthright and creative."

The trio began to put flesh on the bones of the Metalheadz concept through DJing, making and distributing mixtapes and playing sets on pirate radio. Storm's skills as a frenetic selector were honed during those early years of experimenting and ricocheting between the influences of the other DJs and producers surrounding her.

"I've always said Grooverider taught me how to select, Fabio taught me how to tell a story, and Randall put the mix in perspective," she explains. "When he came on, you were like, what is he doing in the mix? You'd be almost scared. Is he going to come out and be on time? But he always did. It was so exciting and that's the one thing I've always maintained about DJing, that live remixing you do in the middle of your set is the ultimate buzz."

Alongside Rage, Metalheadz' Blue Note Sunday sessions in east London were among the most important parties in building a community around the fledgling jungle and drum & bass sound the label explored. Influential drum & bass DJs and producers Photek, Bailey and Dillinja were among those to congregate around the night.

"Me, Goldie and Kemi just lived that Metalheadz dream with the club," Storm laughs. "And when you look back on it, it was almost meant to be. He started the label in '94 and the club came along out of nowhere - they gave us this five-week trial to sell our Metalheadz music."

Hosted at the Blue Note in Hoxton Square, the label's night proved to be an essential hub for the scene in helping establish itself and its associated sound despite some critics who were wary of this supposedly dangerous dance music style.

"It was all very exciting, even though some people said there would be devil-worshipping going down there on a Sunday night at the Blue Note," says Storm. "But in reality, it was just amazing music with a thumping sound system. It was also a chance for DJs to impress with their eclectic tastes. When I play on a Sunday, I find myself being experimental wherever I am. I've taken this from all those Metalheadz parties at places like Dingwalls and the Blue Note. It's ingrained within me."

From classic Doc Scott's *'The Swarm'* and Adam F's *'Metropolis'* to more recent moments from Grey Code and NC-17, the Metalheadz' sound, alongside the rest of the drum & bass scene, has contorted and evolved through a variety of moods, phases and musical territories[221]. Those initial drum & bass tracks, much like other styles of electronic music, would often incorporate different sonic motifs betraying where a producer was from.

"Bristol created the bassline that we'd never heard before," DJ Storm explains. "We were always fascinated to hear a release from Krust or Roni Size. When America first got into d'n'b, they came up with this really apocalyptic take. Then, the Brazilian style from the likes of Marky and XRS featured those beautiful acoustic guitars. You'd drop one of those tunes and we'd be having a party straight away."

Jungle and drum & bass, much like the reggae and dub which precedes it, has an almost physical presence when played through a sound system in a club or rave. For Storm, Goldie's music and DJ sets often occupy more than just the ears but also specific dancefloor areas.

"I think this idea comes from when we'd rave with Goldie and we'd make squares and triangles when we were dancing together," Storm states. "That's what we saw and how we felt it. With his sets and productions, I would always see something. I remember one time when he was playing and managed to make this sound which felt like it came from behind you, then slapped you in the face."

The physical sensation of drum & bass is something DJ Storm continues to crave and relish. More than 30 years after she started DJing, she's still thirsty for the drama this sometimes dirty, chaotic, ruff style of electronic music can create.

"It's made up of all these little elements, bits and pieces of where you come from - there are different influences from what you've grown up with, and what you've subsequently been exposed to," she says of the way inspirations combine to create a whole. "The reggae sound is a pillar of drum & bass - but then you could argue that so is hip hop as we stole all their breaks? Drum & bass is a bastardisation of all sorts of dance music and I love it for that."

DJ Rap stands alongside Storm as a drum & bass and jungle pioneer to emerge from this male-dominated scene. Her childhood was spent travelling the world as her family owned a hotel business before they finally settled in the UK. The first club she remembers heading to was Jacqueline's in London's West End.

"This was the first club I went to," she says. "Then another place was a bar in Peckham called Drovers. This is where I first heard rave tunes. That took me to the acid house scene as a lot of this music grew out of pubs before it headed to the fields."

The big outdoors raves such as Sunrise and Genesis parties of this time were important elements in DJ Rap's musical education. Pirate radio also influenced her tastes before she landed an opportunity to play at the Astoria on Oxford Street in central London.

"In those days, girls weren't allowed to play on the main stage with guys," she says. "I was the first one to get these bookings and get paid the same as the men. That happened at the Astoria when Fabio didn't turn up. I had been pestering the promoter for weeks and weeks to give me a chance. When Fabio failed to show, I got to play his set and it became my first real residency. It was a special place for me."

She also cites the importance of AWOL at the Paradise Club in Islington, north London in turning her on to jungle and the darker side of dance music. Hardcore, the earlier sounds of breakbeat and drum & bass, was initially scattered across various UK clubs but when it morphed into jungle, it became much more London-based.

"In my hardcore days, I'd been to the Eclipse in Coventry, Shelley's in Stoke, clubs like the Que Club in Birmingham was where it was at too," she states.

"For me, I felt like a lot of DJs initially left London as it was outside of the capital where the action was. Then they returned as the music became darker. But everyone has a different experience."

Fast forward to today and the bass-heavy musical culture begun by the Windrush generation has splintered into a kaleidoscope of contrasting musical rhythm and sound. Tottenham DJ Josey Rebelle's sets, whether at festivals such as We Out Here, in clubs like London's dearly departed Plastic People or on Rinse FM, embody this contemporary energy. Her style spans jungle, drum & bass, techno, UK grime and more but with a London ability to connect the dots between them and make them dance. Josey's parents came to the UK as part of Windrush and growing up, her brothers and sisters would always be out raving. A deep passion for music formed within her family meant the club environment was a natural fit.

"When my parents first arrived in the UK, they were keen to build a sense of community so someone would be hosting a house party every weekend," she remembers. "Wedding receptions, christenings, even funerals - there would always be a sound system, there would always be an MC. If someone walked in off the street to some of the funerals I've been to over the last few years, then they would think it was a rave. I've been to some where they would even be playing jungle."

This genre of dance music was Josey's gateway into rave culture, a door shoved open further by London's network of pirate radio stations. Listening to Kool FM and Rush FM meant she could embrace the scene, the DJs and the sounds from a very young age and the music quickly became an obsession.

"Back then, I'd visit record shops, get flyers and plaster them around my room. Pirate radio was really important in making me feel like part of the culture before I was able to go out," she says.

As a teenager, when she did take her love for beats and bass beyond her bedroom, it was to an under 18's daytime rave in Clapton just up the road from where she lived.

"I remember going in there with my friends. It was pitch black with a smoke machine, it was really sick. It was amazing seeing these actual people behind the voices I'd heard on the radio," she says. "The first proper rave I went to, I must have been about 14. Then it was Kool FM parties, Jungle Fever, Telepathy, One Nation, Desire, all the jungle raves everyone used to go to. I was absolutely hooked and was always the first person in the queue, then the last to leave."

Kool FM is London's longest-running jungle station. Founded in 1991 by DJs Eastman and Smurf, it's spent 30 years broadcasting jungle, hardcore and drum & bass from the roofs of flats in Hackney, providing an essential platform for these very distinctive Black British voices to be heard. As a kid growing up, Josey would spend her Sunday evenings listening to pirate radio shows rather than getting a decent night's sleep in time for school the next day.

"I loved it as it did feel like a traditional community radio station, something that really could bring people together," she says. "As well as the music, there was also an open forum where listeners could call in and debate topics about the scene and society. I remember sending in a letter and one of the MCs read it out on air which totally blew my mind."

DJ Wildchild was a Kool FM DJ and one of the few females on the pirate station and in the world of jungle. The scene was and continues to be a boy's club but selectors like Wildchild, DJ Rap and now Josey herself have been crucial figures in opening up the music and making it more accessible.

"Wildchild was a really important influence as it felt like she was someone from just round the way who was DJing on Kool," explains Josey. "Hearing her was the first time it made me feel like girls like me could do this too and play jungle, although it was still many years before I had the confidence to do it."

DJ Rap was another important female inspiration for Josey. But Wildchild's upbringing nearby and ability to circumnavigate the gatekeepers really left an impression.

"DJ Rap was on a bigger level in some ways and a really positive role model but something about Wildchild coming through from pirate radio made it feel more real," she explains. "It's always been a very protective scene from outsiders, so to see Wildchild making her way and seemingly smashing the door down was inspiring for a young girl like me."

Josey's own DJing career has been steadily rising over the last ten years. She found herself a residency on the then pirate station Rinse FM in 2011 and spun low-end theory at essential London clubs, including long-lost basement space, Plastic People. With an ever-increasing profile - in part thanks to her BBC Radio 1 Essential Mix named the best set of 2019 and an accumulation of hyped club bookings - Josey's DJing has taken her to far-flung dancefloors. It's here where her London roots in jungle and pirate radio have been realised and recognised.

"When I'd play internationally, people would come up to me after my set and say how they didn't know me before but could tell from how I played that I was from London," she laughs. "There's a certain energy from growing up DJing in London and being part of that. For me, undoubtedly, it goes back to my parents, being part of the Windrush generation and the sound system at the backbone of club culture in the UK, particularly in the capital. This melting pot of sounds and communities is behind so many of the genres and styles of dance music that we rave to."

This upbringing amidst a rich variety of musical flavours has given Josey and her peers a unique ability to see the links between different styles. To those from other towns or cities, dancehall and techno might appear contrasting, but in London, they slot together to make sense for heads, heart and feet.

"Those connections are obvious to me, even going back to rare groove and how much of an important role it has played in jungle," she states. "I think it's part of growing up in London, connecting the dots between these styles and sounds and creating energy through the different tunes, highs and lows, the bass. That's my thing, that's the UK thing."

Rinse FM is where many may have first encountered Josey, and she's been holding down her celebrated residency for most of the past decade. Outside the dancefloor and inspired by her passion for pirate radio, Josey feels that the commitment of having to deliver a show has led to her elevating her selections and abilities as a DJ.

"Knowing you have to deliver a new show every week means you have this constant deadline to face," she says. "Looking for new music really keeps you on your toes, whether it's brand new or 50 years old. Having your own show is about creating a space to express yourself in. In clubs, it can be harder to play the full range of all the music you love."

She says that although Rinse has grown into this global broadcasting powerhouse, it's still an important player in the make-up of club and rave music. A wealth of DJs from Horse Meat Disco to the Swamp 81 crew have passed through its studio to showcase varying degrees of musical science.

"With my Rinse show, I joined when it had had an FM licence for some time but still had that community feel," she says. "Now, even though it's expanded far beyond London, it's still important and I'm proud to have been with them for so long. Some outside music talk about radio like it's archaic but it's not; it's still alive and giving people the chance to express themselves, share music and build communities and scenes."

Geeneus is Rinse FM's head honcho and a defining figure in bass-driven sounds and London's contemporary musical landscape. As the broadcaster's founder alongside Slimzee, he helped UK funky, grime, and dubstep emerge from London to take on the mainstream via his station's airwaves. In the early days, Rinse was inspired by local broadcasters, including Kool FM and Pressure FM in Bow in east London.

"There were a few of us - me, Slimzee, Target, Wiley - all trying to find a home on radio and we decided to try and figure out how to get our own station," says Geeneus of their beginnings. "One of our friends owned a dub cutting place in Hackney. This is where the old reggae sound system people used to come and cut dubs and they had a link to someone who could get a transmitter. So we figured it out as we went along. We didn't come from a culture of rave; we came from this culture of pirate radio. We'd spend our evenings sitting on the staircases of the estates listening to it."

The pirate radio Geeneus tuned into when he was growing up ably demonstrated what London was, the personalities and characters of the communities and musical styles within them. Everything from UK garage to house and frenetic jungle would be showcased on stations from Rush FM to Deja Vu.

"London was a bit dark, a bit moody, with plenty of exciting things going on behind the scenes. Radio really represented the city for us and helped us to focus on it," he explains.

Geeneus continues: "If you break it down, you could pin sounds to different places. Jungle from Hackney, grime from Bow, dubstep from Croydon. When you think about how big these sounds have become across the world, it's crazy to think about their roots. You can't say grime without thinking of Bow. It's mad that these genres are so massive but it's just a few little estates that created them."

In his early musical days, before launching Rinse in 1994, Geeneus recalls how there was little cross-pollination in musical styles, even between different boroughs.

"We wouldn't really venture too far away from where we were from," he remembers. "To think about going somewhere like south London, it would be a bit like me now thinking about going to Manchester. Certain sounds would come from certain estates too. We'd be on these staircases chatting, then before you know it, every kid in the area is on a particular style. But the rest of the world never got to see it until it exploded out of there."

Word of Rinse was initially spread through family, friends and extended social circles. The DIY ethos at the station's heart was all about a community of people playing the music they were passionate about. But it just so happened that these were the songs and DJs others would fall in love with too.

"We'd have people on, they would tell their mates and suddenly we'd have ten more listeners," says Geeneus. "As we got bigger and better, we'd start transmitting further and word of mouth spread, then more people came on the radio station and told people to get involved and listen. This was pre-internet. Pirate radio is like internet 1.0, the beta version."

During those early days, the Rinse team's desire for finding a space and broadcasting was like an obsession. They would broadcast on-air as long as there was room for them to set up and make it happen.

"We were always desperate to find somewhere to host the shows from," says Geeneus. "One of my friends got his first flat when he was like 16 just as we were about to turn on Rinse. We convinced him to let us use it and luckily, he was on the 14th floor of a tower block in Bow. We ran the wire straight to the top of the block and were there for a couple of months. We'd spend Monday to Friday looking for a studio, set it up on Friday so we'd be ready to go that night. We were relentless."

Part of Geeneus' role with Rinse as it began broadcasting was to avoid being caught by the authorities and having their precious equipment confiscated. This would involve ensuring the transmitter was hidden and nothing of any consequence was in their studio. As challenging as this sounds, Geeneus believes that the arrival of the internet has made pirate radio and the music industry Rinse FM inhabits trickier to navigate than ever before.

"It was complicated back then but now it's more complex than ever," he laughs. "These days, you're competing with the whole world as it's become local to you. We're in this big ocean of radio, music, and platforms like Spotify. There's no real home scene where you can grow and mature. Which is a shame. I know the world moves on but when we started out, we could just concentrate on doing one thing really well. Now you have to focus on Instagram, Facebook, radio, live streams and everything else."

At the heart of Rinse and Geeneus is a restless desire to innovate, to embrace new technologies to get their message and music heard by as many people as possible. It's this commitment that has seen their venture grow from pirate radio to becoming a powerful multi-media brand.

"People criticise you for moving on," Geeneus explains. "When we went online, there was a backlash. But people have to understand we will use whatever tools we have to show people the music and talent we want them to see. Rinse is a London-based, British culture, underground-led music platform and we have changed as the city has. From jungle to grime, via funky, it's all about what's going on on the street."

Rather than resting on their laurels of past achievements, this process of evolution is a concept Rinse is constantly focussed on. Geeneus is always looking to what's next in a bid to take the brand into the future.

"It's not about the result; it's about the journey, so for me, to get someone like Katy B to sell three million records is amazing," he says. "I believed in her talent and we sent her music to labels but they weren't interested. So to release it ourselves and get a massive hit is great. I don't think we're sellouts. We took someone great from the underground and helped them on their way to the top. If I can keep doing that, then I will."

Cultural critic and professor at King's College London, Paul Gilroy, came up with the concept of 'Black Atlantic' to delineate a distinctively modern, cultural-political space. "This is not specifically African, American, Caribbean, or British, but is, rather, a hybrid mix of all of these at once"[222] and something the sound system exists in today. While the sound system has and continues to hold great sway over the bottom-end of certain modes of club music, the traditional form persists too. Albeit, fighting to keep its speakers above water.

"We're starved of venues," says Dr Julian Henriques. "It's similar to the ways in which clubs are suffering, as the planning laws promote gentrification ahead of local community interests. But there's a real lack of available spaces for sound systems right now. Before, there was also the infamous 696 form[223], used by the police to inhibit Black music. This would put a heavy onus on promoters and venue owners to complete all kinds of paperwork and was another way of attacking and suppressing the culture."

In Jamaica, many of the dances and sound system operators can avoid the challenge of securing a venue thanks to the warmer climate. Instead, many dances can be held outdoors without the risk of rain stopping play.

"In the Caribbean, you don't have these problems as you can play outside all year round," says Julian. "That is a big plus, although there are still struggles in Jamaica in terms of the noise abatement act, and the police can lock down your dance."

Issues for sound systems in the UK looking to put on dances in cities and town centres are around noise. Negotiating with the authorities over the volume of a dance is a key stumbling block for many promoters wanting to host an event in a town or city.

"As the sound system scene is a grassroots one, you'd expect it to clash with the authorities - and it does," Julian says. "You need to guarantee certain noise levels, which is a big challenge. The big dances like Channel One have infrastructure in place to do this but for the smaller ones, it's a nightmare."

Another ongoing problem for today's sound system operatives and dance organisers is regenerating audiences to attract a younger crowd. Julian says he's concerned that the scene could be at risk of dying out if the best spaces to entice the next generation of music fans can't be found.

"Younger music lovers might be into grime or drill, and these scenes have a heritage connected to reggae and sound systems," he says. "However, the average young Black person has never set foot in a dance. So if we're not able to find the venues to attract them, then it is in danger."

Despite the risks sound system culture faces, different UK towns and cities have strong scenes surrounding them. London might have had a higher proportion of Windrush immigrants and associated sound systems but towns and cities across the UK have welcomed them too. Location and environment are crucial for the participants within this musical world.

"There are strong connections with sound systems which are similar to how football fans follow their local club," he says. "You have a geo-location of passion and you support your club or your sound. Historically, Huddersfield was very central to the British sound system scene in the eighties and nineties. Bristol has a strong music scene with connections to sound systems in terms of trip hop and dubstep. Nottingham and Birmingham have plenty, too, while Glasgow has the brilliant Mungo's Hi-Fi."

April Grant - known as sound system operator Rusty Rebel - is one of the current wave of female sound system owners doing her best to stake out new territory for women in what has long been a very male-dominated musical scene. Based in Birmingham in the Midlands, her Rebel Rock Sound System has been rolling since 2015 and has taken her across the UK and beyond to play at dances[224].

"It is a discriminatory thing," she says of the sound system gender imbalance. "I've previously experienced someone saying that I should just play with women and we should have our own dances but I don't think that's right. It's unfair that anyone would want to stifle the growth of women in this scene by not allowing us opportunities. Music does not have a gender, so the scene needs to be more inclusive."

April's first musical adventures began on pirate radio, including stations such as the People's Community Radio Link and Metro.

Alongside broadcasting, her expertise extends to sound engineering and a deep knowledge of the technical side of her audio equipment.

"It started in my pirate radio days, I just loved all the music but I realised that I really loved reggae," April states. "I saw connections with some of the pop and soul/reggae, even music that had made it into the charts."

Her Rebel Rock Sound System is an extension of the roots music shows she would play on the pirates and is named after a reggae riddim. While April's sound system has travelled to France, Amsterdam and Switzerland, alongside UK spots including the Custard Factory in Birmingham and the West Indian Club in Hornsey, her sets are more an expression of her own emotions to show how she feels rather than a connection to a specific location.

"With roots, I'd always just play what I thought I should to get my message across," she explains. "The location has never impacted me in that way and I would play some of the same tunes regardless of where I was as long as it captured what I was thinking and wanted to express. It's all about what I'm trying to say."

There are discernible regional differences in style among the musical genres associated with sound system music. According to Rusty, Birmingham is the roots capital of the UK, while Wolverhampton and Leicester have important scenes too.

"Leicester has a vibrant culture of sound systems, particularly as it has more spaces which will accept them," she says. "London is influenced more so by other genres - soul and lovers rock for example - there are other influences within roots. Those influences, wherever they are coming from, are slightly diluting the sound. Here in Birmingham, the sound is unadulterated hardcore reggae."

Like Julian, April is concerned by the lack of spaces for hosting dances. Traditionally, community halls have welcomed events inside them but she fears their number is diminishing, meaning the sound system is struggling for air in our cities and towns.

"Without these kinds of halls, it's tougher for sound systems to express who they are," she says. "The venues need to be protected; otherwise, the scene is going to fade. In another 10/20 years, our children won't be interested. If we don't have sound systems in these community centres where people can access it, it will die."

"You have Star Trek conventions - so why don't we have our own too?" April laughs. "If we could put on daytime events, then we could avoid any potential noise issues without compromising on the sound. As a community, it's down to us to ensure it doesn't disappear for good. We're in the minority when you think about the music industry. If you lose it, young people will never understand that this has been an important part of their culture."

The Axis Valv-a-tron Sound System calls the Yorkshire town of Huddersfield home and is run by audio expert Paul Huxtable. The market town has had a long history connected to sound systems with dances held in its basements and back rooms from the sixties and seventies with a series of reggae stars, including Jimmy Cliff and Burning Spear, all visiting and performing. They would often play at the Silver Sands Nightclub on Venn Street[225], a route within the city that provided a place for Black music in the heart of Huddersfield's nightlife. The town was home to around 30 different sound systems during its heyday[226]. Although the scene is not as fertile as it once was, Paul is working hard to continue to spread the word. He runs events as the Axis Valv-a-tron Sound System, custom-builds speakers and systems and with Mandeep Singh wrote *'Sound System Culture: Celebrating Huddersfield's Sound Systems'*, a history of the town's relationship with this form of music culture.

Since he was a kid, Paul has been fascinated by the concept of sound reproduction. From building an intercom system between his and his sister's bedrooms as a youth, as he grew up, he became deeply immersed in tape recording, sound and PA systems.

"It's the way my brain is wired," Paul says. "Back then, the only way you would be exposed to bass was at a fairground, a cinema, or a church organ and I was really intrigued by all three experiences."

Growing up in Preston, his first dalliances with sound systems were at venues in the town such as the Caribbean Club and Jalgos. He then worked in the Paradise Club, where he would serve pints from behind the bar at dances too. A subsequent trip to St Lucia crystallised his love of reggae and ambitions to develop his own system.

"I went to St Lucia for 12 months, then came back and built what I called the Axis Valv-a-tron Sound System," he says. "I wanted to play old reggae music, so tunes from the sixties, seventies and early eighties, pre-digital, as that's where my heart was. I was a joiner by trade, so that came in handy when building all the boxes and speakers. I played that around Preston and no one was interested in the old reggae at the time. They are now but back then, it was seen as grandad music."

As the internet took off, Paul's reputation for his bottomless record collection, DJ sets, and the system began to spread, leading to bookings across Europe. His older reggae style also became popular, which fortuitously aligned with his tastes and the impressive archive of music he'd amassed.

"Now I build electronics, speakers, and whole sound systems," he says. "I left the building trade, and my full-time job is constructing amplifiers in the old fashioned way, so working on valve amps, valve equipment and early pre-amps, all the gear the old reggae guys used to use."

Paul initially aimed to move to Leeds from Preston but didn't find it to his tastes. Instead, he was drawn to Huddersfield by its smaller size, cheaper housing and more vibrant reggae scene.

"This was eventually run down by out of towners coming in and ruining the dances," he says. "But I've been here 25 years now. I like the attitude and how towns like Huddersfield are smaller, friendlier, cheaper, and easier to live in. There's more of a sense of community than in a bigger city."

In the reggae sound system world, Paul describes how there are disparate different styles within it, all striving to be heard, although some are far louder than others. From the digital roots of Iration Steppas and Aba Shanti-I to sound systems pushing lovers rock and the soul and old-school reggae preferred by him.

"Sound systems such as Iration Steppas are so powerful that only a few venues are capable of handling them," Paul says. "These spaces are usually big, in the middle of nowhere and are expensive to hire due to their size. So the scene is now split between large scale and more intimate events. My revival sound system events are at this 120 capacity venue in Huddersfield. I've played to 2,000 people in a tent at a festival but these days, I prefer playing events which feel more personal."

In today's musical world, the audience's make-up and behaviours surrounding sound system events are changing. A crossover in tastes with techno-loving ravers has meant some sound system fans want their music to be heavier and more propulsive.

"There's this speaker worshipping in Europe which comes from white people who previously followed house and techno," says Paul. "They like the energy levels to be high, a kick drum on every beat and the music to be full of exciting, stimulating sounds; otherwise, they get bored. There's definitely a connection between rave and UK roots steppas alongside the free parties of the nineties."

Paul's own dances exist amid a more meditative space and tempo. Rather than thrashing the ears and bodies of attendees with bass, his events focus on audio quality to reveal the nuances of the music and the messages.

"My music is more about what they call 'the one drop' in reggae," he explains. "This is where I drop the bass and kick drum on the third beat of every four. It leaves you in a different place after four hours of this when compared with more aggressive sounds. I play a lot of tunes about love, peace and harmony, and that actually has an effect on people in the dance. At my dances, I get everybody from 16-year-olds to 66-year-olds. I'm into humans and if you're human, you can come in as long as you behave yourself."

Paul's experiences with sound systems suggest that getting the most from them is easier to achieve when hosted in their original home of Jamaica. As most of the dances take place outside in high humidity, this can help realise a better audio quality.

"As sound waves travel, they are often arrested by this bulk of humidity," he explains. "It's like having a crowd in front of the boxes; it sucks up the direct reflection and colouration of the sound. Here, we're usually always inside because of the weather - so it's always been harder to get a natural sound indoors. It's better when you have more people in there as they act like acoustic sponges to stop reflections."

He continues: "Getting the mid-range right is as important as the bass. It's the most difficult frequency to get correct. But it's an important frequency as the voice is the main communicator and lives there with the instrumentation too. When I listen to my speakers, I'm always looking for good clarity, presence and warmth."

Paul believes that the concept of the dance predates technology, going back to the early days of mankind. The energy and emotions created by people coming together create a "natural phenomenon" that far surpasses the individual.

"When I go to town and play a sound system, this is no different to what cavemen did around the fire hundreds of thousands of years ago," he says. "Sound systems, rave culture, reggae, whatever form this takes, it's still ultimately a mix of heavy rhythmic repetition and storytelling. This is as old as mankind itself."

The concept may have been with us for thousands of years but that's not to say bass lovers or sound system operators are incapable of embracing the future. Roots revival music is what April Grant's Rusty Rebel Sound System is known for but she's expanded her musical community by adapting to the digital world. April took her music online during the pandemic.

"No one really considered this before but it has worked really effectively," she says. "Broadcasting is very compelling and has grown quickly over the past year or two. It has become a really important community, especially with viewers interacting. It's as though we're gathering in a great space of like-minded music lovers."

For jungle, drum & bass heads, Julia Toppins cites the power of online and social media networks in bringing people together and fostering a renewed sense of community around the scene. Partly fuelled by the pandemic, this new digital version of rave culture is more inclusive than ever before.

"Online has created all these pockets of communities which is brilliant," she says. "It's brought all these people together who would have previously lost touch. I think this jungle revival has been powered by Facebook groups or people chatting on Twitter; you can access things on YouTube now. My friend Penny [Wickson] was talking about a track from this EP by DJ Marky. I went straight to YouTube and found it, whereas before, I wouldn't have been able to access it. This is a great thing. It's opened up the music and democratised the elite DJ culture of the peak rave era."

Since the pandemic hit, DJ Rap has utilised online opportunities to maintain energy and engagement surrounding her music. After she moved back to the UK, Covid-19 suddenly wiped out months of bookings and work. In response, she was among the first to launch a home entertainment online subscription platform for fans on her website to create and develop a close-knit community around her music by offering exclusive content.

"It's been amazing for me and just goes to show that you have to embrace change," she says. "If I see a wave coming, I'm not going to dive into it - I'm going to ride it all the way to the beach. By setting up my own platform, I'm less reliant on other social media platforms. I have a new community of fans I'm deeply connected to. It's a full-time day job but it's been wonderful for me and really satisfying."

These examples show how the combination of music and networks can have a hugely positive and important role in community-building. It takes us full circle to the arrival of the sound system in the UK and its importance to Britain's Black communities in facilitating different forms of creativity.

"The sound systems became an important cultural expression," says academic and dance music expert Caspar Melville. "They were a creative industry, technology lab, popular art studio, political forum, spaces of conflict, love and joy, at the very heart of Black London but open to all and the most important influence on the musical culture of the city."

This ability to harness innovation and bring people together has always been at the centre of the UK's sound system culture and its longevity. Despite their mighty physical presence, this form of musical expression has been highly adaptable to the spaces it has found and called home. Author, journalist and sound system owner Lloyd Bradley goes back to how the DIY operations surrounding them saw new technology as opportunities rather than threats, whether it be pirate radio to music making software such as Garageband beloved by some producers.

"It allowed their efforts to reach a far larger audience than their dances, and they tapped into the notion that the British music-buying public is far more adventurous than the big record companies had been giving them credit for," he explains. "By staying true to the sound system way of doing things and keeping things in-house – a significant proportion of grime, garage and jungle artists have sound system backgrounds or heritage - the likes of Congo Natty, Dizzee Rascal, Skepta and so on have been able to keep what they do fresh and fearless."

Producers of lovers rock reggae along with the junglists and grime stars have always had an urge to hone their music on their own terms and let the mainstream come to them rather than the other way around. This independent spirit defines the sound system culture and its standing in our ears and eyes.

"People like Soul II Soul's Jazzie B knew urban culture in the UK was changing as they'd grown up with it and was hitting so many youngsters," says Lloyd. "The underground knew it was simply a matter of time before the large audiences picked up on what they were doing and the mainstream was forced to play catchup. The likes of Jammer, Stormzy and Shut Up & Dance held all the cards; it's a bit of a myth that they need anybody's sympathy or help."

# CHAPTER 9

## FUTURE, PAST AND PRESENT SOUNDS OF LONDON

*"It's the clubs that make property prices go up. They pull people in, then they get booted out. I've seen it happen in the East Village in New York, Shoreditch, Hackney and now in Tottenham. It happens time and time again"*[227].

Colleen 'Cosmo' Murph

"London's urban environment, how it has been developed over centuries and how it has been regulated has, of course, been critical to the kinds of musical culture that have emerged from the city."

Caspar Melville, academic and author of dance music history, *'It's a London Thing'*, is reflecting on the relationship between the capital's sprawling geography and the genre-bending club culture it is so revered for. As the biggest city in the UK with a population of more than nine million and rising[228], it is also the busiest too. London's population density is 5,701 people per square kilometre, a figure some ten times higher than that of England's second-most densely populated region in the north-west[229]. With such a wealth of people and space, London is undoubtedly one of the world's leading cultural hotspots, defined by a rich diversity of musical styles, locations and artists. It's drawn up by those born here but also by the many outsiders who flock to it and adopt it as their home. As the late, great poet Benjamin Zephaniah says in *'London Breed'*: "The music of the world is here, The city can play any song, They came to here from everywhere, 'Tis they that made the city strong."[230] But each of the 33 boroughs has its own local council alongside the Greater London Authority. With so many stakeholders involved in planning and development, the city's hefty size is reflected in its chaos and unwieldy infrastructure.

"London is a hodgepodge, a patchwork; you might say it's a bloody mess," Caspar says. "It has never been subjected to the kind of grand rationalising design like the one which transformed Paris in the 1860s; it continues to be a mixture of mediaeval lanes and alleys, industrial buildings, housing estates, corporate developments and very un-joined up local authority schemes."

According to Caspar, there has been an ongoing tension between legal and unlicensed venues for parties in the city for years, with the music played, heard and danced to in illicit spaces usually the more future-forward sounds lighting up the path ahead. London's acid house scene might have taken off in clubs like Ziggy's in Streatham or the Astoria on Tottenham Court Road during the eighties but it was in the illegal spaces where it began - they "were more exciting, freer and more musically innovative".

"But following the concentrated effort to stamp out rave in the early 1990s, and the simultaneous rewriting of the licensing laws which created 24-hour venues like Turnmills and Ministry of Sound, rave moved back inside licensed nightclubs," continues Caspar. "The economic and racial diversity of London, the rises and falls in its economic fortunes which opened up empty space for club culture, the unplanned nature of its infrastructure, the sheer number of people and creativity to tap into from all over the world; all have had a direct impact on the shape and development of club culture in the city."

Suppose you're looking to find a visual representation of the rate of change in London's ever-shifting urban landscape and its subsequent impact on nightclubs. In that case, the area surrounding St Pancras and King's Cross station is as good a starting place as any. Visitors entering the city by train - either from Europe or elsewhere within the UK - are now greeted by a gleaming new gateway that contrasts sharply with its former self. Now home to Google, Facebook and Universal Records[231], the area's £3 billion facelift has been in development since 2000[232]. This fresh glossy incarnation, led by developer Argent, is at odds with its grimier past as a red light district and home to some of London's best night-time spaces, including long lost clubs The Cross, The Key and Bagley's. Not only has this project created a radical reperception of this part of London over the last decade but demonstrates just how quickly such a transformation can happen. Argent is currently getting its teeth into reimagining Tottenham Hale, a few miles to the east of King's Cross, where similar fresh starts are promised and more than 1,000 new homes set to be unveiled[233].

"I remember King's Cross used to be as shady as fuck in the nineties," laughs DJ, producer and record label boss Luke Solomon. "It would be a bit scary if you ever found yourself in an altercation."

Luke heads up Classic Records, is closely affiliated with Defected Records and has been a lynchpin in London's electronic music scene for more than 20 years, both on and off the dancefloor. His formative raving experiences were in the West Country before he was sucked into London's booming nightlife and clubs, including Bagley's, Bar Rumba, The End and Ministry of Sound. He remembers King's Cross as a creative if slightly gritty hub for dance music during the nineties before Argent's redevelopment started.

"After me and my DJ partner Kenny Hawkes met on pirate radio station Girls FM, we did these Jelly Parties," he says. "They took their name from ecstasy made in a gelatin form which was a thing for a minute as it supposedly helped with any come down. But we did these in a film studio round the corner from Bagley's where we had to support the ceiling with scaffolding. The whole area was quite a hive for DIY club culture and even though they were proper venues, they were always a bit rough around the edges. They were organic places to party and all the better for it."

The clubs located in King's Cross closed their doors during the winter of 2007 with a series of final raves to send them off. But since the redevelopment, the area has been overhauled and is far less frightening. The site where Bagley's once used to welcome thousands of ravers over a weekend is now home to Coal Drops Yard. This new shopping destination is named after the huge railway sheds located here during the nineteenth century for coal storage and distribution. As eye-opening as the revamp looks, this cycle of regeneration with clubs having to head to the outskirts is a familiar story, taking place in many big cities from London to New York and beyond.

"It's similar to Soho in central London too," says Luke of the tensions between the city's geography and nightlife. "Many London clubs have had to look elsewhere in the same way that promoters in New York are now having to go beyond Williamsburg to host their parties. I feel there's a level of economic sustainability which can only go on for so long before these places change again."

The West End, loosely defined as the areas surrounding Oxford Street, such as Holborn and Covent Garden, has long been associated with the starry eyes of bright nightlife, particularly around the network of tiny streets that make up the sparkling yet crooked vibes of Soho. Crackers was a seventies club on Wardour Street in the heart of this area and, from first glimpse, resembled a slightly rum-looking disco. But it was this unassuming venue that set alight the music careers of many of London's most important DJs and electronic music players.

As young clubbers, drum & bass hero Fabio, Soul II Soul's Jazzie B, Norman Jay and Terry Farley all visited the venue to hear resident DJ Mark Roman play an upfront mix of jazz-funk, soul and disco.

"Crackers in Soho between 1975-78 is one of the most important clubs for me," says Terry. "The West End, like most of the UK, certainly had a door policy of restricting the amount of Black lads admitted on one night. The Crackers DJs Mark Roman, then George Power demanded this stop and, to my knowledge, made it the first West End club to drop those policies."

Ashley Beedle was among those who visited Crackers for their Friday lunchtime sessions when George Power was the main DJ. He would head to school in the morning, then disappear into the West End at lunchtime to listen to the mix of disco, jazz and funk played at Crackers.

"By 11 in the morning, I'd be in the toilets getting changed, then sneaking out of the school gates to get from Harrow to the West End," remembers Ashley. "Quite a few of us would go, so there would be plenty of empty seats in the classroom in the afternoon."

"But that's where I met people like Norman Jay and Terry Farley," he continues. "I remember having a tiny notebook and a pencil and I'd go up to the DJ booth. Paul 'Trouble' Anderson was George Power's boy/apprentice at the time and I'd ask him what the tunes were and write them down. It was amazing because it was such a mixed crowd. Then after you'd been, you'd hang out in the West End and search for the records you'd heard."

DJ and broadcaster Norman Jay admits to being a serial clubber from the mid-seventies and visited many important nights, including Crackers alongside parties at the 100 Club on Oxford Street to follow DJs including Mark Roman and Greg Edwards.

"The music in London back then was so upfront and the idea of a disco club really came of age at that time," he states. "Mark Roman was an institution at Crackers, as was Ronnie L at the 100 Club and Norman Scott at the big Global Village club under the arches at Charing Cross. That was a really important venue with Norman playing a proper mix of gay disco."

Global Village operated between 1973 and 1979 as a roller disco, cinema and location for the filming of various movies and television series from that period before opening its doors again as another nightclub, Heaven. According to Mark Ellicott, Heaven's previous General Manager, the structure wasn't purpose-built as a club. Instead, it used to be a warehouse owned by Charing Cross station, located directly above the club.

"The part of Heaven now known as the Stage Bar (previously known as Sound Shaft in the eighties and nineties) was used as a mortuary during the First World War," says Mark of the club's past lives. "The bodies of British and Irish soldiers who died on the battlefields of France and Belgium during the conflict would be returned to Charing Cross and stored there before being repatriated."

From Mark's 13 years in post, it seems this past has quite literally continued to haunt the building. Despite being a self-confessed sceptic when it comes to supernatural occurrences, he says that there have been dozens of "unexplained incidents" over the years.

"I have struggled to rationalise many of them," Mark explains. "Seeing figures (invariably young men dressed in what is sometimes described as 'period' costume or 'old fashioned military gear') that dart through doors or behind bars and then seemingly disappear, sudden drops in temperature, shimmering black shapes moving around, objects moving without any force seemingly applied to them. There is a distinct 'atmosphere' in the venue that even those without any belief in the afterlife notice."

Unsettling paranormal activity aside, the opening of Heaven represented a huge step forward for London nightlife, a space that became a "focal point for what had until then been a fairly understated gay scene"[234]. The club was opened in 1979 only 12 years after homosexuality between consenting adults aged over 21 had been decriminalised. However, "the stigma and prejudice associated with homosexuality in 1979 weren't so very different from 1967," and gay nights up to this point were hidden away. Heaven responded by flinging its doors open to welcome as many queer revellers as it could.

"Heaven was unashamedly a gay club and a haven for many as it was the one place they could openly be themselves without fear of judgement or the threat of violence," says Mark. "There wasn't a precedent for Heaven. It was the first. And when you're the first, you can lay claim to leading the pack thereafter."

London's nightlife at the end of the seventies and early eighties was gradually becoming more colourful, particularly in and around Soho, an area referred to by the Wag Club's Chris Sullivan as a "a vice-infested square mile that housed a red light above every door and on every floor"[235]. Since the 1700s, word of its notoriety for drinking dens, music halls and sex has spread, with the first brothel appearing in Soho Square in 1778[236]. Artists and creatives have continually run amok through its tight, yet unruly avenues while it's also a home for the LGBTQIA+ community with venues like Comptons[237], which renamed itself from the Swiss Tavern in 1986, operating as dedicated queer spaces. Within this world of smoky rooms, late nights, and debauchery, DJ and S'Express producer Mark Moore enjoyed his first taste of nocturnal thrills.

"The first club I ever went to was with a friend of mine called Bowie Teresa who said we had to go to this club in Soho," he remembers. "She said it's full of freaks, socialites, prostitutes, dykes, punks. It turned out to be Billy's run by Steve Strange and Rusty Egan playing music."

Opened in 1978[238], Billy's was the precursor to the infamous Blitz club and featured a cast of brightly drawn characters such as Boy

George and Marilyn dancing to a soundtrack of David Bowie, Roxy Music and Yellow Magic Orchestra, all spun by Rusty Egan. Bedazzled by this world, Mark immersed himself in the capital's clubbing music scene, falling for alternative soundtracks created by DJs 'Evil' Eddie Richards and Colin Faver at the Camden Palace. Their sets would feature music from artists including Soft Cell and Killing Joke, as well as proto-house tracks from the Peech Boys and Gwen Guthrie.

"Colin is so overlooked as a DJ and his contribution to the house explosion. He's one of my biggest influences," explains Mark. "They'd be playing such amazing music and he and Eddie were mixing as well, which a lot of people weren't doing at the time."

Mark's first forays into DJing started in 1983 at Philip Sallon's Mud Club before Heaven asked him to play at their night Asylum, later known as Pyramid. His crowd was more style and fashion-orientated, but increasing numbers of imports from Chicago and Detroit began to creep into his sets as he continued to DJ. This new house sound fit seamlessly with the fashionable electronic music he was already playing.

"We were one of the first London clubs to host nights where lots of house music was played," Mark explains. "In the early days, the established music business wanted house music to take off and really pushed it. If you look at The Face and i-D, there were articles on the scene there from around '85 or '86. But after the success of hits like *'Love Can't Turn Around'* and Steve' Silk' Hurley's *'Jack Your Body'*, it didn't really happen and was left to go underground before it returned again."

The impact of AIDs during the mid-eighties before the house music explosion cast a long shadow over London's nightlife during the decade. Mark remembers that the initial craziness of the style party scene was tempered and people started disappearing.

"Sometimes you'd just never see them again," he says. "AIDs hit badly in the mid-eighties, and it became very dark and depressing for a while. There was this real sense of people who were known for dressing up freakily no longer wanted to."

During this period, acid house continued to bubble in London as well as other parts of the country. Mark's Pyramid night was well-attended and saw Mr C, who would later go on to enjoy chart success with The Shamen, rapping over the microphone before leaving the club in the morning to tend to his milk round. Other increasingly popular parties included Shoom at the Fitness Centre and Delirium at the Astoria from Noel and Maurice Watson. But it wasn't until 1987 that it really began to bubble over. Mark remembers how DJ Paul Oakenfold hosted his Spectrum night at Heaven on a Monday, initially only attracting a few hundred people. But word quickly spread and attendance ramped up rapidly, demonstrating just how infectious acid house could be.

"Monday was the only night they could get at the venue and to start with, there weren't many people there," says Mark. "It was a brilliant night despite this lack of attendees. Then the next week, the amount of dancers had doubled, then within four weeks, there were queues around the block. House music went crazy after brewing and brewing for all this time.

Alongside Spectrum, Nicky Holloway's night The Trip at the Astoria and Danny Rampling's Shoom all added to the intensity of house music's arrival on the capital's clubbing scene. As The Grid and Beyond The Wizard's Sleeve, Richard Norris is a DJ, producer and journalist whose career has spanned all of dance music's contemporary timeline. He distinctly remembers the transformation house music wrought on London's club scene.

"There was a sudden change in the sound. The more mainstream West End clubs were playing rare groove but this shifted in a matter of months and suddenly everyone was playing house music," he says. "The different clubs had their own individual vibes. Spectrum at Heaven would have this sense of drama and an amazing sound system. One of the opening tracks would be A Split Second's *'Flesh'*, which was this really theatrical new beat tune."

In contrast, Shoom was a much smaller, more intense affair, famously held at the old fitness centre on Southwark Street close to London Bridge. The combination of dry ice, heat and hypnotic beats conjured up a different yet equally special experience.

"You'd barely be able to see in front of you and they'd play these acid records, tracks like *'Work it to the Bone'*," says Richard. "They'd have locked grooves and be more trance-inducing alongside other poppier tunes. There's definitely something about certain types of music working in a particular club setting."

The impact of house music and the strong bonds it forged is something Richard has experienced throughout his life. The enduring longevity of some of those friendships made on the dancefloor is at odds with the transience of the club settings where they were created.

"You'd be out walking and see someone in a Spectrum t-shirt, so you'd definitely notice the lesser spotted acid house aficionado out in the wild," he laughs. "It's interesting how the memories people have are so strong; they run deeply and are held for a long period of time. But then the places themselves are temporary, full of smoke, mirrors and have this haziness around them. I've made friends for life in the club and know 100s of people through 30 odd years of clubbing. Yet, I hardly know anyone from school."

More than three decades later, Heaven still has a place in Mark Moore's heart. For him, the most magical and special venues have always been on the fringes of mainstream culture.

"The best club nights took place in spaces that either shouldn't function as a club night or attract those who weren't welcome anywhere else," he says. "Or it might be at a club that was magical for one particular party, but then when you went again, it would feel like an unfaithful lover and be doing something musically you wouldn't approve of."

Alongside the legitimate clubs of the eighties, the underground warehouse party scene was also in full swing in London, with illicit events taking place within its many nooks and crannies. Abandoned spaces such as shopping centres or old factories would be hijacked for various party antics.

"These nights would be amazing as they would feel so risky," Mark says. "There would be holes in the floor where you could potentially fall to your death. No one cared about health and safety, which made it really exciting. The Mutoid Waste parties in warehouses were legendary too. I'd be DJing in one corner; there would be a huge fire in the middle of the room, then Soul II Soul's Jazzie B in another part of the space. At the same time, you can have a great venue, a state of the art sound system, but if you've got a shit crowd, it's no good. It's the people that make it for me."

Located south of the Thames, Elephant and Castle is another area of London going through significant changes. The old shopping centre was why many knew and loved this part of the capital but was sadly demolished in 2021[239]. A new town is now under development with part of the plan focused on overhauling the tube station and the new London College of Communication unveiling, slated for 2030[240].

Nightlife has been an integral reason why you might be tempted to visit this part of the capital. The art deco theatre, The Coronet, was a brilliant space for big, one-off club nights with the likes of house music hero Armand Van Helden tearing it in two back in 2010. Nearby, the raw, smokier vibes of Corsica Studios loiter under an archway and consistently pull in more underground and leftfield DJs and producers.

The club is a favourite of Lukas Wigflex who has played and promoted plenty of parties there including a 24 hour event with Niche favourite Big Ang.

"It's run by a mate of mine who I know through Nottingham who used to manage Stealth," he says. "It's a simple, no frills venue, underneath the arches, massive sound system, it's dark, the lights are subtle, they do it for the right reasons and are real heads. They are artists putting on parties as opposed to business men."

Ministry of Sound is a very different nocturnal beast despite living only a few minutes away on Gaunt Street. This nightclub offered a state-of-the-art clubbing experience when it opened back in 1991. More than 30 years later, it is a global, multi-media brand. This venture initially stemmed from the brain of DJ Justin Berkmann, a young raver who had his mind blown by the energy and excitement of nightlife experiences in eighties New York.

"We went to some of the best parties and incredible clubs like Save the Robots, the White Party at the Saint and Paradise Garage," he says. "I came back to the UK really inspired to find that there were brilliant parties kicking off here too."

Justin timed his UK return impeccably. Almost as soon as he stepped off the plane, the acid house scene was beginning to ignite among those in the know. Nights including Shoom, Delirium and Hedonism were all London parties Justin danced and even DJed at. These were where "the dream started" for his own club venue.

"There was no reality to what I wanted to do," he says. "I didn't have the relationships in place to help bring this to life. It was a freak connection with a very hungry entrepreneur who was looking for something different that made it happen. It was a fluke meeting."

Justin met entrepreneur James Palumbo and his friend Humphrey Waterhouse and their coming together began the process behind the evolution of Ministry. First of all, they needed somewhere to house their club but a strict set of parameters around what they wanted meant landing a suitable venue amid London's urban sprawl "was like finding a needle in a haystack".

"It was all about the sound and having the club contained in a box so we could make plenty of noise without disturbing anyone else," he states. "In effect, we wanted to soundproof this fuck off sound system inside a sealed, studio-style room. You could have as much fun as you wanted in this kind of setting."

It took Justin a whole year of driving around London searching for the perfect space before he came across the Elephant and Castle location. The site wasn't even up for sale but despite the building's dilapidated state, he knew this was the one.

"The frontage attracted me, especially how it looked like a garage. I thought I could have my own, different version of the Paradise Garage," he laughs. "There was no deliberate idea about it being in Elephant and Castle or south and north London. It was just whatever would work. We were driving past, caught a glimpse of it and there it was. It was an impossible site to get as there were so many different landlords; it was a colossally complex deal."

Alongside difficulties with the transaction surrounding the space's acquisition, Justin recalls that the area was "very rough and a bit scary", while opening the club was fraught with challenges. From planning applications to sourcing money and navigating health and safety issues, there were multiple obstacles to overcome, although the latter was solved by unfortunate circumstances.

"There was one problem we couldn't get around. We had the fire officer who wanted us to put another fire exit in the box, which would have made the club a lot smaller," says Justin. "Then the poor guy had a heart attack and died. His replacement thankfully didn't ask for it, so we continued unabated. If that hadn't happened, the club may never have opened."

Justin's dedication to the club and an unwillingness to compromise drove its design forward. The shape of the space was influenced by the quality of the sound system and these ambitions to make it as close to sonic perfection as they could.

"We wanted to ensure that the sound was as tight as possible, which is why the room had five sides rather than four," he says. "We were trying to take the Paradise Garage concept one step further by building a nicely designed room, then putting a good system in it. Theirs was the benchmark of perfection we all aspired to - and we got close, especially when Larry Levan came over and we spent time tuning it together."

Larry Levan and Francois K were two of the most notable DJs to visit Ministry of Sound during the early months of its opening. Both of these American legends were more or less retired and Justin had to do his best to coax them over to the other side of the pond for one last time. Larry was in New York and Justin met him at [New York club] the Shelter.

"I had to be patient and look for Larry as he wasn't easy to find," says Justin. "But when I did get this hero of mine to come over and bless the club, it meant everything. To me, it was the equivalent of getting the pope to visit the church I'd built and perform mass."

Larry put Francois forward and Justin racked up a huge phone bill on calls, gently convincing him why it was so important that he come over to the UK to play in London.

"When Francois came, there were only 15 people on the dancefloor at the end of the party as it was too sophisticated for the London crowd," he says. "A lot of people didn't get it but those who did were inspired. Those left at the end were some hardcore clubbers who had flown over from Tokyo and some of London's A-list DJs. Normally at the close, you have the dregs of the party but here, it was boiled down to the essence. This wasn't about huge crowds; this was about exposing a genius to London."

Justin's relationship with Ministry slowly changed over the years but he returned to help expand the brand in Asia in 2005. In 2022, London and Ministry are in different realities from when the club first opened. Through the fug of Brexit, the pandemic and cost of living crisis, it's tough to see whether a club as ambitious as Ministry would now be given a chance. And if it was, whether it could send the same shockwaves through our nightlife system as it did when it opened.

"London and the UK are still in this transitory point where Brexit is changing the country," he says. "If there is a seventies-style decline, the advantage could be lots of spaces opening up. If the economic dip is only short, then clubbers will need to become more inventive. There are always ways of hosting nights and people are always building buildings."

"In tough times, people tend to party harder," Justin continues. "It is cyclical; it goes around. As long as they are owned and run by someone who loves clubbing, then clubs should survive and hopefully thrive."

Hosted at Turnmills near Farringdon, Trade opened in November 1990 and, as with Ministry, ushered in a new world of clubbing in the capital. One where sleeping was considered cheating.

"Both these clubs were important as they were the first two to have really late licences," says Bill Brewster. "Until they arrived, most London clubs would close at two or three in the morning, which for a massive city was a bit laughable. But Trade didn't even start until 3am."

House DJ Smokin' Jo was among the Trade residents who helped establish the night as a destination for ravers who take their partying (but not themselves) seriously. Growing up, Jo used to live near Portobello Road in London's West End and spent her formative clubbing years dancing at nights at the Mudd Club and the Wag.

"I used to go to the parties at Clink Street too," she says. "I was there from the beginning of the birth of the scene, then I felt lucky going to the big outdoors raves like Sunrise. Hearing that music a lot of the Black DJs were playing, like Paul 'Trouble' Anderson and Kid Batchelor, Tony Humphries, that kind of vibe really drew me in."

While working in the Junior Gaultier clothes shop in Soho, Jo first began obsessing over records and investing her wages in feeding an untameable vinyl habit. At the same time, she'd be out almost every night of the week, expanding her knowledge of club bangers soaked up via the dancefloor.

"My job was at the shop in Newburgh Street, which was very close to Blackmarket Records in Soho," she says. "I'd go in every lunchtime as I knew Ashley Beedle, who worked there, and he would put aside a bag of tunes for me. I wanted to DJ but I didn't see any women behind the decks. Still, I just threw myself into it."

It was a bold move that paid off with Jo taking her blend of funky, upfront house to some of the world's best clubbing institutions. From Ministry of Sound to nights in Ibiza and Panorama Bar in Berlin, she's very much a leading light in dance music circles. But it was amid the sweat, late nights and banging soundtrack at Trade that Jo first established herself.

"It was the first place that was given a legal licence to go really late," she says. "When Trade opened, it was at a time when a lot of the raves were getting stopped or broken up, so it became really hard to do these warehouse parties."

"It was amazing to have the opportunity to go somewhere like it and this 3am opening attracted a very eclectic bunch of people. It was mainly a gay crowd but you'd get promoters coming down and other

DJs after their gigs. It became this great place for people to meet up and the music was just phenomenal too. From very deep house to garage and nose-bleed techno, it was just amazing and made London feel exciting."

The record label Ninja Tune was established the same year as Trade opened but offered electronic music of a more experimental, eclectic nature. Since its inception, Ninja has been defined by an appetite for innovation, with the DJ Food concept among the first records released. Initially more aligned with ambient sounds and hip hop, over time, it has expanded its remit to engage with visuals, beats and anything else it could consume, then spit out via its own creations. Strictly Kev (known as Kev Foakes) has been a key driver behind this artistic vehicle, making music, designing artwork and DJing under its banner. As he moved to London at the start of the nineties, acid house euphoria was tearing through the speakers of many of the city's clubbing destinations. But he found himself attending a mixture of live gigs and "electronic dance music all-nighters" hosted by The Orb and promoters Megadog alongside the Tribal Energy happenings in squats around Camberwell and New Cross in south London.

"These parties showed me that we could do something similar but more tailored to our tastes," he says. "So my housemates and I started putting on our own ambient parties around '92/'93 called Telepathic Fish with the help of Mixmaster Morris and Matt Black from Coldcut. From there, I became more involved with Coldcut, their Solid Steel radio show and label Ninja Tune and really started learning the craft of a club DJ, travelling in the UK and Europe. In 1995 with Ninja, I started a residency at the Blue Note in Hoxton at a night called Stealth which has been one of my favourite clubbing experiences."

Growing up in Reigate to the south of central London in the pre-internet age, Kev's tastes initially led him to hip hop and graffiti but he struggled to find like-minded souls to connect with and an audience to impress. Despite their scarcity, they bonded quickly when he cast his net wider to neighbouring towns and met the few aspiring turntablists and graffiti artists in his area. Each would urge the other to go further in pursuit of expanding their musical knowledge and skills.

"There were maybe five or six of us learning, teaching each other, trying to get house party gigs," he explains. "That's what was good about communities, they are small and word got round quickly, even back then. With the web today, it's even quicker and happens on a global scale."

Moving to London was decisive for Kev's musical education and sudden exposure to a rich seam of pirate radio, DJ equipment shops, bars, clubs and more. Heading to the capital meant there were not only more ways to discover new sounds but greater opportunities to connect with potential collaborators and music lovers with similar passions.

"Suddenly, you weren't confined to what was booked at the one night club in your local town or the scraps of info you'd read in magazines," he says of the lustre of London's fecund music scene. "Instead, the culture was happening all around you."

"It's been proven that scenes can germinate in rural areas quite easily - the Cornwall base for Aphex Twin, Luke Vibert, Rephlex Records and Global Communications, for instance," Kev continues. "But they could only be the sum of the influences they could access, be that their parent's and friend's record collections, local shops or parties. Of course, I'm talking about a pre-internet world here, I'd imagine it's way easier for today's generation to take their music out of the sticks without the need to move but the sheer numbers in cities make the odds better in building up a scene in any meaningful numbers."

As a music-maker in Attica Blues on the Mo' Wax label in the nineties, to his current manoeuvres as selector par excellence alongside founding the Run Dem Crew collective (where his work has seen him receive an MBE)[241], Charlie Dark's life has been defined by movement and communities of all kinds - whether that be from running marathons to playing club music in basements. With his clubbing experiences starting in the mid-eighties, it was in Camden at Dingwalls where he was first exposed to sound systems.

"My parents are from West Africa, which was important for me as a kid as it meant I was under curfew when my friends were not," Charlie says.

"Gilles Peterson and Patrick Forge both played records in the club and I used to go on Sunday afternoons to get immersed in the jazz dance world. It was also an easy journey from my house in south London and I could tell my parents I was studying at my friend's house, then get home before they suspected anything. Although they probably knew what the reality was."

Back then at Dingwalls and the Soul II Soul at the Africa Centre in central London, everything was about dancing. The idea of attending a club night to be seen or noticed hadn't yet made it to these spaces.

"People would say, if you're not here to dance, then fuck off," laughs Charlie. "For me, I was at a point in life when I didn't think I was being seen, my future was being dictated to me by my parents. I was trying to find my voice and music and clubbing allowed me to discover who I was."

Charlie's DJing exploits followed his initial moments at Dingwalls before he started going to warehouse parties towards the tail end of the eighties. His motivations went further than dancing or digging new music - he was also driven by ambitions to extend his social circle and meet as many new people as possible.

"I felt very landlocked by my postcode," he says. "It was exciting to go somewhere to meet someone different who you could connect to via music or via their sense of fashion. London was very territorial back then."

"I loved this idea that you'd go to a party, end up back at someone's house, and there would be drug dealers, criminals, models, journalists, media people, all these different people from different walks of life."

While these after parties would be a diverse mix up of London society, door policies at many clubs were not so welcoming with many having quotas on the number of Black people they allowed in.

"Discussions about race have been erased from clubland - but that's the reason why people would do their own thing as they couldn't get a foothold in the mainstream venues and clubs," says Charlie.

"As a young Black male trying to go clubbing, it was really hard in the eighties and for some of the nineties. You'd get dressed up to go to the Wag Club, then get turned away. So next time, you'd take two outfits so if you did get rejected, then you could go round the corner, get changed, and try again. People ask why didn't you go to a particular club? You'd be like, I didn't get in!"

Hoxton's Blue Note was an East End institution opened in the early nineties that Charlie remembers fondly. Although associated with Goldie and the Metalheadz label, Mo' Wax hosted a party at the club called Dusted and, as part of the label's Attica Blues act, Charlie was among the DJs to play. Charlie remembers Shoreditch being a "wasteland" at the time - not the sticky tourist trap it's now become.

"Dusted was a super great night, you can always tell it's great if you've got the producers in the room from other scenes," he says. "If they are in your club, then you know you're doing something right. It was a real cross pollination of different people from different scenes all hanging out, it was great. I miss that club a lot."

Now with years of experience as a DJ, Charlie's life and career have taken multiple twists and turns. As founder of Run Dem Crew, he stepped away from nightlife for a time before re-entering via radio broadcasts on Worldwide FM during lockdown. Now his focus is on playing more intimate spots such as Gonzo in Norwich Bath Hotel and Cosmic Slop in Leeds. With rich and varied experiences, he feels that dancefloors respond differently to sounds depending on where they are located - certain spaces react to the snare, others to a rubbery bassline.

"I did a talk with Susan Rogers, an engineer with Prince, and we were talking about how you have to EQ certain records in certain ways for different countries," Charlie explains. "For example, if you go to South Africa, you play a broken beat record and it's at 126 bpm, you have to pitch it down to 120. There are all types of subtle things in the music."

In the UK, there are also different perspectives on the way people move and party. Charlie makes sure that his sets respond to the environment around him, something he sees as an essential part of the DJing craft.

"I love playing in London but people can be more vocal about what they like and don't like outside it," he says. "That's why I love playing in Manchester, Liverpool and Leeds at parties like Cosmic Slop. The people are real, if they're into you, they'll let you know - you couldn't have Cosmic Slop in London. As it's in Leeds, it can percolate and brew under its own steam. It's such a special place and I wish there were more clubs like it in the UK."

"I came into Smithfield, and the shameful place, being all asmear with filth and fat and blood and foam, seemed to stick to me", remarks Pip, the protagonist in Charles Dickens' nineteenth-century novel, *'Great Expectations*[242]. As a visitor, Pip's first experiences of London saw him almost gobbled up by the meat market's stench. For many of London's 'techno tourists' during the last 20 years, the sights and smells of Smithfield may have been less overpowering, but still among their initial experiences of the city. Club culture is a relatively new concept when compared with the livestock market's presence in EC1. This dates back hundreds of years but despite its roots in blood and guts, the market was a modern hub for trade with more than 100,000 tonnes of meat and allied products sold annually until it closed in 2022[243]. Since Fabric opened up in 1999 in a disused storage facility located close to the market, what goes in in the three rooms of the club was linked with its former neighbour. As Fabric's blog wrote when it announced its London Unlocked series in 2021: "[Smithfield is] a place that we pass through and queue up in the shadow of at the start of the night in EC1, and end the night with the meat trucks unloading their products as we leave the club in the morning"[244].

The idea for Fabric came from the vision of co-founders Keith Reilly and Cameron Leslie as a reaction to what the electronic music scene they'd loved so much had become. With a history in warehouse events and parties, both had lived through the evolution of dance music and were uncomfortable with where it had landed. As Keith said of the electronic music scene: "By the early to mid-nineties, London had been taken over by the most ghastly, garish mutations of what we thought was ours. It was a complete distortion of everything that was beautiful about this music"[245].

The 1,500 capacity club's ambitions were aimed at resetting the scene by focussing on incredible sound, leftfield music programming and a dedication to championing new talent. This is the recipe Fabric has continued to adhere to and ensured that the club continues to be at the top of its game after years of risks and challenges. By contrast, Home, the much-hyped West End superclub which opened in Leicester Square the same year, only stayed open until 2001 before closing. Author and journalist Bill Brewster describes Fabric as "a superclub which didn't have superstar DJs playing in it".

"It represented a break in the superstar phenomenon which had been started by clubs like Ministry, Cream, Golden and Gatecrasher," he explains "They were reliant on massive names and it became like a pop version of acid house. Fabric was a move away from that, so they'd book DJs who weren't that well known but they liked. People would go for the night rather than the name as they knew they'd book really interesting music. You'd put your trust in them."

As Fabric's Promotions Manager, Judy Griffith has been an integral part of the team since the club's early days, helping to programme epic parties, book talent and steer the venue through its eventful lifetime. Her raving roots lie in some of the most talked of London spaces, including The Trip at the Astoria, Family Funktion, the Shake and Fingerpop warehouse parties, as well as numerous fields and spaces dotted along the M25. From Judy's perspective, the location near the famous meat market played in the club's favour on opening.

"Because of the market's unconventional hours, there were already establishments used to being open 24 hours or from 6am to service the meat market staff," she says. "It's because of its unique location and set up in the city that we received one of London's first 24 hour licences for a nightclub in 2005."[246]

At the beginning of her dance music love affair, Judy enjoyed a decade of raving and parties before she found a job with house music record label Strictly Rhythm and turned her musical obsession into a full-time gig. When Fabric first opened, she was a regular on the dancefloor with the club's programming in tune with her own tastes. Persuaded by Nicky Smith, who was then responsible for booking acts for Saturday nights, Judy went along for an interview for the role of Programming Assistant when the opening appeared.

"Fabric was like all the small underground clubs I was going to at the time, all rolled together in one big space," she says of her attraction to the venue and the job opportunity. "They were booking all the DJs that were influencing and inspiring me. Then when I met the team, it felt like I had instantly connected with my family. Here was a crew that was thinking like me, living like me and sharing all the values of the electronic community that I lived by. Fabric was a bigger club but they weren't interested in huge numbers; it was all about music and how it was presented, almost operating outside of the margins of mainstream clubs."

Since joining Fabric, Judy has never looked back and helped piece together an aural aesthetic for the club, which spans genre, style and time, particularly when some parties last for a sleep-defying 42 hours[247]. Some will love the club for the lengthy techno sessions with Fabric resident Craig Richards alongside DJs Seth Troxler and Ricardo Villalobos. Others will adore it as a trailblazer, leading the way with grime via the Butterz label sessions or electroclash and indie adventures through nights such as Adventures in the Beetroot Field or Blogger's Delight. Every shade of electronic music, from minimal techno to dark dubstep and euphoric disco, has been pumped through its impeccable sound systems and you'd be hard-pressed to find any clubber who hasn't revelled inside it at one time or another. Back in 2009, I danced to the tough tech of Modeselektor on a Thursday night and inadvertently arrived at work very late on Friday afternoon clutching a litre of water and a brace of apologies for 'sleeping in'. It's the kind of place where you can get totally lost in the sound, lights and experience.

"It has evolved musically from championing different sounds on Fridays from breaks to drum & bass through dubstep, grime, garage, hip hop, all the way through the urban musical landscape," says Judy. "Then Saturdays from tech house/house to minimal glitchy to the rise of electro, techno and more harder forms and now to a varied range of sounds. We represent the underground in all its guises and evolve with the scene around us and the community we serve. Always looking forward and using the past to shape the future."

Since the club reopened after the Covid-19 restrictions were lifted, the Fabric team has taken the space through a significant overhaul. A ban on phones has been reintroduced to prevent images from any of its nights being captured and shared while the DJ booth in Room Two has been moved into the centre of the space. A refreshed team of residents, including London DJ and producer Josh Caffe alongside the drum & bass of Rupture's DJ Mantra, shows Fabric still has its finger very much on the beating heart of London's underground nightlife.

"Our ethos aims to support the underground and provide a platform for new, upcoming artists by placing them alongside established artists so they can shine," says Judy on their talent booking approach. "London thrives on its diversity, integration and progressive thinking and our line-ups are increasingly more balanced, inclusive and reflective of the world we live in. This is something we really want to continue putting in the work with until it's normalised."

Of course, Fabric's life has not been without incident. Infamously, the club was forced to shut in 2016 after two drug-related fatalities and at the time, it seemed like the party was finished with Islington Council decreeing that security had been "inadequate and in breach of the licence"[248]. But the clubbing community rallied around in its defence. An online petition calling for Fabric to be kept open attracted more than 160,000 signatures while more than £300,000 was raised in support[249].

"The police called war on us and played the old narrative that clubs are dens of illicit drug-taking, damaging to the moral fabric of society and tried to put a case against us using that as the story," says Judy of the difficulties Fabric experienced.

"But we all know clubs have evolved into places of music education, providing inspiration for artists of the future. They are modern-day community centres, safe havens, creative hubs, and escapes from oppression. The authorities were way behind with their way of thinking. We resisted. We campaigned. We appealed - and only with the love and strength of our people coming together to highlight our values - we won."

Fabric eventually reached a deal with the local council and reopened to great fanfare in January 2017. Ravers on the first night back were greeted with a banner in Room One acknowledging the power of its community with the words 'You Saved Fabric'. Conditions of the agreement included a ban on anyone under 19 entering between 8pm on Friday and 8am on Monday. Anyone found in possession of drugs or attempting to buy drugs will receive a lifetime ban from the venue. Following this, Fabric continued to pack in party people weekend after weekend without further incident until the Covid-19 lockdowns arrived in March 2020.

"Now it is still tough to survive in this area. Conditions, licensing, regeneration alongside overheads are very high and profits are thus low or non-existent," says Judy. "But we feel we've evolved into a necessity. We are there to serve London and the wider music culture. So long as we can continue doing so without fear of being shut down, then it's more of a win than any money can bring. Our priorities have to change to stay in that location."

Despite being shut for 18 months due to the pandemic, Fabric was one of the only nightclubs to apply for and receive support from the Arts Council's Culture Recovery Fund to the tune of £1.5 million[250]. Four other venues including Sage Gateshead's parent company North Music Trust and ACC Liverpool Group received support - but Fabric was the only venue specifically catering for clubbers and electronic music. In collaboration with the Arts Council, Fabric staged an ambitious series of London Unlocked streamed events hosted from some of the city's most iconic spaces, including the Royal Albert Hall and the nearby Smithfield Market.

In a statement, the club said this was a way of paying "homage to our home city's incredible contemporary culture and the legendary, ever-evolving and diverse electronic music scene"[251].

"To finally get recognised as not just a nightclub but a cultural institution during lockdown was a huge progressive step forward for the whole of London's nightlife," Judy explains. "It was very validating for us and maybe if we can finally be seen by our peers in the same way as the Barbican or the Tate, then the way we are treated by the authorities will change too and we can get the support that's needed from these people to exist."

Mark Ellicott, former general manager of Heaven, recognises these challenges for many venues across the UK. It could threaten his past club's livelihood in the future as the boundaries of the city's residential areas ebb and flow. The Arts Council backing a club like Fabric is a huge moment for nightlife but elsewhere, clubs are still striving to have their value to the "local cultural economy" recognised rather than just being viewed as a noisy annoyance.

"As more and more parts of the city become residential when perhaps more than 30 years ago they were largely devoid of residents, so the complaints directed at places such as Heaven increase," he explains. "Remember, residents have the vote. Businesses such as this do not. Local authorities listen to their electorates and if the local residents are well organised enough, it isn't difficult for them to get the local authority to review a club's licence and subsequently make it difficult for them to operate."

The power of nightclubs has been diminished in this debate as increasing numbers of "well-heeled, predominantly middle-class professionals" have invested in property in areas previously considered 'no-go zones'.

"Residents were conspicuous by their absence but many of these incomers have found that living next door to a busy nightclub venue is not conducive to a good night's sleep," he laughs. "Hence the greater regularity of conflict between residents, nightclub operators, local authorities and the police as this new reality has to be contended with. My attitude has always been - 'we were here first. If you want peace and quiet, go and live in the suburbs or the country'."

Strike out east to the London borough of Newham and you'll eventually find yourself in Canning Town. Previously, this part of London was notorious for high levels of poverty and crime as well as slums during the early years of the 20th century, which became so unsafe, the local authorities orchestrated a clean-up operation during the 1930s[252]. Yet, in the present day, the area has changed beyond all recognition to become one bulging with what overzealous developers would describe as 'redevelopment potential' in their PR blurb. Well-connected by tube and overground train and in close proximity to London City Airport and Stratford International station, the promise of the place is being realised by a £3.7 billion regeneration project aiming to change "the area for the better, physically, socially and economically"[253]. Amid this shifting world is nightclub FOLD, a venue that set up shop in 2018 with a 24-hour licence and no-phones policy to ensure what happens in Canning Town stays in Canning Town. The Shapes Collective established the club that lives above a print factory on Stephenson Street. Alongside Seb Glover and marketing director David Conde, venue co-founder Lasha Jorjoliani, aka artist Voicedrone, wanted the club to offer London's nightlife an alternative shot in the arm.

"It was our only chance to make a difference and to create something inspirational, liberating, and welcoming for a community that has been forgotten and mistreated by the current social state," he says.

"Now FOLD is not just a venue, it is an important movement that will continue to grow, make changes and break chains until we reset the system."

The musical policy at the centre of the club is decidedly leftfield, enabling a bombardment of harder, more experimental electronic artists to emerge from the shadows. The industrial techno of Perc and acid techno of Chris Liberator's Stay Up Forever label are some of the DJs and collectives to play inside the 600 capacity space. By shrouding running times in secrecy for their 24-hour parties, FOLD wants to challenge its audiences and instil greater trust in the club's programming rather than just allowing audiences to follow the headline acts.

"The future is always going to be places like FOLD that are set up in an industrial, derelict area," says Chris Liberator. "20 years ago, that would have been out in the sticks but now Canning Town is not seen as too far away."

FOLD came as a response to the boundaries Voicedrone sensed were cemented in place within the techno scene. Rather than be confined by these kinds of restrictions, the club aimed to offer a safe space for ravers of all identities and a sense of release from the pressures of the outside world.

"UK dance music, techno in particular leaves very little space for queer identities, and even less for queer feminine identities," Voicedrone explains. "We work with the community to create comfortable, queer spaces in nightlife and are committed to continuing to do so. LGBTQIA+ communities have been integral to building FOLD's reputation. The unfortunate widespread queer and alternative club closures meant that they were seeking space within a largely straight male-centred industry."

When Covid-19 hit, FOLD was still a relatively young venture but managed to survive by innovating and diversifying its offering outside the dancefloor. The studios surrounding the main room of the club were hired out for video and photography shoots, while a series of livestreams with DJs closely connected with the club were beamed to the wider world. FOLD even offered up its space to the NHS when the pandemic first landed, providing "the potential for a range of uses that goes from NHS administration all the way to critical or specialist care"[254]. The club was also helped by financial support from the Music Venue Trust's Emergency Grassroots Music Venue Fund. Now back open, the sense of disconnection caused by the pandemic has only sharpened the focus of FOLD's parties and the importance of place in "shaping tastes and attitudes".

"Our audience has worldwide links but being in a room together as one has built a certain sound and mindset," says Voicedrome. "Together, we have found that unique sound and style and hopefully, this time out for the clubbing community will make the UK government understand that clubs are carrying more cultural weight than they think. Spaces like this are essential for our cultural growth and the future in general."

In 2022, development on residential and commercial properties continued around Canning Town after the regeneration plans were disrupted by the pandemic. For now, it still offers a brilliant home for FOLD to flourish outside of the mainstream. According to Voicedrome, the greatest clubs have always existed in the margins of our towns and cities. "Ultimately, clubs were never meant to be in the city centres; they always belonged outside, far away from everything and everyone," he says. "Clubs should be places where people can escape jobs, problems, and everyday routines. It is a political movement, our way of protest which is rooted in the time when reality sleeps."

The rallying cry of 'Make Peckham shit again' increased in recent years as a response to this south-east area of London's rapid transformation. Previously known as the home of Del Boy and Rodney from *'Only Fools and Horses'*, like so many other parts of the capital, it's been given a bath, a haircut, a flat white and suddenly been reborn as a much-vaunted 'hipster hotspot'. Crime has declined while property prices have soared; between 2010 and 2020, they more than doubled[255].

Rye Lane cuts through the heart of Peckham and is where much of the nocturnal action happens. The Bussey Building - a former gun factory and shooting range located just off this route - is a hub for various creative endeavours from recording studios to Kanpai, a sake brewery and taproom. Among them is Rye Wax, an independent record shop, restaurant, bar and event space located in the basement and co-founded by Tom Steidl. They have since left this creative hub but now manage the nearby Peckham Audio club as well as helping run the Rising Sun Collective. Tom's musical adventures began as a party promoter at the Red Star in Camberwell, booking DJs such as DJ Oneman and Ben UFO during the early years of dubstep. Another party known as Wavey Tones led them to the Bussey Building, where they had the opportunity to set up Rye Wax with like-minded instigators.

"The Bussey Building director reached out to everyone for new ideas to develop in the space," Tom remembers. "I'd been wanting to open a record shop and work with Medlar and [music producers] the FYI Chris guys who are close friends and Rye Wax was born. After five years, I ended up leaving, then had some time off before getting the job at Peckham Audio. I absolutely love Rye Lane in all its many guises and feel very fortunate to still be a part of it."

Their influences stretch from Plastic People in Shoreditch to Volks in Brighton, "which doesn't get enough shine really for being such a great grubby spot that seems unchangeable". Although Peckham Audio is licensed, the spirit of the illegal raves Tom attended in their formative years have left an impression on the vibe and energy they want to instil in their events.

"I was largely inspired by squat parties and clubs like the Red Star that existed on the fringes," Tom says. "That sense of family and the crowd, security, staff and management sharing the responsibility of care is something that I feel comes from the underground, not more legit venues."

Peckham has undoubtedly changed over the last decade with an ever-increasing array of nights and cultural events. The dreaded word of gentrification is one associated with it and other similar areas in London, such as Brixton or Dalston, which were previously considered run down. The fact that the latter's Kingsland Road now has an M&S Food Hall might have seemed inconceivable ten years ago. Tom is against how these changes can negatively impact communities, and feels the dialogue should focus on the potential displacement it can cause.

"It's always hard to know how much, even as someone totally against gentrification in most ways, I have tacitly contributed to it," Tom states. "The conversation is sometimes too led by things like clubs and stuff like that cereal cafe in Dalston and not the fact they knocked down the Heygate, moved everyone to Luton and replaced it with empty glass towers."

As a 200-capacity space, Peckham Audio is a more intimate club than other London venues and caters for more underground names featuring electronic DJs Ivan Smagghe, Scott Fraser, Supa D and Shy One on its line-ups. This commitment to showcasing leftfield talent, particularly the South African strain of dance music amapiano, has earned the club a loyal crowd but it was almost lost due to the proposed development of encroaching flats.

"For a long time, a big issue for clubs has been having flats built near them and then getting shut down by noise complaints which apparently there is protection against now, but how effective that will be remains to be seen," states Tom. "Ironically, the building Peckham

Audio is in was going to be luxury flats until some of the community, including Rye Wax, organised a big push back against it and somehow won. There are a lot of times it's gone the other way, of course, and London is going to rapidly lose its cultural identity if more isn't done about the recklessness of development."

If you take a walk up Rye Lane, then the vibe persists with Peckham now a Time Out-approved destination for nightlife and the culture it breeds. Spots like Frank's Bar atop of a multi-storey car park amid the Bold Tendencies' art installation are now a well-established part of London's entertainment offering, while the Bussey Building continues to be a hit with weekend warriors. Canavan's pool club was a legendary dancefloor and home to the much-lauded Rhythm Section but has closed due to the impact of the Covid-19 pandemic. The energy levels on the street are reflected in the rapid turnover and reimagining of its places.

"Peckham and London, especially the areas of south, east and north that were considered rough have changed vastly in my lifetime," says Tom. "Some of it has been really bad, particularly led by the housing crisis and communities being rapidly displaced. Some of it hasn't, and I imagine the 'Make Peckham Shit Again' brigade are not wanting to go back to it being the no-go zone in the postcode wars. No one misses that and there's a danger of fetishisation of violence in some of these narratives."

Located in nearby Canada Water, the mighty Printworks offered a very different nightclub experience to Peckham Audio or FOLD. Although it closed its doors in May 2023, the venue provided a jaw-dropping clubbing experience compared with other smaller or more tucked away spaces. Originally home to what was the largest printing factory in western Europe, many of the features from its past life were retained, while it was large enough to accommodate up to 6,000 ravers across multiple rooms. The Inkwells retained the industrial aesthetic, having originally been used to house giant ink tanks which printed newspapers such as the Evening Standard and the Metro. When it was open, Ajay Jayaram, Printworks' Head of Music, believed the building was an integral part of the appeal and something he first experienced at a Secret Cinema event as part of their *Empire Strikes Back* season.

"The collective refrain from all of my friends was that I had to find a way to host a party there," he laughs. "It speaks to the idea that people are always interested in experiencing things in a slightly different way. The flipside was I thought this was almost too challenging. But we were able to pull it off and it shows how you can make any kind of space work if you have the desire and inclination."

Event management business Broadwick Live was in charge of the venue. Alongside other ventures such as the Depot Mayfield in Manchester and Magazine London, they focus on sourcing exciting and unusual spaces for their programming.

Broadwick Live's Managing Director Bradley Thompson says: "We saw the Printworks building and were just blown away by the scale. It's an incredible space. We aimed to leave many of the unique architectural elements in place and bring these out in our productions. We always want to find spaces that are unusual, where we can tell a great story."

Rather than overhauling the building, much of it was left as the Broadwick Live team found it. The scale of the space was breathtaking due to the height of the main room and industrial feel. As the Independent described, "it felt like a futuristic place of worship rather than a factory or a club"[256].

"It was a totally unique venue," says Ajay. "The idea that people could come, listen to some of the best artists on this exceptional sound system is wonderful proof that it's still possible to create a genuine sense of awe in what we do - and that's due to the architectural cathedral where we can host these events."

Bicep, Sink the Pink and Glitterbox all performed or ran nights at Printworks, demonstrating the variety of what it could offer. Since the club shut, the team at Broadwick have moved their ambitions to Tottenham and taken over the site of a former IKEA with their new Drumsheds venue. The 608,000 square foot space has welcomed the enigmatic Sault to its stage and is billed as a "hybrid venue" rather than a club[257]. It's a description that can also be applied to the Outernet, a new entertainment district and one of the grandest of assets in the capital's nightlife crown, full of bold ambitions and glittering technology. The Outernet has opened in the centre of London next to the newly designed Tottenham Court Road tube station and Denmark Street - but is several galaxies removed from the rich musical industry histories that previously occurred there and in nearby Soho. This billion-pound immersive media, music and culture location is reported to have installed the world's largest deployment of LED screens[258].

"In London, the reality is that the majority of people only go out to see DJs on Fridays and Saturdays," says Karrie Goldberg, Founder and CEO at The Kagency and Co-Founder and Co-CEO of Outernet Venues. "So because real estate is so expensive in its centre, you have to be able to 'sweat the asset' as they say."

Karrie is responsible for its two venues, Here, an 1,800 cap space and the Lower Third, a bar and grassroots music venue. Her initial musical experiences were in Chicago with her life always surrounded by electronic music culture.

"In Chicago, you'd go out and you'd always end up in a house music club and dancing," she says. "No one was too good to be out dancing, no matter what you were wearing, who you were with or where you were."

"When I moved to New York in 2002, I was shocked at how stale nightlife was there and how people were more interested in sitting and buying a 500 dollar bottle of champagne than getting on the dancefloor."

Karrie's music career was forged in Cielo, a nightclub located in New York's meatpacking district. She remembers it pushing the metropolis' dance music scene forward before many nightclubs moved out to Brooklyn.

"It was a rectangular room with a sunken dancefloor and a Funktion-One sound system, one of the first in North America," she explains. "There would be tables on the perimeter so if you wanted table service, then that would work. The dancefloor was absolutely the central focus (as this is where the speakers were positioned). We would have Francois K, Louie Vega, Roger Sanchez had a residency there, then Depeche Mode's Martin Gore and Coldplay (or Roger Taylor from Duran Duran) would come and hang out. It was underground but nice enough to not have the sticky floors that would put these people off."

Karrie's experiences after Cielo have flitted between corporate development and nightlife hospitality with her Kagency business taking her into commercial estate and monetising spaces for developers. Her abilities to build relationships with management, artists and big businesses have all helped push the Outernet's venues into new nocturnal worlds.

"With the venues we manage at Outernet, one of the key ambitions was to build an extremely versatile space," she says. "We wanted to go beyond being a nightclub which is where the longevity for the project comes from. I can have Years & Years or Sam Ryder play, I can have Louie Vega DJ and cater for a brand like Aston Martin too. We can be all these things and no one can get angry about it because we cater for different audiences. It's an entertainment venue rather than a nightclub."

Many of the headlines for the Outernet have come from its large screen and great production kit as well as the artists who have stepped onto its stage. But the flexibility of the various venues are an integral part of its appeal. Artists, promoters and brands can come and use it however they want thanks to Karrie's experiences and skills in bringing these worlds together.

"I work in this space, translating underground and corporate cultures and found a way to bridge them at the Outernet," she says. "Prada was one of our first events and they booked Floating Points and Jamie xx. This is a perfect example of a huge fashion brand and underground DJs working together. The brand wanted the luxury attributes of the venue - massive bars, green rooms, great sound - but also to have the energy of a rave running through its event too."

Changing behaviours and technologies are having a defining impact on nightlife. While Outernet is designed to create Instagrammable moments, social media's presence in all our lives means club culture's business associations are out in the open.

"Social media has changed everything," Karrie explains. "At Cielo, before Instagram, I would do corporate events and these would help fund the overall business but we wouldn't shout about them and there would be little crossover between them and the dance music world."

"Now you can't hide anything any more so it makes sense to collaborate and connect with these brands in exciting and authentic ways."

Clubbing habits are also in a state of flux, with the wallets of ravers hit by the ongoing surge in prices and cost of living crisis. As for so many venue owners and event organisers, Karrie has seen advance ticket sales falling and less people heading out into the night.

"We've definitely felt that and how people aren't spending as much on weekly events or nights. Instead, they're saving their money for bigger 'wow' events at arenas or festivals. As a result, they're still buying tickets really late too so it's hard to predict how sales will do - a show now might not sell out until the day before which makes everything more difficult."

"It means we've kept our strategy flexible - we book a broad range of artists and we've now got a 4am licence. This gives us even more flexibility to book multiple events across our spaces and is really appealing to punters and partners."

Head further east out of the city centre and the Ridley Road Market bar in Dalston is an incongruous location for one of London's most exciting talents to cut their teeth. But for Mute Records' HAAi, this eccentric night-time spot was a vital platform for her to dip her toes into the DJing world.

"I worked behind the bar there initially, then I started out doing a mid-week night where I played psychedelic music from all around the world," she says. "I managed to weasel my way into playing all night long on Saturdays, and that's how I learned to DJ. I remember Andy Weatherall was my biggest inspiration starting out. One of the best nights ever was at Village Underground after I'd come from Ridley Road and caught the last few hours of his set. It was a transcendental experience."

The bar is located in the heart of the market and is one of the area's most intriguing places for a dance and a drink. The market itself first set up shop during the 1880s with a mere 20 stalls but has expanded to now house more than 150 on a busy Saturday. Amid the chopping of meat, reggae sound systems and chaos of London life running through it, the bar stands out as one of the last exciting night spaces in a postcode increasingly overrun by retail chains. Gone are the days when you could stumble down any flight of stairs under a shop on Kingsland Road and find yourself in a sweaty rave-up.

"One of the biggest issues has been losing spaces in east London as Hackney Council haven't been the biggest supporters of nightlife," says HAAi. "When I was at the Ridley Road Market Bar, we had to fight really hard for a later licence and I think part of that was an issue with Ridley Road itself and the potential for flat building around it."

"It felt like there was a time around 2017 where there was some hope for east London and clubbing and there are still great venues like Dalston Superstore. Still, I think it's been a struggle to keep nightlife alive in this part of London."

As one of London's most innovative DJs and producers, HAAi's musical journey has been eclectic. She moved to London as lead singer/guitarist of the much-lauded psych/shoegaze trio Dark Bells but was drawn towards dance music when the band split. Since then, her sets have veered between dark and trippy techno to breakbeats and other electronic textures. Whether it's a festival or club venue, she selects tracks specifically for the space she's in.

"I've been lucky enough to play at The Warehouse Project in Manchester more than ten times but when you play in a space like that, you're playing to thousands of people," she says. "This means your sets are all about high energy and bigger drops. You're probably only playing 90 minutes max, so you need to maintain the vibe and impress people who've probably not seen you before. In a smaller club over a longer set, there's more room to get weirder and bring people along for a ride. I love both environments but there's something special about playing in a dark basement where you can really experiment."

Boiler Room and NTS have been two sources of inspiration alongside London record shop institutions like Phonica in Soho and Kristina Records in Hackney. HAAi has discovered so much great new music she's launched her own Radical New Theory label to champion the talent she has unearthed. As a non-Londoner, she's amassed a wide array of influences connecting local with global sounds.

"I think a sense of place definitely still has an impact on music makers and DJs but there's so much genre-bending and subgenres now," she says. "I hear a lot of DJs playing very versatile sets. So while certain cities will always be linked to their musical past, I feel we're definitely experiencing this fantastic period of shapeshifting sounds."

So where is the nightclub at in London? We've seen just how diverse the current nocturnal world looks at the moment, although this is a fluid setting; nightlife never stays still for too long. Rather than moving of their own accord, external forces often propel clubs to new areas of the city. During the last ten years, London has been mauled by austerity measures and this has had a direct impact on nightlife culture. A Centre for London report showed how councils in the capital have seen their budgets cut by 17%, with boroughs including Hackney, Newham and Tower Hamlets the most affected[259]. In the past decade, more than 130 youth facilities have been lost[260].

"Young people from deprived communities have nowhere to congregate or create," says Caspar Meville. "There has been an increase in gang violence and drug culture, although no one in government can seem to make the connection with this loss of places to go and things to do. UK rappers get it, though, and you can hear this if you listen to Dave, AJ Tracey or Stormzy."

Pressures on clubs have come from gentrification and new residents investing in property near these venues, then complaining when the hip nightlife they wanted to be close to proves too much. Combined with councils revving up their reviews of club licences and there are different challenges nightclub owners need to navigate.

"It seems that club culture is great when it makes the city vibrant and attractive, but not really respected and targeted when powerful voices are raised against it," Caspar explains. "Promoters have responded to this by exploring new parts of the city - Deptford, Tottenham, Walthamstow. In a way, this has always been the case and was a process pioneered by the reggae sound systems."

This trend has been glaringly apparent during the last ten years. Areas previously seen as undesirable are now being fought over by residents hungry to get a foot on the property ladder. Ninja Tune's Strictly Kev feels it's tough to predict where London's nightlife might end up, particularly as the impact of the Covid-19 pandemic and the economic fall out are still being felt.

"Scenes are more likely to coalesce around online social media portals than cities now, I'd guess," he says. "Scenes that existed for years will no longer have their locals, new places will need to be found for new scenes and it'll be a huge reset. I don't think we'll recognise it as we knew it anymore. Soho is a pale shadow of its former glory now, that's never coming back. We may see a brief return to the illegal raves of yesteryear. Probably not on the scale of the eighties but warehouse spaces and squats on the fringes of towns and cities might be the only way for grassroots things to grow."

Innovation is at the heart of club music and those DJs, promoters and venue owners working within it. It is an essential attribute for these stakeholders to cultivate if they are to stay alive in a business landscape that tilts as quickly as the urban world around them. However, in this volatile setting, independent venues could benefit from greater support from the local authorities, whether it be financial or through other vital resources.

"It would be nice to see the importance of independent spaces for music and creativity given more recognition by the government and councils (who could, for example, give venues rate relief or other kinds of financial support)," Caspar says. "London is still bubbling, and it's a big place with a lot of untapped potential, but there are ominous new forms of regulation. Sound system operator Lloyd Coxsone told me that councils have installed sound limiters in their municipal halls - when the volume reaches a predetermined level, the power cuts off - which means that sound systems have fewer and fewer places to play."

London selector, NTS broadcaster OK Williams is renowned for her eclectic sets of cage rattlers and is one of the latest generation to stoke the city's dancefloors with her energetic approach to DJing. She started playing out in August 2017 then became involved in online broadcaster NTS through volunteering.

"I used to go to MOT a lot in Bermondsey before I started DJing. I also used to party at Rising Sun, this pub looked after by this collective who are looking to fundraise to buy the venue," she says. "They have a really cool basement with great parties, bands and DJs. I spent a lot of time there when I first started DJing. Those two places in London were really significant."

OK Williams' experiences have seen her play in many similar spaces, including squat raves prior to the Covid-19 lockdowns. As a DJ and a dancer, they offer a level of comfort and freedom she hasn't experienced as much in nightclubs.

"You can just have more fun with it - there's a vibe, good people. There's something about going into an abandoned building and playing rave tunes that is really freeing," she laughs. "They are more relaxed, more accessible, no idiot bouncer in my face - it all adds to the experience."

While she initially cut her teeth as a raver in Leeds, it's in London where her career as a DJ has taken off. She's optimistic about the waves of new production and DJing talent coming through.

"There's a great calibre of new DJs and people rising up, a lot of sick, cool people who love club music, clubbing and dancing," she explains. "In that respect, I'm optimistic and there's a lot of talent from minorities in the UK - Black people, people of colour and women - but I'm pessimistic about UK clubs. The mainstream ones are driven by money; bookers only care about filling their warehouse or festival. And these events rarely book exciting new talent. They only want those who will help them sell out."

With the clubs gone mainstream, it seems that to preserve the sanctity of the experience, they may need to exist outside of these city centres. As we've seen time and time again, nightclubs might need to head to the outskirts of our cities to give themselves the best chance of survival.

"Central London is this hub of money and capitalism and I think that's what is wrong with club culture in a way, that sense of capitalism seeps in," she says. "Clubs are going to keep going further out, but I'm happy for that to be the case if it means those present want to be there. I want to keep DJing and raving as this amazing precious thing."

For the culture to continue to flourish, Caspar believes spaces still matter but that digital platforms offer an important way for those in a scene to connect and facilitate their networks. Instead of being opposed, the physical and online worlds are more powerful when working in sync. Information can be shared easily to create virtual communities via Eventbrite, Instagram and Facebook, who can solidify these connections by meeting face-to-face.

"I think this has only increased the sense that the actual physical space is not the important thing although some places such as the Union Chapel, The Church of Sound in Clapton and Fabric are amazing," Caspar says. "They can lend a night real charge. But it is the club brand, DJs, musicians, the crowd, that matters."

"Anyone who has been raving in London for any length of time knows that venues come and go, but the music lives on. You can feel nostalgic about lost clubs - I always miss the Astoria when I walk past what is now an empty space or miss mad nights at The End when I walk past its closed door, but there has always been a new option opening somewhere else. We have to make sure this continues."

# CHAPTER 10

## UTOPIAN METROPOLIS /IN SEARCH OF THE NIGHTCLUBS OF TOMORROW

*"This homogenisation of city design stems from a new generation coming of age. They have no connection with a spit and sawdust pub or clubs in damp arches. If you want this sense of escapism that clubs used to offer, then you don't want to be wading through someone else's piss to enjoy it"*[261].

Ian Anderson

"The common denominator of the discothèque is darkness, a small dancefloor and the beat"[262]. This nightclub description may be from the New York Times in February 1965 when this new phenomenon first got us bopping but still feels relevant today with the occupancy of a physical space vital to its existence. By stepping over the threshold into this realm and shutting the door on the outside world, individuals are free to indulge and participate in a club night's rituals. From affirming identities on the dancefloor to connecting with musical peers or just getting blitzed in the corner on Jagermeister and plant food, all of the club's collective and individual experiences occur within their four walls.

Whether in terms of its geographical terrain, laws, music industry infrastructure or in the warm bodies that make up a crowd, the city provides a unique zone for these nightclubs and their events to live and breathe. As the *'Night Fever: Designing Club Culture'* exhibition at Dundee's V&A said in 2021, "clubs belong to the city" and emerge when "the urban fabric offers ample freedom" for them to thrive[263]. But what happens when club culture goes beyond its traditional form to inhabit new and exciting territories?

The locations of electronic music are now more fluid than bricks and mortar, while the scene, styles and sounds are even more wildly disparate. From music festivals in deserts in the Middle East and high-end casinos in Las Vegas to classical concert halls and live streams sponsored by corporate brands, the spaces club culture occupies are multiplying - it has travelled a long way since the so-called year zero of acid house. Manchester United defender turned football pundit Gary Neville took to Twitter to say: "No 10 Downing St should be renamed 'Hacienda'" during the so-called Partygate revelations of 2022. Rather than vilifying the club, Neville inverted the old-fashioned narrative of nightlife being a nuisance to society and used it to shake his fists at the authorities instead. Such a reference illustrates just how deeply nightclubs have penetrated our national dialogue[264]. At least, for those of a certain age.

The fate of our nightlife is arguably governed as much by changing behaviours as the shifting environments surrounding them. We now live very differently from previous generations and there are new defining factors influencing how we enjoy ourselves. Prior to Covid-19, Mintel statistics from 2016 revealed how annual admissions for the UK nightclub industry dropped by almost a quarter between 2010 and 2015[265]. The behemoth that is the music festival season, the proliferation of apps, virtual experiences and all-knowing entertainment platforms such as Spotify and Amazon are all at play, skewing the way we consume and engage with music. During the pandemic, 2021's International Music Summit Business Report showed that €3.4 billion (£2.8 billion), or 78%, was wiped off the value of venues and festivals[266]. Amid this diverse and busy entertainment space where numerous activities are vying for our attention, adaptability and diversity are key for the nightclub's ongoing survival.

Ministry of Sound is a great example of a club space still going strong thanks to its ability to move with the rhythm of the times. Established as an underground venue in 1991 by DJ and co-founder Justin Berkmann and inspired by his experiences in New York's best nocturnal spots, Ministry has since evolved into a huge global brand, incorporating a record label, compilation series and retail arm which have gone far beyond the original, physical manifestation. The club's 30th anniversary in 2021 was celebrated at London's cavernous O2 Arena with many dancefloor classics from across its life reimagined by the 50-piece London Concert Orchestra, underlining how club culture now orbits a more high-brow world, several steps removed from its grittier origins. Or that the original audience, which has grown up with Ministry, now likes their clubbing experiences to come well-packaged in slightly more salubrious surroundings.

In 2015, Ministry explored upping sticks from its long-held physical spot on Gaunt Street in Elephant Castle. They approached The Office for Metropolitan Architecture (OMA) and their research and design studio AMO to create a blueprint for a new London venue next to their historical location[267]. From performing arts centres to libraries and opulent residential villas, OMA dreams up exciting new spaces within our towns and cities. When Ministry's team approached them, they wanted AMO to consider programming and potential 24/7 usage. Many of the ideas AMO created revolved around reimagining the concept of the club, its position within its urban environments and how it needs to be overhauled to remain relevant in the 21st century. Paul Cournet and Giulio Margheri were among the architects to work on the project.

"At the start, our research considered the space and its place in the city," explains Giulio of their contribution. "Usually, clubs are only active for a limited amount of time for a specific schedule during the week. We wanted to question and challenge this model and explore whether the club could be somewhere for a range of activities to happen so it could have a life beyond the weekend."

Rather than only opening for a certain number of hours every Friday and Saturday night, their blueprint focused on creating new routines, different opportunities and extracting greater value from the space.

"A typical club is open for less than 10% of the week," Paul says. "Ministry is not only a club but a label and big entertainment company in the UK and internationally. So the question was not only to make a design for the club but as a space for different activities connected to music."

The team's drawings "proposed a building that changed its shape from night to day, thanks to walls that mechanically lift up and down"[268]. Split across separate floors, the new reality included co-working offices, a spa, vinyl shop, cafe and other entertainment functions alongside different event areas.

"We wanted to consider new opportunities and embrace other activities such as the Morning Glory alcohol-free 'raves' which take place in the morning before people go to work," says Paul. "The idea was for it to act as a space for anything ranging from yoga classes to after-parties, lectures and more."

The design team looked to the past and early club scene for inspiration. From the *'Night Fever'* exhibition, we've seen how clubs can offer more than a place to dance. The eye-catching Yellow Submarine disco was developed in Munich in the early seventies. Named after The Beatles' eponymous album and film, this was situated in Munich's Schwabing area and made up part of the Schwabylon leisure district, an ambitious development aimed at providing 24/7 entertainment activities. According to OMA's research, many of the nocturnal spaces developed during the late sixties were "more similar to experimental theatres than nightclubs"[269], offering platforms for performances with architects and designers entrenched in the programming. These concepts around how nightlife spaces are used could become prevalent in modern times if these ventures are to be reconfigured and optimised.

"We wanted to look to this more experimental past to inform the future," explains Giulio. "Nowadays, many clubs are far more commercial."

"Ministry is coming from a more underground background," continues Paul. "So they wanted to look at the origins of clubs that were more innovative, maybe sometimes more illegal, rather than the big commercial venues you now find in places like Las Vegas and Dubai. One space we found really exciting was Area, this New York club in the eighties. It changed its decor and theme every few weeks so every time you went, the atmosphere would be totally different. We used these experimental references for inspiration."

OMA's designs were ultimately never implemented due to delays in the area's redevelopment plan from the Peabody Housing Association[270]. But the drawings and models the team drafted offer an exciting glimpse of what our night-time spaces could well look like in the future, particularly as today's electronic music scene is radically different from when Ministry first opened its doors.

"Our research shows how the idea of 'clubbing' has changed," says Giulio. "Now bars have DJs and many don't charge an entry fee. Big festivals take place with plenty of DJs on the bill. There is a new dance music entertainment ecosystem which puts the club in a very different perspective."

Paul agrees: "In the past, clubbing was associated with hedonism, heavy drinking and often drugs. Now there is a trend around wellbeing. It's become cool to be healthy and some clubs are spaces offering smoothies and vegan food. It's very different from the past."

Many of the spaces OMA researched to spark their imaginations came from New York in the seventies and eighties. When disco balls first started spinning in this American metropolis, it was a hotbed of nightlife action with its rugged environment rampant with scuzz and smut. From the unveiling of dance palace Studio 54 in the mid-seventies, the scene had a lawless vitality inspired by the carnage of unemployment and a financial downturn crashing outside the dancefloor. DJ and Ministry co-founder Justin Berkmann experienced this firsthand and remembers plenty of exciting venues and spaces he revelled in during the mid-to-late eighties. Back when the city's nightlife was full of neon lights and illicit energy, it was the perfect playground for a fresh-faced twenty-something to find his clubbing feet.

"[After-hours club night] Save the Robots was really naughty," laughs Justin. "The venue was an absolute shit hole but an amazing vibe full of great party people. Then I made all of these other incredible discoveries like the Paradise Garage."

During these early days of house music, he also found venues like the Saint, a club based in a theatre and rammed with hundreds of speakers, as well as enjoying notable adventures at nightclubs like Tracks and Nells.

"It was a combination of all these places which made us want to make Ministry what it would eventually become," he explains. "Ministry was a piece of all these clubs. Area was another space that was brilliant as they built their own sets. It was something I dreamed of doing but could never really afford."

Area opened its doors to the great and the good of New York nightlife in September 1983 to redefine the concept of what a club could do and be. Experimental, arty, and creative, it was run by four friends from California - Eric and Chris Goode, Shawn Hausman and Darius Azari. Their aim was to create a new mode of nightlife entertainment where art, personality and music merged, a way for the proprietors to live out their creative fantasies. As one of the core team members, Shawn Hausman remembers how he and his three Area colleagues had all been at high school together in North California before heading to New York. They initially started out hosting one-off parties inspired by the happenings of the sixties.

"We would do these parties without any budget. We'd go to the dump and use whatever we found to create these environments," Shawn laughs.

This magpie approach to club interior design blossomed into more concrete thoughts around opening their own nightclub. The four friends had all been regular attendees at clubs during the seventies when the discotheque's popularity was in its ascendance. They were inspired to take on their next venture at a club on 25th Street near 11th.

"We never called it anything," he says. "It was in Details Magazine as 'the club with no name' and was very low budget. We had a dancefloor area, a couple of bars and this tunnel we had built inspired by H.R. Giger's Alien. We had some permanent items on display but we would change the place a bit every time we opened by adding new elements of decor."

Following this club, Shawn and Eric's bond with Chris and Darius evolved and the vision for what would become Area began to align. They started looking for a more serious club, eventually finding a location in Tribeca in Lower Manhattan.

"This downtown scene started happening with the Mudd Club in the late seventies," says Shawn. "We had this very eccentric landlord in Tribeca. But he liked us. Eric loved tortoises and reptiles and they really bonded over a shared passion for animals."

The 1,200 square metre space on 157 Hudson Street in Tribeca was taken over by Shawn and his gang in 1983. The entrance of the skinny building Area lived inside opened up into a huge space with three loading bays, which they soon set about transforming. The attention to detail Shawn and his friends went on to demonstrate also manifested itself in its pitch for financial backing.

"We created these handmade, embossed boxes to send out to any potential investors," Shawn remembers. "You'd open it up, press this button and it would activate a cassette player with a voice telling you to look through different envelopes with our bios and business proposals."

For the opening night, they sent out 5,000 invitations which came as blue pills inside black velvet boxes. The instructions told recipients to dissolve the pill in a glass of hot water which would then reveal an invite. This creative sense of theatre was at the heart of what made the club unique and attracted a similarly individual clientele with Andy Warhol, artist Robert Mabbelthorpe, Grace Jones and many more passing through in search of the party. The sets the team installed in Area were partly inspired by their love for the Natural History Museum and the window displays New York department stores had started hosting.

"Bloomingdale's would create these living room set ups, much in the same way that Ikea does now," explains Shawn. "We loved the idea of these environments where they would have people performing in them. Then we came up with ideas for themes. We made sure they were deliberately juxtaposed so 'fairy tales', then 'elements', 'disco', 'cars'… they were always completely contrasting."

With the space changing approximately every six weeks at the cost of thousands of dollars, Area's small team would have to work round the clock to overhaul the interior before flinging open the doors to their star-studded guests.

"We'd make over elements in the main space and area as well as the window displays," Shawn explains. "It was a completely creative outlet, so we could dream up these big ideas, then we'd do the change in three days. We'd have 40 people working day and night to get the job done."

Alongside the design, nights at Area also included performers who would take on different roles to fit the theme. Coupled with projections, films and slide shows, it added an unreal air of dis-reality to proceedings. Shawn feels that the club's success over its three-year life span hinged on how it served to capture a unique period in New York's history. It attracted a cross-section of society and offered a new form of nightlife with artists, hip hop performers, punks, and musicians all clamouring to get inside. These divergent vibes collided to fire lightning bolts of creativity around New York at a time when the city still offered artists cheap rents and large amounts of space to express themselves as recklessly as they dared.

"You had wealthy people, club kids, uptown and downtown people. There was a whole group who were mini-celebrities just from going out all the time," Shawn says. "The doorman was like the casting director for the night, getting the right mix of people. As it was a nightclub, people would drop their inhibitions in that environment - so you would just have this crazy mix. I'm not sure that exists in the same way anymore."

Despite the idiosyncratic community around Area, like many of the most legendary clubs, getting in was never a foregone conclusion, no matter how much of a notorious celebrity party starter you were.

"There would be some unfairness on the door. Those who got in might have been on the list, famous, or just looked attractive or interesting. You wanted the right mix of boys and girls too," explains Shawn. "I remember this girl who lived in Long Island wrote to Details Magazine in New York asking how she could enter Area. So we sent a limo to where she lived with the instructions that she could bring as many friends as she wanted. We sent her a tiara to wear so she could be 'Queen of the Night' and that night, anyone who wanted to come was allowed in."

Over its existence, the club saw 25 different themes featured, covering everything from 'nature', 'gnarly' and 'sport' to 'suburbia' and 'science fiction'. The team took inspiration from their love for the whole spectrum of pop culture.

"'Gnarly' was inspired by Road Warriors, so we built this Mad Max-style car inside," he laughs. "Then for 'natural history', we had live animals inside the club. It's crazy how much work we'd put in. Every time, we'd tell ourselves we'd try and plan ahead better but it never quite worked like that."

The club's position on Hudson Street in Manhattan also influenced how they dressed the venue. Shawn and his friends' club was close to Canal Street, a hub for businesses selling industrial materials and an invaluable resource in bringing their ideas to life.

"This location became essential. You could walk over this footbridge and be on Canal Street, where all these places would be selling surplus goods such as foam, metal, flexi-glass. We'd make more than 50 trips when we were working on something. If that hadn't been there, we wouldn't have been able to pull these events off."

Other important New York club contemporaries of that period in the early to mid-eighties included The Tunnel, The Continental and Pyramid. The Paradise Garage and the Saint were also in full swing, offering slightly different but no less vital nights out. The Palladium was commissioned by entrepreneurs Steve Rubell and Ian Schrager, owners of the also infamous Studio 54, and arrived in 1985. But Area stands out among them all for its astonishing vision and sheer ambition.

"The four of us had these different roles within the club but it was basically whatever we felt we could adapt to," Shawn explains.

"When we finished building it, we had to start running it. This was something none of us had any idea of how to do."

He continues: "It was great but it took all of us to be totally involved all the time to do this. It was the mix of who we were at the time that made up the chemistry. At one point, we discussed taking the club public and doing multiple ones in other cities but we realised that this would be a huge endeavour and wouldn't work without us there. But I learned a lot from Area. It taught me just how much you can achieve in a very short period of time."

Colleen 'Cosmo' Murphy is a DJ, audiophile and broadcaster originally from Boston, Massachusetts, now based in east London. While she's lived in the UK for more than 20 years, it was in New York where she found her love for dance music and greatest inspiration in the form of the legendary David Mancuso and his Loft parties. Beginning at 647 Broadway in New York City's East Village in 1970 with his 'Love Saves the Day' party[271], these events were invite-only gatherings for music-lovers inside the loft apartments he called home. The focus was on bringing people from different backgrounds together in a party situation where they could dance and experience quality sound and records rather than the more commercial club scene which was evolving during the seventies. These converted warehouse spaces were littered all over Soho in New York's East Side and provided the perfect rooms for these events to happen. The lofts were initially built in the mid-1800s for department stores but were eventually transformed to house manufacturing and industrial firms at the turn of the century. By the sixties, there were estimated to be more than 650 manufacturing and warehouse businesses occupying these spaces[272]. However, "structural limitations persuaded manufacturers to relocate to cheaper and more accessible zones"[273], allowing slews of artists the chance to move in and take advantage. Amid this, Mancuso took up residence and began to host his weekly parties. His spiralling DJ sets encompassed everything from disco to psychedelia and dub played through exquisitely tuned Klipschorn speakers.

"The Loft was more than just a party," says Colleen of her late friend and mentor's events. "It changed my life as it was all about the community David created surrounding the event, something he was brilliant at nurturing. But he was forced to move around due to the impact of gentrification."

While this issue still plagues clubs in cities worldwide today, Mancuso famously became embroiled in a legal case with the New York City Department of Consumer Affairs to fight for his right to party. They insisted that Mancuso required a "cabaret licence". However, after the longest hearing in the department's history, it eventually decreed in 1975 that he was free to host his private events as long as there were no food or drink sales. This decision set a new precedent that benefited the Paradise Garage and other private 'members clubs' in the process.

"In the 1970s, Soho was a dump which was great for artists and musicians as the rents were so low," says Colleen. "Crime was high and the city was bankrupt, so rent was cheap. Traditionally, Soho had been a manufacturing area with beautiful buildings and artists started to buy them, set up their studios and live in them."

"By the mid-eighties, it had started to change and the area was becoming more attractive," she continues. "Artists noticed that their property prices were going up but felt the neighbourhood would not be as attractive if there were people from different racial backgrounds and sexual orientations hanging out in the street in front of David's loft, located on 99 Prince Street. The neighbours expressed their disapproval and eventually, the landlord made it untenable for David to stay. With property prices going up, there was less appetite for him to host his parties even though he was partly why people wanted to move to the area in the first place."

David Mancuso's influence on club culture in terms of his events, approach to sound and DJing is huge and enduring. In addition to developing one of the best sound systems in the world, he inspired the likes of Nicky Siano, who set up the Gallery, Mike Brody to launch the Paradise Garage and Robert Williams to open up the Warehouse in Chicago, three clubs at the very root of dance music. David sadly passed away in 2016 and, as his protege and close friend, Colleen's approach to DJing has been to continue to push his aesthetic. She upholds his legacy as a musical host at the Loft in New York City, now in a hired venue in the East Village. In London's East End, she also co-founded the Lucky Cloud Loft Party with David and some friends based on the Loft template's focus on sound, music and community in an intimate setting. These day-time to evening events are open to all (including children for the first few hours) and aim to celebrate a figure who continues to hold great sway over how we dance.

"We host the London realisation of the Loft built on the same ethos," says Colleen. "We started the party with David with the idea to avoid promotion and only invite people via word of mouth."

As a dance music fanatic whose life has been split between New York and London, Colleen is well placed to see the similarities between the two cities and the way each has evolved.

"Manhattan has totally changed," she states. "Party people are heading beyond Brooklyn to host events in random spaces. Club culture keeps getting pushed further out from the centre but it's the clubs that are helping these areas change by making these places livable."

Colleen is one of many contemporary London DJs and venue programmers to take inspiration from the Loft. Mancuso's focus on high sound quality has been adopted by different contemporary London spaces, including Spiritland in King's Cross, Aures underneath Waterloo Station and Brilliant Corners in Hackney. These spots don't so much take influence from the environment they live in but create a special galaxy removed from reality where attendees can luxuriate in a bath of beautiful sounds.

Spiritland moved from being a sound system in residence at the Merchants Tavern in Shoreditch to its own permanent space in King's Cross back in 2016. Its bespoke system was created by audio experts Living Voice and the specially crafted rotary mixer was built for Spiritland by Isonoe. Since launching, the venue has built a reputation for offering a musical experience somewhere more sophisticated than the sweat and flesh of the traditional club experience. As the Spiritland website says in its FAQs when asked if there is a dancefloor, "No, Spiritland is seated, with table service". Instead, the focus is on visitors immersing themselves in the soundtrack in a much deeper way than their home stereos can offer, providing a rich and detailed listening experience. Music critic Alexis Petridis described the sheer physicality of the music on his first visit: "The weirdest thing is that the music doesn't appear to be coming out of the speakers: it seems to be happening in a space just in front of you. It feels like it's in 3D: you could walk around it, you could reach out and touch it. It's astonishing"[274].

Sheffield DJ Solid State has been a regular selector at the venue and enjoys the opportunity it affords to dig deeper into the more esoteric parts of his record collection.

"With no pressure to maintain the dance - which almost never happens in clubs - it becomes far more an exercise in mood-setting," he explains of his approach. "Like all the people who have played at Spiritland, I'm a music lover before I'm a 'DJ' and I've acquired a wide range of music over many years. Some of my collection has been mentally filed away for decades, just waiting for its one 'moment'. If that 'moment' doesn't happen here, you could be waiting a very long time for it to come round again!"

Playing in this setting is more about "morphing the mood" of the room than attempting to lure people onto the dancefloor with party pleasers. DJs can also leave their technical skills at the door and instead focus on ensuring that "the elusive 'vibe' transpires and a quiet magic happens". According to Solid, DJs have to think carefully about the type of sounds and records to play to get the best from this environment. Spiritland is an alternative experience to the classic nightclub, not only for the audience but the DJ as well.

"I've heard other DJs mention that it's hard to predict what will really shine on the Spiritland system," Solid explains. "Bass-heavy tracks, which might sound amazing on a night out, can sound very flat - all thump and no 'air'. Meanwhile, records that in a club context might be considered a bit lightweight or lacking in presence can shine in having superior dynamics, detail and clarity which really draw the listener in."

*Shadow Dancing* by Andy Gibb is a track that really stood out for Solid in his DJ sets at the venue. He is also a fan of hearing any Sly & Robbie production for disco icon Grace Jones come out of the speakers.

"Under the microscope of the Spiritland system, the rule of thumb is that 'real' musicians recorded in a proper studio will always sound superior to tunes recorded on computers which bang in a club," he said. "That being said, sound quality alone should never be held up as the preeminent factor defining 'good music', as Larry Sherman at Chicago Trax would testify."

High-end sonics are also a similar obsession for the team behind Brilliant Corners on Kingsland Road in Hackney. In the 2010s, two brothers Amit and Aneesh Patel, launched this London venue that nestles between a kebab joint and hairdressers, offering another classy audio affair paired with fancy food and wine. They've since expanded their remit with Giant Steps, a travelling version of their sound system. Again, venturing to an event is an extension of David Mancuso's blueprint and an immersive listening experience.

According to Amit: "This London night called Beauty and Beat, the London incarnation of the Loft and David Mancuso himself were the main influences behind what we wanted to do. We used to go to these nights religiously."

Both Amit and his brother used to be lawyers living near Old Street. Inspired by Mancuso's utopian vision of the party, they cast their nets wide and stomped around the streets of east London until they found the perfect location for their own adventures into sound.

"David Mancuso had done the research for us in terms of the system," says Amit. "It's well established that pairing Klipsch speakers with valve amplifiers sound amazing when you put recorded music through them."

The front-end of the sound system at Brilliant Corners is a "constant work in progress", always being updated and improved to ensure it interacts beautifully with the walls around it.

"It's like a sports car," states Amit. "It needs maintenance and we are always doing what we can to make it sound as good as possible. At the same time, everyone will tell you that the room is what you need to get right and we've made structural changes to the space to achieve this. It's fun to have amazing equipment but whatever you do to the room itself has a bigger impact than the gear."

As we've seen throughout, a sense of transience surrounds many clubs in today's constantly moving world. With cities and towns often living in an almost permanent state of regeneration, it's long been a challenge for nightlife to survive and thrive amid pressures from real estate, licensing authorities and party people striving for new ways to enjoy their thrills, spills and bellyaches. Rather than viewing a lack of permanent home as an obstacle, LCD Sound System's James Murphy and Soulwax's David and Stephen Dewaele brothers saw it as an opportunity to create Despacio - a night-time offering that's very existence is defined by its temporary state. They opted to set up short-term homes for their party when the time, money and demand was there instead of developing a long-term location and subjecting its fate to neighbours' complaints or decisions of local councils. It's an example that other clubs might look to for inspiration in the future, although challenging to emulate due to Despacio's unique nature and cost. It's made up of eight speaker stacks each standing at 11 feet while 48 McIntosh amplifiers are reported to have cost £22,000 each[275]. Originally commissioned by the Manchester International Festival (MIF) back in 2013, this roving musical venture takes its name from the Spanish word for 'slow' and is one of the world's best-sounding and looking speaker systems, propelled by the technical knowledge of John Klett, LCD's James Murphy's comrade in audiophilia.

"Despacio was kind of a fluke actually as James wanted my technically "obsolete" take on things," laughs John when quizzed on Despacio's origins. John first moved to New York in the mid-seventies and hung out at the likes of Studio 54, Danceteria and the Paradise Garage, playing in various bands and attending as a punter, all the while feeding his vociferous love for musical gadgets and equipment.

"I was burning my candle at both ends, sometimes even in the middle," John recalls. "I went out to a number of clubs and discos in New York. Back then, I was very sleep deprived and most likely on some sort of 'going out to the club' drugs. So I'm sure nothing I remember from then is terribly accurate. It's like some impressionist memory painting sitting in the attic of my mind."

John's self-deprecation aside, many have pointed to Despacio as one of the most future-facing clubbing experiences despite its bubbling soundtrack drawing heavily on past Balearic classics (including tunes like *'Fly like an Eagle'* by the Steve Miller Band or Chicago's *'I'm a Man'*). On the occasions that the huge speakers have been rolled out into a physical space, the night has focused on what comes from them rather than the Dewaele brothers or James Murphy, who take the decks for the entirety of the evening. Despacio aims to be the perfect club, although, from John's perspective, there have always been challenges in getting the space ready for musical lift-off.

"The majority of Despacio events have been done in less than ideal acoustical conditions," he states. "So mainly in tents and car parks, then once in a while in good spaces but with only a couple days to load in, build the system, and tune it. That tuning part would generally extend into the first show since the acoustical element of many warm bodies has a huge impact."

When quizzed on how to create the perfect dancefloor world, John says the main focus is ensuring the acoustics within the space are on point.

"To get it right, you want a larger volume and good dimensions so that the longer wavelengths can develop and you can control reverb timing within the space," he states. "Larger spaces can have longer reverb times. In this scenario, reverb time is a measure of how long it takes for a sound to decay in a room. If the reverb time is too long, then you lose definition. If it's too short, the energy gets sucked out of the music."

John has very specific requirements for what he believes would offer the best club escapades. He suggests that an old two-storey high bus garage of around roughly 2,000 square metres would be the most appropriate size with a dancefloor between 750-950 square metres although these ideal conditions are rarely achieved.

"Despacio lays out as a roughly 25 metres diameter circle around a dancefloor. With the DJ booth/backstage, you come up with a rectangular space surrounding an internal volume of around 4,500-5,500 cubic metres," he explains. "You are dropping a lighting grid in there and over the top of that, there would be acoustical trapping to bring the reverb time down enough to keep the room under control."

On the perimeter of the space are other support areas such as bars and toilets, which play an important role in soaking up the sound. Part of John's plan for Despacio was to offer these zones to local artists and food trucks and provide an alternative experience outside of the dancefloor. Amid the dance itself, low lighting and DJs hidden in shadows means the room's focus is on the aural silk being fed through the system.

"The emphasis is on listening and enjoying everyone around you rather than checking your phone or bunching up in front of the DJ booth," says John. "The idea is to let your brain go into listening mode where you can really experience and feel the music."

"You shouldn't need to rely heavily on processing to get a good result," he continues. "But in many clubs, the trend seems to be overcoming the acoustics with processing rather than getting the actual room right."

'Despacio is Happiness' is a slogan the sound system has adopted and displayed at the various events it's been taken to[276]. From its initial outing at MIF to Glastonbury, Sonar, Coachella and the All Points East Festival, the trio's mixture of Balearic, italo, new wave, and acid house affirms the positive messaging displayed. This sense of blissful sanctuary is cultivated by the soundtrack and sound system coming together in sonic harmony.

"A really good club experience should leave all participants feeling great and happy," says John. "It should be a recharge station. You should not be leaving a club feeling burnt to a crisp. You may be tired and exhausted but it should feel good. To do this, you want a system that is clean and does not bludgeon you. This means retaining dynamic range, reduced processing and DJs having some discipline as far as they push the system too."

'Club music' now goes far beyond what can be confined within the four walls of a physical space with the last decade welcoming the streaming phenomenon, in part thanks to the arrival of virtual clubbing broadcaster Boiler Room. Now domestic ravers can enjoy DJ sets from around the world without leaving the house with this new spatial context raising questions about how an environment influences sounds. Does location still have any impact on the sound of a club night, now that the internet has made the world so much smaller? Or can any form of electronic music emerge from anywhere now that geographies have collapsed? Part of the vitality of a club comes from how it provides somewhere for individuals to meet and enjoy a shared cultural experience among a certain number of participants. But the internet's limitless capacity has, for better or for worse, removed some of this sense of exclusivity and made more niche sounds available for all. At the same time, the Boiler Room events themselves are almost impossible to get a ticket for. If you do manage to gain access, then you have broken down some third wall between the star DJs, online world and audience. Before it became one of the most dominant broadcasting forces within the global clubbing community, Boiler Room "started with a webcam taped to a wall, opening a keyhole into London's underground"[277]. Now, its deep archive of content features thousands of hours of performances from artists ranging from Tirzah and Four Tet to Richie Hawtin and Solomun.

In these streams, the platform has managed to boil down the essence of the club experience, then beam broadcasts of it into people's front rooms, kitchens or wherever they choose to watch. The visual experience feels authentic thanks to a mixture of crowd shots and static close-ups of the DJ and decks. A chat room also enables participants to create some form of community in real time. However, apart from those lucky enough to land a ticket, most watchers will be unable to feel the sound system rushing through them.

Thristian Richards, alongside Blaise Bellville, was one of the co-founders of Boiler Room. His musical infatuation began as a teenager tuning into Kiss FM and listening to DJ EZ, Steve Jackson and The Dreem Teem. Originally from Hackney, his family moved to Essex while he attended school in west London. Long tube rides to and from school would involve headphones and digging into recorded radio shows.

"It was just me on the tube in the eighties and nineties, this Black kid listening to music," Thristian recalls. "I used to record DJ EZ's shows but I had no context, had no idea of where it came from. I just felt it was related to me."

From school he went to study at Goldsmiths, University of London and threw himself into London's nightlife. Clubs in the capital such as Herbal, Home and Fabric all welcomed him into this newly discovered musical world.

"It was just total immersion in music," he remembers. "It was around 2000 when club music was just this cool subculture and you had a lot of access to great music. My parents were West Indian and I was born in the UK, and this really gave me some sense of identity."

Thristian began running and promoting his own ventures before finding his way into podcasts and studio stints with the BBC. The first flickers of what would become the Boiler Room started while he was behind the counter of Soho record shop, Sounds of the Universe and working for Gilles Peterson on his early morning BBC Radio 1 show. Thristian, alongside the founder of NTS Radio, Femi Adeyemi, were contacted by Blaise Belville, who asked them to record a mixtape for his online magazine Platform.

"Blaise said he was starting this series and I'd done a couple of video broadcasts from the Brownswood record label's basement," he says. "He had a space in Hackney with a sound system which was rare, so we just started it. I posted about it on Twitter and my mates could watch me, which seemed cool at the time. Me and Femi just invited our friends for the first few, so everyone was a mate from DJing, Plastic People or any of the clubs we used to hang out at. Before Boiler Room and online radio broadcaster NTS, there wasn't necessarily a platform for these experiments to exist."

From its humble beginnings in Hackney, the platform has become one of the most important channels in electronic music circles, with millions of subscribers and followers across its various social media networks. Boiler Room went from hosting early sets from Hudson Mohawke and post-dubstep electronic act Mount Kimbie in old factories to Ibiza pool parties with Carl Cox.

"In some ways, I didn't really understand the concept of people watching us hang out online," laughs Thristian. "The Carl Cox session came about as a sponsor had mentioned the prospect of Ibiza. It's not really my energy but we thought this would be the most 'Ibiza' thing we could possibly do. It certainly felt like the optimum way of experiencing this style of dance music was by having a pool party at Carl Cox's house."

Many of the Boiler Room sessions came together by inviting a certain DJ on board, then they would be tasked with building the rest of the line-up around them. An event I managed to attend was hosted by Sheffield's Toddla T, who packed it with friends and family, including DJ Q, DJ Pipes, Walter Ego, Shola Ama and the Forgemasters.

"It would be about communicating with the different DJs and producers and finding out who they wanted to play alongside," explains Thristian. "You're doing something cool, so who are the mates you want to bring with you? When you're doing something every week, it becomes impractical to book four DJs, so instead, we identified someone who could put it together and let us showcase their vibe."

With the unwelcome arrival of Covid-19, clubs were forced to shut, which meant our social media feeds were suddenly drowning in DJs streaming sets and producing online content. With the virtual experience suddenly the main way of getting our clubbing fix, it felt like almost everyone was doing their own take on the Boiler Room.

"It was weird as even Channel 4 was doing what we'd kind of started," laughs Thristian. "But there was no other option. I don't think we can claim responsibility for this way of showcasing DJs. There were people doing it before us; we just took on a niche and expanded it."

From Thristian's perspective, the launch of Boiler Room wasn't born from a desire to revolutionise the dance music ecosystem. But its influence over the last few years is undeniable. Alongside NTS, the depth of the programming has meant more underground music scenes, DJs and artists have had a popular platform and exposure to huge audiences. UK jungle and footwork DJ Sherelle is one whose career went into hyperdrive following a set of pure energy and beats. "I amassed thousands of followers overnight," she told the Observer. "Some of them were DJs and producers who I loved and respected for years. My mind was blown."[278] It was a unique combination of circumstances that led to Boiler Room's birth, then ongoing success thanks in part to the London scene it writhed through. Many of those early online sessions featured artists such as singer-songwriter Sampha, electronic artist James Blake and indie headliners The xx, all now global stars.

"We were just putting music together which was already happening," he says. "I've always thought to myself, 'how can I help in this situation?' I was just looking for a way forward. People still want to rave no matter where it is, which is where Boiler Room came from. I wasn't a fan of going clubbing at the time. I didn't enjoy the bouncer being all over me and feeling tense. I just wanted a space where I could just play music I wanted to hear without bowing to commercial pressure. That's where Boiler Room came from."

The brand has been an undeniably disruptive and sometimes controversial force within the clubbing world during the last decade. Not everyone sees the digital experience as a force for good. On their website, architects OMA lament the plight of the club in today's physical world. They claim that "places dedicated to celebrating the collective encounter of bodies, through the designed or provisional medium of architecture, have lost their relevance. Phone applications open the doors of clubs for remote, individual experiences. A night out at a disco today can be experienced comfortably from our own couch"[279]. However, the Covid-19 lockdowns forced us to get our raving fix via a screen, whether we wanted to or not. It pushed ravers into thinking differently, while DJs and clubs also had to be as creative as possible to sustain their audiences no longer allowed inside physical spaces. We all embraced video conferencing via Zoom in our working lives and this tool permeated nightlife too.

Club Quarantine (also known as Club Q) was one of the most notable virtual events during the Covid-19 lockdowns. This queer online rave brought a global audience together when restrictions were at their peak. Their party, born from the minds of four Toronto-based creatives, was one of the most high-profile digital events, featuring guest turns from megastars Charli XCX and Lady Gaga. Club Q also participated in Discover Tokyo, a virtual nightlife experience that took viewers on a trip into the city via spatial audio. This surround sound means listeners could totally submerge themselves in a soundtrack provided by DJ Nobu and Honey Dijon[280]. Club Q's so-called "unfiltered queer experience"[281] proved to be a viral sensation during Covid-19, with i-D claiming that its innovative take on entertainment and nightclubs came in a long tradition of exciting cultural clout swung by marginalised communities. According to the magazine, the "LGBTQIA+ community have always been at the forefront in developments in internet culture - from early dating and hook-up apps ... to the strong presence we've always had on social media"[282].

Despite its success, Erin Logan, Club Q Community Manager, does not believe that the online experience will ever be able to fully replicate the power of being together in one space, all moving to the same beat. Instead, it offers a refreshing alternative to physical clubbing realities.

"In the virtual club, connectivity manifests in new and beautiful ways," she says. "The possibility of chatting with someone without screaming into their ear, the ability to take space without having to sneak onto a VIP's couch, and ultimately - the accessibility of it all. They're entirely different and wonderful experiences."

During the peak of the first wave of lockdowns, Club Quarantine created an online buzz by offering a platform for heavy-hitting artists wanting to let their music out and express themselves.

"Each performance felt so *intimate*," says Erin of these guest appearances. "Our usual Friday night friends from Toronto came out and merged quickly with people across the world chasing the same high - the space to be ourselves and be a part of something new. This high is what drew me in."

Club Q came from years of collective experience in Toronto's queer community in spaces such as The Beaver, Buddies in Bad Times, and Unit 2. This strong presence and sense of the physical world have influenced and entered the digital sphere.

"Our Canadian ability to recognise frequent familiar faces has allowed us to bond with so many of our regular partygoers and give opportunities to upcoming artists within our community who, in turn, bring their communities," she says. "We still can't wrap our heads around the fact that this has gone global, but the fact that *anyone* can come in and find inspiration within our community is what keeps us going."

Offering a safe space is a key aspect of the queer club. By hosting a Zoom event, Club Q employs moderators who act much like less visible security guards to guarantee this for participants.

"I've taken over moderating after a couple glasses of wine, and it's not an easy job," explains Erin. "You run sound and visuals for the artists, spotlight participating partygoers to give them their moment and ensure nothing (too) weird is happening on video or in the chat. The ease of removing someone who attempts to break our safe space is satisfyingly as simple as a click. We have a full disclaimer before entering, and we're not playing around when it says, *"you'll be removed immediately & your IP barred forever."*

Club Q was not the only virtual club to find a crowd. The Zone was a multi-room club featuring a range of experiences, including a "chill yurt" and "flirtation station"[283] alongside multiple different DJs. It claimed to be "the most real place in the lockdown, the place where your deepest desires come true"[284]. Elsewhere, the United We Stream concept was born out of a group of Berlin clubs coming together to provide a virtual platform for DJs during lockdown and grew to incorporate collectives in more than 100 cities the world over. Acid house veteran Graeme Park has been a DJ at clubs ranging from the Hacienda to Ministry of Sound but when lockdown hit, he found himself playing virtual sets. The freedom afforded by this new reality reminded him of the early days of his career at the Garage in Nottingham, where he had the room to play a huge variety of music.

"I hosted this 12 hour session and had no idea what I was going to play," he remembers. "But I started at midday and didn't play any house music until 9.30 at night. I started with *'Being Boiled'* by the Human League, then followed it up with this Captain Sensible record and it just set the tone for where I was going to go. I ended up playing lots of early eighties artists like Trouble Funk, Chuck Brown and the Soul Searchers. I went through the decades, then ramped it up to full-on banging house for the final couple of hours."

Elsewhere, the nightlife experience, or at least the dance music ecosystem, is entering another realm entirely in the metaverse. This is a combination of multiple elements of immersive technology, such as virtual reality, augmented reality and video, where participants can 'live' within a digital universe via avatars. So far, Club Amnesia has partnered with Decentral to reproduce the club in the metaverse[285]. The launch event took place in October 2021 with DJs Benny Benassi, Paul van Dyk and Luciano all sharing the stage at Decentral Games' SuperClub – the world's first immersive 3D metaverse experience of its kind. The event was designed to demonstrate the potential of this new platform built using blockchain technology. Electronic music aficionado and tech expert Inder Phull is an innovator and disruptive force within the music industry who believes this can go much further. As a co-founder of Pixelynx, he works alongside dance music pioneers Richie Hawtin and deadmau5 to explore bold new worlds where few ravers have ventured before[286]. Inder wants artists to take advantage of opportunities within this virtual space to create jaw-dropping, interactive experiences.

"The metaverse is all about this intersection of entertainment, blockchain and interactive experience," he says. "The moment that kicked off my love for the future of music was when we launched a project where we had a giant synthesiser at a festival. Watching people interact with this really opened my eyes to the kind of experiences we can offer by creating interactive moments. The metaverse offers a new canvas for anyone who makes art or music. It's the next form of creative expression."

In this context, the metaverse can offer much more than a straight-up replication of the club format in a digital reality. The club is possible to recreate but if the tech is in place, then creatives can go much further. Deadmau5 unveiled Oberhasli, an evolving social space and virtual music experience that the artist has described as "like a window into my brain that I can evolve over time"[287].

"Artists need to use the metaverse to create space that you would never be able to experience in the real world," says Inder. "It's not so much about creating clubbing experiences as trying to come up with cinematic, story-filled universes that the music can exist in. It is really exciting for artists who have a conceptual style that informs their work."

Alongside deadmau5 and Richie Hawtin, Bjork and Gorillaz have also delved into this experiential side of their music world. Traces of the ideas powering the metaverse can be seen in the narrative surrounding the Afrofuturism of Detroit's Drexciya. Duo Gerald Donald and James Stinson wrapped their bold, funky take on dance music within a science-fiction narrative that preempted some of the creative possibilities unveiled by the metaverse.

"They created a whole conceptual universe and storytelling," he explains. "If we look back, many of the things we're talking about have already been done a long time ago by artists. It just shows how future-facing the electronic music sector is. If you look at new concepts like NFTs, it's been the dance electronic artists who embraced them much quicker and that's very telling of what the genre is about."

Virtual reality (VR) is an emerging disruptive technology that can offer experiential pleasures within electronic music. Numerous films on the rave experience have been made over the years - from

'Human Traffic' and '24 Hour Party People' to 'Better Living Through Circuitry' and 'Eden' - and have delighted viewers by delving into past clubbing victories. But often these stories and historical recaps follow similar formats - there's hi-jinks, commentary from talking heads and rave veterans but as a viewer, you're removed from the chaos of a life-changing night out.

Darren Emerson's 'In Pursuit of Repetitive Beats' places participants firmly front and centre, providing an immersive experience via chest-pounding (courtesy of a Subpac vest) technological innovation. The 40-minute VR experience offers something less ethereal than the futures imagined by the metaverse - and transports ravers to the heart of the party without warehouse gunk ruining their trainers. Originally unveiled in the summer of 2022 at the Coventry Capital of Culture, the project has been created by Darren's East City Film company. Installed in a designated space where you are free to roam, participants journey back to Coventry during the second Summer of Love, one of many UK towns and cities swept up by acid house culture.

"One of the original Coventry acid house veterans came out after seeing it and said: 'Fucking hell, I'm buzzing mate'," says creator Darren. "I wanted to make something that seems as real and possible. The experience uses an art directed environment and an exhibition of real rave archives (flyers and images) and combines that with technological innovations such as the VR headset, a bass vest that you wear, wind machines that trigger on and off when you enter the room, projections, and soundscapes. It's something that uses as many techniques as we can think of to pull the audience into this world, and the story we are telling."

We're talking after I'd been through the rush of 'Beats' at Liverpool's cultural hub, FACT. This installation followed similar events in Coventry, Texas' SXSW and the Amsterdam Dance Event and takes you beyond conventional content. On entering a darkened room, you are given a Subpac vest, a VR headset, and hand controllers, the main components of a time machine that takes you back to '89 and a night at a warehouse dancing to Joey Beltram's *'Energy Flash'*. After the 40 minutes is up, you leave feeling nostalgic for a past you never experienced first-hand (I was only eight in 1989) while also wondering where the party is at. Darren was also too young to experience the halcyon days of dance music culture although he did dabble in some illicit party experiences as a student in the mid-nineties.

"I went to university near the south coast so we would drive to illegal parties in forests and disused tunnels," he says. "I really used to love the sense of adventure and a lot of my work is about going back to recontextualising things I observed as a young man."

Darren and his company East City Films wanted *'In Pursuit of Repetitive Beats'* to push the classic acid house documentary into new territory. The experience begins in the back of a virtual Peugeot before entering a bedroom full of flyers, with DJs and MCs from Coventry's Amnesia House collective recounting their takes on the time. As it progresses you head past police stations, service stations and pirate radio announcements before arriving at the warehouse. Although based in the West Midlands, *'In Pursuit of Repetitive Beats'* captures a universal nocturnal energy that many of us will be familiar with, whatever age we are. As a dance music lover, it might be a virtual experience but one that makes your mind and heart burst.

"It's always interesting to watch documentaries about rave culture," says Darren. "But I've found myself wanting to be there, to hear and feel it. That's where the idea to create something like this came from."

"There are autobiographical elements, but acid house was a collective shared experience," he continues. "The project is really about being young and going on those first night-time adventures with the people that will shape who you become as an adult. It's about the journey and the nervous excitement, which is why the Subpac bass vest with the visuals and sounds in the headset combine perfectly to make you feel this. VR is a great immersive storytelling tool, but ultimately, it's real gift as a medium is how it makes you feel!"

Darren and his team used 360-degree cameras, drones, 3D modelling, motion capture, volumetric capture, animation and built the whole experience in a game engine called Unity. In VR, users are given 'six degrees of freedom' which allows them to pick objects up and move freely within a space, an approach he was keen to add into the innovative mix.

"It was very challenging to devise the different scenes and make sure we had the right combination of techniques," explains Darren. "We did lots of research, filming interviews with people who lived the scene, and spending a lot of time finding the right artefacts to bring into our virtual world by creating 3D models. I really geek out on making sure all the elements in the experience are authentic to the time, from the clothes people are wearing, to the cigarette packets in the back seat of the car. Everything must be perfect. It's a big team and you need to write it all, directing and producing it in a very hands-on way."

Despite having experienced it thousands of times, Darren is still visibly excited by what he and his team have created.

"There are many moments when the visuals and sound come together in such a way that even myself and the Lead Developer Ollie Lindsay (who had been working on it for the best part of a year) would be so excited. We'd be jumping around the studio, because we knew it was working. You could truly feel it. And that's what great VR has to do."

Increasingly, these experimental spaces are providing a breeding ground for electronic music to enter new realms that past ravers could only dream of. For Ana Ofak, Transmoderna Co-Founder and

Creative Director alongside Steffen 'Dixon' Berkhahn, it was a VR installation at Berlin club Tresor in 2018 that exploded her conceptions of what the dancefloor could look and feel like.

"It really changed the way I perceived the cultural value of pairing electronic music, virtual art - as it was called back then - and clubbing," she says. "I realised that underground culture can be about the expansion of knowledge on new technologies, about unique sensorial experiences, and the club as a vessel for cutting edge innovation."

It's this vision that is behind the jaw-dropping Transmoderna events, a fusion of immersive visual imaginings and Dixon's inspired sets. The beginnings of the project can be traced back to 2018 when the DJ was invited to take up a residency at Pacha in Ibiza. Initially, he turned down the request, deeming the club to be too conservative and commercial. At the same time, exciting creative sparks were flying in Berlin in what Ana describes as "post-internet art". Coders were experimenting with augmented and extended reality and Dixon's team started expanding their club-wear brand Together We Dance Alone, developing shirts with AR components and cinematic Instagram filters. These creatives were then invited to the White Isle to aid and abet Dixon's residency.

"It was an extremely ambitious idea, which in May 2019, when we launched, had no comparable counterpart out there," says Ana. "Not just in Ibiza, but also nowhere else on the globe. It was the first audio-visual experience in a club, decentralising the DJ, and pushing digital arts and the immersion on the dancefloor into the foreground."

During the 20 week residency, DJs, musicians, artists, promoters and myriad industry movers and shakers were invited to take part in the events at Pacha. Initially, these experimental evenings were met with some confusion by dancers not used to witnessing such innovation in a club setting.

"It wasn't until we were halfway through the residency that we reached a tipping point," Ana explains. "The understanding of our ideas increased, and started to change the view of how clubbing intersects with digital art."

Since then, Transmoderna has evolved to install its VR experience in a variety of different locations. From the iconic museum Fondation Beyeler in Basel to Centre Pompidou Metz, Julia Stoschek Foundation, Max Ernst Museum, NXT Museum, and Printworks in London, these events have aimed to push the envelope of what is possible with club music. Work began on their first installation during the pandemic after the Fondation Beyeler director Samuel Keller had the idea of Dixon DJing in one of their exhibition halls with Transmoderna's visual show.

"Sam was inspired by our Boiler Room underwater stream, our first venture into fully virtual streaming at the beginning of 2020," says Ana. "We developed a concept for Fondation Beyeler, where we digitised its architecture, and some of its most renowned art from its collection, while Dixon played his set as an avatar. The digital film *Machiné Concrète* was a gigantic collaborative project that pushed the limits of what is possible in terms of digitalisation, and virtualisation. Turning this digital film into VR seemed like a small step. But involved again making things possible technically that were never done before."

The Transmoderna show at Printworks in 2021 was one of the most talked about events of the now defunct venue's season. The huge former print factory became a sensory feast with Dixon's deep set acting as a soundtrack and guide to the immersive experience.

"We produced the show with Touch Designer as the central processing unit and it was a game changer," says Ana. "Additionally, we work with our own AI app, which generates art worlds in real-time, and audio-reactively. The challenge is to then bring in light, lasers, haze, and even performers into this equation, creating our signature "AI based ecosystem". We have done this since 2021. It's only now that others are understanding that AI is not just about visuals, it needs to be an active collaborator in a show, this has always been our vision."

While much ink has been spilled over the way nightlife is mutating, despite the dazzling technology deployed, the essence of the Transmoderna lies in traditional ideas associated with a club and what it can offer - a safe space for countercultures and subcultures to take root and grow.

"We push our visual, and musical curation to reflect alternative and underground content," says Ana. "We collaborate with artists, who represent that, artists that represent other ethnicities, other sexualities, other social contexts, and worldviews. We are often associated with transhumanism, but we consider our vision of the club to be something encapsulating the present, our relationship with non-human agents, and marginalised beings in the furthest sense possible."

The Transmoderna concept is fluid with the creative team looking to new ideas and technical media into their form of entertainment. But, despite the visuals and sonics at play, as Ana has said, they want to remain true to their underground dance music origins.

"We work with game engine developers to realise our projects. So when we present VR installations or game simulations during our shows, we truly cross-breed clubbing with gaming or creative coding, not just showing commissioned visuals from those households. This is the vision that we will continue to follow, pushing the boundaries of what is considered the future of clubbing, but also the future of exhibiting computational art in museums too."

The internet has created huge opportunities for artists, producers and the electronic music community to collaborate, interact and connect. It's exposed us all to more music of different styles than ever before and brought many of us closer together via our broadband connections. But the changes in music consumption are not without their downsides.

"Everything is caught before it has a chance to develop," says DJ and producer Ashley Beedle. "Back in the day, you could develop something at an underground level but in some ways, it's harder to do that with the instant access culture we're living in."

Ashley's Heavy Disco parties have taken place in venues such as The North London Tavern in Kilburn in west London and the Margate Arts Club, more intimate music haunts than his reputation as a selector suggest. This is a deliberate approach designed to foster a sense of community surrounding their party and for the blissed-out disco, tech and Balearic that's thrown down. It's almost an antithesis to the myriad, forgotten connections we sometimes make on social media and 'Facebook 'friends' we've all amassed.

"We like to make sure there's no more than 150 people and try to get the right people in there to instil that community vibe," says Ashley. "Everyone knows each other and it means we've managed to build up a wicked relationship among the crowd."

The sweat and sound of the club has reached different physical places, too, other than the smaller community spaces that parties like Heavy Disco have sourced. Rather than being in city centres, so-called entertainment complexes now exist as dedicated places for nightlife to thrive. Often they are subject to their own legislation and rules to benefit the businesses that call these places home. The reputation of areas such as Soho in London is all about entertainment and unique nightlife. Mick Wilson, DJ and DJ Magazine editor, says that as these dedicated areas change and become more commercialised, nightclubs leave traditional city centres and open on the outskirts. It's a spatial shift driven by a seemingly unquenchable appetite for real estate.

"When nightclubbing exploded, there wasn't this crazy demand for property like there is now," he explains. "But cities and towns have all changed. The attitude is let's get the clubs out and put something else in."

"Placing entertainment in one area is a deliberate approach. When you go to Las Vegas, you have hotels, casinos, clubs, and restaurants all in the same complex," he continues. "It's all about keeping the footfall in this concentrated area; you'll keep supplying your venue rather than having a destination where you have to go out to. It means everything is in one spot and feeds the club."

Paul Cornet from architects, OMA, says that many of the iconic clubs of the eighties and nineties established a blueprint for these larger, glossier ventures to succeed.

"In our research, we found that many of the great venues like the Hacienda or Ministry, they created the space for the super clubs such as those you now find in Las Vegas, Ibiza or Barcelona," he says.

"These ventures are more commercial and appeal to a different, more mainstream audience - and find it easier to survive than those which offer more experimental music and DJ booking policy. This is a global trend and shows where we are today. Now, nightlife appeals to a larger audience and also has an interesting impact on cities, their ecosystems and economies."

"As far as the underground scene is concerned, these clubs will try and remove themselves as far as possible from these settings," adds Mick. "These kinds of spaces will be in the middle of nowhere, be small, in a cooler, more undesirable part of the town."

One trend that has taken off in different places across the UK is the food hall. Much like the entertainment districts, these dedicated culinary zones often group independent food businesses together to capture an audience all in one place. From Escape to Freight Island in Manchester to the Baltic Market in Liverpool, this model has been adopted all over. DJ and rare groove originator Norman Jay has lent his DJing skills to these new forms of entertainment.

"This is the new going out," he says. "There are a generation of younger kids who've never been to a nightclub. Instead, they go to these open air food places. I like them and I've played at them but these are not nightclubs."

"For some, if they do get together, then it's normally at a festival," Norman continues. "I've spent nearly 50 years in nightclubs; it's what I've grown up on and always loved. But my young nephews, it's different. They'll go to a festival and be at Glastonbury or dance events out in the open. This is a cultural shift."

Oversharing is something many of us are guilty of in an Instagrammable world where posting about an experience online sometimes seems just as important as having it. This is another shift where any sign of restraint on social media is an exception to the norm and a notable, noble ambition. The Secret DJ is the antithesis of this online culture, an anonymous, yet globally-renowned figure with a 30 year plus career in rave. Rather than shouting about his achievements, he's instead extended this masked identity into the clubbing world via his Dark Room parties. Hailed by Mixmag as a night going "against every single bit of accepted wisdom about clubbing"[288], these events take place with "no billed names, phones, lights, visible focus or DJ booth". Instead the emphasis is all about the sound as part of a concept the Secret DJ describes as "simply being the opposite of showbiz".

"The anonymity aspect is vital to present a level playing field where once again we are applauding the composers and performers of the music, instead of the 'curator'," he explains.

"I found in several situations it was very, very interesting that who was playing something mattered more than what was being played. And conversely something that was an excellent piece of music was received less warmly if offered by the 'wrong' person. Another aspect of the Dark Room project is an attempt, win or lose, to achieve absolute authenticity in an increasingly fake world. I'm very aware of Guy Debord predicting our current woes in *'Society of the Spectacle'* and I guess we are trying to fight that cultural inevitability with these 'anti spectacle' events."

With no DJ names revealed either in the promotion or on the night (with the DJs themselves often concealed), the Dark Room transcends time and space to offer a pure, unadulterated clubbing experience. Hosted in London venues such as the Ace Hotel or Hangar, this is a musical happening where all focus is on the energy fizzing between the soundsystem and the dancefloor.

"The main driver was about sound and it being *only* sound," the Secret DJ says. "I tried to look ahead at where the club thing was going and sort of ended up where it all started, in the pitch black with no clue who was playing. I also noticed that younger people were getting more and more dowdy in their dress and seemed to frown on rock 'n' roll excess. Quite puritanical in their own way. That informed the strictness of the Dark Room a little. Plus it is the ultimate 'safe space' perhaps? None of the issues of gender, fashion, race, age, or culture have any meaning in a pitch black box where no one can see or hear you."

While the Dark Room concept aims to take the clubbing experience back to the source, the Secret DJ is no luddite, instead always operating with one eye on the future curve of electronic music culture.

"I'm very wary of Balearic Silverbacks and gatekeepers putting the brakes and padlocks on everything," he laughs. "Things for me are usually an evolution rather than an apocalypse. It's not that hard to remember what it was like to be young, and not impossible for youngsters to enjoy what we consider 'authentic'. There is a venn diagram where all the good stuff meets. I try to inhabit that intersection. Whenever possible."

If we look at our UK cities now, much of the new development we see in places like Manchester, Sheffield, Leeds and Liverpool seems identical, as if they each had access to the same town planner's blueprint around imposing shiny apartment blocks. A cultural change instilled in young people has emerged at the same time as this homogenisation of city design.

"They have no connection with a spit and sawdust pub or the clubs in damp arches," says Ian Anderson of Sheffield's Designers Republic. "My abiding memory of the Limit in Sheffield was that the toilets overflowed every night. If you went in there, it wouldn't be sticky carpets but piss leaking out from the Ladies. But it wasn't unusual to go to places like that back then."

Demands on cities and how we treat them are changing in line with the adoption of new behaviours. Retail was previously a big draw but online shopping has decimated this habit. Many of the biggest department stores have been forced to shut their doors in recent years. In 2016 British Home Stores closed all its UK shops while Debenhams has removed all 118 branches from the high street in the wake of the pandemic[289].

"What do people want from their city centres these days?" asks Ian. "With rising rents, the days of little clubs in old discos like Occasions in Sheffield, for the most part, those days are gone. If you want to run a successful club, then it has to be outside of a city centre, yet still accessible."

"In the old days in Sheffield, we'd go to the Adelphi and you'd never be able to get back as there weren't any taxis. It meant a big part of your evening was about walking back as a group, then finding some shitty burger van to refuel. But that was all part of what you'd be up to. Now, I'm not sure if anyone wants this."

Instead of dancing in nightclubs, Ian believes that the key change is how many of us are shifting towards an 'experience' economy with the emphasis on witnessing an event or happening rather than buying things we don't need. Instead, we want to do more things and share this online, which is why 'club culture' now exists in so many different worlds.

"From looking at my kids, I don't think they aspire to go to nightclubs," Ian explains. "They aspire to have experiences. If you can create this in a spot, hidden away from anywhere where noise is not an issue, then this is amazing for them. We assume each generation will have their own version of clubs but what they appear to be having is their own version of experience. And that doesn't mean paying a fortune to get into a club. Previous generations would say they'd be 'going clubbing' and the word became a noun. Younger generations are now more eclectic; they are channelled into much more than just one thing."

So where will the nightclub travel from here? As we've seen and heard, the traditional sound of the beats and bleeps that soundtrack nightclubs firmly has two feet in the mainstream. You're now as likely to hear dance music in a classical music hall being played by an orchestra as being blasted out of a tinny radio in a supermarket or in a Dubai casino. And, as we've seen, it can be a part of an imagined past or reimagined future. The clubbing community got really innovative when we weren't allowed to have physical gatherings due to Covid-19 restrictions. Gilles Peterson used his BBC 6 Music show to host lockdown where listeners would be invited into different 'rooms' filled with a rich variety of artists and sounds. The pop megastar Dua Lipa embraced the club and pointed us towards Disco 2054, a dancefloor re-imagining of her hit record *'Future Nostalgia*[290]. This nonstop party mix of her album, full of Europop hits and streamed to more than five million viewers, gave those of us watching a rush of excitement for life beyond restrictions. For a contemporary mainstream artist like Dua Lipa to embrace the nightclub also shows how club music is a dominant sound. This hinged around eye-catching production and a sense of spectacle drawing once again on the blueprint for the ever-changing environments dreamed up by the team behind New York's Area nightclub in the eighties.

"We're in this era of Instagrammable, blockbuster experiences and people are excited by this world of amazing location, sound, visuals and curation," says Inder Phull. "This creates challenges and potential opportunities for our clubs. Then some clubs have responded, which is where we might be heading next. Clubs like Studio 338 can have a raw, underground feel or a more mainstream look and sound depending on the event. It paints an interesting picture of how clubs of the future need to be flexible and resourceful enough to come up with different styles and worlds to stay alive."

# CONCLUSIONS

## ESCAPISM / HEDONISM / COMMUNITY / EUPHORIA[291] – THEMES FOR GREAT CITIES

*"For music culture to be sustainable, we need to own our music venues. We need to stop squeezing cultural institutions for profit and forcing them to fight for their survival"*[292].

Lenny Watson (Sister Midnight)

In 2017, the environment towards clubs in our towns and cities seemed more volatile than ever before. London's LGBTQIA+ venues particularly felt the sting of rising business rents, large-scale developments and a lack of safeguarding in the planning system.

Shocking research released by the Mayor of London Sadiq Khan revealed the extent of nightlife's devastation, with more than half of the capital's queer spaces lost since 2006[293]. The Joiners Arms, an institution for the queer community on Hackney Road in east London from 1997, was one of those under threat which I covered in a piece for Mixmag in 2017[294]. Back in 2014, when the writing seemed to be on the wall for the pub's future, campaign group the Friends of the Joiners Arms[295] launched a bid to prevent the much-loved boozer from being another space sacrificed on the altar of development. Their efforts were, at least partly, effective. Although its doors have remained closed since January 2015, developers Regal Homes had their plans rejected in 2017, then amended to meet councillors' fears that the proposal for a replacement queer venue was insufficient to guarantee its viability.

Since then, the lines continue to be drawn between queer venues and property businesses but the Joiners Arms team believe the situation has stabilised despite the impact of the pandemic.

"In Hackney and Tower Hamlets, the blood-flow seems to have been staunched," says Peter Cragg from the campaign group on the situation surrounding embattled queer spaces. "Many of Hackney and Tower Hamlets' venues seem to have survived the last few years, so places like Dalston Superstore, VFD [formerly known as Vogue Fabrics], The White Swan, and The Queen Adelaide are all still here. From what I can see, the pent up demand from Covid-19 created this hunger for the queer community to go out while we still can."

Although the Joiners has been shut for more than nine years, the campaign had some positive news in 2021[296]. Regal Homes agreed to provide a long-term replacement venue in its new development alongside an additional £100,000 to fund a queer temporary space while the work is underway.

"That planning permission was granted in February 2021 but it took the developers until December 2021 to actually sign it," says Peter. "We don't get a sniff of the cash until they not only sign it, but actually start work on the development."

"In the meantime, we're putting on our Lese-Majeste parties. Ironically, the place we were doing them pre-Covid was itself a temporary-use space and has now been closed so it can be demolished and turned into a hotel. So we're using venues like the Bethnal Green Working Men's Club and the Ivy House in Nunhead."

The group now has a grant to help their community share sale for the Community Benefit Society. This will enable them to have a wide section of owners with the power to vote on how and what they operate inside the space. Peter is cautiously optimistic that the work they've put in has led to a slight sea-change in the attitude towards spaces like the Joiners.

"In our very small pond, there's been an improvement," he says. "The planning officer we've worked with has really gone on 'a journey' to understand what the issues are and what we talk about, although I think that's very much a personal thing on his part rather than indicative of something that's come top-down."

"Even though councils are more aware of attracting negative attention and locals kicking off, they are still constrained. But ultimately, if you want safer, sustainable venues that are able to make decisions based on 'values' rather than cash, community-ownership is the way to go."

The nightclub now occupies a very different space compared to when the Joiners campaign began, not only within cities but in our cultural consciousness as the world looks to life beyond the pandemic. Somewhat battered and bruised by the last few years, 'the club' continues to fight on in a landscape more challenging than ever before. The changing lockdown restrictions proved to be a lesion through which hospitality budgets and financial resources drained while more than 80,000 jobs[297] were lost from the sector despite the furlough scheme support. As the UK moved forward, damaging reports were released showing where the nightclub sits in the eyes of certain members of the public. A poll, compiled by market research company Ipsos MORI in collaboration with The Economist and published in July 2021, revealed how more than a quarter of respondents thought nightclubs should never reopen[298]. A further 19% supported the introduction of a permanent 10pm curfew in the UK. Figures subsequently released in the summer of 2023 revealed how over 100 of the UK's independent nightclubs had closed down in the previous 12 months[299].

Against this negative public perception, the challenges for venues and club nights are myriad, with finances balanced more precariously than ever. In these tough times, where running a nightclub seems so tricky, the ownership concept of the Friends of the Joiners Arms could look appealing to anyone attempting to keep a venue afloat. It's also a strategy that a brace of other co-operatives and collectives are simultaneously exploring.

One such campaigning group is Sister Midnight[300], a collective currently working hard to reanimate the former Brookdale Club, a disused working men's club in the heart of Catford.

Previously, the group opened in 2018 as a record shop, music venue, craft beer bar and vegan friendly cafe in Deptford. Due to the pandemic, their space was forced to shut and the group chose to launch a crowdfunder to raise funds to acquire a new venue in the form of an ex-pub, The Ravensbourne Arms.

"I went to visit the Ravensbourne Arms around October 2019 purely out of curiosity; there was no way we could have afforded to buy it back then," explains Lenny Watson from Sister Midnight. "But I instantly fell in love with the space, and it stuck in my mind ever since."

After their original space in Deptford closed, the group began researching what would be required to take on the boozer and how they could source the funds to begin putting flesh on the bones of what they saw as a potentially exciting new musical community.

"Through my own research and the help of the Music Venue Trust, I started learning more about how community ownership could save the pub and make it a sustainable business," Lenny says. "To raise the money we needed for a deposit on a mortgage, we started working towards launching a community share offer, giving our community the chance to invest in the proposal, become members of our democratic society and future co-owners of the pub."

However, ultimately they lost out on this former pub and were forced to look for a building elsewhere. A tip off from Lewisham Council alerted the group to the dilapidated Brookdale Club and they were offered a ten-year lease on the property subject to a peppercorn rent - so without requiring payment. With the majority of their investors backing proposals for the latest site, a new community share offer was launched to push plans for the new space forward. The group has kept the momentum up, launching their own Sister Midnight FM community radio and holding numerous fundraising events. They are continuing to fight for the space while simultaneously ensuring the local community is engaged, supportive and can input into how the venue is managed.

"We want this venture to be a democratically run creative and cultural hub, with local music at the beating heart of everything we do," Lenny says. "There's a long road ahead to getting the doors of the pub open, but acquiring the building is our biggest hurdle."

"The radio station launched in 2024 as a way of engaging with our community without having a physical space," she continues. "It's been a great way to connect with local creatives. Even when the venue is up and running, to have a way to engage with local music culture which doesn't require them to be there is important on many levels."

Such localised spaces seem vital in offering creative playgrounds to develop ideas and innovation in our communities. With Sister Midnight and the Friends of the Joiners Arms, these campaigns are driven by an inherent urge to work closely with their local community and serve their needs as effectively as possible. The Sound Diplomacy agency's work and research explores this placing of music within our towns and cities and how, if deployed correctly, it has a positive impact on these environments. Shain Shapiro works as Chairman of the organisation and Executive Director of non-profit think tank, The Centre for Music Ecosystems. He developed the Music Cities Resilience Handbook, a framework and plan that any city, region or state can use as a roadmap for embracing music[301] and worked up his ideas further through his 2023 book, *'This Must Be the Place: How Music Can Make Your City Better'*.

"We need to define what a club can be," Shain says. "The term itself is problematic to me and creates these binary conversations surrounding our cities. Should we have a nightclub or not? If we think about it like this - so housing versus going out - then it does increase displacement. When you work in binaries, one wins and one loses."

Work is also ongoing to ensure that the cultural contribution of nightclubs is recognised in the same way as other art forms or modes of creative expression. In Germany in spring 2021, the authorities took the bold step to label clubs as "cultural institutions" and gave them the same status and protection as museums or opera houses[302]. After being previously lumped in the same category as "entertainment venues" such as brothels and casinos, this was a significant elevation. This shifting of the needle favouring nightclubs followed months of lobbying and hard work from Clubcommission, a collective of German club owners and supporters[303]. Shain feels other countries should follow this example and officially reassess the worth and contribution of these nocturnal spaces.

"Ministry of Sound and Sydney Opera House are seen differently," he explains. "But there is now a greater opportunity to change the narrative than ever before. When you say nightclub and you don't explain or define it, this often creates a negative perspective in people's minds. We need to do more to showcase what value they bring to a community."

A similar initiative to help clubs gain cultural status has launched in France[304]. Established in November 2021, Club-Culture brought together 38 clubs across France, wanting to legitimise their value. Influential French DJs Laurent Garnier and Jennifer Cardini and venues including Rex Club and I-Boat were behind this initiative to inject nightlife spaces with additional gravitas. In Ireland, the Arts and Culture Minister Catherine Martin has taken a different route to support the electronic music sector alongside other creatives through the provision of a basic income. This is expected to be paid to an estimated 2,000 artists, musicians and other entertainers until 2025[305]. In a statement, she said: "If we look at how far behind we are, look at Berlin where culture thrives at all hours, why does the city's heartbeat have to end at midnight or one in the morning?" These changes add up to the sense of a slow realignment, one with the potential to increase in volume as younger people more familiar with the positive contribution of modern-day nightclubs to our society, towns and cities ascends to power.

"A lot more people who have spent time in nightclubs will be heading into office in cities and towns as generations turn over," Shain says. "Young mayors who come from this background of entertainment, hospitality and media will be very influential. The argument in cities is how you don't build places to live; you build places to live for. Historically, those advocating for these communities haven't been great communicators with governments. This is now changing."

Bristol's inaugural Night-time Economy Advisor Carly Heath was appointed in March 2021 and is leading the fight for clubs and hospitality businesses alongside fellow night-time representatives in other towns and cities. In London, Amy Lame was appointed as a Night Czar in 2016[306] while in Manchester, the Parklife Festival and Warehouse Project's Sacha Lord has been the Night-Time Economy Adviser since 2018. The jobs of these nocturnal representatives and who they report to and work for are different in each city depending on local governance. For Amy, her role sits within the Mayor of London's office and was a high profile appointment in November 2016 to put the Mayor's Vision for London as a 24-hour city into action.

"London has 33 boroughs and the Mayor's office is on top of it alongside the Met and TFL, so she has to navigate this alongside 33 councils, 33 licensing departments and 33 planning departments," Carly explains. "Sacha is an advisor outside the Mayor's office, so he's not politically connected. My role in Bristol is somewhere between the two, sitting between those writing policies and the industry which it ultimately impacts."

Carly's experience within nightlife is as richly diverse as Bristol's clubbing scene itself. From flyering and cloakrooms to running promotion company Don't Panic, she has "spent ten years standing outside every single venue in Bristol handing out flyers", so has plenty of first-hand experience of how the city operates at 3am.

"I'm a massive advocate for this work and think every city should have a Night-time Advisor or Czar," she says. "The local authorities constantly update their policy on decisions such as waste, transportation, economic development, city centre rejuvenation or planning. Having a role such as this means that needs of the night are represented at a city level."

The nuts and bolts of Carly's job cover everything that occurs in Bristol between 6pm and 6am, from clubs and pubs to bars, restaurants and other areas within hospitality and entertainment. Her appointment is an opportunity to reframe how the night is interpreted, so it's seen as something more positive than cross-eyed students stumbling out of kebab shops after pub kicking out time.

"The perceived problems of the night are what the authorities tend to talk about but to me, everything that takes place after dark is the lifeblood, soul and vibrancy of our cities," Carly explains. "I see my role as cultural gardening. The clubbing community is strong here in Bristol and we want to foster an indie spirit that thrives. You don't want to be too heavy-handed and force something to be something it's not. At the same time, you don't want councils to make decisions about areas that don't enable night-time communities to succeed."

The introduction of the Agent of Change principle into the National Planning Policy Framework[307] in 2018 has been important in affording music venues and clubs some protection. Stating that "the person or business responsible for the change is responsible for managing the impact of the change"[308], it means if an apartment block is built near an established club or venue, then developers are liable for any soundproofing. A new venue opening in a densely populated residential area would be responsible for covering these costs. While this has been adopted by other cities, including Liverpool, its introduction has been hard-fought by campaigners, politicians and music venues. Carly says there are technicalities surrounding the policy's implementation, which mean it's not as effective in protecting our music spaces as it could be.

"The problem is that the Agent of Change principle is only a policy, it's not law, so developers don't have to follow it, and it has to be fought on a case by case basis," she states. "Some of the new planning rules also undercut Agent of Change in a number of different ways. For example, it is more difficult to apply to a development if you are turning a pre-existing building into residential property. In relation to current laws, then that building already exists, so Agent of Change doesn't apply. It only applies on new builds."

Bristol's population is growing at a rapid rate, and is projected to increase by almost 70,000 people to reach a total of more than half a million by 2043[309]. With this growth will come increasing pressure on infrastructure and a need for more housing and amenities to accommodate its residents.

"Development has to happen but in a way which is navigated", states Carly. "So triple glazing windows in a densely populated area, trying to place entrances to blocks of flats away from streets with plenty of night-time activity taking place on them. It's about planning for the area it's in and this has to be done building by building."

At the heart of this is clear communication between developers and the local government's planning department. If property builders want to take advantage of the vibrancy created by nightlife, then designated areas must be provided for it to live and grow in, such as squares and other public spaces.

"In Bristol, buildings are now being built upwards as we can't go further out," Carly says. "It means we're using brownfield sites in the middle of the city. We're not creating satellite towns that need transportation in and out. We're developing communities within the infrastructure that already exists."

With old industrial spaces on city centre outskirts now earmarked for redevelopment, these parts of the urban landscape are an opportunity. If temporarily made available for creatives and night-time economy players, then this could be a great additional resource for DJs, musicians and artists.

"When you have areas earmarked for development, then using these buildings as temporary spaces would be fantastic," Carly enthuses. "You can put creatives in there and allow them to do their thing, knowing they only have three to five years to do so. We also need to think about our high streets too as these are often deserted after 5pm. This is something that the night-time economy could really help revive if we were creative with these spaces."

Carly has been living in Bristol since 2004 and witnessed firsthand how the city and its club scene has changed. Its ability to adapt to fluid circumstances gives hope for the future that these places will be capable of responding to the 'new normal' created by the pandemic. If you look closely at the smaller clubs and venues, this is where the real ideas and bold innovation of a local music scene comes alive.

"Bristol is a big city but is a big village when it comes to the dance music community," she says. "This is why Bristol is able to reinvent itself so regularly. Trip hop, jungle, drum & bass, dubstep, house music, techno, now we've got bands like Idles achieving huge international success. It's because we have small communities, producers and musicians from different scenes will get out there and support each other. It leads to cross-pollination and new sounds flaring."

An ability to help give each other a leg up via opportunities and networks is at the heart of Bristol's clubbing community too. This vibrant network continues to enable new talent to bubble to the top.

"Motion is now an internationally renowned nightclub but I remember those first few shows when they were young promoters giving it a go," Carly explains. "There are still opportunities here too, something which the pandemic has cracked open. Lakota has been a cornerstone of Bristol's club community for 30 years and through every generation of the dance music continuum. Post-lockdown, they were one of the first to open up and pivoted their business model to offer food, comedy, fashion shows, all via an outside area in their car park. It shows how this world is constantly evolving and changing, as much by necessity as design."

At grassroots level, clubs are fighting to be heard among the nitty-gritty of planning applications and local government. As these spaces are increasingly recognised by the authorities as cultural spaces, 'club culture' is simultaneously finding its way into more high-brow areas with exhibitions at museums and galleries featuring glow-sticks and rave memorabilia alongside Egyptian mummies and fossils. In September 2020, Berlin's Berghain - regarded by many as the world's most significant and infamous nightclub - reopened as a gallery with an exhibition featuring 115 works made by artists based in the city[310].

At Manchester's Museum of Science and Industry, *'Use Hearing Protection: The Early Years of Factory Records'*, shone a spotlight on the exploits of New Order, svengali Tony Wilson and, of course, their club, the Hacienda[311]. At the V&A in Dundee, *'Night Fever: Designing Club Culture'* explored the relationship between club culture and design. Dr Catherine Rossi, the exhibition's co-curator, says that the research for the project was sparked by the discovery of Space Electronic, a nightclub opened in Florence in 1969 by radical architectural futurists, Groupo 999. As Vice said, "describing Space Electronic as a nightclub would be like describing '*The Odyssey*' as a poem about a boating trip"[312]. Although born out of avant-garde concepts, the club possessed elements that point to the potential multi-functional future of nightclubs.

"It was just this amazing space that had live theatre, music, poetry readings, jazz, an experimental architecture school on the dancefloor. On one notable occasion, they planted a vegetable garden. It was a huge experimental space," says Catherine.

Discovering this nightclub led to further research into nightclub design which became *'Night Fever'*, an exhibition first shown at the Vitra Design Museum in Germany. Among the other notable ideas uncovered was Cyclia, a nightclub designed by Muppets creator Jim Henson. The club never made it past the drawing board but the ambitions to map out "the entertainment experience of the future" were indicative of the ambitious times[313].

"One of the differences between the sixties and now is how nightclubs were a new architectural space," says Catherine. "There was no sense of rules about what they were or what they were meant to do. At the time, it coincided with this huge explosion of music and youth culture. Even if you look at places like the Hacienda, then they had all sorts of different types of nights beyond just being this cathedral of raves. They haven't always been defined by this sense of experimentation, but it's always been there."

Dr. Jochen Eisenbrand, Chief Curator at the Vitra Design Museum, says that if club culture is to survive, it may have to look to the past and stretch beyond the traditional basement-sound-system-dancefloor combination that we all know and love.

"The club itself could be just one part of the offering," he says. "Instead, they become cultural centres with different things happening around them. When we look back to the early clubs of the sixties, they offered exhibition spaces for contemporary artists where this form of expression existed. Maybe it's time to consider these transformative things again, which could serve different purposes at different times."

The trend of club closures, exacerbated by Covid-19, has meant this vital part of our lives is certainly under greater scrutiny than ever. With the wealth of festivals providing alternative experiences and younger generations no longer relying on music as their defining mode of cultural expression, these are undoubtedly challenging times for nightclubs.

"People are now increasingly questioning - what is a nightclub?" says Catherine. "So whether it was Printworks hosting daytime events or places like the Bussey Building in Peckham which have different types of performance and co-working opportunities, people are using the pandemic as a great chance to rethink what a club can be."

So let's try to answer Catherine's question and define a nightclub in the 2020s. As they adapt and change to the pressures of their surroundings, they are increasingly slippery entities to pin down. Dimitri Hegemann, the owner of Berlin's Tresor nightclub, described ambitions to include a nightclub in the redevelopment of Hotel Igman in Sarajevo as creating a "cultural lighthouse"[314]. It's a neat way of capturing how clubs need to work in the future if they want to retain their locations in the heart of our cities. Shain Shapiro from the Center for Music Ecosystems agrees that these spaces need to look beyond the dancefloor to sustain themselves. Any kind of business or service can create more value if used across the entirety of a day or week.

"Nightclubs need to consider themselves more as community centres with a number of strings to their bow," he says. "It's hard nowadays to make money off the dancefloor for eight hours over three nights a week. Instead, they need to consider how to educate, train and open up the culture behind what happens in the club."

Charlie Dark MBE, DJ, producer and founder of collective Run Dem Crew has had many experiences working with brands through his work in the world of running. While many talk about the power of community in sustaining nightclubs, Charlie feels they must go further if they are to survive and thrive.

"I realised during the pandemic that community is a buzzword that is thrown around marketing tables these days," Charlie says. "What you want to create is a movement, which is a community that is empowered and self-sufficient. This means that once the brand pulls out, the community can continue on."

Now, rather than being dedicated to the dancefloor, at least at some level, these spaces are as much about building an ecosystem around it - or movement as Charlie says - as they are about music and lights. The challenges they face are numerous - legislation around licensing, the threat of hungry property developers and other forms of entertainment via social media and digital platforms jostling for our attention. If club culture can infiltrate different mediums, then this is a way of shoring up their defences at a time when the impact of the pandemic has made for gory reading for anyone concerned about the welfare of our night-time. Amid all this chaos stands the Night Time Industries Association (NTIA) and their Chief Executive Officer, Michael Kill. Michael's work has seen him championing the night-time economy, challenging government policy and lobbying for long-term reform while supporting businesses. Beginning his music industry career as a house music promoter, he's since taken on multiple roles within nightlife. Unsurprisingly, the NTIA collaborates closely with the UK's night-time advisers appointed in recent years.

"We were very influential in the UK adopting this European template," he explains. "Ultimately, we want these advisors in every town and city across the UK. Places like Berlin and Amsterdam are way ahead of us in the way their governments really understand the value of cultural tourism."

The electronic music industry has evolved over the last 30 years without much in the way of support from the authorities. But the pandemic exposed the government's lack of understanding surrounding the needs of the night-time industry. The Office for National Statistics confirms that the arts and entertainment sector has been the worst hit by the Covid-19 crisis. A quarter of businesses were unable to operate while 41% saw their turnover fall by half[315]. In an interview, producer Jax Jones told the BBC: "It feels like we are second class citizens, we provide a big revenue for the government and we are a big cultural hub for this country. Our sound is recognised around the world and I just don't think our leaders give it the respect it deserves"[316]. Promoter and DJ Lukas Wigflex goes even further: "Over here in the UK, we've always been demonised for what we do. Our culture is just not seen as a culture." More than ever, the clubbing community's voices need to be united when speaking its truth to power at both local and national levels.

"We've got a responsibility to ourselves that those in charge understand the industry we represent," Michael explains. "Long-term, the strategy has to be about us having recognised representatives within central government while MPs and members of local government need to do more to understand our sector. Then we can start utilising more protective mechanisms such as Agent of Change and heritage protection for club venues like Ministry of Sound or Fabric which should be protected like the Tate Gallery."

As we've seen, the nightclub's digital proposition is an exciting galaxy of innovation that really came to the fore during the pandemic lockdowns. If dancing in small, sweaty basements is going to be out of the question, then the nightclub experience needs to be "pandemic proof" so it can survive in the uncertainty of the future. As with any species at risk, necessity will force innovation, especially if it's a choice between living or dying.

"Undoubtedly, the nightclub's offering must be multi-faceted," says Michael. "We need to be in a position where we can still offer experiences if the physical reality is removed."

Nightclubs capable of switching between digital and physical entertainment could well be where the future of rave culture lies, particularly when city centres seem increasingly inhospitable towards nightlife. Now we have emerged from Covid, the centres of our towns and cities still seem threatening.

"I worry that London has become a hostile environment for clubs and sadly, the pandemic has accelerated that for spaces that were already struggling to stay afloat," says DJ and Rinse FM broadcaster Josey Rebelle. "It's always puzzled me that people will move to London, they will be promised a city based on culture, that they'll be round the corner from iconic cultural spaces like Fabric or Ministry, they move in and they complain and get those spaces shut down. And I thought that was the reason you moved here? That was in the brochure, the reason you bought it."

Shoreditch institution Plastic People closed its doors in 2015, meaning an invaluable venue and its surrounding community were gone for good. The loss was unrelated to concerns about nearby redevelopment, but it still hurt more than most. This was a space where Josey could turn up on any given night and always find a friend or peer to hang out with.

"It had that community feel to it, not to mention that the DJs and sound system were incredible," she says. "The sad thing for a space like that when it closes is that there are so many people who you don't see anymore. I'd see them at Plastic and when the club closed, I didn't see them again."

As the environment around Plastic People has changed, so has Soho, which acted as an amusement park for the New Romantics and Blitz kids of the early eighties. Now it's stacked with Pret-A-Manger sandwich shops. This is great for those who enjoy overpriced, tasteless butties but if you're into arts, independence and creativity, then their ubiquity might not get your tastebuds flowing. S'Express producer and DJ Mark Moore has lived through the changes of recent years and is concerned about the area's future. Previously a glorious den of iniquity, he fears that the party starters, delinquents and rabble rousers will all be erased from this part of town by the relentless march of consumerism.

"In the pre-New Romantic era, we learned that the trick was to find a club which was doing badly and it was far easier to find these kinds of spaces back then," he explains. "There were plenty of people who wanted to go out but with nowhere to go."

Before the pandemic, the West End was teeming with corporate businesses but now the area is at a crossroads. With London's centre less inhabited through successive lockdowns and working from home orders, this could present an opportunity to redress the balance.

"I want people with ideas and creativity to return but I fear that money talks," Mark says. "If you could enable independent entrepreneurs to go in, then you'd see an explosion of jobs and ideas. Clubland does impact everything in this way. You have to have people working inside the venue, musicians, performers, dancers; it grows and grows."

While Covid-19 has impacted the towns and cities we call home, there are potential positives for the soundtrack that keeps these spaces shaking, Carly Heath feels there's always a wealth of great sounds popping in the home studios of dance music producers across the world.

"We're also seeing a proliferation of UK artists performing at festivals and clubs, partly to do with Brexit and partly to do with Covid," she says. "And if we're talking about what the future looks like in terms of our sustainability commitments, is getting artists from the other side of the world to come and play responsible in a world blighted by climate change?"

We've now seen how local scenes are tighter than ever in our communities. We need the physical experience of the club, yet online or digital worlds can help support this and add extra layers of fun and value to their audience. Elsewhere, clubs have to go beyond the dancefloor while the dance music community needs to work harder than ever for their concerns to be listened to by decision-makers. But how about the influence of towns and cities on the sounds of our clubs? There's no doubt that while the online world has broken down boundaries, music makers, DJs and club nights continue to be products of their local scenes. Luis-Manuel Garcia is a Lecturer in Ethnomusicology and Popular Music Studies at the University of Birmingham. Rather than the internet cutting ties between cities and their creatives, he instead argues that these scenes offer definition and focus for dance music producers.

"Scene-specific sounds became an important way for local scenes to be legible to the international, global networked scene," he explains. "These can develop detail and identity through contrasts with the rest of the world. It's not unrealistic to say that scenes become more distinct as they become more exposed."

Luis spent many years in Chicago undertaking research for his PhD. He remembers how the imprint of house music was so strong in the city that most artists who succeeded internationally would be tethered to this idiom.

"There's a certain amount of resentment or frustration that if you are from Chicago, it's in your interests to position yourself as a house DJ or something similar," he explains. "If you do something else, you won't get recognition."

"Back in the early 2000s, DJs would come, visit [world-renowned Chicago record shop] Gramophone, buy a bunch of house records and play them that night. You'd want to see Marcel Dettman play face-melting techno but instead, he's opted for funky house from local producers. It's thrilling for the DJ to try something different in a new location but less so for fans expecting a fresh sound from elsewhere."

Liverpool-based design agency Dorothy[317] has created tangible clubbing maps - *'Acid House Love Blueprint'* and *'Club Together'*. The blueprint was unveiled in 2018 as a map of dance music and rave culture pinned onto the circuit diagram of a Roland 303. *'Club Together'* was inspired by reactions to this first design and is an interactive map that collects clubbers' comments and memories about some of their favourite night-time raving experiences.

"It was such a lovely feeling to see the *'Acid House Love Blueprint'* embraced by so many people and it seemed to open a conversation about the places and nights that really meant something to them," says Dorothy designer Jim Quail.

"People would write to us with nights and venues that they felt we'd either omitted or overlooked or felt we should just know more about," he continues. "You could feel how important these experiences and memories are, of something that they'd been to or been a part of, and we wanted to make something that would allow people to share those memories of places, and post stories or photos or flyers so we started to create *'Club Together'*."

The interactive map allows viewers to search for venues and clubs by space and time period to see what's happening now in your city or what was going bump in the dark in the seventies or eighties. As with this book you're holding in your hands, a personal story is at its heart with '*The Acid House of Love Blueprint*' fashioned through the lens of researcher Ian Mitchell.

"Although it maps lots of clubs, DJs and scenes I have only ever read about, they are mapped (in collaboration with Jim) through their relationship to my lived experience, which I guess includes reading about scenes as well as directly experiencing them," explains Ian on how the narrative was steered. "So for someone else mapping the same culture, the emphasis on certain cities, clubs, or scenes would obviously be different."

From the machine funk associated with Sheffield to the New York disco of the seventies and eighties, Ian's uncovered plenty of personal accounts of how the rave scene took over. It adds up to an overlapping series of stories and shows the similarities of experiences in the clubbing world.

"It seems every northern town had its own really great night at some fairly traditional mainstream club venue," he says. "One of the best things I discovered was the alternative stories to the creation myths that surround certain scenes. For instance, the London-centric dominance that Shoom, and the mythical Rampling-Oakenfold Ibiza visit has over our understanding of acid house's arrival in the UK. As any northern DJ or clubber from that time will tell you, people in the north of England were dancing to house music en masse several years before it hit London. But even this is an oversimplification of the story."

According to Ian, one of the most intriguing untold stories he learned was surrounding the nightclub Hedonism[318] and how, over four nights in 1988, this club helped galvanise a London nightlife "that was far more tribal and cliquey" than is often thought.

"We tried to represent as many of these less well-known venues and artists as well as acknowledging the dominant narratives," says Ian. "The Hacienda probably plays too big a role in our understanding of the history of dance music in the north of England and Manchester. Cities such as Nottingham and Sheffield were equally as important and in Manchester, there will be those that cite somewhere like the Thunderdome as far more significant."

Clubbing seems increasingly fragmented - and the underground and overground more distant from one another than ever. Still, there are some striking similarities between now and the glory days of acid house, particularly amid a turbulent political climate. Recent 'Kill the Bill' demonstrations have taken place against the police, crime, sentencing and courts bill, with certain sections of this legislation condemned by campaigners as attacking our right to protest. In some ways, mirroring the infamous Criminal Justice & Public Order Act of 1994, the simmering volatility suggests that despite 30 years between now and the acid house raves, relations between the authorities and the UK's counterculture haven't progressed as much as once thought. From those I have spoken with, there's an obvious tension between the clubs and those in charge of our towns and cities, with the authorities now doing what it can to tame club culture as it matures from its wilder years. As long as this culture moves more towards the mainstream and allows itself to be managed, then it might be allowed to continue existing in our cities. Music, sound, and space reverberate in the crosshairs of this tension. In this game of cat and mouse between nightclubs and legislators, community ownership appears to be something that tips the balance in favour of clubs. Although there are still plenty of challenges for groups, campaigners and activists to contend with.

"We don't see our current home as our final home as we generally believe we'll eventually be pushed out for one reason or another," said Gut Level's Hannah Brere when we spoke back in 2021.

Her premonition became a reality shortly after the first edition of this book was published in the summer of 2022. Back then, the Sheffield queer collective were based at a building on Snow Lane in Shalesmoor but suddenly found themselves forced to move out and find a new location. The sense of transience surrounding Gut Level may have persisted since their birth back in 2019 but their bold ambitions to fulfil a community need is embedded within them wherever they might be[319].

"I feel there has always been a lack of parties/collectives led by women/ non-binary/gender queer people, particularly in the north," says Gut Level's Hannah Brere on how the collective started life. "Growing up in Sheffield and feeling like it isn't your place to put on parties was definitely a big driving force for myself to start Gut Level."

This galvanised Hannah, alongside friends Adam Benson, Katie Matthews, Frazer Scott and Dan Watson, in their ambitions. Local DIY spaces and friends including Hatch and Delicious Clam were inspirations alongside similar groups, Wharf Chambers in Leeds and Partisan Collective in Manchester.

"It was pretty clear to us all that there was room and demand for another space in Sheffield, where people of all ilks can gather, express themselves safely and just listen to good music without being ripped off," says Adam. "It's possible for good clubbing to exist without emphasis on the name and status of the main act and how many ticket sales that name can generate."

Gut Level has marauded across Sheffield's nooks and crannies ever since, seeking a home wherever they have been welcomed. Initially, the group was housed under a railway arch in Attercliffe on the outskirts of Sheffield's city centre, before heading to a Grade-II listed cutlery factory in Shalesmoor. After they were told this building was to be redeveloped, their attention turned to another city centre spot on Eyre Street in Sheffield.

"We weren't able to host late night events on Eyre Street, so this led us to pour more time and energy into our community-focused arms such as FLAW and Working Them's Club," says Hannah. "We've found there was a real appetite for queer-focused community creative projects and workshops as the community should have a place to exist beyond hedonism."

Over the past year at Eyre Street, Gut Level's programme has seen events of all kinds take place within its wall. From queer speed dating, DIY kink gear workshops with Leatherdyke, to tabletop games meetups, patch printing workshops, communal meals, craft socials, a QTIPOC film club, and sex worker meetups.

"I believe a really strong part of creating a community means going beyond late night partying," says Hannah. "I think operating as a members club definitely creates a local community within Gut Level as we see the same people at our events who respect and understand what we're about."

Stil, the story of the group only offering temporary pleasures is ongoing with the Eyre Street location also subject to redevelopment. It meant that they were forced out once again in October 2023. At the time of writing, Gut Level has taken over a space on Chapel Walk with a five-year lease and are cautiously optimistic that this will be their home for the foreseeable future.

"Losing Eyre Street really gave us the extra push we needed to pursue renting a commercial property with a lease," says Hannah. "It gets draining having to constantly move alongside spending loads of time and money doing up spaces when there's no certainty on how long you'll be able to stay there for. Hopefully if everything goes to plan we'll still be sailing the Gut Level ship in years to come."

The demise of these numerous Gut Level spaces - like so many other nocturnal ventures and venues - can be connected to the peace and quiet demanded by new city centre residents. This right to silence is enacted by the urban dwellers via the idea of how ownership gives them authority over non-owners. As this system is one signed off by local government, validation is given to a system that all too often sides against the creatives. Because of this, Lenny Watson from Sister Midnight describes how the existence of music venues "is highly political these days" and the fight is ongoing to keep them in these areas in our towns and cities.

"For most music venues, a lot of these threats come down to ownership," she states. "New luxury property developments drive up property prices, which for UK music venues [93% of whom are tenants rather than owners of their buildings[320]] means unaffordable rent increases. Many venues have been direct victims of redevelopment, being evicted from their spaces to make way for luxury flats that few in the local community can afford. On top of that, most venues can't afford to invest in necessary infrastructure improvements to their spaces to keep them in good condition. When they do, it just gives landlords a reason to increase their rent."

As with some of the other ventures now starting, a new ownership model is essential if music culture is to be sustainable and survive. Without them, our towns and cities would be much quieter, less exciting and unattractive to those people or businesses looking to invest somewhere.

"We need to stop squeezing cultural institutions for profit and forcing them to fight for their survival," Lenny says. "We need our creative and cultural spaces to be protected by community ownership so that we can't be forced out of cities by unscrupulous landlords or property developers. We want to see power put into the hands of local communities, empowering them to lead the way on urban regeneration."

For the Secret DJ, gentrification is a circular process with areas of London taking it in turns to move between various states of splendour and dilipadation.

"What has changed is that developers have become wise to the cycle," he says. "So they do things like support and even build clubs and cultural community projects in some places with the full intention of pulling the plug on them the moment it suits the wealthy new residents."

As we've seen, with councils seeing financial cuts, many are forced to turn to private investors for capital to maintain their areas, often from property developers and puts local culture and communities at risk.

"There can't be a person reading this who doesn't know of a local pub, serving it's community for possibly hundreds of years, suddenly being attack by new, wealthy neighbours who arrive tempted by the 'colour' and 'vibrancy' the estate agents promised and promptly being terrified by the 'colour' and furious at the 'vibrancy' within moments of unpacking," he says.

This is part of a wider problem the UK powers that be have with its culture and an inability to champion it. Instead, it is "something to be eradicated".

"Conversely, hard times produce great art," the Secret DJ states. "There is a silver lining in that you just cannot stop youthful energy. It's Newtonian in nature, that you cannot destroy energy, only move it around. Like putting up wallpaper, you find a bubble and press it down and it just pops up somewhere else. The underground can never die. There's too many of us, and way too few of them."

By taking on ownership and landing in the community, we've seen how spaces can set a precedent for the future although this can be uncertain until the new club owners have the keys in hand. However, from Sheffield to Manchester and London, their adoption is cause for optimism, suggesting that perhaps we're not out of space just yet. In fact, there's plenty to go around across the 250,000 square kilometres of the UK[321] as long as we budge up and make enough room for each other. Rather than the future of clubs looking like something out of *'Star Wars'* or *'Blade Runner'*, grassroots culture is continuing to grow and demonstrates just how resilient and innovative club culture can be. Despite all the changes our lives and cities have witnessed, Judy Griffith, Fabric's Promotions Manager, says the equation for a successful club has been and continues to be simple. "Great clubs are those that have managed to build a community, a family vibe of like-minded people, that serves up quality, authentic music and delivers it with love and attention. These rarely go wrong. When our community comes together united in music, only magic happens…"

# ENDNOTES

## INTRODUCTION

1 Acid House Memories and Memorabilia exhibition | Tate Liverpool (1996) muhka.be/programme/detail/163-energy-flash-the-rave-movement/item/13933-do-you-remember-the-first-time
2 Kafka, George | How Architecture Transforms the Clubbing Experience | Electronic Beats (April 2020) https://www.electronicbeats.net/the-influence-of-club-architecture-berghain-b018/
3 LGBT+ venues in crisis | London has lost 58 per cent since 2006 | London.gov.uk | Press Release (July 2017) https://www.london.gov.uk/press-releases/mayoral/mayor-pledges-support-to-lgbt-venues-in-london

## PREFACE

4 Coney, Brian | Over 100 independent UK clubs shut in the last 12 months, report reveals | DJMag.com (August 2023) https://djmag.com/news/over-100-independent-uk-clubs-shut-last-12-months-report-reveals
5 Ottewill, Jim | Oppose the Developers | Mixmag (August 2017) https://mixmag.net/feature/oppose-the-developers-london-is-fighting-to-protect-its-lgbt-clubs
6 Number of clubs in the UK has almost halved | Mixmag (August 2015) https://mixmag.net/read/number-of-clubs-in-the-uk-have-almost-halved-since-2005-news
7 Coultate, Aaron | London's Dance Tunnel to close in August | Resident Advisor (April 2016) https://ra.co/news/34256
8 Where have property prices increased the most since 2010 | Rightmove PR (October 2020) https://www.rightmove.co.uk/news/articles/property-news/asking-price-increases-since-2010

9  Rawlinson, Kevin | London nightclub Fabric to close permanently after losing its licence | The Guardian (September 2016) https://www.theguardian.com/music/2016/sep/07/london-nightclub-fabric-close-permanently-licence-revoked-drugs

10  Cafe, Rebecca | Last Call: What's happened to London nightlife | BBC (October 2016) https://www.bbc.co.uk/news/uk-england-london-37546558

11  How much does nightlife benefit the UK economy | NTIA (October 2021) https://www.ndml.co.uk/articles/how-much-does-nightlife-benefit-the-uk-economy/

12  Frishberg, Hannah | A safe haven for freaks: Pyramid Club closes after 41 years | New York Post (April 2021) https://nypost.com/2021/04/01/a-safe-haven-for-freaks-nycs-iconic-pyramid-club-closes/

13  Rossi, Catherine | An Incomplete History of Clubbing | Museum of Youth Culture https://www.museumofyouthculture.com/club-culture/

14  The Prodigy | 'Out of Space' (1992) https://www.youtube.com/watch?v=a4eav7dFvc8

15  Dandelion, Pink | Religion and Youth | Susan Luckman citation (2010) https://www.google.co.uk/books/edition/Religion_and_Youth/AXe1buvTt7UC?hl=en&gbpv=1

## CHAPTER 1

16  Baines, Josh | How Did a Beardy Scottish Folk Duo Write the Best Song About Going Out Ever? | Vice/Noisey (July 2016) https://www.vice.com/en/article/53aw4z/arab-strap

17  Neil Landstrumm, Glaswegian producer/DJ | Out of Space interview

18  Beatson, Jamie | Bakery's 24-hour hot pie vending machine proves roaring success with revellers | Daily Record (December 2013) https://www.dailyrecord.co.uk/news/scottish-news/bakerys-24-hour-hot-pie-vending-2900638

19  Glasgow City | Britannica | https://www.britannica.com/place/Glasgow-Scotland

20  Brocklehurst, Steven | Govan: A shipbuilding history | BBC (November 2013) https://www.bbc.co.uk/news/uk-scotland-glasgow-west-24820573

21 Clydeside: When the workshop of the world shut up shop | BBC https://www.bbc.co.uk/legacies/work/scotland/strathclyde/
22 Lowndes, Sarah | Social Sculpture: The Rise of the Glasgow Art Scene | p21 | Luath Press (June 2010)
23 Williams, Craig | Every Glasgow street named linked to slavery | Glasgow Live (June 2020) https://www.glasgowlive.co.uk/news/history/glasgow-history-slavery-street-names-18369259
24 Forgotten Glasgow : when Glasgow helped clothe the world | The Herald (April 2019) https://www.pressreader.com/uk/the-herald-on-sunday/20190414/281500752639296
25 Buckle, Becky | Glasgow's iconic venue The Arches is set to re-open after eight years | Mixmag (September 2023) https://mixmag.net/read/glasgows-iconic-venue-the-arches-is-set-to-re-open-after-eight-years-news
26 Lost Glasgow Facebook Group | Sub Club (December 2017) https://www.facebook.com/251032471675283/posts/hard-to-believe-that-glasgows-sub-club-now-the-longest-running-underground-music/1341202289324957/
27 Sub Club | Optimo Return Home - a Brief History https://subclub.co.uk/optimo-return-home-a-brief-history/
28 Sub Club | Heritage https://subclub.co.uk/heritage/
29 Lowndes, Sarah | Social Sculpture: The Rise of the Glasgow Art Scene | p25 Luath Press (June 2010)
30 Social Legislation | Electric Scotland https://electricscotland.com/history/articles/mackenzieact.htm
31 Williams, Craig | Remembering the gig that saw Glasgow ban punk music | Glasgow Live (May 2019) https://www.glasgowlive.co.uk/news/history/remembering-gig-saw-glasgow-ban-16318101
32 O'Neill, Christina | Glasgow punk show ban saw scene explode in Paisley as music fans look back in new documentary | Glasgow Live (June 2021) https://www.glasgowlive.co.uk/whats-on/whats-on-news/glasgow-punk-show-ban-saw-20884337
33 Steven, Colin | Wham! Bam! Thank you Slam | The List (March 1990) https://archive.list.co.uk/the-list/1990-03-23/68/
34 Brown Laura | Claude Young Interview | Higher Frequency (August 2004) http://higher-frequency.com/e_interview/claude_young/index.htm

35  Fred Deakin: Irreverence and Interaction | Elephant (March 2018) https://elephant.art/fred-deakin-irreverence-interaction/
36  Philp, Ray | Nightclub: Edinburgh's Pure - Scotland's Greatest 90's night | Red Bull Music Academy (January 2014) https://daily.redbullmusicacademy.com/2014/01/nightclubbing-pure-scotland
37  Cooper, Neil | Fred Deakin: 'I wasn't running clubs to get famous' | The List (April 2023) https://list.co.uk/news/43351/fred-deakin-i-wasnt-running-clubs-to-get-famous
38  Industrial decline of Glasgow and Clydeside | The Scotsman (June 2017) https://www.scotsman.com/whats-on/arts-and-entertainment/industrial-decline-glasgow-and-clydeside-captured-pictures-1446925
39  Bread Party | Old Glasgow Blog (February 2015) https://oldglasgow.tumblr.com/post/110459788341/in-business-for-120-years-before-going-bust-in
40  Thorpe, David | Is Glasgow being Regenerated or Gentrified? | Smart Cities Dive  https://www.smartcitiesdive.com/ex/sustainablecitiescollective/glasgow-being-regenerated-or-gentrified/293166/
41  Stewart, Catriona | Glasgow venue sets its sights on being heart of cultural map | Evening Times (October 2019) https://www.pressreader.com/uk/evening-times/20191022/282067688713862
42  Clyde Waterfront maintains momentum (October 2009) http://www.clydewaterfront.com/our-journey/expert-articles/clyde-waterfront-maintains-momentum
43  Scott, Kevin | How a business focus helped SWG3 to become the hottest arts venue in Glasgow (December 2017) https://www.heraldscotland.com/business_hq/15711990.business-focus-helped-swg3-become-hottest-arts-venue-glasgow/
44  Philp, Ray | RA in Residence: Sub Club | Resident Advisor (September 2016) https://ra.co/features/2815
45  Boiler Room | Jackmaster | Boiler Room DJ set (February 2017) Jackmaster Boiler Room Glasgow DJ Set

## CHAPTER 2

46 Justin Robertson, DJ and producer | Out of Space interview

47 Kelly, Ben | Behind the scenes of the Hacienda's opening night | Vinyl Factory (May 2017) https://thevinylfactory.com/features/photos-hacienda-opening-party/

48 Quincey De, Thomas | Confessions of an Opium Eater | 1821 (Excerpts from) https://www.berfrois.com/2013/10/confessions-of-an-english-opium-eater-thomas-de-quincey/

49 Griffin, Emma | Manchester in the 19th Century | British Library Article (May 2014) https://www.bl.uk/romantics-and-victorians/articles/manchester-in-the-19th-century

50 Llangollen Advertiser Denbighshire Merionethshire and North Wales Journal (August 1868) | National Library of Wales https://newspapers.library.wales/view/3286744/3286747/9/SR%20Jones

51 Haslam, Dave | Manchester, England: The Story of the Pop Cult City (1999) p4 | Fourth Estate Publisher

52 Where was Cottonopolis | History House https://historyhouse.co.uk/articles/cottonopolis.html

53 Disraeli, Benjamin | Coningsby (1844) https://www.victorianlondon.org/etexts/disraeli/coningsby-0024.shtml

54 The Way We Were: When cotton was king | Manchester Evening News (September 2013) https://www.manchestereveningnews.co.uk/news/nostalgia/way-were-cotton-king-manchester-6085736

55 Schofield, Jonathan | A short history of Manchester: the rise and fall of Cottonopolis | Confidentials, Manchester (June 2018) https://confidentials.com/manchester/a-short-history-of-manchester-the-rise-and-fall-of-cottonopolis

56 Jacobs, Jane | Quoted in by Wheeler, Paul | Rebranding Manchester: A success or failure | GeoFile, Series 37, Issue 1 (September 2018) https://intranet.kes.hants.sch.uk/resource.aspx?id=263402

57 Greg Wilson | Biography/About section https://blog.gregwilson.co.uk/about/

58 Final Interview with Twisted Wheel DJ Roger Eagle | Modculture (June 2018) https://www.modculture.co.uk/final-interview-twisted-wheel-dj-roger-eagle/

59 V&A Collections | Orchestral Manoeuvres in the Dark Record Sleeve (1984) http://collections.vam.ac.uk/item/O148309/record-sleeve-kelly-ben/record-sleeve-ben-kelly/

60 Bolton, Jonathan | The Blunt Affair and its impact on literature, television and film in the 1980s | Manchester Hive (December 2020) https://www.manchesterhive.com/view/9781526148476/9781526148476.00005.xml

61 Fus-Mickiewicz, Maksymilian | The Hacienda Must Be Built (August 2012) https://thehaciendamustbebuilt.wordpress.com/2012/08/15/the-hacienda-must-be-built/

62 Spring, Martin | The making of Manchester | Building.co.uk (January 2006) https://www.building.co.uk/focus/the-making-of-manchester/3061734.article

63 Haslam, Dave | Manchester - Nightclubs and the city (August 2001) http://www.davehaslam.com/#/manchester-nightclubs-the-city-the-times-august-2001/

64 Kennedy, Maeve | Manchester's Hacienda and Pete Hook inspire new university's masters course | The Guardian (June 2012) https://www.theguardian.com/uk/2012/jun/26/hacienda-peter-hook-university-masters

65 Cons, Paul | 'Gaychester': Remembering Manchester's early 1990s gay scene | The Guardian (February 2013) https://www.theguardian.com/uk/the-northerner/2013/feb/07/manchester-gay-scene-paul-cons

66 Flesh at the Hacienda - Photos of Manchester's legendary gay clubnight | British Culture Archive (September 2021) https://britishculturearchive.co.uk/flesh-at-the-hacienda-photos-of-manchesters-legendary-gay-clubnight/

67 Binnie, Jon | Cosmopolitan Urbanism | New York, NY: Routledge (2006) https://archive.org/details/cosmopolitanurba00binn/page/n242/mode/2up

68 Needham, Jack | Saluting Sankeys: How a disused soap factory became one of Britain's best loved clubs | FACT Magazine (January 2017) https://www.factmag.com/2017/01/28/sankeys-soap-manchester-club-closing/

69 Luvdup (Adrian and Mark) | Manchester Digital Music Archive https://www.mdmarchive.co.uk/biography/4471/Luvdup_(Adrian_and_Mark)

70 Brett, Davey | Inside the old school boozer fuelling Manchester's rave school | The Face (July 2023) https://theface.com/music/the-derby-brewery-arms-manchester-pub-white-hotel-djs-music-scene-meat-free-rave-queer

71 Partisan Collective | https://partisancollective.net/

72 Piccadilly Station air-raid shelter remains | 28DL Urban Exploration (March 2011) https://www.28dayslater.co.uk/threads/piccadilly-station-air-raid-shelter-remains-manchester-march-2011.60324/

73 Pellant, Georgina | Inside Mayfield Depot - the Warehouse Project's new home for 2019 | I Love Mcr (September 2019) https://ilovemanchester.com/inside-mayfield-depot-warehouse-project

74 Escape to Freight Island | About https://www.escapetofreightisland.com/

## CHAPTER 3

75 Andy Carroll, Liverpool DJ | Out of Space interview

76 Graham, Bill | Embrace the Contradictions: The Strange World of ... The KLF | The Quietus (February 2017) https://thequietus.com/articles/21674-the-klf-justified-ancients-of-mu-mu-bill-drummond-jimmy-cauty

77 Cohen, Sara | Decline, Renewal and the City in Popular Music Culture : Beyond the Beatles (2007) https://tinyurl.com/4u8pea6r

78 Liverpool and the transatlantic slave trade | Liverpool's Maritime Museum https://www.liverpoolmuseums.org.uk/archivesheet3

79 Guy, Peter | Pete Fulwell of Eric's dies | Get Into This (February 2020) https://www.getintothis.co.uk/2020/02/pete-fulwell-of-erics-dies-a-liverpool-music-legend-and-miracle-worker/

80 Jamieson, Teddy | Holly Johnson on life in and out of Frankie Goes To Hollywood | The Scottish Herald (July 2019) https://www.heraldscotland.com/life_style/arts_ents/17779905.archive-holly-johnson-life-frankie-goes-hollywood/

81 Grady, Helen | The English city that wanted to 'break away' from the UK | BBC (November 2014) https://www.bbc.co.uk/news/magazine-29953611

82  Hansard | Parliament (July 1983) https://hansard.parliament.uk/commons/1983-07-04/debates/7669d4e2-68b0-4afc-a18b-09d87be34054/Liverpool(Unemployment)

83  Hughes, Lorna | 35 years after the Toxteth riots, this is what the people of L8 are doing today | Liverpool Echo (July 2016) https://www.liverpoolecho.co.uk/incoming/35-years-after-toxteth-riots-11559186

84  Ryder, Elliott | Quadrant Park signalled the emergence of modern Liverpool | The Liverpool Echo (July 2021) https://www.liverpoolecho.co.uk/news/nostalgia/quadrant-park-signalled-emergence-modern-21135475

85  Bona, Emilia | Cream: How a Liverpool club night became a global superstar | The Liverpool Echo (May 2020) https://www.liverpoolecho.co.uk/news/liverpool-news/cream-how-liverpool-club-night-18321707

86  Live Nation buys out Cream Group in £14m deal | Insider Media (May 2012) https://www.insidermedia.com/news/north-west/70410-live-nation-buys-out-cream-group-14m-deal

87  Castillo, Arielle, Domanick, Andrea, Matos, Michelangelo | 50 Most Important People in EDM | Rolling Stone https://www.rollingstone.com/music/music-lists/50-most-important-people-in-edm-30822/

88  Saunders, Lawrence | Liverpool superclub to get top honour | YM Liverpool (April 2017) https://ymliverpool.com/liverpool-cream-top-honour/25532

89  McLoughlin, Jamie | How did Liverpool's Baltic Triangle gets its name and where does it begin and end | The Liverpool Echo (November 2017) https://www.liverpoolecho.co.uk/whats-on/whats-on-news/how-liverpools-baltic-triangle-name-13944484

90  Baltic Creative | Its Story  https://www.baltic-creative.com/about/story/

91  Houghton, Tom | Anger as developer plans threaten future of 24 Kitchen Street | Liverpool Echo (December 2019) https://www.liverpoolecho.co.uk/news/liverpool-news/anger-developers-plans-threaten-future-17360424

92  Sonic Yootha | Instagram  https://www.instagram.com/sonicyootha

93  Garlands | There's no place like Garlands | Liverpool Museum https://www.liverpoolmuseums.org.uk/stories/theres-no-place-garlands

94  Bona, Emilia | Inside Sonic Yootha - the club night that saved Liverpool's gay scene | The Liverpool Echo (July 2017) https://www.

liverpoolecho.co.uk/whats-on/music-nightlife-news/inside-sonic-yootha-club-night-13310952
95 Groove, Aria | Mele Interview | Electronic Groove (November 2017) https://electronicgroove.com/mele-interview/
96 New Half Man, Half Biscuit Album | The Voltarol Years (February 2022) https://halfmanhalfbiscuit.uk/new-half-man-half-biscuit-album-2022/
97 Wirral Intelligence Service | Wirral Population https://www.wirralintelligenceservice.org/state-of-the-borough/wirral-population/
98 Koncienzcy, Rebecca | Birkenhead's decline from 'New York of Europe' to town of deprivation | The Liverpool Echo (March 2021) https://www.liverpoolecho.co.uk/news/liverpool-news/birkenheads-decline-new-york-europe-20259856
99 Ferguson, Ryan | Why Central Park in New York is based on Birkenhead Park in Wirral (July 2019) https://ryanferguson.co.uk/blogs/wirralist/why-central-park-in-new-york-is-based-on-birkenhead-park-in-wirral
100 McKeon, Christopher, Morgan, George | Merseyside's left behind neighbourhoods at risk of slipping further due to the pandemic | The Liverpool Echo (July 2020) https://www.liverpoolecho.co.uk/news/liverpool-news/merseysides-left-behind-neighbourhoods-risk-18656194
101 Future Yard | Leftbank Soundtrack https://futureyard.org/the-leftbank-soundtrack/

CHAPTER 4

102 Stephen Mallinder (Cabaret Voltaire), artist and producer | Out of Space interview
103 Sampson, Stacey | The rise and fall of Gatecrasher - the UK's spiritual home of trance | Vice (September 2016) https://www.vice.com/en/article/3de5ev/gatecrasher-trance-feature-uk
104 Designers Republic website https://www.thedesignersrepublic.com
105 Gatecrasher West One Apartments https://westone-gatecrasherapartments.com/about-gatecrasher-sheffield.php
106 Hill, Jenny | Sheffield's stainless steel legacy | BBC (January 2013) https://www.bbc.co.uk/news/av/uk-20929986

107 A Vision of Britain through Time | Sheffield population statistics https://www.visionofbritain.org.uk/unit/10076882/cube/TOT_POP

108 Centre for Cities | Sheffield report (2014) https://www.centreforcities.org/wp-content/uploads/2014/09/11-10-17_Sheffield_Appendix.pdf

109 Wright, Ron and Schofield, John | How Industry and Electronic Music Forged Sheffield's Sonic identity | Taken from Music and Heritage : New Perspectives on Place-making and Sonic identity | Routledge (2021) https://books.google.co.uk/books/about/Music_and_Heritage.html?id=FSL5zQEACAAJ&redir_esc=y

110 The Shock of the Modern | The Yorkshire Post (October 2018) https://www.pressreader.com/uk/yorkshire-post/20181026/281921659035584

111 Sheffield Music Map | Western Works | Mal's Cabaret Voltaire Tour https://www.dhi.ac.uk/mobile-tours/sheffield-music-map/tour/location.php?app_id=1&tour_id=8&marker=57&n=7

112 Musician biographies | Cabaret Voltaire https://musicianguide.com/biographies/1608000257/Cabaret-Voltaire.html

113 Mallinder, Stephen | Sheffield is not sexy | Nebula | (September 2007) http://www.nobleworld.biz/images/Mallinder.pdf

114 Sheffield Music Map | Mona Lisa's Jive Turkey https://www.dhi.ac.uk/mobile-tours/sheffield-music-map/tour/location.php?app_id=1&tour_id=24&marker=303&n=1

115 Burns, L Todd | Nightclubbing: Jive Turkey | Red Bull Music Academy (November 2013) https://daily.redbullmusicacademy.com/2013/11/nightclubbing-jive-turkey

116 Wray, Dylan Daniel | Sheffield's post-punk explosion: synths, steel and skinheads | The Guardian (December 2019) https://www.theguardian.com/music/2019/dec/12/sheffields-post-punk-explosion-synths-steel-and-skinheads

117 King, Richard | How Soon Is Now? The Madmen and Mavericks Who Made Independent Music 1975-2005 | Ref: FACT Magazine | Faber and Faber Ltd https://www.factmag.com/2012/04/17/oh-my-god-what-have-we-done-the-secret-history-of-warp-records/

118 Anniss, Matt | Warp Records | Label of the Month | Resident Advisor (November 2019) https://ra.co/features/3557

119 Ahmed, Aneesha | Mira Calix Obituary | Mixmag (March 2022)

https://mixmag.net/read/mira-calix-experimental-warp-records-artist-died-news

120 Brown, Dr Adam | Music policy in Sheffield, Manchester and Liverpool | Manchester Institute for Popular Culture, Manchester Metropolitan University and Institute for Popular Music, University of Liverpool (1998) https://e-space.mmu.ac.uk/12468/1/musicpolicy3cities%20-%20brown2.pdf

121 Moss, Linda | Sheffield's cultural industries quarter 20 years on: What can be learned from a pioneering example? | International Journal of Cultural Policy (Vol 8 2002) https://www.tandfonline.com/doi/abs/10.1080/1028663022000009551?journalCode=gcul20

122 Casey, Andy | Out with the old and in with the sort of new | BBC (September 2003) https://www.bbc.co.uk/southyorkshire/clubbing/gatecrasher_one_opening/

123 Historic England | The Wicker Arch, Sheffield https://historicengland.org.uk/listing/the-list/list-entry/1270747?section=official-listing

124 Planet Zogg https://planetzogg.co.uk

125 Lo Shea | DJ Profile | Resident Advisor https://ra.co/dj/loshea

126 Wray, Dylan Daniel | Nightclubbing: Niche | Red Bull Music Academy (September 2015) https://daily.redbullmusicacademy.com/2015/09/nightclubbing-niche

127 Deadman, Alex | Deadman's Blog | Steve Baxendale Interview | Naughty but Niche (July 2010) http://alexdeadman.blogspot.com/2010/07/feature-niche-true-story-from-steve.html

128 Deadman, Alex | Deadman's Blog | Steve Baxendale Interview | Naughty but Niche (July 2010) http://alexdeadman.blogspot.com/2010/07/feature-niche-true-story-from-steve.html

129 Twells, John | Sheffield's iconic Niche to be demolished | FACT Magazine https://www.factmag.com/2016/05/12/niche-nightclub-to-be-demolished/

## CHAPTER 5

130 Lai Power, DJ and producer | Out of Space interview
131 Tony Child (Surgeon), DJ and producer | Out of Space interview
132 Cole, Matt, Dr | Spaghetti Junction at 50 | University of Birmingham

(May 2022) https://www.birmingham.ac.uk/news/2022/spaghetti-junction-at-50-what-does-it-mean-to-you

133  Bray, John | Spaghetti Junction at 50 - What lies beneath | BBC (May 2022) https://www.bbc.co.uk/news/uk-england-birmingham-61482844

134  Foot, Joe | Defining Moment: Spaghetti Junction opens, May 24 1972 | FT (June 2009) https://www.ft.com/content/e76ce4fc-4e5a-11de-a0a1-00144feabdc0

135  Bounds, Joe | Birmingham: It's Not Shit - Reason No. 7: The things that might be under Spaghetti Junction | Paradise Circus (May 2022) http://paradisecircus.com/2022/05/23/birmingham-its-not-shit-reason-no-7-the-things-that-might-be-under-spaghetti-junction/

136  Birmingham City Council | Population and Census overview | https://www.birmingham.gov.uk/info/20057/about_birmingham/1294/population_and_census

137  Shire, Robert | Why the Midlands is the best place on earth | The Guardian (March 2014) https://www.theguardian.com/uk-news/2014/mar/26/why-midlands-is-best-place-in-britain

138  Took, Rebecca | The BBC managed to perfectly describe the nation's prejudices against Birmingham – and Brummies like me are sick of it | The Independent (July 2020) https://www.independent.co.uk/voices/bbc-archive-tweet-birmingham-olympics-bid-prejudice-midlands-investment-a9639531.html

139  Birmingham : It's not shit | Paradise Circus (Website) http://paradisecircus.com/bins/

140  Taylor, Harry | Tory MP apologises for calling Birmingham and Blackpool 'godawful' | The Guardian (June 2022) https://www.theguardian.com/uk-news/2022/jun/10/tory-minister-calls-birmingham-and-blackpool-godawful

141  Madden, Sophie | What is happening in bankrupt Birmingham? | BBC (September 2023) https://www.bbc.co.uk/news/uk-england-birmingham-66730165

142  Press Release | Birmingham 2022 contributes £870 million to UK economy | Gov.uk (January 2023) https://www.gov.uk/government/news/birmingham-2022-contributes-870-million-to-uk-economy

143  Aston University | Vice-Chancellor tells Birmingham Tech Week that region's 'superpower' of diversity and collaboration vital for innovation

(October 2023) https://www.aston.ac.uk/latest-news/vice-chancellor-tells-birmingham-tech-week-regions-superpower-diversity-and
144 Birmingham City Council | Why Birmingham's super-diversity is a strength and not a surprise (November 2022) https://www.birmingham.gov.uk/blog/birmingham-blog/post/1205/why-birmingham%E2%80%99s-super-diversity-is-a-strength-and-not-a-surprise
145 Birmingham University | Handsworth Area Profile | https://www.birmingham.ac.uk/generic/upweb/partner-countries/united-kingdom/handsworth-area.aspx
146 Jacobs, Jane | The Economy of Cities | Pelican, p91-92 (1972)
147 Birmingham Music Archive https://www.birminghammusicarchive.com/
148 Whelan, Kez | The Mermaid | Home of Metal Presents At the Mermaid
https://homeofmetal.com/grindcore-at-the-mermaid/
149 The Samuel Johnson Birthplace https://www.samueljohnsonbirthplace.org.uk/
150 Brown Jr, DeForrest | Waajeed constructs Afrofuturist realms from the seed of Detroit techno | Document Journal (December 2022) https://www.documentjournal.com/2022/12/waajeed-constructs-afrofuturist-realms-from-the-seed-of-detroit-techno/
151 Seenan, Gerard | Bird's Custard going up for sale | The Guardian (November 2004) https://www.theguardian.com/uk/2004/nov/10/foodanddrink
152 Taylor, Nick | In The Que tells the social, cultural and political history of the '90s venue | Resident Advisor (January 2023) https://ra.co/news/78314
153 Richards, Will | XOYO to open new club in Birmingham | NME (August 2023) https://www.nme.com/news/music/xoyo-to-open-new-club-in-birmingham-3478966
154 Farrington, Dayna | BOXPARK to open huge food hall and events area in Digbeth | Birmingham Mail (October 2023) https://www.birminghammail.co.uk/whats-on/food-drink-news/boxpark-open-huge-food-hall-27938179
155 Young, Graham | The Rainbow pub roars back as live music venue | Birmingham Mail (October 2021) https://www.birminghammail.co.uk/whats-on/whats-on-news/rainbow-pub-roars-back-live-21738599

156 Geraghty, Hollie | One third of nightclubs closed by end of 2022, report shows | NME (January 2023) https://www.nme.com/news/music/one-third-of-uk-nightclubs-closed-by-end-of-2022-report-shows-3385828

157 Birmingham City Council | HS2 Benefits https://www.birmingham.gov.uk/info/50028/transport_information/502/high_speed_2_hs2/2

158 Birmingham property market expected to boom from the 'Commonwealth Games' effect | Property Wire (August 2022) https://www.propertywire.com/blog/feature-birmingham-property-market-expected-to-boom-from-the-commonwealth-games-effect/

159 Knowles, Kate | It's Brum as Fuck: 30 Years of House of God | Resident Advisor (October 2023) https://ra.co/features/4216

160 Gallop, Joe | NTIA appoints 30 Night Time Economy Ambassadors across the UK | Access All Areas (October 2023) https://accessaa.co.uk/ntia-appoints-30-night-time-economy-ambassadors-across-the-uk/

161 Birmingham City Council | Lawrence Barton appointed as Birmingham Night-Time Economy Champion (November 2022) https://www.birmingham.gov.uk/news/article/1218/lawrence_barton_appointed_as_birmingham_s_first_night-time_economy_champion

162 Witts, Sophie | Alex Claridge made Night-Time Economy Advisor for West Midlands | The Caterer (April 2023) https://www.thecaterer.com/news/alex-claridge-night-time-economy-birmingham-wilderness

163 Collins, Jez | Discussion paper about the Night-time Economy in Birmingham | Birmingham City Council (July 2018) https://rb.gy/omctyo

164 Harris, Catherine | The Birmingham Economic Review 2018 | Birmingham University (January 2019) https://blog.bham.ac.uk/cityredi/the-birmingham-economic-review-2018-people-population-and-employment/

CHAPTER 6

165 Mick Wilson, DJ Mag/producer as Parks and Wilson | Out of Space interview

166 Lavelle, Emma | How did Todmorden become one of England's biggest UFO Sighting Hotspots | The Culture Trip (April 2018) https://

theculturetrip.com/europe/united-kingdom/england/articles/how-did-todmorden-become-one-of-englands-biggest-ufo-sighting-hotspots/

167 Himefield, Dave | Yorkshire's 'alien abduction capital' eager for Pentagon UFO report | Yorkshire Live (June 2021) https://www.examinerlive.co.uk/news/west-yorkshire-news/yorkshires-alien-abduction-capital-eager-20869149

168 Todmorden Information Centre website https://www.visittodmorden.co.uk

169 Unemployment Statistics | Hansard | February 1981 https://api.parliament.uk/historic-hansard/written-answers/1981/feb/24/unemployment-statistics

170 Williams, Ben | Austerity Britain - A Brief History | Sage Publishing (March 2019) https://journals.sagepub.com/doi/pdf/10.1177/2041905819838148

171 Humphries, Steve | Britain's motor city: how Coventry's car industry roared | History Extra (September 2021) https://www.historyextra.com/period/20th-century/coventry-motor-city-car-industry-history-rise-fall-timeline/

172 Dowd, Vincent | UK City of Culture 2021: Can Coventry rise up from grimy decline? | BBC (December 2017) https://www.bbc.co.uk/news/entertainment-arts-42278355

173 Coventry raves: 'People were hugging each other and dancing' | BBC (October 2021) https://www.bbc.co.uk/news/uk-england-coventry-warwickshire-59009784

174 Criminal Justice and Public Order Act 1994 https://www.legislation.gov.uk/ukpga/1994/33/section/63

175 Cawley, Laurence | Milton Keynes: The middle-aged new town | BBC (January 2017) https://www.bbc.co.uk/news/uk-england-beds-bucks-herts-38594140

176 Dunn, Frankie | Celebrating the forgotten home of UK rave culture | i-D Magazine (December 2021) https://i-d.vice.com/en_uk/article/y3vwzk/sanctuary-90s-rave-culture-exhibition

177 Gone To A Rave 60-Eddie 'Evil' Richards Interview | Ransom Note https://www.theransomnote.com/music/playlists/gone-to-a-rave-60-evil-eddie-richards-from-camden-palace-to-sunrise/

178 Bainbridge, Luke | The heart and soul of Stoke-on-Trent | The Guardian (November 2010) https://www.theguardian.com/travel/2010/nov/06/stoke-on-trent-northern-soul-weekend

179 Barker, Nigel, Brodie, Allan, Dermott, Nick, Jessop, Lucy, Winter, Gary | Margate's Seaside Heritage | English Heritage (2007) https://historicengland.org.uk/images-books/publications/margates-seaside-heritage/margates-seaside-heritage

180 Burrows, Tim | When Did England Abandon its East Coast? | Vice (March 2015) https://www.vice.com/en/article/bnpg43/eastern-promises-east-kent

181 Live Margate | Kent County Council | Regeneration Policy https://www.kent.gov.uk/about-the-council/strategies-and-policies/regeneration-policies/live-margate

182 Lucking, Liz | London's decade of dominance: City led UK in 10-year price growth | Mansion Global (December 2019) https://www.mansionglobal.com/articles/londons-decade-of-dominance-city-led-u-k-in-10-year-price-growth-210553

183 City Population | Margate | 2020 https://www.citypopulation.de/en/uk/southeastengland/kent/E35001458__margate/

184 Hirst, Ian | Praise for 'fantastic progress' on cutting the risk of flooding in Calderdale | Halifax Courier (November 2021) https://www.halifaxcourier.co.uk/news/environment/praise-for-fantastic-progress-on-cutting-the-risk-of-flooding-in-calderdale-3445184


CHAPTER 7

185 Tommy Smith, organiser of the Blackburn raves | Out of Space interview

186 Simms, Sara | History of the Rave Scene: How DJs built Modern Dance Music | DJ Tech Tools (December 2013) https://djtechtools.com/2013/12/19/history-of-the-rave-scene-how-djs-built-modern-dance-music/

187 Titmus, Stephen | Boy's Own: A History | Resident Advisor (January 2010) https://ra.co/features/1139

188 King, Richard | The Lark Ascending: The Music of the British Landscape | Faber (2019)

189 Warwick, Oli | Let Us Be Your Fantasy: How Fantazia brought UK rave to the masses | DJ Magazine (January 2020) https://djmag.com/longreads/let-us-be-your-fantasy-how-fantazia-brought-uk-rave-masses

190 Barden, Benita | Why did raves become illegal | BBC (June 2020) https://www.bbc.co.uk/news/newsbeat-53170021
191 Margaret Thatcher: A life in quotes | The Guardian (April 2013) https://www.theguardian.com/politics/2013/apr/08/margaret-thatcher-quotes
192 Chester, Jerry | Castlemorton Common: The rave that changed the law | BBC (May 2017) https://www.bbc.co.uk/news/uk-england-hereford-worcester-39960232
193 Reynolds, S. (1998) Energy Flash, Pages 135-140, Picador ISBN 0-5712-8914-2
194 Oliver, Scott | The Raving Crew Who Were Named 'The Most Dangerous People in the UK' | Vice (August 2014) https://www.vice.com/en/article/xd38mq/diy-25th-anniversary-scott-oliver-125
195 Guest, Tim | Fight for the right to party | The Guardian (July 2009) https://www.theguardian.com/music/2009/jul/12/90s-spiral-tribe-free-parties
196 I am a Mutoid: A Glastonbury Hero | Film (June 2021) https://www.bbc.co.uk/iplayer/episode/m000xh3q/glastonbury-i-am-a-mutoid-a-glastonbury-hero
197 Jeffries, Stuart | They thought we were terrorists: meet Joe Rush, master of mutoid art and King of Glastonbury | The Guardian (June 2021) https://www.theguardian.com/tv-and-radio/2021/jun/24/joe-rush-i-am-a-mutoid-mutoid-waste-company-glastonbury-g7-mount-recyclemore
198 Mutoid Waste Company | Berlin https://cargocollective.com/MutoidWasteCo/Berlin
199 CBS News | Why half of London's nightclubs have shut down for good (September 2015) https://www.cbsnews.com/news/why-half-of-londons-nightclubs-have-shut-down-for-good/
200 The Criminal Law Act 1977 | Section 6 https://www.legislation.gov.uk/ukpga/1977/45/section/6
201 Chris Liberator | Bag | Discogs (1995) https://www.discogs.com/release/268536-Chris-Liberator-Spectrum
202 Taylor, Hugh | Lasers, robots and DJ Lara Croft's Dentist: the rave lunacy of Bang Face | The Guardian (March 2019) https://www.theguardian.com/music/2019/mar/20/lasers-robots-and-dj-lara-crofts-dentist-the-rave-lunacy-of-bang-face

203 Ottewill, Jim | Bang Face Review | Resident Advisor (May 2010) https://ra.co/reviews/7497
204 Club your way to an intimate encounter | Metro (June 2009) https://metro.co.uk/2009/06/11/club-your-way-to-an-intimate-encounter-187221/
205 Rising Sun Collective https://www.risingsun.space/
206 Talora, Joe | London is 'epicentre' of housing crisis as 250,000 Londoners await council homes | The Evening Standard (October 2021) https://www.standard.co.uk/news/london/london-housing-crisis-sadiq-khan-council-homes-b960327.html
207 Rightmove | Where have asking prices increased the most since 2010 (October 2020) https://www.rightmove.co.uk/news/articles/property-news/asking-price-increases-since-2010

CHAPTER 8

208 Paul Huxtable, sound system owner and builder | Out of Space interview
209 30 Years of Rage | Fabio and Grooverider | Bandcamp compilation (May 2019) https://aboveboardprojects.bandcamp.com/album/30-years-of-rage-part-1
210 Ward, Paul | Sound System Culture, Place, Space and Identity in the UK 1960-1989 | Edge Hill University (June 2018) https://research.edgehill.ac.uk/ws/portalfiles/portal/20119304/WARD.docx
211 History of Sir Lloyd Coxsone | Biography https://sirlloydcoxsone.com/bio/
212 Finch, Jennifer | The Cultural Impact of Migration: The Impact of Sound System Cult | Halcyon Wax (June 2020) https://www.halcyonwax.com/post/the-cultural-impact-of-migration-the-impact-of-sound-system-culture-on-britain
213 DJ Don Letts | Biography https://www.donletts.com/dj
214 Dance Can't Nice: Exploring London's Black music spaces | Horniman Museum and Gardens (Exhibition July - October 2021) https://www.horniman.ac.uk/event/dance-cant-nice-exploring-londons-black-music-spaces/

215 Toppins, Julia | They're Not In It Like The Man Dem (September 2019) https://www.bloomsburycollections.com/book/media-narratives-in-popular-music/ch3-they-re-not-in-it-like-the-man-dem-how-gendered-narratives-contradict-patriarchal-discourse-in-electronic-dance-music

216 10 Things You Didn't Know about Norman Jay | Ministry of Sound blog (June 2018) https://www.ministryofsound.com/posts/articles/2018/june/10-things-you-didnt-know-about-norman-jay-mbe/

217 Norman Jay | Red Bull Music Academy (2010) https://www.redbullmusicacademy.com/lectures/norman-jay-public-mbe-no-1

218 Shulman, Alon | The Second Summer of Love: How Dance Music Took Over the World (2019) shorturl.at/kpMVY

219 Loben, Carl | Children of the Windrush Generation: The Pioneering DJs who paved the way for UK dance music | DJ Mag (June 2020) https://djmag.com/content/children-windrush-generation-pioneering-djs-who-paved-way-uk-dance-music

220 Shock Sound System | Facebook Page https://www.facebook.com/shocksoundsystem/

221 Tryggvason, Karl | Various Artists - 15 Years Of Metalheadz | Review | Resident Advisor (November 2009) https://ra.co/reviews/6840

222 Kaisary, Philip | The Black Atlantic - Notes on the Thought of Paul Gilroy | Critical Legal Thinking (September 2014) https://criticallegalthinking.com/2014/09/15/black-atlantic-notes-thought-paul-gilroy/

223 Brett, Sian | What Was Form 696 | Horniman (November 2021) https://www.horniman.ac.uk/story/what-was-form-696/

224 Snaith, Emma | Sound system innovators: The women shaking up the UK scene | East London Lines (January 2018) https://www.eastlondonlines.co.uk/2018/01/sound-system-innovators-women-shaking-uk-scene/

225 Hirst, Andrew and Raleigh, Emma | Why Huddersfield is leading the sound system culture revival | Yorkshire Live (March 2018) https://www.examinerlive.co.uk/whats-on/music-nightlife-news/huddersfield-leading-sound-system-culture-14404919

226 Simpson, Dave | Champion Sound! When Huddersfield ruled the British reggae scene | The Guardian (July 2014) https://www.theguardian.com/music/2014/jul/31/champion-sound-huddersfield-ruled-british-reggae-scene

## CHAPTER 9

227 Colleen 'Cosmo' Murphy, DJ and broadcaster | Out of Space interview

228 Mayor of London/London Assembly Datastore (2021) https://data.london.gov.uk/dataset/londons-population

229 Population Estimates for the UK, England and Wales, Scotland and Northern Ireland | Office for National Statistics (May 2020) https://www.ons.gov.uk/peoplepopulationandcommunity/populationandmigration/populationestimates/bulletins/annualmidyearpopulationestimates/mid2019

230 Zephaniah, Benjamin, 'The London Breed' | Taken from 'Too Black, Too Strong' | Blood Axe Books (September 2001) https://www.iispandinipiazza.edu.it/wp/wp-content/uploads/2016/06/The-London-Breed.pdf

231 King's Cross Redevelopment https://www.kingscross.co.uk/about-the-development

232 Wainwright, Oliver | The £3bn rebirth of King's Cross: dictator chic and pie-in-the-sky penthouses | The Guardian (Feb 2018) https://www.theguardian.com/artanddesign/2018/feb/09/gasholders-london-kings-cross-rebirth-google-hq

233 Heart of Hale | Argent https://www.argentrelated.co.uk/developments/tottenham-hale

234 Heaven Nightclub | History https://heaven-live.co.uk/about/

235 Sullivan, Chris | Billy's Club | We Can Be Heroes : Punks, Poseurs, Peacocks and People of a Particular Persuasion | The Blitz Kids (2012) http://www.theblitzkids.net/billys-club-by-chris-sullivan/

236 Cruickshank, Dan | Soho: A Street Guide to Soho's History, Architecture and People (2019)
https://tinyurl.com/3hnrnuym

237 Comptons | History https://www.comptonsofsoho.co.uk/comptons

238 Perrone, Pierre | Steve Strange: Lead singer with Visage and club owner who became the leading light of the 1980s New Romantic movement | The Independent (February 2015) https://www.independent.co.uk/news/obituaries/steve-strange-lead-singer-with-visage-and-club-owner-who-became-the-leading-light-of-the-1980s-new-romantic-movement-10045777.html

239 In Pictures: The Demolition of Elephant and Castle Shopping Centre | The Londonist (January 2022) https://londonist.com/london/art-and-photography/in-pictures-the-demolition-of-elephant-and-castle-shopping-centre

240 Rogers, Dave | Delancey defeats challenge to 1,000-home Elephant & Castle regen | Housing Today (June 2021) https://www.housingtoday.co.uk/news/delancey-defeats-challenge-to-1000-home-elephant-and-castle-regen/5112182.article

241 Barraclough, Alice | Charle Dark MBE: It's amazing the doors that now open | Runner's World (July 2023) https://www.runnersworld.com/uk/news/a44439492/charlie-dark-mbe/

242 Tindall, Gillian | Smithfield's Bloody Past | Spitalfields Life | Citing Charles Dickens' Great Expectations (September 2016) https://spitalfieldslife.com/2016/09/06/smithfields-bloody-past/

243 Smithfield Market | London Wholesale Markets http://www.londonwholesalemarkets.com/smithfield.html

244 Fabric Blog | London Unlocked at Smithfield Market with Object blue, batu https://www.fabriclondon.com/posts/london-unlocked-at-smithfield-market-object-blue-batu

245 Considine, Claire | Fabric: An Oral History | Red Bull (October 2018) https://www.redbull.com/gb-en/fabric-nightclub-an-oral-history

246 Fabric's 24 hour Alcohol Licence | Resident Advisor (November 2005) https://ra.co/news/7357

247 Wheeler, Seb | Fabric announces 42-hour reopening weekend | Mixmag (March 2021) https://mixmag.net/read/fabric-reopening-weekend-open-when-nightclubs-news

248 Music Law Updates | London nightclub Fabric to close permanently (October 2016) http://www.musiclawupdates.com/?p=6979

249 Ellis-Petersen, Hannah | Fabric nightclub to reopen under strict new licensing conditions | The Guardian (November 2016) https://www.theguardian.com/uk-news/2016/nov/21/fabric-nightclub-to-reopen-under-strict-new-licensing-conditions

250 Cameron, John | Fabric awarded £1.5 million from Arts Council England | Selector (October 2020) https://selector.news/2020/10/26/fabric-london-1-5-million-arts-council-england/

251 Fabric London | Fabric presents: London Unlocked A series of streams

from London's most iconic spaces, with the UK's leading electronic artists https://www.fabriclondon.com/posts/newsflash-announcing-london-unlocked-a-series-of-streams-from-iconic-london-locations

252 Oakley, Malcolm | History of Canning Town East London (March 2014) https://www.eastlondonhistory.co.uk/visit-canning-town-east-london/

253 Regeneration Project: Canning Town and Custom House | Newham Gov.uk https://www.newham.gov.uk/regeneration-1/regeneration-project-canning-town-custom-house

254 Fielding, Amy | London Club FOLD offers NHS use of space amid Coronavirus Pandemic | DJ Mag (March 2020) https://djmag.com/news/london-club-fold-offers-nhs-use-space-amid-coronavirus-pandemic

255 Curtin April | London house prices | The parts of London where house prices have more than doubled | MyLondon (November 2020) https://www.mylondon.news/news/property/london-house-prices-parts-london-19336358

256 Townsend, Megan | Printworks : From Evening Standard Printing Press to World Famous Nightspot | The Independent (August 2018) https://www.independent.co.uk/life-style/design/printworks-nightclub-evening-standard-printing-press-london-a8506851.html

257 Gallop, Joe | Banging the Drumsheds: Broadwick Live's Simeon Aldred on venue's impact | Access All Areas (January 2024) https://accessaa.co.uk/banging-the-drumsheds-broadwick-lives-simeon-aldred-on-venues-impact-so-far/

258 Warrington, James | Outernet signs deal for world's largest LED screen deployment | City A.M. (November 2019) https://www.cityam.com/outernet-signs-deal-for-worlds-largest-led-screen-deployment/

259 Brady, Dominic | Inner London authorities 'hit hardest by budget cuts' | Public Finance (May 2019) https://www.publicfinance.co.uk/news/2019/05/inner-london-authorities-hit-hardest-budget-cuts

260 Berry, Sian | London's Youth Service Cuts 2011-2021: A Blighted Generation | City Hall Green (August 2021) https://www.london.gov.uk/sites/default/files/sian_berry_youth_services_2021_blighted_generation_final.pdf

## CHAPTER 10

261  Ian Anderson, Designers Republic | Out of Space interview
262  Lawrence, Tim | Love Saves The Day: A History of American Dance Music Culture 1970-1979 (2003) citing the New York Times (Feb 1965) shorturl.at/ghHS5
263  Night Fever: Designing Club Culture | Exhibition at the V&A, Dundee (May 2021 - January 2022) https://www.vam.ac.uk/dundee/exhibitions/night-fever-designing-club-culture
264  Ross, Gemma | Gary Neville on 'Partygate': Downing Street should be renamed the Hacienda | Mixmag (January 2022) https://mixmag.net/read/gary-neville-on-partygate-downing-street-should-be-renamed-hacienda-news
265  Last Orders for Nightclubs : UK nightclub attendance drops by 34 million in 5 years | Mintel (September 2016) https://www.mintel.com/press-centre/leisure/last-orders-for-nightclubs-uk-nightclub-attendance-drops-by-34-million-in-5-years
266  Chapple, Jon | Dance music festivals and clubs lose 78% of value | IMS Business Report | IQ Magazine (July 2021) https://www.iq-mag.net/2021/07/dance-music-festivals-clubs-lose-78percent-value-ims-business-report/
267  OMA Ministry of Sound II | Commissioned Study (2015) https://www.oma.com/projects/ministry-of-sound
268  Frearson, Amy | OMA reveals cancelled designs for Ministry of Sound nightclub with moving walls | Dezeen (January 2017) https://www.dezeen.com/2017/01/09/oma-scrapped-design-ministry-of-sound-nightclub-moving-walls-london/
269  OMA | Ministry of Sound II project  https://www.oma.com/projects/ministry-of-sound
270  Coultate, Aaron | Ministry of Sound confirms it tried to build a new club with moving walls next to current location | Resident Advisor (January 2017) https://ra.co/news/37816
271  Gonsher, Aaron | Love Saves the Day Turns 50: Hear 12 of the Loft's Essential tracks | New York Times (February 2020) https://www.nytimes.com/2020/02/13/arts/music/love-saves-the-day-loft-playlist.html

272 Sussman, Anna Louise | How Artists Fought to Keep SoHo Rents Affordable - and Why It Matters Today | Artsy (July 2017) https://www.artsy.net/article/artsy-editorial-artists-fought-soho-rents-affordable-matters-today

273 The Loft | The Legacy of David Mancuso | Tim Lawrence (November 2016) http://www.timlawrence.info/articles2/tag/The+Loft

274 Petridis, Alexis | Audiophiles: Are they hearing something we're not? | Esquire (July 2015) https://www.esquire.com/uk/culture/news/a8618/are-the-audiophiles-hearing-something-were-not/

275 Spice, Anton | The 50,000 watt Despacio | Vinyl Factory (July 2013) https://thevinylfactory.com/features/despacio-james-murphy-2manydjs-soundsystem-interview/

276 McCallum, Rob | 10 massive tracks from one of the world's greatest clubbing experiences | DJ Mag (May 2018) https://djmag.com/content/10-massive-tracks-one-world%E2%80%99s-greatest-clubbing-experiences-despacio

277 Boiler Room | About Boiler Room https://boilerroom.tv/about

278 Iqbal, Nosheen | Dance Revolution: Has Boiler Room changed club culture forever | The Guardian (September 2019) https://www.theguardian.com/music/2019/sep/28/electronic-dance-revolution-boiler-room-online-djs

279 Ministry of Sound II | OMA Design (2015) https://www.oma.com/projects/ministry-of-sound

280 Price, Joe | Resident Advisor and Asahi debut Immersive Discover Tokyo Virtual Experience | Complex Music (March 2021) https://www.complex.com/music/discover-tokyo-virtual-experience

281 Kheraj, Alim | How Queer Clubbers created 2020's Biggest Virtual Party | Vice (December 2020) https://www.vice.com/en/article/g5b5m4/club-quarantine-biggest-party-2

282 Greig, James | How digital clubbing became the saviour of queer nightlife during the coronavirus pandemic | i-D (March 2020) https://i-d.vice.com/en_uk/article/939jvp/queer-digital-clubbing-coronavirus-pandemic-club-quarantine

283 Lhooq, Michelle | People are Paying Real Money to Get into Virtual nightclubs | Bloomberg (April 2020) https://www.bloomberg.com/news/articles/2020-04-14/virtual-nightlife-grows-past-dj-livestreams-to-paid-zoom-clubs

284 Dumas, Daniel | I've Never Been a Club Guy but in Quarantine I've Become One | Exquire (April 2020) https://www.esquire.com/entertainment/music/a32256114/best-dj-live-streams-dance-parties-clubs-online-during-coronavirus-quarantine/

285 Amnesia enters the metaverse | EDM.COM (October 2021) https://edm.com/events/decentral-games-amnesia-ibiza-metaverse-superclub-launch

286 Pixelynx | Business About  https://pixelynx.io/about/

287 Deadmau5' interactive music experience in the metaverse | Grateful Web (October 2021) https://www.gratefulweb.com/articles/deadmau5-interactive-music-experience-metaverse

288 Dick, Duncan | The Secret DJ's Dark Room party rips up the standard clubbing template | Mixmag (December 2018) https://mixmag.net/feature/the-secret-dj-dark-room

289 Bryant, Miranda | Empty Shops could be the next studios for Bacon or Hirst, says leading curator | The Guardian (February 2022) https://www.theguardian.com/cities/2022/feb/12/empty-shops-artist-studios-whitechapel-gallery-director

290 Hikino, Kara-Bodegon | Dua Lipa takes 5 million fans into the world of disco parties | Bandwagon Asis (Decembers 2020) https://www.bandwagon.asia/articles/dua-lipa-club-future-nostalgia-online-concert-studio-2054-5-million-viewers-gig-report-november-2020

## CONCLUSIONS

291 Corbyn Shaw | Escapism, Hedonism, Community, Euphoria | Brett, Davey | Queer Up North - Homobloc, masculinity and the art of rave | Confidentials Manchester (December 2021) https://confidentials.com/manchester/homobloc-corbin-shaw-art-flags

292 Lenny Watson, Sister Midnight | Out of Space interview

293 LGBT+ venues in crisis - London has lost 58 per cent since 2006 | Mayor of London | London Assembly | Press release (July 2017) https://www.london.gov.uk/press-releases/mayoral/mayor-pledges-support-to-lgbt-venues-in-london

294 Ottewill, Jim | Oppose the Developers | Mixmag (October 2017)

https://mixmag.net/feature/oppose-the-developers-london-is-fighting-to-protect-its-lgbt-clubs

295 Friends of the Joiners Arms   https://thejoinersliveson.wordpress.com/

296 Lloyd, Kate | Friends of the Joiners Arms to get pop-up queer space funded by developers | Time Out (January 2021) https://www.timeout.com/london/news/friends-of-the-joiners-arms-to-get-pop-up-queer-space-funded-by-developers-011221

297 Beaumont-Thomas, Ben | Night-time cultural sector hit with 86,000 job losses due to Covid-19 | The Guardian (October 2021) https://www.theguardian.com/music/2021/oct/11/night-time-cultural-sector-hit-with-86000-job-losses-due-to-covid-19

298 Hawthorne, Carlos | 26 percent of UK citizens think clubs should never reopen, according to new poll | Resident Advisor News (July 2021)  https://ra.co/news/75651

299 Ross, Gemma | Over 100 independent UK nightclubs have closed in the last 12 months, says report | Mixmag (August 2023) https://mixmag.net/read/100-independent-uk-nightclubs-closed-12-months-study-ntia-report-news

300 Sister Midnight Collective   https://www.sistermidnight.org/

301 Sound Diplomacy | The Music Cities Resilience Handbook   https://www.sounddiplomacy.com/better-music-cities

302 Jhala, Kabir | It's official - Germany now declares its nightclubs are now cultural institutions | The Arts Newspaper (May 2021) https://www.theartnewspaper.com/2021/05/07/its-officialgermany-declares-its-nightclubs-are-now-cultural-institutions

303 Clubcommission   https://www.clubcommission.de/

304 Thomas, Katie | French clubs launch initiative to gain cultural status | Resident Advisor (November 2021)   https://ra.co/news/76216

305 Ahmed, Aneesha | Irish government to pay artists 'basic income' | Mixmag (January 2022) https://mixmag.net/read/basic-income-artists-ireland-news

306 Night Czar | Mayor of London | London Assembly  https://www.london.gov.uk/what-we-do/arts-and-culture/24-hour-london/night-czar

307 The National Planning Policy Framework  https://www.gov.uk/government/publications/national-planning-policy-framework--2

308 What is Agent of Change and why is it important | Music Venue Trust https://musicvenuetrust.com/2014/09/what-is-agent-of-change-and-why-is-it-important/

309 The Population of Bristol | Report | Bristol Government (September 2020) https://www.bristol.gov.uk/documents/20182/33904/Population+of+Bristol+September+2020.pdf/69aa0aa1-290a-ccf2-ec4f-13a7376b41a8

310 Rodorigo, Clara | Berghain from club to gallery | Domus (September 2020) https://www.domusweb.it/en/art/gallery/2020/09/14/berghain-from-club-to-gallery-olafur-eliasson-wolfgang-tillmans-and-115-other-artists-on-show.html

311 Use Hearing Protection | Museum of Science and Industry | Manchester (June 2021-January 2022) https://www.scienceandindustrymuseum.org.uk/what-was-on/use-hearing-protection

312 Schwarz, Erin | The Futuristic Italian Nightclub with Vegetable Gardens and Toga Parties | Vice (February 2019) https://garage.vice.com/en_us/article/evexb7/italian-futurist-nightclubs

313 Jim Henson's Red Book | Cyclia (July 2011) https://www.henson.com/jimsredbook/2011/07/7-1967/

314 Tapper, James | Restoring Hope: 'Why can't we recreate the old energy of Sarajevo?' | The Guardian (January 2022) https://www.theguardian.com/world/2022/jan/09/restoring-hope-why-cant-we-recreate-the-old-energy-of-sarajevo

315 Hewison, Robert | How the UK Government Failed to Save the Arts | Arts Review (September 2020) https://artreview.com/how-the-uk-government-failed-to-save-the-arts/

316 Connolly, Jim | Nightclubs reopen but fears remain for the industry's future | The BBC (July 2021) https://www.bbc.co.uk/news/newsbeat-57867865

317 Dorothy | Design Studio, Liverpool https://www.wearedorothy.com/

318 Cheeseman, Philip | The Story of Hedonism https://hedonism1988.co.uk/history/

319 Gut Level | Website https://gutlevel.co.uk/

320 Grassroots Music Venues: Recovering from the Pandemic and Building Back Better | Music Venue Trust | Parliamentary Evidence (February 2022) https://committees.parliament.uk/writtenevidence/106304/pdf/

321 UK Land Area | Worldbank https://data.worldbank.org/indicator/AG.LND.TOTL.K2?locations=GB

# ACKNOWLEDGEMENTS

As befitting a book about club culture, much of this has been written at night. Appropriately for a book about space, it's also been written in a variety of different places, often enroute between them. From Tottenham to Fife via Liverpool and Sheffield, on trains to London, in airport lounges, kids' A&E at Alder Hey... Big up to these places for existing and all the wonky public Wi-Fi spots I've bled dry.

Massive thanks to all those I interviewed or helped set up interviews. Thanks for being so open, enthusiastic and generous with your time and telling me your stories. In no particular order (and apologies to anyone I've inadvertently left out), praise be to:

Mike Grieve (Sub Club), Slam (Stuart McMillan and Orde Meikle), Harri Harrigan, Graeme Park, Domenic Cappello, Dr Sarah Lowndes, Mutley (SWG3), Fred Deakin, Neil Landstrumm, Yogi Haughton, Carole Kelly, Nightwave, Lynn Macdonald, Richard Chater, Dave Haslam, Meat Free, Anton Stevens at Hidden, Ben Kelly, Justin Robertson, Greg Wilson, Jon DaSilva, DJ Paulette, Emma Warren, Balearic Mike, Jay Wearden, Suddi Raval, Danielle Moore, Sophie Hayter (Partisan Collective), Kevin McManus, Jayne Casey, Matthew Barnes (Forest Swords), Chris Torpey, Chris Amoo (The Real Thing), Ian Usher (Sonic Yootha), Saad Shaffi (24 Kitchen Street), Andy Carroll, Dorothy (Ali Johnson, Jim Quail, Ian Mitchell), Barry Collings, Mele, Richard Anderson, Matthew Flynn, Stuart Hodson (909), Caspar Melville, Stephen Mallinder (Cabaret Voltaire), Richard Hardcastle (Solid State), Greg Zogg,

Anwar Akhtar, Chris Duckenfield, Liam O'Shea, Gut Level, Simon Mander (Green), Toddla T, Dan Sumner, Chantal Passamonte (Mira Calix), Big Ang, Alan Deadman, Alex Deadman, Ian Anderson, Matthew Conduit, Ann Andrews (Funktion One), Tony Andrews (Funktion One Founder), Giulio Margheri (OMA), Paul Cournet (OMA), Emma Webster, Colin Dale, Caro Smart, Raif Collis, Adelphi Music Factory, Terry Farley, Harry Harrison, Mick Wilson, Evil Eddie Richards, Ian (Sound of Milton Keynes), Russ Malland, Gig/Matthanee Nilavongse (The Golden Lion), Louis Sweeting (The Golden Lion), Joe Rush (Mutoid Waste Company), Cymon Eckel, Cath Mackenzie, Alex Zawadzki, Scott Bowley (Rising Sun Collective), Shawn Hausman (Area), Stéphane Sadoux, James Bangface, Chris Liberator, D.A.V.E. The Drummer, Gizelle Rebel Yelle, Tommy Smith, DJ Rap, DJ Storm, Geeneus, Josey Rebelle, Julia Toppins, Penelope Wickson, Julian Henriques, Imre van der Gaag, Amit Patel (Brilliant Corners), Luke Vandenberg (Margate Arts Club), Freya van Lessen, Dave Seaman, Stuart Patterson, John Klett, Friends of the Joiners Arms, Michael Kill, Ashley Beedle, Norman Jay, April Grant (Rusty Rebel), Thali Lotus, Shawn Hausman, Thristian, Colleen 'Cosmo' Murphy, Richard Norris, Mark Ellicott, Matt Walsh, Hannah Holland, Jason Kinch (JFK), Dubplate Pearl, David Rudlin (Urbed), Debbie Griffith, Lloyd Bradley, Judge Jules, Paul Huxtable, Voicedrone (FOLD), Tom Steidl (Peckham Audio), Ajay Jayaram (Printworks), Brad Thompson (Printworks), The Secret DJ, HAAi, Inder Phull, Erin Logan (Club Quarantine), Luis-Manuel Garcia, Dr Catherine Rossi, Dr Jochen Eisenbrand, Tom Steidl, Rebecca Salvadori, Hannah Brere (Gut Level), Adam Benson (Gut Level), Smokin' Jo, Anthony Breach (Centre for Cities), Kirsty Hassard, Ian Bowerman, Mark Moore, Lenny Watson (Sister Midnight), Bill Brewster, Luke Solomon, Richard Norris, Smokin' Jo, Justin Berkmann, FOLD, Strictly Kev, Judy Griffith (Fabric),

Rebecca Salvadori, OK Williams, Shain Shapiro, Carly Heath, Joe Ruckus, Isis O'Regan, Liam O'Reilly, Lukas Wigflex, Charlie Dark, Man Power, Abigail Ward, Ruf Dug, Doris Woo, Tony Child, Joe Ruckus, everyone at Melodic Distraction (RIP), Karrie Goldberg, Darren Emerson, Adam Regan, Mo Jones, Neil Spragg, Jez Collins, Neil Rushton, Bobby Friction, Chris Finke, Emily Jones, everyone at Selextorhood, Lai Power, James Stammer, Coorie Doon, Apricot Ballroom, Banana Block, Cobalt Studios, TAAHLIAH.

Massive thanks to Craggsy, Tom James, Pete Hoppins, Ravina Bajwa and Alex Turner (aka Gag Reflex) for your input on my words and look and feel. Big high fives to Velocity's Colin Steven for giving me the opportunity to write this and sticking with me despite Covid. Big up to Matt Evans for giving me a chance as a music writer at the Sheffield Telegraph back in the mid-2000s when I was pretty wet behind the ears and pretty clueless. His weekly listings in the paper were some of the best music writings I've ever read and he was always there with an encouraging word, a beer and the energy when you needed him. Matt sadly passed during the writing of this but everyone who met him will know what a special soul he was. Rest in Power Matt. Finally, maximum love vibes to Kathy, Dre and Stan and my fam for keeping me going when writing this. You guys are everything.

Thanks to everyone who pre-ordered the book: Paul Adams, James Anderson, Anton Ardakov, Luna Atkins, Waq Aziz, Simon Baggley, Ravina Bajwa, Louis Bartlett, Andrew Barlow, Jennie Barratt, Frederik Birket-Smith, John Boddy, Jefferson Boss, Alex Bowen, Ben Boyce, Andjela Buncic, James Cain, Karen Campbell, Paul Caulfield, Timothy Child, Oliver Chrimes, Nick Clarke, Ewen Colquhoun, Vanessa Colquhoun, Jez Collins, Pete Cowasji, Jonathan Coxhead, Tom Darke, Huw Davies, James De Gray Birch, Gary Dobson,

Daniel Douglass, Markus Drese, Jason Drew, Yvonne Duffield, Kieran Duggan, Mar Ealand, Zoe Ellsmore, Neil Elkins, Jakob Falk, Andy Faulkner, Richard Fogarty, Paul Francombe, David Franklin, Richard Garner, Andy Gee, Tim Gibney, Pippa Gillam, Gary Grant, David Griffiths, Rob Hale, Christopher Hammond, Jon Hannan, Dan Hawes, Terry Hilton, Thomas Hnatiw, Mark Holmes, Katherine Hoppins, Peter Hoppins, Andrew Hough-Smith, Michael Hughes, Fabian Huismans, Tom James, Minseung Jeoung, Benjamin Jones, Wiy Jones, Tim Kantoch, Tom Keeley, Anna Keenan, John Kell, Ben Kelly, Carole Kelly, Si Kemp, Ben Latham, Victoria Lawson, Seewoo Lee, Al Livesey, Tim Long, Andrew Low, Mufeed Mahmood, Jenny Marzano, Darryl Matthews, Emily McCunn, Ian McGee, Steve McLay, David McLennan, Luke Melling, Goran Mikulic, Matt Milnes, Vimal Mistry, Chris Moore, Karenza Moore, Poppy Moroney, Joe Morrison, Joerg Mueller-Kindt, Tarek Musa, Paul Nichols, Christian Nockall, Richard Norris, Ollie Oak, Francesc Vila Oliveras, David Osborne, Liam O'Shea, Natalie Ottewill, Sarah Ottewill, Luke Palin, Sam Pearse, James Peel, Chris Perks, Robert Pointer, James Pooley, Katherine Potsides, Antony Price, Sareta Puri, Tom Ralph, Damien Ratcliffe, Claire Reilly, Steph Robinson, Craig Rose, Jaime Rosso, John Rowlands, Kate Russell, Jenny Sargent, Jane Scarlett, Derren Sequeira, Jean-Christophe Sevin, Jes Sewerin, Paul Sleaze, Pablo Smet, Gregory Smith, Michael Smith, Astra Spyrou, Dominic Stanley, Dobre Stavrov, Craig Stedman, Nate Stevens, Darren Stewart, Jacob Stone, Leigh Strydom, David Sutheran, Louis "Longshot" Sweeting, Steven Taylor, Joe Todd, Ian Townsend, Alex Turner, Saki Tsukasaki, Paul Twomey, Richard Vokes, Chris Ward, Max Ward, Ambrose White, Matt Williams, James Wilson, Brian Wolohan, Mark Wood, Benjamin Woods, Kai Wu, Eleanor Young.

# ALSO ON VELOCITY PRESS

## JOIN THE FUTURE

### MATT ANNISS

Matt Anniss's critically acclaimed alternative history of UK dance music in the acid house era returns in updated and expanded form. Named by Rolling Stone UK as one of the best books on British music culture, Join The Future puts forward a persuasive new argument about the origins of UK club culture's long-running love affair with bass.

A mixture of social, cultural, musical and oral history based on five years of research and hundreds of interviews, Join The Future tells the previously hidden history of 'bleep' for the first time. It brings forth the untold stories of bleep's pioneers and those that came in their wake, moving from mid-80s electro all-dayers and reggae soundsystem clashes in the North and Midlands, to the birth of breakbeat hardcore and jungle in London and the South East in the early '90s.

Now expanded to include more interviews, analysis and a brand-new 'afterword' chapter, Join The Future is one of the most revealing and significant books on dance music in years.

"A significant contribution to the canon of dance music literature" – Matthew Collin, author of Altered State and Rave on

'Brings to the surface a hidden cultural history and a scene that reverberated around the world' Lanre Bakare

velocitypress.uk/product/join-the-future-book

# FIRST FLOOR VOL 1

## SHAWN REYNALDO

First Floor started small. At first it was just a newsletter, an outlet where veteran electronic music journalist Shawn Reynaldo could write and share his ideas without having to contend with outside editors or cater to social media algorithms. It was a blank canvas, and Reynaldo began to fill it with his extended thoughts on not just electronic music itself, but the culture and industry that surrounded it.

Just a few years later, First Floor now stands as one of electronic music's most influential platforms, particularly as Reynaldo continues to put many of the genre's thorniest issues under the microscope. First Floor Volume 1 collects his most thought-provoking pieces and provides a nuanced, wide-ranging look at contemporary electronic music culture as it comes to grips with systemic challenges and a time of profound transformation.

"Shawn is at the forefront of critical thinking and analysis of the greater electronic music industry. His thoughtful and often emotional opinions of issues within our scene are balanced by years of experience and a talent for zooming out to articulate thoughts from a wider perspective." Richie Hawtin

"For anyone who cares about electronic music, Shawn Reynaldo's First Floor is essential reading." Philip Sherburne

velocitypress.uk/product/first-floor-volume-1/

# THE RADIO PHONICS LABORATORY
## JUSTIN PATRICK MOORE

The Radio Phonics Laboratory explores the intersection of technology and creativity that shaped the sonic landscape of the 20th century. This fascinating story unravels the intricate threads of telecommunications, from the invention of the telephone to the advent of global communication networks.

At the heart of the narrative is the evolution of speech synthesis, a groundbreaking innovation that not only revolutionized telecommunications but also birthed a new era in electronic music. Tracing the origins of synthetic speech and its applications in various fields, the book unveils the pivotal role it played in shaping the artistic vision of musicians and sound pioneers.

"From telegraphy to the airwaves, by way of Hedy Lamarr and Doctor Who, listening to Hal 9000 sing to us whilst a Clockwork Orange unravels the past and present, Moore spirits us on an expansive trip across the twentieth century of sonic discovery. The joys of electrical discovery are unravelled page by page." Robin Rimbaud aka Scanner

"In this captivating exploration of electronic music, Justin Patrick Moore unveils its evolution as guided by telecommunication technology, spotlighting the enigmatic laboratories of early experimenters who shaped the sound of 20th century music. A must-read for electronic musicians & sound artists alike." Kim Cascone

velocitypress.uk/product/radio-phonics-laboratory-book

# EARS TO THE GROUND

## BEN MURPHY

For the biggest artists to the most underground, field recordings have become the vital spark of electronic music. Whether documenting nature, sampling the city or capturing the atmosphere of archaeological sites, musicians are using found sounds to make sense of our world.

Ears To The Ground explores the relationship between electronics, landscape and field recordings in the UK, Ireland and around the globe, discovering how producers and artists evoke the natural world, history and folklore through sampled sounds. Author Ben Murphy takes you on a journey to discover how field recordings can create context, emotion, atmosphere, humour and meaning - and examine the most pressing topics of our times.

"Recording or celebrating 'place' in art and music feels increasingly relevant, as our environment faces more serious threats than ever before, and Ears To The Ground is a timely examination of this development." Ultramarine

velocitypress.uk/product/ears-to-the-ground-book/

# A DARKER ELECTRICITY

## MARK ANGELO HARRISON

At the time, it was unclear why the UK government targeted the Spiral Tribe travelling sound system. Even after arresting many key members and launching one of Britain's biggest court cases against them. Was it really because they were a marauding horde of anarcho-techno-pirates, their outlandish music calling a generation to rebel against conservatism, convention, and even consensus reality?

Or was it because, as pioneers of the 1990s free party movement, championing the new British breakbeat and European techno sound, they were reclaiming social space in warehouses and out under the stars? Each weekend they pulled ever bigger crowds away from consumer culture. No superstar DJs, no door policy and everyone dancing together as equals. An inspiring, unifying force of creativity.

As Spiral Tribe's co-founder and visual artist, Mark Angelo Harrison has a unique perspective to tell their inside story. He vividly charts their nomadic journey and the rapid escalation of their popularity - and notoriety. From small squat-scene parties in London to enormous warehouse raves and free festivals. From one little overloaded van to the mighty convoy of matt-black military vehicles that instigated the teknivals of Europe.

"Expounding his anarcho-mystic creed, Mark has the visionary gleam of a prophet in his eyes… Yet despite the cultic, almost Manson-like aura, a surprising amount of what Mark and his acolytes say makes sense." Simon Reynolds, author of Energy Flash

velocitypress.uk/product/a-darker-electricity/

# DREAMING IN YELLOW

## HARRY HARRISON

Emerging from Nottingham in the summer of 1989, the DiY Collective were one of the first house sound systems in the UK. Merging the anarchic lineage of the free festival scene, the cultural and political anger of bands like Crass with the new, irresistible electronic pulse of acid house, they bridged the idealistic void left by the moral implosion of the commercial rave scene.

Written by Harry Harrison, one of DiY's founding members, this book traces their origins back to early formative experiences, describing in detail the seminal clubs, parties, festivals and records that forged the collective. Dreaming in Yellow is an attempt to distil the story of DiY's tumultuous existence and the remarkably eclectic, outrageous and occasionally deranged story of them doing it themselves.

"Full of wild tales from the highest of times, this is the story of an intrepid crew of idealistic hedonists whose quest for freedom and joy created some of the peak moments of Britain's rave counterculture." Matthew Collin (author of Altered State and Rave On)

velocitypress.uk/product/dreaming-in-yellow-book/